AGE OF SECESSION : VINDICATO

DISSOLUTION

In memory of John Alfred Peter Ruffles

AGE OF SECESSION : VINDICATOR TRILOGY PART I

DISSOLUTION

Third Edition
Published in Great Britain by Roger Ruffles, February 2018

www.ageofsecession.com

First published by Roger Ruffles, October 2013

Printed by CreateSpace, An Amazon.com Company

ISBN : 978-1493579785

Also By The Same Author

Age of Secession: Vindicator Trilogy
#1 : Dissolution
#2 : Rosicrux
#3 Shadow
#4 Vindicator – Full Trilogy

Age of Secession: Blood Money Trilogy
#1: Crying Moon
#2 : Blood Feud
#3: Cost of the Hunt
#4: Blood Money – Full Trilogy

Age of Secession: Ascent of Mars Trilogy
#1 : Oncoming Storm
#2 : Darkness of Mars
#3: Rise of the Diadochi
#4: Ascent of Mars – Full Trilogy

Age of Secession: Standalone books:
The Unchained

Out Early 2018:
Pay Dirt: Dishonest Intentions

Coming 2018/2019:
Augmented Genocide
The Lost Kindred
Adare's Legacy: Kingdom of Blood
Collective Misdirection

www.ageofsecession.com

+++ Jacking Into Datasphere +++

+++ Datasphere Connection Confirmed +++

+++Incoming Transmission +++

JOINING THE AGE OF SECESSION

If you want

- early access to new eBooks months ahead of official releases
- Special offers and exclusive competitions
- Direct communication with the author and creator of the series

Then send an email requesting to join the age of secession to:
ageofsecession@gmail.com
or go to www.ageofsecession.com and register your details there.

Your details will NOT be passed to any third party,
and you have the right for deletion of those details at any time.

+++ Transmission Ends +++

Chapter I

The red planet Mars rotated imperceptibly on its axis, uncaring of the destruction that had been wrought in its name, or of the devastation that had been laid all around it. In the distance Earth twinkled in the darkness of space reproachfully.

Mars was ringed by no less than six defensive starbases, vast military complexes that covered every angle of approach to the planet. It was an excessively heavy defensive ring of the very best military technology mankind could design, and yet it had not been enough to defend the capital planet. On the surface of the planet, the nuclear explosions had finally died down, and calm was slowly being restored to the red planet in increments, city by city, as the False Emperor's supporters fought on despite the loss of their leader. Even these actions were now thankfully minimal, the main battle having being fought to its conclusion.

Every starbase showed signs of the tremendous battle that taken place around Mars, but by far, the worst hit was Starbase 1. Once, it had been shaped like a ball that had been sliced in two, the two halves extended outwards along a thick column. Three rings had circled the main column, each on six spokes from the body, the docking rings of the mighty station. Now, one of the gigantic half-spheres was missing, blown into nothingness, debris still rocketing away from the massive rupture that had torn it apart. Huge holes peppered the entire surface of the station, power crackling around them as the station entered its death-throes. The reactor was about to go nova, and totally destroy the stricken station. Every single one of its rings had been broken apart, spokes pointing out into space as if to accuse the perpetrators that were pulling back from the expected blast radius. Bodies flew through the void, the ones that had not burst in the vacuum due to lack of life-suits. Entire decks of the station were missing, and one part of the main body had actually lifted away, and was in danger of detaching. There was widespread decompression throughout the station, and even the partial surrender of the False Emperors forces had not allowed enough time for repair crews to make it to the starbase. It was to be abandoned to its fate.

Starbase 1 was just one example; the others were also damaged to greater or lesser degrees. Beyond the starbases, however, there was a scene of devastation much worse.

A large naval action had taken place on the approach to Mars. Wreckage and debris filled the entire approach vector the invaders had taken, some of them defending ships, some of them attacking. The history books would come to call this the largest naval battle in memory to date.

Some ships still had some power, although not enough to fight, barely sufficient to keep their surviving crew members alive. Others had been completely broken apart, and lay in various states of destructive disassembly. A number had been completely vaporised, and only small shattered remnants survived in an expanding cloud of annihilated superstructure.

Other ships were damaged, but still moving. The False Emperor's forces had surrendered, and the ships had mostly been boarded by the Loyalist forces. Support ships had jumped into the Sol System, and were acting as prison ships, ready to begin transferring their prisoners to moons of Saturn where there were proper holding facilities for them.

It was impossible to tell physically any difference between the surviving military starships, because beyond different classes of capital naval assets, there was no difference in design - this had been a civil war, fought between the elite guard of the former Red Imperium. Such a civil war had been unthinkable, once.

The Loyalist Praetorians, the elite of the Red Imperium and the personal army of the one True Emperor, had been victorious. The False Emperor Praetorians, as they would become known, had been vanquished, at least in the Sol System. The False Emperor himself now lay dead, but the cost had been high and it was a pyrrhic victory at best.

The Empire was no more.

Commander James Gavain disconnected from the datasphere, requiring a moment of relaxation, a respite from the continuous flow of data. His internal modem dialled down as he unjacked, and he stood up from the command chair to stretch his tense muscles. The suspensor seat gently deactivated, the frame lowering itself into its docking port.

He surveyed the damage to the bridge of the *ISS Vindicator*. His gaze first fell to the body of Captain Evanleigh. They had been boarded during the battle, and the very bridge itself had been penetrated by the enemy marines. The fighting had been fierce, and much of the bridge crew lay dead in the places where they had fallen, those few who were wounded being removed by the medical teams some hours ago. They had almost lost the boarding action. Out of the two thousand naval crew, nearly a quarter had died, nearly two hundred of those to the boarding action.

Captain Evanleigh had taken a number of short-range laser pulses to the chest and head. His face was unrecognisable, a charred mess where the series of bolts had slammed through and out of the back of his head. The metal walls behind the command chair still had burn marks in them, the reinforced alloy much more resistant to the blasts than his body had been.

James Gavain had seen many actions in his time in the Praetorians, and seen much death. Evanleigh had been a friend, however, and it never became easy to witness the violent end of a friend, or to look at his or her body afterwards.

He raised his eyes from the body, and walked forwards. One of the weapons consoles, directly in front of the command dais, had been utterly trashed, and the power-armoured body of a boarding marine still lay sprawled through its remains. He gestured at it, "Have that removed," he ordered calmly, tonelessly.

"Aye, sir!" a marine sergeant, stood on guard at the edge of the bridge, turned to give orders to one of his squad. They both stepped forwards, genderless within their own power armour, and began to lift the boarder's body out of the wreckage.

Commander Gavain felt almost as dead inside. It was a shock reaction, the payback of when the adrenalin and the tension-stress faded. He was genetically engineered for battle and military service, it was the entire reason he had been cooked up from bioengineered molecular soup in a biovat many decades ago, but no matter what the training and psychological conditioning was, and no matter how much they tried to turn you into a heartless killing machine, the human element remained. In fact, the Red Imperium's bio-artificers had realised centuries ago that keeping the human element, the personalities and the rest, reduced psychosis and made a better soldier or navvy.

He walked towards the length of the long, rectangular bridge, a raised walkway with control pits to either side. Beyond the immediate semi-circle of the more important stations around the command chair, such as helm, navigation, defence controls and weapons controls, the others were arranged in recessed pits to either side of the walkway, which led up to the massive main viewer at the end of the control centre.

As he descended the steps to the walkway from the command dais, he had to tread carefully over the spilt blood of one of his crewmembers. Sandra Illyvich, he knew, recalling the moment the boarder had smashed the life out of her with one power-assisted punch through the chest and spine. He personally had used his own handlas to shoot the armoured marine, for all the good it had done against the power armour. One of their own defending marines had blasted the invader to pieces in the end. He closed his mind to the memory.

He looked up at the ceiling, stopping momentarily. At one point in the battle, the blast shields had taken such a battering that one section of them had crumpled, and the hull far above the bridge had been ruptured by a glancing hit from a torpedo. Even as the torpedo had rocketed back off into space, the minor rupture had been instantly sealed by a protective forcefield, but even so, the couple of seconds of decompression had been enough to suck two crewmembers screaming out into space. That had been after the boarding action.

It had been worse on decks ten through thirteen, he knew, amidships. A major decompression event had taken place, and many had died before the emergency forcefields could snap into place. The lucky ones had been atomised by the trio of torpedoes that had struck it in tight formation.

He shook his head. He felt numb. Even as he smelt the ozone in the air, the tang of the emergency force field with the coppery-iron taste of blood in the air assaulting his senses, inside he felt drained, destroyed. It was more than just the after-effect of the battle stress, he suddenly realised. Life as he knew it was coming to an end, and something altogether new would be taking its place. He just did not know what, and that brought an emotion he was genuinely not used to – fear. As he began to feel anxious even thinking about the future, he used his internal regulators to blank the feeling. This was not the time.

"Sir, sir, sorry sir, I didn't realise you still weren't in the datasphere," an orderly had come running up to him.

"Yes?" he asked, turning to face the comms lieutenant.

"There's a message that has come from the surface. It's for all ship captains, sir."

"I'll take it in the ready room." He immediately began to head for the private quarters, the personal office of the commander of the ship. With Evanleigh dead, command had fallen to him, so it was his now.

As he headed towards the ready room, Lieutenant-Commander Julia Kavanagh raised an eyebrow in query. "I'll speak to you after, Jules," he told her quietly, and then mercifully the doors hissed shut on the wreckage of the bridge.

Marine Major Ulrik Andryukhin stomped along one of the main pedestrian thoroughfares in the capital city, towards the parked HAPC. The *King Cobra* class command HAPC was one of the best of its kind, and this particular vehicle had been his home on many a campaign, both in the name of the Emperor and the False Emperor – before the civil war. Its repulsor engines were deactivated, and it nestled on the ground on its extended supporting struts. There was still an alert marine stationed in the shielded twin las-cannon pod on top of the vehicle, despite the fact that the city had gone quiet hours ago.

"Not how you thought it would be, eh?" he said through his helmet's vocaliser. The heads-up-display which was projected onto his retinas by the helmet identified the officer stood by the side of the HAPC as Corporal Naomi Calaman, his personal adjutant.

"What do you mean, sir?" she replied. The power armour suit hid the fact she was a woman. She still had her chameleon field activated, the suit's coloration changing to match the dusty red of the surrounding environment.

"I meant Olympus Mons City," the Major replied, gesturing around him. "I always thought Olympus Mons was a huge mountain, but you don't even know you're stood on top of a great big frikking volcano, do you? Ground looks flat."

Olympus Mons City was the capital city of the Red Imperium, built on Olympus Mons, the biggest mountain on Mars, the capital planet. There were other mountains of approaching size, all bearing their own, similar cities, which had also been invaded by the Praetorian Marines of the gigantic armada up in space.

"Well, sir," said Naomi, "That's because the incline's so gradual. The mountain's a shield volcano, and so large that the curvature of the planet means we can't see the base of it –"

"Yes, yes," the Major interrupted. "What about this city, then? You'd have thought the capital of the Red Imperium would be grand and majestic, but this bloody red dust covering everything makes me think of an old American Western movie."

"When we blew the shield-dome the dust got in, otherwise it would be clean. It is one of the biggest cities in the Imperium, Major," Calaman replied, almost reproachfully. "The skyscrapers alone are some of the tallest in the colonised galaxy." The scrapers were towering over them to either side of the wide pedestrian street.

"You see one Imperial city, you see them all," Major Andryukhin replied. "I thought this would be a bit special. I think I preferred Emerald City on Cavius III, that was a beautiful city, pre-Imperium architecture. Before you joined us, mind. Underwater it was, the sun so strong that it shone through the green sea and bathed everything in a rippling glow when they opened the dome-shields. Fantastic," he breathed, the vocaliser robbing his external voice of all the wistfulness and making it toneless.

"Yes, sir," Corporal Calaman said carefully.

"Major Andryukhin," a voice suddenly crackled in over the datasphere, sent directly into his brain by the internal modem, an image of Sergeant Jack Inman accompanying it, "A message is coming down from the *Vindicator,* sir. The approaching dust-storm and the orbital debris is causing interference though, you will have to use a booster to get it."

"Thank you, Sergeant," he replied. "Later, Corporal," he said cheerfully, as he began to walk around to the rear of the *King Cobra* HAPC. In the low gravity, it would have been very hard to prevent bouncing without the special gripping surfaces on his power suits armoured boots. Here on Mars, with the shield-dome deactivated during the invasion, not only had the ubiquitous red dust been blown into the city with the invaders but the special gravity generators under the street had failed, and the atmosphere had blown out, killing most of the civilians on the streets and not in the sealed buildings. It was a tragedy, but unavoidable.

He paused at the door to the *King Cobra*. The HAPC was parked near to a huge slanted block, one of the scrapers that had fallen over during the orbital bombardment. A deflected shot, probably aimed at the police station where a number of the False Emperors forces had taken cover, which broke the tall building into two. The building had collapsed into the one opposite the street, killing those within both buildings as the oxygen bled out. The fighting on Mars had been brutal - as well as civilians, there were Praetorians of both Imperial Loyalist and False Emperor leanings lying dead around the street. They had taken the police station, however.

He clumped up the ramp, and slapped the panel sensor that would close it. Once the boarding ramp had sealed, he sat down at the comms station within the empty HAPC, secure in the knowledge that the Marine up top would hear nothing in his sealed weapons pod. He tapped the booster to activate it, cycled through the list of incoming comms and found the one addressed to himself. A personal encrypted hail from Commander Gavain, secured against general interception. He opened up the channel, a miniature holographic image of the Commander behind Captain Evanleigh's desk coalescing into existence in the middle of the deserted armoured personnel carrier.

"Major Andryukhin," the Commander nodded. "Hail, in the name of the True Emperor. Rest his soul." The traditional greeting had become amended, once the rebellion had started against the False Emperor.

"Commander Gavain," the Major replied. "Hail, in the name of the True Emperor. Rest his soul. Where's the Captain?"

"Dead," was the typical short reply from Gavain. There was no emotion on his face. Andryukhin, however, still encased within his suit and face hidden by the visored helmet, winced and then frowned. Evanleigh had been a friend of all of them; the command staff of the *Vindicator* had always been very tight. Then, the psychoanalysts of the Imperium made sure the personalities assigned to a ship were compatible, so it was typical and to be expected amongst most naval ships both inside and outside the Praetorians.

"When this is over, we will all have a drink to his memory, James," Andryukhin said quietly.

"Yes, we will," Gavain nodded, face still blank. He was a cold bastard sometimes, the Major reflected, but he knew that underneath the blank exterior was a very powerfully emotive man. "Are you aware of the situation on Mars?"

"Yes, I'm up to date," Major Andryukhin replied. "I've read everything on the official channels, anyway. Olympus Mons City has been quiet for a couple of hours, but I understand there's still some residual fighting in Ascraeus Mons and Pavonis Mons. This is despite the False Emperor being killed. How did he die, do we know?"

"Shot through the head," Commander Gavain replied. "Probably for the best. StarCom will not be happy, they wanted him for trial, but we do not answer to them."

"Yeah, bugger the commies," he replied.

"I've also had some orders through," Gavain replied. "Have you had any contact from your Divisional HQ or Marine Command?"

"The last order was to hold position, a general order from Marine Command, and that was a number of hours ago," Major Andryukhin replied. When in a large operation, and this certainly counted as one, involving multiple landing forces from naval ships, a temporary chain of command would be set up for all the marines and they would be detached from their normal chain of command, which was typically to the commander of the starship they were stationed upon.

"Hmmmm. Probably just taking them a while to get all the orders out, then," Gavain said. The Major knew that one; in the chaos of winning, things could get confused. "You'd better chase to see if you've been missed out accidentally or if there's a hold-up. Marine Command are going to release all the ship-assigned Marines back to their naval chain of commands. It will only be temporary, however."

"Why only temporary?" Major Andryukhhin asked.

"Well, there's quite a bit that's going to happen," Commander Gavain suddenly looked pained, his usual mask slipping, which told Andryukhin volumes of information. "The Praetorians are going to be dissolved, Ulrik. We will be no more."

There was silence on the line for a while.

"Why?" Andryukhin asked eventually. Like Gavain, the Praetorians were more than his life, it was the reason for his life. However, as he thought, he suddenly realised that reason no longer existed.

"No Emperor, no False Emperor, no need for us," Gavain replied simply. "There will probably never be another Emperor again. The Empire is falling apart, Ulrik, we both know this - parts of the Empire seceded even before we invaded Sol. The Empire has already begun to shatter into hundreds of little pieces. The Commander-In-Chief, in his message, said that officially it is the joint decision of the Revolutionary Council and Praetorian High Command that we are disbanded. There will be a Dissolution Order issued officially across the galaxy in a matter of hours. He said privately that his own opinion is that the Council views us as a threat, and also, he could see why they might think that. We are the largest military force in the galaxy. The StarCom President initially asked for the Praetorians to transfer into their control, and he refused - they are not to have their own military force by ancient Imperial Decree, and if they did, he said, he fears what they would do in the power vacuum we now have."

"So what happens to us? What's next?" the Major asked, aghast.

"We have one last mission before dissolution," Commander Gavain replied. "The False Emperor kept a large number of the Lords and Solar Administration family member's prisoner, hostages against rebellion. They're being freed, and the *Vindicator* is one of the ships tasked to transfer some of the released hostages back to their home systems. Other ships, those too damaged by the battle, are being scuppered here and their crew assigned elsewhere or released from duty."

"I see," Major Andryukhin replied.

"I will download a list of the people we are to take," Gavain replied, "and their current locations. When you are released from the Marine chain of command, I want you to go and find them, and escort them back to the *Vindicator*. I know the situation down there is reported as stable, but you know as well as I that strange things happen in cities following their fall."

"Yes, Commander," Andryukhin replied. "What's next though? What happens after we've transferred all the released hostages?"

"We will be disbanded, our ship scuppered or sold to the highest bidder, most likely," Commander Gavain replied tonelessly. "I'm told we will all get pay-offs to ensure we have some money whilst we find some other thing in life to do."

"No," Andryukhin shook his head. "They cannot do this to us."

"It is the only safe thing for the galaxy," Gavain replied. "The Praetorians are too large. In the wrong hands, we could bring yet more devastation to mankind, and the False Emperor has done enough damage with us already."

"That's –"

"We have our orders, Major," Gavain had a sudden sharpness in his voice. "Get your release from Marine Command, and then do as I have said." His voice softened. "We will talk later. *Vindicator* out."

Lieutenant-Commander Kavanagh stood leaning with her hands braced on the rail, watching the military lander complete its docking procedure through the observation ports in the docking bay mustering hall.

The observation port's reinforced windows were large, allowing her an almost completely unrestricted view of the docking bay. There were eight such docking bays in the belly of the gigantic V-Class *Vindicator* battlecruiser, each capable of swallowing one such Freiderich-class multipurpose adaptable lander. All eight of the *Vindicator*'s landers were returning, minus some Marines and their equipment and vehicles. Shaped like large old-fashioned shuttles without the wings, these landers could be internally adapted to carry different make-ups of their military cargo. Their chameleon paint had been electrically changed from the camouflage pattern used during the assault on Mars, back to the standard "dress" colour of deep Imperial Red with black trimmings.

A black and gold stylised imperial eagle lay across the nose, back and sides of the lander she was watching, and it brought a pang to her heart. The end of the Empire, she reflected, it cannot be. The gold-bodied and black-lined eagle on the nose stared at her upside down, haughty, proud, golden eyes boring into her soul. In order to dock, the lander had to turn so its belly was mated to the roof of the bay. Far down below, amber lights turned red as the massive blast doors began to slide shut, each one as thick as the armour and outer skin of the *Vindicator*'s main hull.

She backed away from the observation port, walking over to the massive airlock gate for docking port 1. Standard disembarkation procedure dictated that the Marine foot-sloggers would leave the lander first, and then the vehicles in ascending size order, first the HAPCs, then the tanks, SPGs and artillery, cargotrucks, then finally the massive battlewalkers. The walker pilots always complained about it, as they were the first on and the last off; the foot-sloggers would be washed and eating or sleeping by the time they were just getting into the mustering hall.

The mustering hall was large, a cavernous expanse in the lower portion of the battlecruiser. Holding pods lay waiting at one end for the entire vehicular arsenal of the Marines to be strapped in during transit, and an entrance to the arsenal and fitting rooms was at one end, an exit to the barracks and canteen at the other.

Finally, the amber lighting strips all around the airlock gate turned green, and the doors began to open. The widening crack that appeared from top to bottom was many, many times taller than her, designed as it was to allow the egress of the battlewalkers.

Striding through the white light like an avenging angel was a tall, bulky figure in red "dress" coloured power armour, also trimmed in black. A golden eagle had spread its wings across his breastplate, the insignia of the Empire. Heavy armoured boots clanked on the floor, other figures of similar size marching behind. The figure stopped in front of her, the upper body canting forwards slightly, a black visored V in the helmet staring down at her. One arm ended in a deactivated power claw and stubbed lasrifle, the other mounted a heavy duty rotary projectile cannon. A multiple missile launcher lay at rest across the back, tubes stretching into the air at an angle over each shoulder.

The visor snapped back suddenly, the helmet parting into two and retracting into the collar of the suit. A handsome if hard face suddenly smiled at her, a smile on the large lips and perfect white teeth showing. A buzzcut of blond hair framed the head, and stubble covered the square jaw. Genetically modified, all Marines were tall, muscular, and almost un-Human in their physiological makeup.

"Hail in the name of the True Emperor, rest his soul," Lieutenant-

Commander Julia Kavangh saluted. As a Lieutenant-Commander, she ranked below the Marine Major, which was a rank equivalent to Commander in the navy. Commander Gavain was senior to the Major however, as the naval rank always superceded the Marine rank within the Praetorian Guard.

"Hail," the Major used the short form, saluting with the power claw casually. "It's good to see you, Jules. Why don't you walk with me whilst I get -" and here he laughed " - changed?"

Julia smiled back, knowing exactly what he meant. "Again, Ulrik? You have the strangest ways of getting a girl's interest."

"You're not a girl, you're a woman, and a beautiful one at that," he replied, sighing. "Come on."

They began walking across the suddenly busy mustering hall. Two of the other airlock gates had opened, and there was a rush to head towards the fitting rooms. "Are you glad to be back?" Julia Kavanagh asked, self-consciously straightening out her red-and-black uniform. As a senior officer, she had the black triangle on the dress jacket where it buttoned down to the left hip from the right shoulder, as well as the gold epaulettes.

"Oh yes, Mars is nothing like what we see on the holoretta," he replied. "I was unimpressed to say the least, just ask Corporal Calaman." He gestured at the Marine who was striding along a couple of metres behind him. All the Marines looked the same in their power armour, beyond variations in weapon load-out, Kavanagh would never have known it was Corporal Calaman. His voice went surprisingly soft for such a monster of a man. "When are we having Evanleigh's funeral?"

"After our next jump," Julia replied. "James wanted it to be private, just us and the crew. I can see his point - things are a bit crowded in Sol at the moment."

"That makes sense," Andryukhin replied. "I was sorry to hear of his death. Did you know, I first met him over ten years ago, when I was a Sergeant-Major and he was your rank?"

"Yes," Julia nodded. "You've mentioned it many, many times," she smiled somewhat sadly. She shook herself slightly, as if having a cold shiver. "But everything's changing now, Rik."

"Aye," he frowned darkly at her. "It's the end of the Empire, so the rumours go. The Emperor Himself knows what's going to happen to us when our last mission is over."

"Speaking of which, where are our rescued hostages?" the Lieutenant-Commander asked.

"They're coming up in the HAPCs," said the Major. "They're a strange bunch of people, but then what do I know about civvies, especially the higher-ups. Do you know who they are?"

"Yes, Commander Gavain briefed me earlier."

They had no less than five House Lords and their surviving retinues, as well as a House Lady coming up from the surface. There were also two Planetary Governors, and two Solar Administrator Chancellors. They had eight destinations to drop them off, the Planetary Governors each belonging to one of the House Lords they were conveying. The journey would take some three Standard months, at the end of which, they would cease to be Praetorian Guard.

"Frikkers, some of them," he said shortly. You never were one to keep your opinions to yourself, Kavangh reflected. They were getting near the fitting rooms, and the mustering hall was full of noise - a number of the other landers had also docked. The battlecruiser had nearly five hundred of its six hundred Marines returning home.

"What makes you say that?"

"House Lord Cervantes, is someone I would trust as far as I could throw him. House Lady Sophia Towers, she's nice, calm and collected, but House Lord Mannerton, oh Emperor, is he a spoilt brat. He's the only son of the Lord Senator, and did not stop whingeing all the way back. I could say more about the others, but it's ruining my Karma," he sniffed dramatically, then laughed as they entered the fitting room.

"You're just saying that because they are humanists," said Julia Kavanagh.

"It's not a borgite - humanist thing," the Major replied. "Some of them are borgites, after all. Although, I have to admit, I do find the unaugmented humans frikking backward. I think because we're all borgs they have an issue with us. The frikking barbarians."

Lieutenant-Commander Kavanagh found it wise to say nothing. There were many different people in the galaxy, from those born in vats from molecular soup, to others cloned from other people, to assisted fertilisation, to naturally born. The real dividing line, however, was between the cyborgs, the augmented borgites, and the unaugmented humans, the humanist. There were also the neutral free-thinkers, who did not care about the differences, but they - and the humanists - had been persecuted by the False Emperor. It had only further divided the Empire's populace, with many humanists forced into augmentation against their will, and others interred in special camps or labour prisons.

Praetorians were all augmented, and tended towards borgite leanings, or free-thinking. Kavanagh herself was a free-thinker, although she knew the Major and even Commander Gavain were borgites politically, the Major of an even more extreme nature than Gavain, who merely found the unaugmented uncomfortable.

They crossed to one of the disengagement pods. He tapped in his personal code, allowed his retinas to be scanned, and then turned as the disengagement pod opened. "Ready to see me naked?" he winked.

"Just do it," she laughed.

He stepped back into the pod, and it's clear membrane closed over him. The pod began to peel back his armour, disconnecting the power suit piece by piece. As it was pulled apart, it became obvious that it was grafted onto his body, the connecting ports closing over synthetic flesh. A huge muscular chest was revealed, then bronzed legs rippling with muscle. Finally, the membrane peeled back, and he stepped out, modesty covered by tight red underwear.

"Your weaponry seems smaller out of your armour, sir," Lieutenant-Commander Kavanagh said playfully.

"Hah," he snorted. "You should see it when it's armed and ready to fire."

James Gavain entered the bridge from the ready room. Instead of the usual bustle, the bridge was fairly quiet. All the crew looked at him, shock in their faces. Five minutes ago, the Dissolution Order had been received from the Commander-In-Chief. It had been sent personally to every Praetorian Guardsman across the galaxy.

First we turned traitor to the False Emperor, Gavain thought. Then we destroyed the False Emperor, assaulted the homeworld of the entire Empire, and lost friends in the process. We were created in biovats to serve the true Emperor in his elite guard, and then, we are told that the organisation that is the very reason for our existence is to be decommissioned.

He strode confidently across the bridge, knowing that he had to project a reassuring image to the crew. As he neared it, the command chair activated, repulsors lifting it out of its docking station, and he sat down in the frame. Lieutenant-Commander Kavanagh sat in a control chair by his left side.

He closed his eyes out of habit as he jacked into the datasphere. He felt the familiar rush as he connected, became part of the interconnected web of minds and thoughts of the entire crew of the *Vindicator*. In a sense, he now was the battlecruiser, jacked into its mainframe.

<Captain on the bridge,> Kavanagh sent in transmission to the bridge crew. She then opened a private mind-link to Gavain. <Congratulations, sir.>

<Thank you,> he replied. He then turned his attention to the new second-in-command, who had transferred over from the *Retribution*, which had been damaged so badly it would require at least a month of repair work. The command staff had only met Commander Lucas De Graaf a couple of hours ago, when the replacement crew had transferred over. The majority had come from the *Retribution*, some from other ships.

Gavain was not sure what he thought about De Graaf. The man seemed pleasant enough, although somewhat reserved, and there was something in his eyes and manner that almost spoke of resentment. Still, these were turbulent times, and in De Graaf's case, he had lost his fellow officers on the *Retribution*, transferred to an unfamiliar ship, and all against the background of the Dissolution Order.

<Commander, status?> he asked across the datasphere.

<The jump initiation capacitors are at full and ready to discharge, and the warp accelerators are at green status. We have traversed to the correct heading, Helm reports. Engine status is nominal. All stations report readiness, all decks are locked down. Navigations reports that we have clearance from operational control to jump. We are ready for the order, Captain.> When someone new joined an established datashpere, it was often impossible to read inflections in tone or voice, so Gavain glanced at Commander De Graaf. There was a hard set to his face, which could mean anything. Gavain wondered why he was so concerned about the attitude of this new Commander - experience had taught him long ago to go with his gut instinct,

<Very well, Mister De Graaf,> Gavain replied. He then leaned back in his chair, and once again closed his eyes. He widened his use of the datasphere, pinging every crewmember so they knew he wanted to speak to them. The two thousand five hundred navvies and the six hundred Marines registered full attention, the backwash of confirming links sending a thrill through him. He was addressing the whole ship.

<Crew of the *ISS Vindicator*,> he began. <By order of High Command, I have been promoted to the rank of Captain. We welcome aboard Commander De Graaf, and all the other transferee's. We will hold funeral services for those people we lost in the battle for Mars, and the new crew are more than welcome to attend if they wish to show their respects to fellow servicemen.> He felt that would be a good way of bringing some unity to the crew. In the Praetorians, people transferred between ships all the time, but so many lives had been lost, and there were so many new faces on board ship, experience taught him that there was always that period of adjustment where the old crew had to learn to gel with the new and vice versa.

<All crew, in relation to the Dissolution Order issued by Praetor Commander-In-Chief Cisko, we fall under one of the exceptions he gave whereby some of us have last orders. Our very last mission together as Praetorians will be to escort a number of high-ranking Imperial officials back to their homeworlds or designated drop-off points. In a galaxy where we are witnessing the probable end of the Empire, as well as our own organisation, their safe conduct is a priority. This mission will take approximately three months, at the end of which, we will all be honourably discharged from the Praetorian Guard. It is a consolation that

we will provided with a pay-off to make our way in the world.

<I will tell you now, I do not know what the future will bring. These are uncertain times. Much will happen during the next weeks, months, and years. Have faith, in me, your command staff, and your comrades in arms. Let us not be despondent in the face of our duty, and have trust in the Emperor's guiding light, rest his soul.

<All hands, prepare to jump.>

He disconnected from the datasphere's general communications channel, noting the number of forums that were cropping up within it as departments began to speak about his announcement. He would review them all later, to better understand what his crew thought.

<Engage the capacitors,> he ordered.

<Capacitors engaging,> the Lieutenant in charge of engineering replied back, from down in the Engine Room.

Quietly, Gavain called up an image of the *ISS Vindicator*. It appeared to be floating in front of the command dais, although in reality it was only a projection in the datasphere, within his own mind. He shared it with De Graaf and Kavanagh.

The *Vindicator* was a large battlecruiser, a relatively recent class. It was still possible to see the damage along its hull from the Battle of Mars, as the news media were already naming the last action in the civil war. With a thick main body, a series of three dome-like bubbles along its back, a boxy and bulky rear, and two extensions almost like landing gear but of an incredible size jutting down and to the side from each flank, it kept to the distinctive standard Martian Industries design format.

Right now, around the image, a large bubble was growing, a field of energy. The warp field was what would allow the ship to jump into hyperspace. Hyperspace was just a term which meant faster than light travel, as the ship would actually transit at unimaginable speeds towards a destination. The travel time could not be kept up indefinitely, so there was always a safety limitation on the so-called 'jump', otherwise the structural stresses would begin to tear the ship apart. As it was, even with a jump, special force fields had to be used to maintain structural integrity or it would fall apart within seconds of entering the hyperspace mode of travel.

<Warp field is at maximum, Captain,> De Graaf said eventually.

<Jump!> Captain Gavain ordered calmly.

The warp accelerators flared into life along the two support struts on either side of the ship, and the one that was centrally located in the rear, igniting with the warp field surrounding the ship, and in a flare of white light, the *Vindicator* jumped into hyperspace.

Chapter II

They were in transit time.

Captain James Gavain sat in the upper deck's relaxation lounge. There were three such places on the battlecruiser, the upper lounge, the lower, and the marine canteen. Each lounge, besides serving food and offering a place to relax, had a fitness centre adjoined to it. Beyond that, there were no other concessions to the crew in terms of rest and relaxation besides the officers' mess, and even the fitness centres doubled as training rooms. Each lounge was designed to hold just less than five hundred people comfortably, as that would be the maximum off-duty at any one time. Accordingly, they were usually busy places, and today was no exception.

He was jacked into the datasphere, but only to take advantage of the support functions, not to communicate with anybody. He could have been doing his work in his ready room, but he felt it was important for the crew to see him. Comms had sent him an early report of the forum discussions on the Dissolution Order; it made grim reading. He had a ship full of people very fearful for the future, with a great deal of anger directed at High Command, the Revolutionary Council, all mixed with a feeling of betrayal. The worst thing was, he could not disagree, as he felt all of that himself.

He held a cup of hot synthesised coffee in front of him, sipping from it gently. Everything shipboard was synthesised, it saved on stock space, although they did carry some real food for special occasions and celebrations, rare as those were nowadays. He always felt that real coffee tasted better than this stuff, synthesised from molecular soup - much in the same way as he had been all those years ago, he reflected. Did that mean that synthesised humans were less human than those born naturally, he wondered not for the first time.

He looked up from the coffee, to stare out of the large observation windows. The upper deck lounge had almost complete vision of the space around it when the blast shutters were peeled back. In transit time, there was not much to see, just a streaking of black with the odd red and purple colour mixed in. Scientists told them this was from the way in which the eyes interpreted the visual spectrum during a hyperspace jump, but he always wondered if this was actually true; it was beautiful, if not a little disturbing. You never saw stars in transit time.

A ship jumped into hyperspace, which was not another dimension as was romanticised by the sillier children's novels, but merely a term describing faster than light travel. Once it had been thought that such a thing was impossible, but those antiquated theories had been disproved long ago. For the people on board, there was always a couple of hours between entering the hyperspace speed and leaving it, but for an observer who could hypothetically stand in both the system the ship was leaving and the one it was arriving in, the time difference would appear to be nothing more than a couple of seconds, nearly instantaneous. Therefore, you had real time, the galactic Standard time, and transit time, the period of time travelling in hyperspace that did not exist at sub-light speeds. It would appear that the ship 'jumped' from one system to the next.

He looked back down at the display hovering just before his coffee cup. It was not a real display, existing in his mind and supported by the datasphere, but it helped the mind to translate it as a holographic representation hovering in the air just in front of him. It was a map of the stars, drawn back to small scale, showing the route they were going to take. It was almost semi-circular, leaving the centre of the core and heading partway through the mid-sectors towards the outlying systems although never coming near, before turning around on itself and heading back corewards.

Although a ship could jump tremendous distances in no apparent outward realtime at all, they could typically only manage two or three such jumps at full capacity, each time travelling the maximum distance they were limited to by the structural integrity fields. The longer a ship travelled in hyperspace, the greater the stress, and eventually, the ship would disintegrate. Beyond that limitation, the capacitors could only hold a finite charge, before they would have to be re-energised from the main engine drives in an emergency (called hotwiring, which would eventually damage the capacitor), or more commonly from the sun of the system they were in, or special fusion rechargers at space stations. The structural integrity fields also needed time to recharge and reenergise. The recharging of the jump capacitors could take days or weeks depending on a number of factors, all of which meant that they would take three real-time months to carry out what was a total of nineteen jumps across an unimaginable stellar distance. To the crew, it would effectively be closer to five biological months in their lives.

Their first jump would take them to the Exeter System, to drop off one of the Solar Chancellors. Then it would be another jump to an uninhabited solar system, for a recharge over two days, before jumping twice to the Roshnetak System to deliver a House Lord and his Planetary Governor. They would lay-up at the space yard there for a two-week refit and repair to the damaged battlecruiser.

Gavain did not wonder why they were bothering to repair the battlecruiser; the High Command was most likely going to sell it to raise funds for the Praetorian Guard's pay-off following Dissolution.

Did we really win this war, he thought to himself.

"Captain, could I have a word?"

He looked up from the map display, into the eyes of Solar Chancellor Hans Luger, of the Exeter System. He was tall, and obviously the recipient of rejuvenation treatment, as his file said he was nearly two hundred years old. His skin was almost perfect, his white friendly smile creating barely a wrinkle in his cheeks. His hair was blond and not grey, his hands unspotted with age and not a collapsed capillary to be seen.

"Of course, Chancellor Luger," Gavain replied. With a mental command, he deactivated the holo display and it minimised into nothingness, before he unjacked from the datasphere. "Sit down."

Luger sat down in the chair opposite Captain Gavain. He wore the long white robe of an Administration Chancellor, only the puffed sleeves and the high-backed collar - which rose above his immaculate blond hair - coloured in imperial red. It was trimmed in gold, the sign of his rank near the apex of the Administration of the Empire. The Solar Administrators had once kept the Empire running, although as the Empire cracked, so did the Administration.

"May I just say, thank you for taking me home," said Luger, laying his hands on the table. "I really appreciate it."

"Certainly," Gavain replied noncommittally. He cocked his head slightly to one side; the unaugmented human's heart rate had increased slightly, as had perspiration, despite the constancy of the computer-regulated environment. He was nervous.

"Uh, yes," the Chancellor said. "I have to say, my stay with the False Emperor was not a pleasant one."

"So I understand," Captain Gavain replied. The conditions the hostages and prisoners were kept in varied greatly, depending on the circumstances of their arrest and what they were suspected of. Judging by Luger's condition, he had not been considered any great threat to the paranoid False Emperor, merely an inconvenience.

"I was accused of being too close to the House Lord Senator of my system, his own loyalties being under question. And of course, I am fully human and not borg, which did not help matters. Unfortunately, Gunther Weiberg died whilst being questioned. His son Ibbe Weiberg has inherited the Senatorship of the seven systems of House Weiberg earlier than expected. I was due to be questioned in his place, suspected of 'treason', when thankfully, members of the Praetorian Guard - like yourself - decided the False Emperor had gone too far."

"Yes," Captain Gavain replied, "this was all in the file. House Weiberg, under Lord Gunther and then Lord Ibbe, was one of the many that were active in the Revolutionary Council."

"I can see you cut to the chase, Captain -"

"I do. I'm a busy man, Chancellor," Captain Gavain interrupted pointedly.

"Sorry," Luger held his hands up, open-palmed. "Well, obviously, I had turned my back on the Empire, and had agreed to support House Weiberg rather than the Empire." He paused. "Just saying that still seems strange. It would have been death to say that to a Praetorian, even just a few months ago .... anyway. It cannot have escaped your notice that the Empire is disintegrating, Captain. A number of Houses have already declared independence, and I suspect it is only a matter of time before the Empire breaks apart completely. There is no Emperor, no successor - no leader of the Empire. The Revolutionary Council has no interest in assuming control."

"Interesting," Captain Gavain shrugged slightly, meaning in relation to the Revolutionary Council. He had wondered whether they would try to assume control of the Empire. "But of relevance to me because ....?"

"You are not an easy man to converse with, Captain, so I will just come out and say it." Luger took a deep breath. "The Exeter System, as with all systems under control of House Weiberg, announce its independence shortly, shortly after I return to the system. And we are only a few hours away from me leaving this ship, Captain, as I'm sure you know. The Weiberg nation will be born, our seven systems forming it. I tell you this in the knowledge that there is nothing that can stop it now."

Captain Gavain just nodded, once, acknowledging that he had registered the information. Of course, he reflected, until the Praetorian Guard revolution and resultant civil war, much less the removal of the False Emperor, House Weiberg would never have dared declare independence. It would be the first of the central core Houses to do so. In terms of transit, it was virtually next door to Earth, and the False Emperor would have been merciless in his response to their rebellion. Some planets he had completely destroyed from orbit for their defiance, even when trying to fight against elements of his own Praetorian Guard. With no Emperor, however ......

"Before we left Sol, the Dissolution Order was announced by the Commander-In-Chief, although of course, I had foreknowledge from Lord Ibbe of it. I understand you have your last mission to complete, but after that, there will be no further Praetorian Guard, no need for you."

The feeling of resentment rose strong and powerful within James Gavain. "Yes," he said shortly.

"The nation of Weiberg will require its own fleet and army, Captain."

Ah, Gavain thought, the resentment suddenly replaced with understanding and surprise. That is what this is about. "Yes, Chancellor?"

"Lord Ibbe has asked me to approach you with an offer of employment. You, your crew, your ship. These are going to be fiery, chaotic times, Captain. The galaxy will burn. You need a home, and we need defence. What do you say?"

Captain James Gavain's first instinct was to reject it. Then something made him hesitate. The world as he knew it, as they all knew it, was ending. Part of the reason for rejection was that the person in front of him was a humanist, he knew that, and so was not really likely to be very supportive of an all-out borgite. Another was pride; he was a Praetorian, unbribable, loyal to .... and that was the problem, was it not? Loyal to who, he realised with shock. Not the dead False Emperor, certainly. The Praetorian High Command? Yes, of course he would do what they told him to, but that was duty, respect for the chain of command, not loyalty.

But then, he had turned his back on duty once, the duty to protect the False Emperor. Why not do it again?

"The *Vindicator* is not my battlecruiser or my property," he said shortly, warily.

"This is true," Chancellor Luger suddenly smiled, and from his eyes Gavain could see that he thought this conversation, which he had almost given up on, had swung in his favour. "But who knows what will happen in the next couple of months?" The Chancellor looked like he was about to say more, but suddenly decided not to. "It may be possible that when your mission is over, you think differently. After all, who is going to take it from you?"

"The Praetorian High Command," Captain Gavain replied quickly.

"As I said, who knows what will happen. Let us suppose that you think you are in a position in a couple of months to do what you want with it. Humour me, please?"

This is strange, Captain Gavain thought. What do you know?

"Then there is the matter of the crew. Not all of them may want to work for House Weiberg."

"We would offer land to each and every one of them, property, a home," the Chancellor came back with rattlesnake speed, displaying the iron that had taken him close to the top of his profession. "That is something none of you have right now, beyond this ship."

"A Praetorian's home is his ship," Gavain replied.

"And look at how unsure you are of that, right now," Chancellor Luger spread his hands wide. "We offer stability, Captain. To you and your crew. In return, we ask that you join the House Navy. You could always offer your crew a vote on it, and only bring the willing. We could sort out terms later, but it need not be forever if you want a retirement date, although of course I know that Praetorians have always served until death. Then again, maybe some of you will want something different apart from military service in our brave new world."

Gavain said nothing. He did not even move apart from to blink, whilst he thought about the possibilities. His instinct still said no, but that same instinct also prevented him from saying it. The Chancellor had a point –

who could say what was going to happen in the very immediate future?

"The others may well ask the same of you," the Solar Chancellor continued into the silence. He noticed the quizzical look on Gavain's face. "The other Houses, I mean. I will say to you now, whatever they offer, we will match."

Captain Gavain reached a decision. "Very well," he said. "I will not reject your offer, but at this time, it's unlikely I will accept. The High Command has the final say on what happens to this battlecruiser, and maybe even to me and my crew."

"Maybe?" Chancellor Luger smiled. "As I said, let's see what happens, hey?"

"Thank you, Solar Chancellor," Captain Gavain inclined his head. "This ..... discussion .... is over. I must return to my work, and we will be arriving in the Exeter System in less than an hour and a half. You must prepare for disembarkation."

"Yes, Captain. All I ask is you consider it. The door is always open." Solar Chancellor Luger nodded, and offered a hand as he stood. Captain Gavain ignored it. Still smiling as if he had won some concession, Chancellor Luger left the captain's table.

*

Commander-In-Chief Cisko finished his starter, and placed the eating wand very carefully onto the empty plate.

The Senator's Hall was large, lying as it did close by to the Senate. For centuries, the House Lord Senators had dined here after session in the Senate, or at least those that had attended in person and not by interstellar HPCG had dined here. It was grand and majestic, with stained glass windows at regular intervals depicting different scenes from Imperial history. They were reinforced against the Martian atmosphere of course, but the integrity of Olympus Mons City's shield-dome had been returned, and oxygen levels were returning to normal outside already.

C-I-C Cisko looked up at the roof. The ceiling had a defaced picture of the True Emperor, his face obscured on the orders of the False Emperor. It was monstrously huge, the Emperor sat in the Imperial Throne of the Red Palace. Pillars stood between each of the windows, reaching almost to the ceiling, and atop each one there sat an imperial eagle, wings in various degrees of stretch. There were alcoves near the base of each pillar, and statues of some of the more prominent figures from Imperial history.

They were only using barely a fifth of the Senator's Hall, long tables laid out in a square with the occasional gap for the waiters. The entire Praetorian High Command sat around the tables, along with some members of the Revolutionary Council's more senior activists who had been present on Mars and had supported the invasion, with some of the more senior members of the Star Communications Network, and the Interstellar Merchant's Guild. Those Solar Administration Chancellors who were known to be sympathetic to the revolution were also present.

The Commander-In-Chief noted the absence of some people he thought should have been in attendance. This was the victory dinner, after all. The Head of the IMG was absent, as was the StarCom President, and notably the Solar Administration Chancellor for Sol. The President had sent her Ops Director, who was in charge of the state media arm of StarCom, who unfortunately had been seated close to the C-I-C. Most of the Revolutionary Council was out-system of course, even in the more open days of the rebellion it having been dangerous for all of them to reveal themselves, much less gather in one place.

"Did you enjoy the seafood mix, Commander-In-Chief?"

"Yes, I certainly did," Cisko ran a hand through his greying hair. He had fallen far behind on his rejuvenation treatment. "It was from Earth, I take it, and not synthesised?"

"That's correct, sir," the waiter bowed his head as he collected the plate. The serving staff were all borgs. Once upon a time, the borg serving staff had been joined by full humans, under the True Emperor, but the False Emperor had purged all the fully human staff years ago.

"Excellent," Cisko commented into his napkin, as the waiter moved up the table.

The Commander-In-Chief leaned back in his chair, whilst he waited for the main course to be served up, and watched what was going on around him. The Admiral of the Fleets and the Marine Field Marshal were seated either side of him, the Field Marshal already drunk on the real alcohol. The Ops Director of StarCom's media arm sat next to her, hopefully not picking up on anything useful. Cisko had warned all of his High Command staff to be careful what they said in earshot of the head of the state media.

He wondered what the future held. He had been offered a position within StarCom, but had refused. They wanted to build their own military force, but he saw no reason for it, and besides which, they were banned by an old Imperial Decree.

He did not trust this President of StarCom. The StarCom network was already too powerful as it was, one only had to see how they played all sides in the Revolutionary Council to appreciate that. They had complete control of every HPCG communications station across the galaxy, the system that linked one solar system to another, and control of the only media in the galaxy beyond localised planetary media networks, which even then were under a licence monitored by StarCom. They were even trying to subsume the Interstellar Merchants Guild, which relied upon their services, and the Exploration and Colonisation Corps, not that there had been much colonisation for the last couple of decades. He suspected that ExCol would probably become part of StarCom without much fuss, although he was less sure of the IMG.

"Ah," he said to himself, as he watched the first wave of the waiters returning with the main courses. Each dish was within a covered silver plate, and as the waiters arrived at the appropriate person, they removed the domed covers with flourishes. The smell of different types of food began to fill the Hall, and made his mouth water. Following the Battle for Mars, this would be the first proper meal he had eaten. That was not good for someone of his age.

It seemed to take forever for one of the waiters to head towards him, eyes locked on. As the waiter approached, Cisko vaguely registered that the man seemed to be nervous. He stopped in front of Cisko. The man tried to open his mouth, but nothing issued forth.

"Mine I take it –" Commander-In-Chief Cisko began, then as the waiter removed the cover, "- what the hell! –"

There was a round circular device sat in place of the expected plate of food. A red light was running around it, and even as Cisko watched, the circulation of the red light sped up, as if it had detected the removal of the cover.

The bomb exploded.

"It is done," said the assassin, watching the explosion through the reinforced window of the Star Communications Network Tower.

"Yes, a good job, it would seem," replied the President of StarCom. "What are the chances of survivors?"

Through the window, in the particular, deserted office they had chosen, they could see the Senator's Hall in the distance. Most of the stained glass windows had blown out, and a significant portion of the rear of the building was already collapsing in on itself. It was as if it had been struck by an orbital turbolaser. The light from the explosion had lit the entire section of Olympus Mons City, and the noise was still reverberating around under the reactivated dome shield. Orange-red fire had vented in every direction it could, indicative of the inferno that had been ignited within the heart of the victory dinner.

"Zero," the assassin replied. "The radiation will ensure that any survivors are damaged beyond medical repair, and the bomb itself was configured to make sure that all diners within the seating plan would be caught in the blast radius. All of them will have been incinerated. I overcompensated on the strength of the explosive compound, to be sure."

President Rebecca Nielsen considered this, and actually laughed to the assassin's mild disgust. "At least I am rid of my Operations Director, as well as the High Command."

"Payment is due," the assassin said blankly, uncaring.

"It will be transferred into your usual account," President Nielsen said.

"When? The terms of contract stated that on successful detonation, I would receive payment."

"I will do it now," the President said. She jacked into the datasphere, accessed the algorithm that she had prepared in the mainframe, and activated it. Almost immediately, confirmation of the payment transfer came back to her. "It's done."

The assassin paused and then said, "Yes, payment has been received."

"Then we are done, until next time," President Nielsen replied.

"If you want me again, contact me through our associate," the assassin said. "Good day, President Nielsen." With that, the assassin simply turned and walked towards the door.

At that present moment, the assassin was a shapeless, androgynous figure, with no particularly noticeable features. As it walked towards the door, its body changed, the simple black jumpsuit it wore on personal business turning into a StarCom uniform seamlessly, its features changing into that of an old man, bone moving sickeningly in the head as it changed shape, shoulders widening. Even the gait of the walk altered.

It was a cybernetic biomorph, and to this day, President Nielsen had no idea whether it was male or female. Apart from the androgynous black jump suited, featureless figure she saw when in private, she had never seen it in the form twice. Male, female, young, old, no disguise was the same. She could not even be sure she had met the same assassin, although she had not exactly had that many meetings with the hired killer.

As the door hissed shut behind the assassin, she shivered, and not for the first time thought about paying the assassin a retainer to ensure loyalty, or have the assassin killed. Still, she knew the last House Lord to try doing that to the Faceless had been found in several different pieces in several different locations, his entire household guard murdered, and his palace destroyed.

She was willing to bet that the assassin could have taken down the False Emperor, if it had ever been employed to do so. The underworld's guild of assassins, the Faceless, had always refused any contract on either of the Emperors. Many rumoured that they had been illicitly supported by the Emperors. She would probably never know.

She put such thoughts out of her mind, and turned back to the window to look at the devastation wrought secretly in her name. The High Command of the Praetorians, completely obliterated. All of a sudden, there were a lot of armed men and ships in the galaxy with no-one to command them or provide them with direction.

Commander-In-Chief Cisko had been suspicious of her, President Nielsen knew, but he had severely underestimated the lengths her ambition could go to.

Chapter III

The darkness of the void in the Roshnetak System was suddenly torn asunder by a flash of light, and an image of blurring on a large scale, as the *Vindicator* battlecruiser arrived in-system. It appeared to be stretched out as it arrived, snapping back into normal parameters as it exited the jump.

<The translation into realspace has been successful, Captain,> Navigations Lieutenant Chu reported.

Captain Gavain sent an acknowledgement through the datasphere.

<Structural Integrity Field collapsing,> Commander De Graaf said. <Warp Accelerators going off-line - exit complete.>

Out of sheer habit, Captain Gavain called up an image of the Roshnetak System. As he studied it, he listened to the activities of his crew through the datasphere.

The Roshnetak System consisted of seven planets, all of an extraordinary size by normal standards, and that alone marked it out as being fairly unusual. The first planet, Roshnetak I, was completely uninhabitable on its surface, close to the sun and baked to a cinder, but rich in all sorts of minerals and metals, which fed a thriving mining industry that even now hollowed out the inside of the planet. It was on the far side of the sun, invisible to the *Vindicator* from its current position, a computer tag identifying its position on the map as an estimation.

Roshnetak II was large, five times the size of Mars, and on this side of the system from where the *Vindicator* had jumped in. The planet was hot, 1.3 gravity, heavily populated, engaged in heavy industry, and famous for its gangs and crime. Roshnetak III, which was actually further away than Roshnetak IV because of its current position in its orbit around the sun, was cooler but equally as large, and as dangerous. Roshnetak IV was slightly smaller, but was the capital of the system, and the closest planet to the *Vindicator*'s position. In astronomical terms it was still some distance away, but every system had permitted jumping points marked on the Imperial Charts, to prevent accidents with local shipping, and the battlecruiser had jumped in on one of them.

Roshnetak V and VI were gas giants, both of them failed stars, both of them mined for their gas. They were hulks, both so far away they appeared tiny at this distance. Roshnetak VII, the last and the coldest planet, was the smallest, but still three times the size of Mars, frigid and utilised as a military base by the House Navy and Army. The Roshnetak System was one of the main systems that fell under House Cervantes, and Cervantes was an exceptionally powerful house. Lord Simeon Cervantes, who the *Vindicator* had escorted to the system, was the first born son of the

Lord Senator.

It was the objects located within the system that Gavain paid attention to, however. There was a large linear asteroid field close to Roshnetak IV's orbit, and less than half an hour's travel from here. At the edges of that asteroid field was the gigantic shipyard they were going to take advantage of, to affect repairs from the battle around Mars.

The House Navy was active here, that much was obvious. No less than three battlecruisers were moving slowly away from Roshnetak VII into another jump point, a general band which ran around the entire outside of the system. Roshnetak VII also had a vast number of military transporters in orbit. A star-carrier was nearby, tactical already assessing from preliminary scans that it was fully loaded with starfighters, just cresting the asteroid field, heading to the shipyard. There were two frigates actually in the shipyard, with a civilian cargo-freighter. There were another seven military ships and three major civilian ships in system at various distances away, besides countless small interplanetary shuttles, and those were just the ones they could see.

<Tactical reports all is normal, no threats> said Commander De Graaf, but there was something in the tone of voice. The blond haired, blue eyed, handsome man had put his chin on his hand, eyes alive with interest as he assessed his Captain.

Gavain broadcast openly, <An old habit, Commander.> He did not flick the tactical display off, merely minimising it. <Drop the firewalls, and begin downloads.>

<As you command,> came the traditional reply from the Lieutenant in charge of Communications, Ms. Forrest. Within the second, the mainframe reported that the protective electronic firewalls were dropping, the powerful super-modems were dialling in to the dataspheres of the planets, and already the daily download was on its way. Every solar system had regular updates for visitors, consisting of a package of rules of the system, facts, figures, news updates, military updates, and announcements both Imperial, House and local, amongst other things.

<Put me through to Lord Simeon,> Gavain commanded.

The communicator panel woven into the skin of his right hand suddenly flared to life, the metallic surface appearing through the pores of the human flesh. In a moment or two, the implant had emerged completely. He raised the back of his hand to his mouth, the communicator already connected to Lord Simeon's own personal communicator.

"Lord Simeon, Captain Gavain. We have just jumped into Roshnetak. Your journey with us is at an end. Are you and the Planetary Governor ready to leave?"

"Yes, Captain, we are."

"Then make your way to –" Captain Gavain paused as he checked the datasphere "- shuttlebay four. We have a shuttle prepped to take you to Roshnetak IV, whilst we repair at the shipyard."

"How long will the journey be?" the House Lord demanded, in an imperious tone.

"No more than six hours, my Lord," Captain Gavain replied.

There was a dissatisfied sound at the other end. "Very well. Adios, Captain."

"My Lord." Captain Gavain deactivated the communicator, plunging wholly back into the interconnected web of data with a small feeling of relief.

Briefly, Gavain thought of the Solar Chancellor Luger that they had dropped off at the Exeter System. As Commander De Graaf very competently oversaw the operations of the ship post-jump, something which Gavain watched with interest, he accessed the news downloads that were coming in over the automatic beacon. In moments he had found the news article on the Exeter System, and digested its contents as pure text in less than a second.

<Look, Jules,> he opened up a private channel to Lieutenant Commander Kavanagh. <House Weiberg declared independence whilst we were in transit.>

Julia Kavanagh accessed the same article. <Wonders never cease, James. That's why Chancellor Luger made his offer to you. He knew what was going to happen.> Gavain had shared the offer Luger had made with all his command staff; it had never occurred to him not to.

Another channel opened up in his mind - seeing as it was ship's business, he signed off from the comms with Lieutenant Commander Kavanagh. Lieutenant Forrest said <Captain, you have an exceedingly large number of messages from all number of sources out-system. There is a priority alpha message from the President of StarCom. It's a personal message. I thought you might like to know, sir.>

<You were correct,> Gavain said with typical brusqueness. He accessed the message in text format, to absorb it quicker.

His heart almost stopped, he was sure. "It can't be true," he said aloud.

<James?> the inquiry popped into his mind.

<Later, Jules,> he said. He needed to see the video message in full. He stood, looking directly at Commander De Graaf. He disconnected from the datapshere completely. "You have the bridge, Commander."

With that, he walked to his ready room, only clenching his fists once he was on his own and the doors had shut.

Lieutenant-Commander Kavanagh walked into the ready room cautiously, as her Captain had given her permission to do so. Once the immediate post-jump operations had taken place, only one member of command staff needed to be on duty.

"Is everything alright, James?" she asked.

"No," he replied with typical shortness. "Why? Is it that obvious?"

"Not really," Kavanagh replied, feeling a small white lie was appropriate. "I know you, and I can see when something is wrong."

James Gavain leaned back in his seat, and gestured wordlessly at the one on the other side of the desk with his left hand. His right held a steaming cup of coffee.

Even after all this time, she could not read James Gavain that well. His face was giving nothing away, but she thought she could see some signs of worry in his eyes. When he suddenly sighed as she sat down, she knew he was deeply concerned. In short order, so was she.

James Gavain was not ugly, but nor was he particularly handsome, at least to her. His short hazel brown hair was light in some places, dark in others, running to thinness. He was only forty years old, which was hardly any age at all in a time when people lived for centuries. He was young to be a Commander, let alone a Captain. Taller than average, thin, with what was called an athletic build, he hardly dominated a room. He managed that with the pure iciness of his personality, the familiarity with command and the respect others gave him willingly.

"What is it, James?"

"I've had a .... startling, message from StarCom." He looked out of one of the windows to his left, staring into space, before snapping his head back. "I cannot believe it is true."

"What, James?"

"The Praetorian High Command. There was a bomb, at the Senator's Hall. It has wiped out the entire Command."

Lt-Cdr Julia Kavanagh blinked rapidly several times. There was no point in asking him to repeat it. "There have definitely been no survivors?"

James Gavain shook his head. "Complete and total extinction of life. Apparently, investigations are under way."

"It's not been on the StarCom News Media."

"No. The communication came from the President of StarCom. Apparently, they are delaying news of the 'event' until they have something concrete to report, a story to spin to the masses."

Julia noticed that James kept saying the word 'apparently', and she knew why. "You don't believe this."

"Absolutely not," he took it as a question. "Especially not because of what else President Nielsen said in her message."

"Which was?"

"She did a Chancellor Luger. She offered to take us on directly into StarCom, to form a military force. She's offered it to all the Praetorian Guard. She pointed out that we have no High Command, so many of us are on our own."

We are, aren't we, Julia reflected. The *Vindicator* was part of Tenth Fleet, and their Admiral had been in the High Command. The Vice-Admiral and two Rear-Admirals had been killed in the Battle for Mars, and the third Rear-Admiral had remained loyal to the False Emperor, as had both Commodores. There was nobody above Captain Gavain - he had no chain of command any more. There were other ranking officers, of course, but they were not in Tenth Fleet, and the Praetorians had always been very, very strict about chains of command. No-one remained to give Captain Gavain an order, not a person in the galaxy.

"What do you intend to do?" she asked.

"Follow my recent orders. They still stand. We must return the lords and ladies and the governors and the chancellors to their homes. And then the Dissolution Order takes effect."

"And then, what do you intend to do?" she swallowed. "After all, with no High Command, there is no-one to look after us, no-one to give us direction when the Dissolution Order applies to us. No-one to sell the ship, give us our pay-off. What will you do?"

He paused for a long time. "I don't know," he looked down at the coffee cup.

She looked at her friend carefully. This was a rare admission, without doubt. She thought quickly, then she softened her voice, aware she was one of the few who would dare speak to James like this. "Well, you have a couple of options, maybe. The best thing to do is to think about what those options are, and then take your time to decide. There is no need to make a decision now, especially as the SCNM haven't released the news to the galaxy yet."

"They will eventually, and then I will have to provide some reassurance to the crew." It was said as a challenge, not as someone who was lost, but Kavanagh could see Gavain was completely in space over this.

"And you will, when the time comes, I'm sure you will, James. Just think about what to do, take the time you have. You know this." She waited for him to nod. "So it was a bomb that took the High Command out. Is there anything said at all about who did it?"

"No," he shook his head, anger suddenly flaring. "But, when you take C-I-C Cisko's warning about StarCom's ambitions, then their suspiciously fast offer to form a military, which old Cisko had refused, it looks –"

All of a sudden, their conversation was interrupted as the ship went to red alert, and the battle stations call sounded out.

Commander De Graaf sat in the command chair, watching the datasphere, ensuring that all was right with the ship. He felt somewhat ill-at-ease. He had come from an R-Class destroyer, not a V-Class battlecruiser, and the *Retribution* was a very different ship from the *Vindicator*. Even their bridges were different. Everywhere he looked, he was reminded of what he had lost.

He was not sure what to make of this Captain Gavain, either. He was young for a Captain, and De Graaf knew the command had only been offered in very unusual circumstances. He seemed stand-offish, almost arrogant to the point of rudeness sometimes. As for Lieutenant-Commander Kavanagh, she seemed nice enough, a very relaxed individual, but he did not trust it. There was no possible way she could not resent his being re-assigned to the *Vindicator*, essentially blocking her promotion. Although with the Dissolution Order, perhaps it did not matter to her. She never showed any sign of animosity, but that could just as easily be two-facedness. The Marine Major, the other member of the command staff, he had only met the once, and definitely did not like. He was too loud, too opinionated, and too confrontational.

De Graaf felt like throwing it all in. He had lived his life for the Praetorians, for the Empire, and he had watched in horror as the False Emperor had taken power and shown his true colours. He had rebelled willingly, and then watched as the civil war tore all he had known apart. Somehow, he found himself here, on this ship, witnessing yet more change. He felt he could not cope, and he tried not to think about it if he could help it, but everywhere he looked the reality of his situation was hammered back into his consciousness by the strange surroundings. He could not let it all go.

He felt like he was falling apart as fast as the Red Empire was, sometimes.

<Commander,> the call came, <we have a problem, sir .... a data-virus has just come across from the auto-beacon.>

Instantly, De Graaf was alert, almost glad for a problem to concentrate on. <What sort of virus, and what exposure do we have? I need a Situation Report, Sub-Lieutenant.> he demanded. He was pleased to note, pulled out of his reverie, that the rest of the crew had suddenly also become more alert at the data-tac officer's warning. He knew it could not have got far into their systems, as the automatic alert had not been sounded, or the computers would have failed. It was not uncommon for viruses to remain in systems and get transferred accidentally, but then, it was not exactly expected either.

<I'm not sure,> the data-tactical officer, Sub-Lieutenant Woolfe was leaning closely into the station pod, shoulders tense as she worked. <It was detected and isolated fairly quickly by secondary viral checkers. I've no ident on the source code. No danger to ship's systems, Commander, but it was designed to deactivate the mainframe and redundancies, and leave us

dead in the water. It would have played havoc with a civilian ship, but for us, no problem, sir.>" Praetorian technology was the most advanced in the Imperium, and even very few of the most competent House militaries could match it.

Commander De Graaf said <Well done, Sub-Lieutenant,> and almost felt the pride radiate from the officer. It was probably designed to incapacitate a civilian freighter, but such viruses were more common in the outer regions of the Empire where pirates could take advantage of a disabled ship, not this deep in the core, even nowadays.

<Raise the firewalls,> Commander De Graaf ordered. <Just to be safe.>

<Firewalls going up, Commander> Woolfe replied, then, <Firewalls active.>

De Graaf considered informing the Captain, but decided there was no immediate danger, and he had taken appropriate action. <Begin an intensive sensor sweep for ships running on silent,> he ordered the scanners section. It would not hurt to be sure that there was no-one out there, a pirate waiting to take advantage of a disabled civilian ship. He would be surprised if that was the case this deep into the core, but he had heard of it happening before, and attended the aftermath of such surprise attacks. Only in the outer systems, though.

<Sir, we're under attack, two military-grade viruses have just hit the firewall!>

<Ident?>

<One is definitely House Cervantes source code, sir! ... and yes, so is the other one>

<Red alert, battle stations, all hands to battle stations,> Commander De Graaf ordered. His mind was racing - this was not coincidence, it could not be. The red alert sounded throughout the entire ship at his words, the computer mainframe picking it up immediately.

<Sensors?> he demanded.

<Nothing yet, sir,> was the reply.

<Weapons hot and ready, Commander,> the tactical officer, <Shields going up.>

<Contact System Command, and ask them why we came under data attack from one of their viruses,> Commander De Graaf said, even as his peripheral vision caught the door to the ready room opening. <Put it nicely, though. Captain on the bridge!>

He stood, vacating the command seat, moving to his secondary chair, even as the senior tactical officer reported that the shields were now at full power, and all blast covers had been engaged.

<SitRep,> Captain Gavain demanded, even as he crossed the command dais to his own position at the head of the bridge.

Commander De Graaf updated him quickly, all his thoughts of before forgotten in the face of the immediate situation. The red warning panels of battle stations flashed all around the bridge incessantly.

<Torpedo launch, torpedo launch!> the senior tactical officer, Lieutenant Meier, suddenly called out. <Three incoming .... make that five, another two from a second source. Two ships running on silent located.>

<Defensive fire, abort course to the following heading> Captain Gavain ordered calmly. De Graaf was amazed at how calm Gavain was; with his augmetics, De Graaf could see that Gavain's heart rate had not even increased, or his perspiration or body temperature, the typical reaction in a battle situation. This man was icy cold.

De Graaf activated a data-map, setting it just in front of him, Gavain and Kavanagh. The tactical map displayed the position of the *Vindicator*, the likely location of the two assailants, and five rapidly moving dots showing the tracks of the torpedoes. They were still out of range of the battlecruiser's defensive batteries, but at their speed, it would only be a matter of seconds.

<Three more torpedo launches, a third ship identified,> Lieutenant Meier called out.

<Commander, find out who is attacking us,> Captain Gavain ordered, even as Meier was reporting that the four of the torpedoes had been taken out by turbolaser fire. The fifth smashed into their shields, but all it did was drain the energy of the protective force fields.

<Target the suspected location of target alpha, and fire six torpedoes, maximum spread,> Captain Gavain ordered. <I want one of those ships found, people.>

De Graaf was reviewing the sensor logs, following orders, but there was precious little information. The ships were still running on silent, although now they were moving, there was a minimal energy signature. They would have special low-energy force fields up to mask their energy signatures, undetectable at long distance like this. They would have their communications capabilities deactivated, even their protective shields. Chameleon fields would have been activated, to make them invisible, all the running lights that a ship typically used would have been extinguished.

<Sensors are reporting that the House Cervantes star-carrier is launching fighters, and has changed direction towards us, Captain,> De Graaf said. <I can't make the stealthed ships out there, but it's reasonable to assume that House Cervantes is attacking us, especially as the military viruses had Cervantes source code.>

<Agreed, Captain,> Lieutenant-Commander Kavanagh said, <It seems the most likely identity of our attackers.>

<Strike!> Lieutenant Meier interrupted. <Second strike on target alpha. Their chameleon field is failing ......>

De Graaf called up a visual. With no shields possible when running on silent, when the first torpedo had hit the attacker, it had punched into bare, unprotected hull. One of the other torpedoes had automatically changed direction, and ploughed into the other side of the starship. The others had been on too wide of a spread to react.

The visual showed what was undoubtedly a frigate. As the chameleon fields failed, and the ship was revealed in all its infamy, the colours of House Cervantes could be seen on the hull.

<Fire at will, Lieutenant Meier. Destroy that frigate.> Captain Gavain ordered. Then he activated the private command channel. <Options, people?>

<Withdraw,> Commander De Graaf said promptly. <We have enough of a jump-charge to make an emergency jump out of the system, and we will be outgunned if we stay.>

<There's nothing to gain by staying,> Lieutenant-Commander Kavanagh added.

<Very well.> Captain Gavain gave the order to prepare to jump.

<Incoming message from Roshnetak IV,> comms Lieutenant Forrest said, <It is from the House Lord Senator Cervantes. He demands that we power down and turn over the *Vindicator* to House Cervantes.>

<Tell him to fuck himself,> Marine Major Andryukhin's voice came over on the private command channel. He and all his marines would be fully suited up by now, ready for anything.

<No reply,> Gavain simply ordered Lieutenant Forrest. <How long until we can jump?>

<Two minutes,> Commander De Graaf replied. <I've selected an uninhabited system, not on our plan, Nav have the co-ordinates.>

<Adjust heading, ready for the jump> Captain Gavain ordered the Helmsman.

<Captain!> the scanners officer Lieutenant Agrawal shouted across the datasphere, <The three battlecruisers at the edge of the solar system have just jumped .... they're re-emerging here!>

De Graaf could not believe the desperation. It was an incredibly dangerous manoeuvre to jump such a relatively short distance, but House Cervantes had probably detected the *Vindicator*'s jump preparations, and wanted to prevent it at all costs. To jump such a short distance risked burning out their accelerators, or complete structural failure of the ship. Even now, De Graaf could see that one of the battlecruisers had overshot completely, and had almost materialised within the gravity well caused by the asteroid field. If it had translated there, it would have been pulverised into nothingness by the interference of the gravity well.

Gavain had seen that one of the battlecruisers had actually jumped so close to the *Vindicator* it was within middle-range of their secondary weaponry. It could very easily have collided with the Praetorian Guard ship, and if it had at hyperspace-exit speeds, there would have been nothing left of either ship. <All fire on target epsilon. We need it incapacitated before we lower shields for the jump.>

<The other two frigates are going hot,> Lieutenant Meier reported, <All fire commencing, Captain.>

The dark void between the *Vindicator* and the House Cervantes battlecruiser closest to it became alive with light. The target had no shields, as it had just exited the jump, and the *Vindicator* let rip with a spread of torpedoes from its starboard and upper hull launchers, turbolaser fire flickering across the distance from all of the batteries it could bring to bear. Magnetic Acceleration Cannons hurled projectiles at the target, whilst close-range disruptor emitters fired beams capable of breaking down the actual molecules of the target. In the space of ten seconds, the hull of the target battlecruiser had actually rippled, and then, with a massive explosion, a large portion of the battlecruiser literally disintegrated, an equally large section flying away into space.

The *Vindicator* was still firing on the frigate that was target alpha, and was doing significant damage, but it had now raised its shield fully. Shortly, it would be within turbolaser range.

<Target epsilon is losing power!> Lieutenant Agrawal called out, sounding like he could scarcely believe it.

<We are jump-ready, Captain,> Commander De Graaf reported.

Captain Gavain acknowledged, and then paid close attention to the tactical map. He waited, watching as the latest spread of torpedoes from the target gamma frigate almost drained away their rear shields completely, and then judging it to be the safest time, gave the jump order.

The *Vindicator* dropped its shields quickly, and engaged its warp accelerators. A wave of turbolaser fire lanced into it from target zeta, doing some damage to the hull. The accelerators reacted with the jump field around it, and with a blur, the *Vindicator* dived into hyperspace.

Chapter IV

Major Andryukhin exited the lift onto the bridge. He was in full power armour, minus the helmet which he had retracted back into the suits collar. The status panels throughout the entire ship were flashing amber, a downgrade from red alert, but hence the reason why he was still fully armoured. He crossed the bridge, and entered the ready room.

"Sorry I'm late," he said, jokingly.

"You're not," Captain Gavain shook his head, taking him seriously, as he lifted his steaming cup of coffee to his mouth. Andryukhin rolled his eyes as he clumped over to the small conference table in the room, taking a seat. He liked James, but the man's sense of humour needed some adjustment in his opinion. He was always the last to a command staff meeting, as he had further to come than the others.

"Hey, beautiful," he winked at Lieutenant-Commander Kavanagh, noting how Commander De Graaf reacted to the lack of respect. "I heard there was some kind of scrap?"

"You could say that," Jules Kavanagh replied drily. "You got out of it with having to do nothing, again, I noticed."

"I've gotta let you star-gazers have some of the fun," Andryukhin grinned. "I didn't see you lot getting your boots dusty on Mars though, did I?"

"Come on, people," Captain Gavain interrupted. "To work. Our current status, Lucas?"

Lucas De Graaf looked equally surprised to be addressed on first name terms. He would learn, thought Major Andryukhin. The command staff were very close on this ship, and he could either be a part of it or not. Personally, he was beginning to dislike the stuffy commander, and doubted he would fit in.

"We are in system DL-27984," Commander De Graaf began, blinking his blue eyes a couple of times. "It is uninhabited, and has a relatively weak sun. It will take about nine days to recharge the capacitors to full, but we would have recharged enough that we could make an emergency jump in slightly less than three days if we are found by House Cervantes –"

"- if they decide to chase us," Major Andryukhin pointed out.

"We must assume they will, for our own security. Continue, Lucas," Gavain nodded.

"Thank you, Captain," the Commander said stiffly, and Andryukhin instantly felt a wave of irritation at the stuffy commander. "In terms of damage, our shield generators held well, although we need to recharge them as we almost lost protection on our rear shield. We should be at full on all shields in less than two hours, however. We did take some turbolaser damage to the port and upper hull sections from target epsilon, but no loss of life or hull breaches occurred."

"We were lucky," Major Andryukhin interrupted again. "It could have been so much worse, the frikkers. Why the bloody hell did they do it? I mean, why then? They should have waited until we'd docked at the shipyard and then boarded us, surely?"

"Don't know," said Gavain. "They wanted the ship, that much was clear. It looks like something went wrong in their plans - they only started firing once we started actively scanning for threats."

"We would have found their hidden frigates eventually, Jamie," Kavanagh said. "Someone on their frigates got jumpy, perhaps they thought we'd found them. The first one fired, and then the second, whilst the third held for a longer period of time."

"That's the problem with a small squadron running on silent," Captain Gavain pointed out. "Can't talk to the other ships if something goes wrong in the plan."

"Whatever the reason, though, we were lucky," Lieutenant-Commander Kavanagh said. "What's the plan going forwards? We've deviated from our original flight plan, and our guests are going to start asking questions soon. I've already had two enquiries as to what is going on."

"We tell them the truth," grunted Ulrik Andryukhin. "We were fired upon by House Cervantes. Let the frikkers think about what happens when the Praetorians are betrayed. That battlecruiser's not going anywhere for a long time. We should have shot bloody House Lord Simeon's shuttle out of space when we had the chance."

"We stay here," Captain Gavain said slowly. "We recharge to full, unless we are discovered by Cervantes chasers."

"We shouldn't be," said De Graaf. "There were over thirty-nine systems we could have jumped to on the vector I chose, it would take them a long time to find us. And we don't even know if they will try."

"Even so," Gavain leaned back in his chair. "We never take the risk of jumping into an inhabited system without back-up jump charge. From now on, we go to restricted jumping - one jump, and then recharge in that system. I want two jump charges in the tank in case we have to escape on short notice again."

"That will alter our flight plan," Julia Kavanagh pointed out.

"Work it out and tell the Lords and Ladies, Jules," Gavain ordered. "But we will not communicate it outside the ship, and I want all their communications monitored to prevent them leaking it. We will have to apply stricter operational security to all our movements. I'm not taking the risk of something similar happening again. Whenever we jump into an inhabited system, we go to green status and run full checks on everything, including active scans."

"What about the repairs to the ship, Jamie?" Kavanagh said. "We were going to use the Roshnetak shipyard to repair. We're damaged, with at least two weeks-worth of downtime. We have to trust somebody at some point," she said gently.

"We were just frikking lucky we weren't damaged worse than we were," Andryukhin interrupted.

"Leave that to me," James Gavain gave a rare smile. "I have a .... friend .... on our journey who will be able to help. Commodore Harley Andersson, at the Janus Shipyards in the Andes System."

The Janus Shipyards were a Praetorian Guard owned facility, secreted from public knowledge. Most Praetorian ships had stopped there for repair at some point in their life history, at least those that operated in the core.

"What of our guests?" Andryukhin asked. "They can't bloody well see it, can they?"

"We keep them on ship, and confined, during the layover," Gavain said simply.

"They'll love that," Andryukhin snorted.

"So, *why* did the House Cervantes attack us, full stop?" Julia Kavanagh asked.

"Bloody obvious, isn't it," Major Andryukhin snorted. "The galaxy's going to hell in a piss-pot. The Empire's falling apart. Look at the House Weiberg declaration of independence. It wouldn't surprise me if House Cervantes declares it's seceding from the Empire. They wanted to build up their own military for the frik-storm that's coming, and couldn't pass up on a Praetorian starship."

"There's going to be more war, isn't there," said Julia Kavanagh quietly.

"Too damn right," Major Andryukhin slapped an armoured fist on the table with a metallic crunch. "The civil war was the beginning, not the frikking end of it."

"It does appear that we are becoming sought-after property," James Gavain interjected, gravely. "This is not to go to the rest of the crew, but Cervantes only tried to do by force what Weiberg tried to do with money." Andryukhin listened with surprise as James explained the offer Solar Chancellor Luger had made.

"Bloody hell," he swore. "He couldn't have been serious."

"I'm taking it seriously," James said, looking at all three of them. "There is more." Then he explained about the Praetorian High Command bombing, and the StarCom offer. "I was in the process of telling Jules when we were attacked," he said, "this is the first chance I've had to share it with you."

"What do we do?" Commander De Graaf spoke for the first time in a while. He looked pained, to Andryukhin, and the Major wondered what was going on in the man's blond head. "We ..... well, we're alone, now, aren't we?"

"There are other Praetorians," Gavain pointed out gently. "But none in our chain of command. People - we need to have a think, all of us, about what we do. I'm determined we will carry out our last order to convey these nobles back to their home systems, but after that, as far as I am concerned, the Dissolution Order takes effect and we are no longer in the Praetorian Guard. The ship is ours, and all we have is each other."

"We've got two offers on the table," Julia Kavanagh said. "One from Weiberg, one from StarCom. Or we could always scupper the ship, and go our separate ways – but I have to say, I don't want to do that. I think most of the crew will feel the same."

"After all," said Major Andryukhin, quietly for him, "Where the hell do we have to go? We have no home apart from this ship – we were all frikking vatborn on Deimos. And I don't want to go to StarCom either, I'll tell you that for frikking nothing either."

"Whatever we do, at the end of our mission, we will do together, and everyone in the crew will have a say," James Gavain replied.

"Are you suggesting a vote, sir?" Commander De Graaf asked. "That's highly unusual, Captain. Think of morale?"

"These are unusual times. A vote on our future is appropriate, I think, once we've decided what the options should be. And please, Lucas, call me James or Jamie. We're all friends here."

There was a moment of silence, as everyone looked at De Graaf. Quite surprisingly, he turned a bit red. Andryukhin felt that wave of irritation again with the Commander. Don't bet on it Jamie, he thought to himself.

"Have you had any chance to catch up on what else is happening out in the galaxy?" Julia Kavangh changed subject slightly, with her typical sensitivity to other people.

"According to the news we downloaded, five more Houses have declared their systems independent," Gavain said, with a certain deadness in his voice. "From personal messages, I had one from Admiral Haas of Eighth Fleet, saying he had gone over to StarCom, and urging me to take the President's offer up. It was a round-robin, copied to every ship captain in the Guard. I also had a follow-up message from Captain Reichenburg, saying that he and a number of Eighth Fleet had deserted and jumped out-system. They're all going their separate ways, but it put the lie to what Haas said."

"Haas always was a frikking idiot. I had a message from one of my friends in the Marine Corps, Second Division, Fourth Regiment" Ulrik Andryukhin shrugged. "It just said he and some of his unit were stood down completely by the Dissolution Order. The very next day House

Devereux invaded, and they could do nothing about it. They've all been offered individual commissions in the Devereux House Army, and he thinks most of them are going to accept. They've no way off-planet anyway, the fuckers impounded all their frikking transporters!"

"It was in the news that the Interstellar Merchants Guild have formally declared that they will not become a part of StarCom, and will maintain their independence," said Julia Kavanagh. "The Head of the IMG says he will continue to work with President Nielsen, and they will stay close as they always have, but he also wants to continue to offer all his services to all of the Houses. He has also declared that they won't collect shipping tax whilst this is ongoing, until it is clear what is going to happen with the Empire, but they will still act as a neutral bonding commission for merchant contracts, at a reduced percentage."

"How's that going to work?" Andryukhin snorted.

"It's quite clever, actually," said Kavanagh. "If you read between the lines, why should all the Houses that have gone independent pay the shipping tax? It's always been resented. With more and more systems declaring independence, especially, why bother? But everyone needs to trade, and whilst the merchants and businesses don't need the shipping tax, they do need an independent service that will guarantee they get paid. The buyer places the money into the IMG, the seller delivers the goods or service, and the IMG releases the money. With so much uncertainty in the galaxy, they're probably going to make a killing in monetary terms."

"It spits in the eye of Imperial Law," said Gavain severely.

"There won't be a frikking Red Empire in a few more weeks at this rate," Major Andryukhin snorted.

There was once again silence at the table. "Well," said Gavain, "If no-one else has anything to add, we'll call this meeting over? No? Very well then - dismissed."

*

"Are we not done yet?" President Nielsen demanded.

"Er, yes, madam President," the servant stammered, moving the applicator device away from the most powerful woman in the entire solar system of Sol, let alone the mighty galaxy-spanning organisation that was the Star Communications Network.

"Get gone, then," she waved the servant away. With a palpable look of relief, he did not even wait to properly stow the applicator into its case, merely shoving it all onto the floating tray by his side and dragging it away towards the exit.

Nielsen leaned back in her chair, a small smile on her face. The next to feel her wrath would be the three-man holo-projection crew, who were still making adjustments to the suite's equipment. If it were a borg-only conference all this physical paraphernalia would not be necessary, as it would all take place in a virtual environment within a secured datasphere, but there were unaugmented humans within the forthcoming interstellar meeting, so that would not be possible.

How did the unaugmented cope, she wondered? She was not quite as extreme as the False Emperor had been in his beliefs, but as a borg with a borgite philosophy, she found the unaugmented humans - whether they be humanist or free-thinking in their beliefs - somewhat distasteful and almost barbarian in their acceptance of non-augmentation. Where once in history the great divider had been religion, in modern times the issue was implant technology.

"How much longer?" she demanded. "The conference starts in less than a couple of minutes."

"We're almost there, madam President, almost," someone who she took to be the head of the crew said quickly.

"Well, hurry!" she slapped a hand down on the desk surface before her. It was an ancient antique from pre-Industrial era Europe. The True Emperor had been a great history lover, apparently, and so the False Emperor had destroyed much of what he had liked on Mars. This holo-suite was based deep within the StarCom Network's grand headquarters on the red planet, and neither Emperor had concerned themselves much with visiting the facilities of the various organisations that operated in their name.

She straightened the uniform that she wore. As President, she wore the dark green colours of StarCom, with Imperial red as a secondary colour, and golden trim. A long cloak covering one shoulder was Imperial red. A golden eagle of the Red Empire, its wings outstretched, was emblazoned across her chest and on the back of the cloak, but in its claws it held a golden representation of Earth, with a laurel wreath wrapped around it. The earth-and-wreath was the traditional symbol of StarCom.

The very next thing I'm going to do, President Rebeccah Nielsen thought, is change this damn uniform, and get rid of that eagle. In reality she would most likely wait, as change had to happen in increments to be accepted, but it was a nice thought.

"Less than one minute ..." she drawled.

"We're done, madam President," the crew leader actually saluted before he led the others off the floor.

She glanced up at the gallery. The holo pit she was in was slightly sunk into the floor, the desk she was seated at had been moved to one side of the huge circular depression, almost against the wall. When it was fully activated, the holo-images of the other participants would appear around the circle, and the speaker's image would flash into the middle of the pit.

The gallery hung above the pit, out of view of the participants, deliberately off-camera. She currently had her senior support staff up there. Her new Operations Director was sat there, as was the Head of the StarCom News Media, an old supporter. Her new Commander-In-Chief of the StarCom Armed Forces was there, a former Praetorian Guard member. The Communications Director sat a little way from the others, probably worried about his future in an organisation where his support was rapidly dwindling, the Security Director staring at him openly. There were a number of senior managers from all the various arms, the Solar Administration Chancellor of Sol, the Planetary Governors of all the planets and planetoids in the system.

A large audience to watch this historic moment, she thought. Witnesses were essential, and of course, the whole conference would be recorded and replayed through the StarCom News Media, suitably edited of course.

"Three ..... two ..... one ..... we're go!" the amplified voice of the stage manager flowed through the holo suite.

The lighting dimmed suddenly, and a green light mounted in the ceiling went red. She levelled her gaze, staring in front of her, and put on her best smile.

The HyperPulse Communications Generator in Olympus Mons City would even now be pumping its beam into the sky, the signal going into Hyperspace. Whereas in other times they could fire once, dumping data in one quick pulse, the HPCGs could now fire continuously, sending a continuous stream of live data across the entire galaxy with little more than a slightly noticeable delay in realtime. A ship using hyperspace was limited by its need to maintain structural integrity, but a low-level laser beam of pure data had no such problem. Rather, the only limitation was the possibility of the HPCG overheating, in which case they would simply switch to another without any drop in signal.

Even now, the continuous signal was jumping into an untold number of systems. Such a widely dispersed multiple continuous signal would mean swapping out the HPCG almost every minute, but it would be worth it for almost-live conversation with all the most powerful people remaining in the galaxy.

"President Nielsen present," a robotic voice sounded out in the holo pit. It would be played out in all the holo pits across the galaxy, where these people who suddenly blipped into existence around her would be sitting.

She gazed around, flashing each her smile. The holo pit was full of various people, and she could see that she was the last to attend. She would have that holo crew's heads, she decided. All these people were the members of the Revolutionary Council, those who had survived the civil war.

She nodded only briefly at the Head of the Interstellar Merchants

Guild. Well played, she thought, your latest gambit was excellent, if a trifle lacking in ambition.

She tapped the speak panel in front of her. The Revolutionary Council did not have a chairperson as such, all being equal in the Council, but she wanted to be the first to address the conference. Her late entrance had prevented that, and she had lost her chance. The holo crew would definitely pay, she decided.

The image of House Lord Yassin Al-Zuhairi, leader of a large tract of systems covering the Frontier and the Boundary, flickered into the centre of the holo pit. Tall, dark and handsome in a cruel way, when the unaugmented humanist spoke he had the accent of the outer colonial systems.

"Lords, ladies, my friends," he began, "We must keep this brief. Even though a part of our success, StarCom decides to charge us a fortune for this gathering. The Praetorian Guard who joined us have been successful on Mars, and the False Emperor is dead. The revolution has been bloody, but it has been won. The loss of Commander-In-Chief Cisko is very regrettable, a tragedy that must be investigated, and those who caused it held accountable.

"However, we must focus on what is to come. We were always focused on the removal of the Emperor, and left until now the question of what would happen afterwards. Nevertheless, many of us spoke about it in private as well as in council, and we all have our own thoughts and feelings on the matter. We here represent nearly a third of the Red Imperium, and whilst our votes cannot be binding on the entire Empire, we are, at the moment, the ones who are best placed to determine the future.

"With that in mind, I put forward the following proposition. The Revolutionary Council should become the ruling government of the Imperium, with one leader chosen by democratic vote on a regular basis. Let us leave the question of the leader for the moment, but we invite the other House Lords, even those who have taken their systems independent, to join. The vote I put to you is this; to sustain the Imperium, but on a democratic, rather than an autocratic, basis, with us at the forefront. I submit to you the vote."

With that Al-Zuhairi bowed, and his image flew back into his place around the circle.

Everyone's voting panels flashed up. President Nielsen did not even pause, but hit the 'No' panel. She felt she knew how this would go – the Revolutionary Council consisted of a wide number of House Lords and Ladies, all with their own viewpoints and disagreements. Even under the Empire they had not particularly gelled well, and the Revolutionary Council had been formed as an expediency of people who for once wanted the same thing - overthrow of the False Emperor. No-one here could agree on much else.

The counter in the centre of the holo pit revealed the truth; twenty-two per cent for 'Yes', nine per cent 'Abstain', and sixty-nine per cent for 'No'.

The speaking panels flashed again, and President Nielsen was slightly too slow in slapping it. The image of House Lady Lucija Korhonen, Senator for a number of systems in the Mid-Sectors, flickered forwards to the centre.

"I would ask a general question, in that case, for us to vote upon. Should we formulate a new government to rule the Red Imperium, regardless of how it is put together, or should we abandon the Empire. Do we want to take the Empire forwards, or do we want to dissolve it? Yes for we should take the Empire forwards, no for complete secession of every House territory represented here. Remember, please, as you vote, that as Al-Zuhairi pointed out, we only represent about a third of the Houses, and the other two thirds may have their own ideas on this matter."

As her image flicked back into place, the gasp from the gallery was audible to President Nielsen. The faces in the circle displayed a wide range of emotions, but only a few of those displayed shock. They were the fools, most likely, the ones who did not think through what the ultimate outcome of the revolution would be.

Nielsen hit the 'No' button.

The votes came back as twenty-four percent for 'Yes', two percent for 'Abstain', and seventy-four per cent for 'No'. The StarCom News Media would be blasting the news all around the galaxy in mere moments.

And so the Empire dies, Nielsen thought.

*

James Gavain finished his lap in the zero gravity tank, and grabbed hold of the rung on the wall. Sweating with the exertion, he pulled himself down to the ground of the tank and waved his hand over the sensor that would activate the localised gravity generators. Slowly the gravity returned to normal, and wrapping a towel around his shoulders, he emerged out into the fitness centre's main room.

It was busy, fitness training being mandatory for all crew, an essential part of the military life. The entire centre was a cacophony of grunts, the sounds of exertion, the smell of sweat and physical exercise.

Major Andryukhin was sat on a bench outside, dressed similarly to Gavain in a pair of trunks and nothing else. He was drinking from a bottle of energising liquid thirstily, in such a way that just happened to show off his extreme genetically modified musculature to the trio of women at the other end of the bench.

Gavain gave a rare laugh at the picture. There seemed to be very little to laugh about these days.

"You poser, Rik," he said quietly to Andryukhin as he sat down next him.

"Jamie, Jamie, Jamie," Ulrik Andryukhin tutted, "Just because it's not your thing, don't spoil my fun. Here, have some of this."

James finished the bottle and disposed of it.

"Ah, here comes trouble," Ulrik nodded his head.

James looked in the direction he had indicated, and spotted the House Lady Sophia Towers walking towards them. She was the daughter of Erik Towers, the Lord Senator of a number of systems on the edge of the Core. Tall and graceful, she wore a long one-piece dress of pure enijholle emerald green silk with a stole of real meerhal fur, a chain of large-cut diamonds around her neck, an ensemble that was probably worth a planet in itself. The House of Towers obviously did not lack for money.

Her presence was causing a wave of looks and muttered comments as she walked on a direct line towards Gavain and Andryukhin. It was probably not just the richness of what she wore, but her natural beauty as well; even James could appreciate that.

"Hello Captain, Major," she smiled, with perfect white teeth between full, red lips. "May one join you? It will only be for a moment of your time."

"We can go somewhere more pleasant than in here, if you wish, my Lady," James Gavain replied quickly.

"No, no, not at all," she made calming motions with her hands, as she sat down next to both of them. Her eyes lingered for a moment, not on Ulrik's insanely large musculature, but on Gavain. He was uncomfortably aware that he was almost completely naked apart from the trunks, in front of one of the House Ladies of the Imperium. Her eyes flickered back to his. "One finds this quite an enjoyable and interesting place to visit. The view is so much better, my dear Captain."

Ulrik snorted quietly, and Lady Sophia Towers laughed gently, a teasing a look in her eyes. Gavain felt colour rise to his cheeks.

"How can I help, my Lady?" he asked quickly.

"One wonders how our journey is progressing? Especially after all that unpleasantness with House Cervantes."

Unintentionally, Gavain traded a glance with Ulrik, using the pause to consider his answer. His instructions regarding operational security were very clear, and he had to follow them himself. "On the next jump, we head into the Phaero System." That much had been revealed to the House Lord concerned less than an hour ago, as in their current location there was no possibility of an interstellar communication getting away from the ship without his knowledge. "After that, a number of jumps, and a lay-over in a system I cannot disclose at this time. Sorry, my lady." They would be staying at the Janus Shipyards for a refit.

He was expecting a loud complaint, an angry demand, at least a serious insistence on the details - he had received a range of reactions to his decision to maintain secrecy about their altered course - but it did not occur. Instead, Lady Sophia merely displayed that suggestive smile, touched him lightly on the knee, and said "Surely you could trust me with our journey, Captain?"

"It is for all our safety, my Lady."

"One is entirely in your hands in that case, my dashing Captain," she inclined her head slightly, eyes never leaving his.

"Ah ... glad you feel that way," he replied weakly.

"One would be honoured if you could find the time to dine in one's quarters, at your earliest convenience? Perhaps when we have our lay-over?"

Gavain pulled himself together, and replied with a measure of confidence he did not feel. "Yes, my lady. It would be my honour."

"Excellent. When you find yourself in position to let me know when will be convenient, please do get into contact. This is the code to my personal communicator." She handed over a data-wafer; she was obviously unaugmented, or it would have been sent over the data sphere.

"Thank you, my lady."

The House Lady Senator stood gracefully, bowed ever so slightly in a gesture of a respect, and said, "With your leave, Captain. Major."

They both did not say a word until she had disappeared into one of the changing cubicles, her small retinue of two staff members taking up station outside the door.

"You've got an admirer, then," said Major Andryukhin with mock jealously, before suddenly letting out his booming laugh. "It's such a shame she's barking up the wrong tree, eh?"

"Shut up," Gavain replied.

Ulrik laughed again. "Still, y'know, it's not that often a House Lady invites you to dinner. Especially not when the dinner's going to be in her frikking quarters. I think you'll be dessert."

"Shut up."

"At least she likes being entirely in your hands."

"Rik. Shut up."

"Whatever you say, my dashing Captain."

*

President Nielsen smiled into the holo camera. After this recording for the StarCom News Media, her image would be beamed by hyperpulse communication all across the galaxy, to every colonised system within the former Red Empire.

"People of the colonised galaxy, there was an ancient curse from one of the former nations in old Earth times. It said, 'May you live in interesting times'. We are certainly living in interesting times; as many if not all of you are aware, the Revolutionary Council, which so successfully led the action against the False Emperor, have voted to disband the Red Empire. The former Imperium will hopefully secede into its constituent parts in a peaceful manner, following so much blood, sweat and tears in recent months and years.

"These are interesting times for all of us indeed, but I believe wholeheartedly that this will prove not to be a curse for most of us, but a blessing. We are in transition, all of us, from a monolithic imperial nation, unhappy and at war with itself, into what will hopefully be a collective of individual nations led by the former Houses of the Imperium. I sincerely wish all of you the best of luck for the future, with all the prosperity, and hopefully security that future will bring.

"However, for all that I speak of the future, there will be some systems where that secession and how it is to occur will not be clear. There may yet be further conflict. Look at the bombing of the Praetorian High Command as an example of continued violence. Look at the numerous stories the News Media, both StarCom and local, have been carrying. Where this conflict happens, I hope that it is limited, and that the parties involved can find resolution and bring to an end the hostilities as soon as possible, for all our stakes. We, the people of the Red Imperium, have suffered so badly.

"With the end of the Empire, I must as President of a large Imperial organisation, look to what the future holds for the people and the assets under my care. My intention is to ensure that StarCom continues to provide the service it always has; to safeguard the communications of the human race, to enable us to talk and to enable the sort of resolutions I alluded to just now. In the future, this service may change in nature, but we will remain a constant.

"The centre of the Imperium was always Mars, next door to Earth, the birthplace of our race, and long-acknowledged as the Star Communication Network's base of operations. In order to protect the Sol System from any predations or further conflict, and in order to repair the vast damage that has been done to it during the course of the rebellion, I hereby name the entire Sol System a protectorate of StarCom.

"I further wish to inform you, that from henceforth, we will be known as the Star Communications Federation."

There was a long pause, to allow the sentence to sink in to the viewers of the recording.

"As our own independent nation, we will seek to put in place the internal systems and organisations that enable a nation to function. We will continue to provide a communications service to other nations in the former Imperium, wherever and whatever form they take, and we will remain neutral in all cases. We will continue to operate the HyperPulse Communications Generators in those nations, but we will also see these as our property - any attacks on any of our installations will result in immediate excommunication for the House concerned, and reprisals. This also applies without doubt to our stargates, the mass-transit conveyances which kept the Empire united.

"To protect our interests and assets, I have extended a hand to every former Praetorian Guard member, and the StarCom Army is now fully operational. We have the means to protect the Sol System, and the means to protect our assets abroad. We are ready to assist wherever we are asked to, by the people, by you, should you require a neutral force to provide safety and prevent humanitarian atrocities. We will only intercede without a direct invitation, where and when our assets are attacked. Any House is more than welcome to request our installations to close and vacate their territory, but they should remember, as the only people with the technology to allow interstellar communication, in the forthcoming world we enter, this would be a severe handicap.

"Lastly, allow me to extend the hand of peace to every person in the former Imperium. If you should need sustenance, escape from any form of persecution, be it borgite or humanist, you will not find us ignorant of your desires. We will accept all immigrants and refugees, and I implore every House Lord and Lady of the former Imperium to secede your nations in a calm, orderly, and above all, peaceful manner, much as the StarCom Federation has.

"I am President Nielsen, and I wish you all well for the future - whatever it may bring."

Chapter V

Silus Adare looked up as he saw shapes approaching his cell beyond the energy field. The sparkling green haze was designed to keep him isolated in this small room that had been his home for months, acting partly as a barrier to prevent his escape and partly as a screen to prevent him seeing out into the corridor beyond. The shapes appeared as fuzzy indistinct forms, humanoid but genderless, even when they were stood directly outside the visually painful energy screen.

Many people had gone mad in the prison cells of Saturn, incarcerated for decades or even centuries, with no-one to talk to, and only the ever present, never-ending ripple of the energy screen casting its green glow over everything.

He had no idea which one of the many uncountable Saturnian moons he was imprisoned within. Following the success of the rebel Praetorians, he had been taken from his ship and transported in silence to this modern dungeon of a jail. There was an occasional shudder across the whole facility, which suggested regular impacts, so he suspected one of moons closer to the ring system rather than one of the outer bodies. The gravity had cut out once, and he had almost been pressed to the floor, so the decking was obviously lined with anti-gravity plates. In the night, he could hear them hum in counter point to the throb of the rippling energy barrier.

Today, he knew, was going to be different from the inane existence he had been forced to endure to date.

With a snap, the energy barrier disengaged, dissolving into nothingness. A sharp tang filled the immediate atmosphere, re-oxygenated and recycled air zapped with the ozone of the energy field disengaging.

"Rear-Admiral Adare," the woman on the other side of the rectangular entrance to his six-by-four metre box greeted him with a raised eyebrow. She was dressed in the robes of a StarCom official, and two burly Marines stood behind her in full power suited armour.

He did not recognise the uniforms at all, either the robes of the StarCom official or the Marines. He only knew they were members of StarCom from the picture of the planet Earth wrapped in its laurel wreath, a golden symbol on the chests of all three figures. The uniform colour itself was a white and regal blue, with sky blue trim.

There's been a lot of change while I've been locked away, he thought. He had been allowed to see President Nielsen's broadcast, and then the offer had been made.

He saw himself as a true servant of the Imperium. He despised and hated the usurpers, the rebels, the Revolutionary Council. He detested President Nielsen's declaration. He felt emotionally repelled by the very thought of the Red Empire being torn apart by the greed of its supposed best. He had been loyal to the Emperor, the one they called the False Emperor, and he had been proud of being a Praetorian.

They had offered him membership of the StarCom *'Federation'* Army. Him! How dare they. For a long time, his anger had reigned supreme. How could they ask him to join their rebellious, traitorous, duplicitous organisation?

He had also had a long time to think within his prison cell. He was nothing if not practical. He took the anger, and the hatred, made it into a hard ball of spite which he buried deep within his soul, and resolved he would wait until the right moment to let it explode.

"So, Rear-Admiral Adare," the woman said. "I am Special Agent Caterina La Rue, and I have come to ask you only one question. Do you accept the StarCom Federation Army's offer of a commission?"

"Yes," he replied without hesitation. "I accept."

Suddenly the Special Agent smiled. "This is excellent Admiral, we were hoping so. You're a free man, congratulations. Come with me."

She turned her back to him, he stood and stepped outside his cell for the first time since he had entered it, and the two Marines followed them at a respectful distance, a reminder that he was not fully trusted.

"What made you decide to accept the offer?" the Special Agent La Rue asked.

They walked down another one of the never-ending corridors. This entire facility appeared to have no end to them. Many of the cells were empty, but this particular corridor, somewhat higher up in the facility he knew from their use of a turbolift, had no cells coming off from it. They had passed a number of security checkpoints, and the decor had changed from a steely grey to more a pleasing blue, with even the occasional holopicture mounted on the wall and data-points at waist-height, so he guessed they had emerged from the detention centre into the outer areas of the prison facility.

"It's better than prison," he grunted. With his short military buzz-cut hair, scarred and heavy features, and deep bass voice, he was known as an intimidating person. Even his walk spoke of a stalker hunting its prey, a confident easily controlled gait. In another life, Silus Adare could almost have passed for a genetically modified Marine.

"Is that the only reason?" the Special Agent pressed. He was not fooled by the apparent nicety of Agent's tone.

"I cannot profess any loyalty to StarCom, and you would not believe me if I did," Silus Adare grimaced. "I would not lie either. There is no Empire any more. There is no Praetorian Guard any more. There is nowhere for me to go any more, even if I were not within a Saturnian prison cell. What were my choices, exactly, Special Agent?"

"This is very true, I'm sure."

"So why did you join the StarCom Federation then?" he asked.

"What a strange question to ask," Special Agent La Rue replied. "Why ask that?"

"You're not StarCom born and bred, you have a Boundary accent. You smell like one of the Imperial Intelligence operatives to me. Am I right? Were you a spook, Madam La Rue?"

She glanced at him, that pleasing smile seeming to harden somewhat around the eyes. "You are very observant, Rear-Admiral Adare."

"Yes, then."

She paused in her speech, but continued on through the corridor. It straightened out from its gentle curve, and at the end was a large double door. Eventually she said, "I was in Imperial Intelligence, but I cannot tell you which division. I was always loyal to StarCom, however. I was one of many, many double agents who also worked for the Star Communications Central Intelligence Department. It was always much larger than anyone ever suspected, as the history books will doubtless show one day. My point is that I have previous loyalty to StarCom, Admiral, which is more than can be said for you."

"A loyalty you hid under false allegiance to the Empire. I will take your oath, Special Agent, but do not ask for any more loyalty than that. There will be no fanaticism from me. This is expediency, nothing more."

"It will be enough for me, and for the President," Special Agent La Rue shrugged. "You are about to see what happens to those who refuse to give us even that."

Rear-Admiral Adare said nothing, as the double doors opened and he entered a reasonably sized lounge. It was an observation lounge, much like many that you would see the galaxy over, one entire wall taken up with a large viewing window which doubtless looked out onto a shuttle hangar or mustering hall.

The lounge had a number of occupants dressed similarly to himself, some of whom he recognised, one or two he even knew from previous operations and missions. The ten or so Praetorians were all ex-prisoners, loyalists who had supported the Second Emperor against the rebels. They were all of Commander rank or above, and he was willing to bet that they all had command experience. Every single one of them had a Special Agent by their side, and two burly Marines stood behind them.

"So, you're not as special as I thought you were, Special Agent," Adare commented in a neutral tone of voice.

"A small number of officers accepted the offer," Agent La Rue offered as an explanation. "This was perhaps not surprising considering the terms, and that you were once Praetorian Guard. Every one of you will have your own Agent, and an armed escort, until such point as your loyalty is proven."

"I have to prove my loyalty as well as take an oath to StarCom and the President?" he asked wryly. "The trust is truly heart-warming."

"I am sure you understand." La Rue began to walk towards the observation window. He followed, mindful of the two Marines stood behind him. His large frame appeared in the black window, and the other officers were crowded towards it. He was obviously the last to arrive.

They waited in silence for a short couple of moments, and then the opaqueness of the window began to fade. The vista beyond was revealed slowly.

It took some time for the window to become transparent, and then Adare could discern that it was indeed a shuttle hangar. It was bereft of shuttles and small vehicles, being filled instead wall to wall with hundreds of Praetorian uniformed service personnel. They stared about them, some of them fully aware of what was about to happen to them. Some were accepting it stoically, a couple were banging uselessly on one of the many exit doors to the hangar. A couple of dead bodies lay on the floor, testament to the fact that they had not all gone willingly like sheep to the slaughter.

"All of these people refused the StarCom Federation's offer," La Rue whispered to him, and his augmetics picked up similar whispers being made to the other officers in this room.

Out of sheer habit, Adare glanced at the status indicators above the massive blast doors that would lead to the void outside. Each status panel across the top of the blast doors showed that the hangar was sealed, the redundancies in place.

Even as he watched, the status indicators began to flick from constant amber to flashing red.

"Of course, this is a crime under Imperial Law, by Imperial Decree of the Emperor Himself," Admiral Adare said.

"What Imperial Law, Admiral? Show me where the Empire rules now, and then talk to me about Imperial Law."

He paused, and thought for a moment. His eyes never left the blast doors, as secondary lighting strips showed that the force fields had been disengaged. There was a rumble as massive actuators prepared to pull the doors open.

"You have a point," he nodded slowly.

"And your psychological profiling suggests you have a high degree of sociopathic tendency, Rear-Admiral, so I doubt my point concerns you overly much," La Rue shrugged.

The screaming and yelling started the very instant that the mighty blast doors cracked open, and he could imagine the whistling shriek as the hangar bay decompressed violently. It had not been cycled down properly, he knew from the status panels, to give the people inside oxygen for as long as possible and to ensure the people were fully flushed out into space, but also unfortunately prolonging their last few seconds of life.

Through the widening crack, he could see the pure black of space, and the twinkle of stars.

"I can't disagree," he shrugged.

Bodies began to lift from the floor, the crack disappearing as the people within were sucked towards the gap by tremendous forces they could not fight against. Some still tried, attempting to hold on to various fixtures, but it would be a race between their strength failing and violent decompression popping their bodies.

It was a hopeless struggle.

And that is rather the point, he thought.

*

The *ISS Vindicator* had translated into the Andes System at its outermost reaches, far beyond the point where even in an inhabited system the heat signatures and electromagnetic disturbances would be detected by anyone further in-system. The Andes System was very much dead, or at least appeared to be.

They were automatically detected by a handful of the small robotic drones that patrolled the entire system, which self-destructed before the *Vindicator* fully emerged from the jump and could detect their existence. Before self-destruction, they sent a message to the secret installation further inside the uninhabited solar system.

The secret installation went onto high alert, the nerves of the people inside the enormous facility only heightened when long-range scanners detected the battlecruiser heading directly for them, running silent.

They only stood down when the *ISS Vindicator*, satisfied that there were no other ships present - that they could detect, anyway - sent a communication to the Janus Shipyards. It was accompanied by a personal message from Captain Gavain. The *Vindicator* itself only stood down from amber alert when Gavain had received a personal message back from Commodore Andersson, the base commander of the Shipyards.

The whole journey took upwards of two days, a period of time in which the remaining nobility were kept largely incommunicado and in the bowels of the ship, so they could not identify which system they had arrived at.

In the asteroid belt, just at the edge of the seven planets around the incredibly weak sun, there were a number of particularly large asteroids, bigger than some moons and planetoids. One of these was codenamed

Janus, and as the *Vindicator* approached, it dropped its camouflaging force fields, revealing the gigantic maw that led inside to the hollowed out rock and the Shipyards facility.

As the *Vindicator* disappeared inside the asteroid, docking at one of the many ports for the Shipyard, the force fields rose back up and it was if the *Vindicator* and the Janus facility itself had never existed.

Captain James Gavain entered the holo-pit auditorium, saying a quick thank you to the two Marines from the base security which had escorted him there. They saluted, the doors closed, and he was plunged into the semi-darkness of the auditorium.

It was semi-darkness because the only source of light came from the holographic map gently revolving in the centre of the pit. Even at this distance, the Captain could see that it was a full map of the entire colonised galaxy.

He walked down the stairs built into the auditorium, heading for the centre. He found it slightly irksome that the Commodore had not come to greet him, but he understood the necessity of maintaining the illusion. They both had their positions to think of – or at least, that had always been the case in the Guard. Nowadays, who knew whether that was still relevant?

"Ah, James Gavain," Commodore Harley Andersson gestured with an airy wave of one hand. "A Captain now, I understand?"

"Yes, Commodore," Captain Gavain saluted.

"Excellent, well done. I wish this reunion was under better circumstances. Do you know these officers?" he gestured then at the other people stood with him.

"Captain Elena Jarman, yes," Gavain nodded, "I saw the *Solace* in the docks." They exchanged quick pleasantries. The Commodore introduced the others.

"Well, I believe we're finished," Commodore Andersson said by way of dismissal. The officers all saluted, and left the auditorium. Neither he nor Gavain said anything until the doors had shut.

Commodore Harley Andersson stepped forwards, a big smile creasing his face. He embraced James in a bear-hug, then pulled back, hands still on his shoulders.

"It's good to see you, James."

"And you, Harley."

"It's been too long. It seems like years ago when we last stood here."

James smiled, his usual impassiveness disappearing, holding the gaze a while before he looked around the auditorium. "Last time this place was full of loyalist Praetorians, before we made the journey to Mars. Never had the time to talk before I left, did we?"

"It was a crazy time," Harley Andersson shook his head. "The roads we've walked, hey? So many didn't make it out of Mars as well, I've seen the lists and reports. I never knew if I'd see you again, but I was glad you made it."

"It was close." James paused. "It was hell – I've never seen anything on that scale before."

Andersson nodded. "We can talk about it later if you like?"

"Yes."

"I see the *Vindicator*'s taken fresh damage as well?"

"Had a run in with House Cervantes." James briefly explained the story of the ambush, and the measures he had taken to prevent a similar one.

"Well," Harley Andersson said, "there's no problem with you refitting here. You can have full replacements for load-outs, vehicles, food, and stock, whatever it is you need. Give it two weeks and we'll have the *Vindicator* fully repaired as well, as good as new."

"Thank you, Harley. It will give us a chance to catch up, as well."

"Yes," Harley smiled.

"You had any trouble with the end of Empire?"

"Some," Andersson grimaced. "Two False Emperor Praetorian ships, but they never had a chance. Luckily, the Revolutionary Council and High Command left me a small garrison when you lot all went off to Mars for your fun. They never even got close. Nothing from any of the Houses, but then, they don't know about the Janus Shipyards – yet."

"You're expecting them to?"

"Of course. There's still some False Imperium Praetorians out there, rogue or gone pirate. Then there's the loyalist Praetorians, some of whom are joining the Houses or doing what you're doing, and stopping off for refits. Some have joined StarCom. Some of the intelligence agencies know about us, I'm sure. It's chaos since High Command went."

"And what do you think of that?"

"High Command? It's highly suspicious. I don't believe this rubbish put about by StarCom News Media, about rogue elements and terrorists. It was someone on the Revolutionary Council, it had to be. Mars might have been hell, Jamie, but it's going to be nothing compared to the dissolution of the Red Imperium."

James pointed up towards the holo-map, still revolving slowly in the air above their heads. "What's this?"

"The current starmap, as up to date as we can make it, showing all the new divisions that have occurred since the Council announced dissolution. The secession of the Houses, it's being called on SCNM, and it truly is. There's conflict erupting everywhere, Jamie, and alliances cropping up in all sorts of places. The Empire's splintering into mini-states all across the galaxy – but then, I guess that's what the Empire always was, a group of states and Houses that didn't like each other and was held together by the might of the Emperor."

"That would have been treason once."

"Maybe." Andersson shrugged. "But not anymore, with no Empire and no Emperor." He then proceeded to take James through what had been happening.

As he spoke, James took the chance to study his old friend.

Harley Andersson was young for his rank, much as Gavain was, but in a time when people could live for centuries that was a very relative judgement to make. His blond hair was probably only just a result of rejuvenation treatment, and the deep blue eyes sparkled in the half light of the holo image revolving gently above their heads. A short man, Harley raised a hand into the air unnecessarily and waved the image down, so that it was all around them. Despite his short stature, and a very small amount of being overweight - at least in comparison to Gavain's super lean thinness - Harley was well-built, and moved with a confidence that Gavain admired and had perhaps even come to emulate.

James tore his attention away from Harley and listened with half an ear as he jacked into the local datasphere. The holomap became even more alive, allowing him to download information on each action throughout the Former Imperium, just looking at one of the delineated groups of systems automatically bombarding him with the details of what that particular House had done since the break-up of the Empire. There were no Hyper-Pulse Communications Generators here in Janus, so it was fully reliant on information taken from downloads of visiting ships, and the bi-weekly data-run that one of its disguised corvettes performed to neighbouring solar systems.

The StarCom Federation appeared as a small regal blue colouring, a small dot covering only the Sol System slightly off-centre of the colonised part of the Galaxy, the centre of what was known as the Core. On touching it with the eyes, webbed links took it to almost every part of the colonised galaxy, apart from where big black crosses appeared.

"I think calling it a Federation is a bad sign - a Federation of what, exactly?" Harley was saying. "If you listened to her speech, I think it's obvious that she has plans to extend the scope of their reach. The webbed links show where they currently have operational assets, which is most of the colonised galaxy of course, but the black crosses show where the HPCG stations have been captured by the local Houses. President Nielsen will have to respond to that. None of the stargates have gone yet, but it is only a matter of time. I expect to see a reaction coming out of the StarCom Federation very shortly; they've subsumed a massive part of the former Praetorian army, and of course they have the factories around Mars to produce a new army and navy."

Much of the galaxy was shaded grey, with hazy lines, to show that the Houses and their territories had yet to publicly declare their intentions. Out towards the Boundary, Harley directed Gavain's attention to what now called itself 'The OutWorlds Alliance', a large tract of solar systems belonging to the peripheral Houses which had joined together. The OWA was to hold democratic elections - amongst its ruling House parties, with no hope of their vassals being allowed to vote - but the outcome was widely predicted to be the Revolutionary Council member, Lord Yassin Al-Zuhairi. On the holomap, it was shaded a sunburst orange, with a brown trim.

"The OutWorlds Alliance have made noises about taking the HPCG stations and the one stargate in their territory, but I wouldn't expect to see anything happening until after Yassin Al-Zuhairi gets the position of First Lord." Harley commented.

Almost as large as the OWA was the single territory of the Household of Korhonen, with some twenty-three solar systems in the Mid-Sector, glittering a deep, dark green in the holo-map. Lady Senator Lucija Korhonen had declared her territory fully independent, with herself as Arch-Chancellor. Korhonen had always been mainly a borgite territory, but a pogrom had begun against the small percentage of humanists sheltering within her estate. There was a major outflow of refugees, and there were rising tensions with the neighbouring and predominately humanist House of Van Hausenhof, who were extremely anti-borgite.

"This is just the start, of course," Harley said. "The Van Hausenhofs and the Korhonens have always been antagonistic towards each other, even within the Empire scheming and plotting against each other. The humanist-borgite hatred has always been deep there, and they have any number of historical reasons to begin fighting. The borgite Korhonens probably hope to take advantage of the humanist Van Hausenhof's current war with humanist Cervantia - it could turn into a three-way conflict, that one."

Gavain reflected that borgite Korhonen had been pro-revolution, as had humanist Van Hausenhof and Cervantia. It was not surprising, the rebellion bringing together many houses of different political persuasions and pro- and anti-augments for all sorts of reasons. Van Hausenhof had been in it because of the False Emperor's persecutions of the humanists, whilst Lucija Korhonen hated the False Emperor because of his destruction of their homeworld. Despite this, as a borg, whilst he did not share the extreme borgite viewpoint like Major Andryukhin, he nevertheless could not support the extreme anti-humanist hatred Korhonen appeared to favour. He wished Van Hausenhof luck, both in their war against Cervantia and their possible upcoming conflict with Korhonen.

That, he reflected, was what made the civil war and the subsequent emergence from it so messy. But perhaps the end of the rebellion was only the start of the true, real civil war. This holo-map certainly suggested so.

He spotted the small nation of Weiberg, close to the StarCom Federation, amongst dozens of other smaller local house nations. It was one of a handful that had declared themselves independent. "They are going to be swallowed by the StarCom Federation," he pointed at them as they revolved past.

"I suspect the StarCom Federation will find an excuse," Commodore Andersson agreed. "Look across here at Cervantia, as House Cervantes are now calling their territory. These old friends of yours have tried to do something similar to President Nielsen, in subsuming many ex-Praetorian units - sometimes by force. House Krzarjic have done the same, and now they are using them to invade the declared independent nation of House Solomon."

"Praetorian Guard, fighting for the houses," Gavain shook his head. "Still, I don't what I'm going to do with the *Vindicator* once our last mission is over."

Harley Andersson looked as if he was about to say something, but Gavain continued. "House Devereux, they're expanding rapidly. With Praetorian units I assume?"

"Yes," Harley Andersson nodded, continuing to explain this particular drama. House Devereux had named their nation after their capital planet, which was New Amiens. The nation of Amiens, led by Jacques Devereux restyling himself as 'the Archon', was showing unparalleled aggression, ripping through neighbouring territories in a form of blitzkrieg. He was displaying an amazing grasp of tactical acumen that had not manifested itself in Imperial days.

He seemed to be veering away from the newly formed Republic of Varrental. Golden coloured on the holo-map, the Republic consisted of a joining of four Houses, all of which had inter-married and formed their own nucleus of territories within the Mid-Sectors region of space. They were due to hold elections, open to all the people of their territories, to elect a President. Interestingly, some of the house territories were predominately borg, and some predominately human, but their overall political leaning was in the centre, being free-thinking in nature. They were vast, at over forty-nine systems already, but Gavain wondered whether the young nation would survive with so many different forces at play within it. Perhaps that was why when they all met at Varrental to agree their constitution, they had decided to have an open vote for all their people. It was a level of democracy that had not been seen in the Empire for centuries.

"I thought that we won the war," said James Gavain, looking almost in despair around him at the vista of the Empire's downfall. "I never expected this."

"Well, what did you expect?" Harley almost laughed, but there was no humour in it. He placed a warm hand on James' arm to take away the sting. "That we would de-throne the False Emperor, and they would all band together? The Empire always hung by a string, and it was only both Emperors and the might of the Praetorians that kept the Houses and their own private armies in line. The Emperors created more Houses, not less, so this was even more inevitable. The old Houses want their old territories back, the new Houses want to keep them, and then you have all the old hatred of the hard-core borgites and the humanists, with the free-thinkers in the middle. The Empire shredded most of the neutrals in *that* particular disagreement, with persecutions and stoking the hatred. Add in old inter-House rivalries based on trade disagreements, family arguments and a myriad of slights, even the sanctioned House Wars that the Red Imperium used to grant, and the break-up of the Empire was almost pre-ordained."

"So why did we do it then?" James asked.

"Because the False Emperor was going too far," Harley said simply. "He was insane, and evil, and had to be stopped. Remember the massacres, the destruction of entire planets in his name."

James just nodded slowly. At heart he was still an Imperial man, but he had to face reality. There was no more Empire, and the man who had led it at its end had not been his Emperor.

"If you look at history, this sort of thing has always happened," Andersson continued. "Humanity goes through cycles of forming great organisations, crossing boundaries and territories physical and natural, but we always end up breaking them up again, usually because the nations become so big they can't possibly satisfy all the identities and the conflicting priorities of those within their sphere of influence. The Empire lasted a long time, by allowing those individual conflicts and identities, and it suffered when it tried to squash them. Unfortunately, history always shows us that the end of a nation is never peaceful."

James looked at Harley. He had always listened to the elder man, and he probably owed some of his career to the senior officer. He had yet to hear bad advice from his friend.

"So what shall we do?" he asked. "What do you intend to do, with Janus?"

"Unfortunately, too many people know about it," Andersson's face became sad. "There are Praetorians who were on both sides, with their new loyalties, who may sell us out to their new masters. Some of the intelligence ministries, either House or former Imperial, will know. I only have four frigates, two strikecruisers and a star-carrier to defend the base, and I'm more inclined to blow it up and leave than let it fall into anybody else's hands."

"Really?" Gavain asked, shocked.

"Definitely," Andersson said firmly. "I will keep it running for as long as loyalist, rebel Praetorians need it, and then when we come under assault, I will do them damage whoever they are and blow the base."

"And then what?"

Andersson sighed heavily. "This is why I watch what goes on in the galaxy. I could join a House, or maybe scupper the squadron and then disappear into the ether, but I won't. I'll never join the StarCom Federation like so many of our erstwhile colleagues. I don't have the stomach for piracy, it goes against what I believe in. I will become a mercenary - fighting is all I know, in fact, it's what we were created for in the first place. What will you do?" he asked.

"Follow my last orders," said James. "I will convey the few remaining nobles to their chosen systems, then make up my mind. We've talked about it, the command staff, but I don't know."

"The High Command no longer exists," Harley pointed out. "The Praetorians no longer exist as a force, really. Do you want to know what I would do in your position?"

"Yes," James looked at his friend, mentor and more, much more, willing to accept the guidance.

"I would become a mercenary," he said without hesitation. "It doesn't have to be forever. The Interstellar Merchants Guild has maintained its independence, and the new nation states and Houses are posting contracts with them for skilled soldiers. With the way the galaxy is going, you won't be short of work. The *Vindicator* is your property now, I would say, so use it. This is a time to look after yourself, Jamie."

"A mercenary," James repeated the word. "It would be better than being tied to a house."

"If you do, you can always come here for repair. Whilst we survive, at least."

"I - I just don't know, Harley."

"And I'd forget your last orders as well," he said sternly.

"What do you mean?"

"Well, look. No High Command, no Praetorians, no Empire. Why do it? Stop thinking as a Praetorian soldier, James, and think for yourself - after all, you did when you joined the rebellion. Take the remaining nobles to a system, off-load them, and let them get home on their own. Look at what happened with Cervantia and House Cervantes - it could happen again, and you may not escape next time."

"And what do we use as a base of operations?" he asked.

"Here, or make your own arrangements with one or two of the Houses, some of them are offering that as well," Andersson replied. "I may come and join you as a merc if you do, once I have to leave Janus. As I said,

James, think for yourself, look after yourself and your people. That's what I'm doing."

James breathed deeply. "I'll think on it," he said, not sounding convinced.

"Do," Harley said. His tone softened considerably, and he stared into James eyes. A hand touched his arm again. "I'm on shift officially, but I will be off-duty tonight until tomorrow morning. Why don't you come and do your thinking in my cabin tonight, over a glass of real wine, and a plate of real food. For old times' sake - and for the sake of making new times between us."

James felt his heart lurch. "That would be good," he gave a small hint of a smile, and a nod. It was what he had come here to this room for anyway, if he were truthful.

"I will see you later, then," Harley Andersson replied.

Lieutenant-Commander Julia Kavanagh sat in the command seat of the bridge on the *Vindicator*. Jacked in, she did not have to check her internal chronometer, but she knew that Commander Lucas De Graaf was running late to relieve her from the duty shift. She would give him ten minutes, then find out where he was.

In truth, she was not in much of a rush. Major Ulrik Andryukhin had gone over the docking tube to the main part of the shipyards, so she would not be seeing him after her shift. Captain James Gavain had relaxed their normal safety protocols, the ones he had instigated after the Cervantian episode. Jamie himself was over in the main part of the hidden space station, reacquainting himself with Harley. She knew their history, knew what they meant to each other, and so had not even objected as De Graaf had when Jamie had announced he would be taking several days shoreleave. She knew why he wanted it.

Ulrik had told her of Sophia Towers' obvious attraction to James, and she had laughed with him when she heard. It was pretty pointless when it came to James. She could not really see the attraction herself, preferring people of Ulrik's build, but Gavain had the lithe athleticism some people found irresistible. James was too cold for her, but obviously not for Commodore Harley Andersson.

She busied herself checking the status of the ship for the hundredth time that shift. Nothing had changed. They were at dock, within the protection of an armoured behemoth many times their considerable size, so there was not much to do beyond the humdrum. The ship was at one-fifth power, a quarter of its crew were on their share of the shore leave rotation, but out of the command staff there had to be at least two on board ship at any one time, one on duty and one off. That meant herself, De Graaf or Gavain; Ulrik Andryukhin was a Marine and could not command the ship.

Still, she reflected with typical optimism, in two weeks they would be on their way again, fully repaired for the first time since Mars. It would be good, and they would all feel safer again.

There was another call waiting on the datasphere from one of the nobles for her on the comms network. She considered not answering, but that would have been rude.

She answered it brightly, "Lieutenant-Commander Julia Kavanagh speaking."

"Lieutenant-Commander?" the voice on the other end of the comms call was highly born, every vowel of Standard High Imperial slotting into place perfectly. "Is Captain Gavain not the commanding officer on this ship? One does apologise for disturbing you, one did request the commanding officer."

"I am the duty officer, Lady Sophia," Kavanagh replied, recognising the tones of Lady Sophia Towers. She was unlike the other nobles on board, in that she did not pester constantly and demand special treatment. The other House Lords on board had been incandescent at not being told where they were being held for two weeks, or what system they were in, but Lady Towers had accepted the reasons of operational security without question. "Captain Gavain is on shore leave temporarily."

"Ah, in that case one would appreciate it greatly if you could let one know when he returns from shore leave. He has been invited to dinner, and one did not want him to think it had been forgotten."

"Of course, Lady Sophia," Lieutenant-Commander Kavanagh managed to keep her voice level, without betraying any of her amusement.

"Have a good day, Lieutenant-Commander."

Lady Towers signed off from the call.

The turbolift doors hissed open, and Kavanagh glanced to her side as the presence of Commander De Graaf was announced as he arrived on the bridge, by his jacking into the datasphere.

She stood slowly from the command chair as he approached. Her eyes took in his dishevelled uniform, the growth on the chin, the unruly hair. His classically handsome face had circles under the eyes, which themselves were redlined and bloodshot.

<Hail in the name of the True Emperor, Commander De Graaf,> she said over the datasphere by way of greeting.

<Hail. You are relieved, Lieutenant-Commander,> he replied, with no apology for being late.

<As you command,> she replied, glad that the datasphere hid the uncustomary stiffness she would have put into the tone of voice if she had been speaking with her vocal chords.

Then, Lucas De Graaf came within arm's reach of her. She could smell the alcohol coming from the man. She looked at the way he sat down heavily, and realised the man was still drunk.

Oh dear, she thought, turning quickly as she realised she was staring. For a brief moment she thought about reporting him, but decided against it. Gavain, as much as she counted him as a friend, was the sort of person who would come down heavily on the officer regardless of circumstance, and she had no desire to create a problem of that nature. In truth, although it was not acceptable to be drunk on duty, they were in dock in a shipyard, and there was not much to do. They were all having a difficult time of it, so she would let the poor man be.

Chapter VI

"So, my dear Captain, are we still likely to depart tomorrow?" Lady Sophia Towers asked with her consummate politeness.

"Yes," he replied shortly. He was in her quarters, having the meal he had put off for weeks. James Gavain was not really one for networking, and the constant amusement of Jules and Ulrik had made him delay this even more, but he had run out of excuses. He found this sort of thing excruciating, but as Harley had reminded him, regardless of his intentions he needed allies amongst the houses, and House Lady Sophia Towers had offered no trouble in comparison to the others on board his ship during this journey.

"How have the other nobles taken your announcement from earlier today?" she asked.

He glanced briefly at the unaugmented human in front of him, and then looked away. At least the flirting had ceased today, for some reason. The quarters they sat in were not that spacious, and not at all luxurious, this being a military ship and not a passenger liner. They were considerably better than the bunks most of the crew shared in barracks, and of a similar size to his own and the other command staff quarters, which was not very big at all. There was barely enough room for them, this table, the bed, a two-seater suspensor sofa in its docking port, and the very anxious servant who loitered in the doorway to the showerhead.

"Mixed," he replied. "You were kind enough not to complain, my Lady, as always, but the rest voiced their opinions loudly and often."

"One is not surprised," Lady Sophia Towers gentled spooned a delicacy from the dessert into her mouth. It melted on her tongue quickly, and she continued, "Please do not under any circumstances take this as a criticism, as one understands the reasons why. But, we have been delayed significantly, and now you announce that you are abandoning your final orders to convey us to our chosen destinations, and we will all be asked to leave the ship in a system you will not identify to us for operational security. This is not a criticism, Captain, but one understands their point of view."

Is that why you were so insistent for this meal today, he wondered to himself. "Abandoning my final orders is very strong, my Lady," he said, keeping his voice neutral without any effort. It was one of the reasons for his reputation for iciness. "The orders were given by an organisation that no longer exists. The Praetorian Guard is no more."

"And one can see how that hurts and concerns you," Lady Sophia inclined her head in submission, almost. "One can certainly understand your position – it is surprising that you have continued this far along your journey."

"You are very kind, my Lady."

"Not at all," she dabbed at her mouth with a napkin, and then pushed the plate away gently. A glance at the servant was all it took for both their plates to be picked up, and then the servant left the room without a word.

"One hopes the system you will ask us to leave ship in is carefully chosen? These are dangerous times, Captain."

"It is, yes," he said. He would offer no more. His sense of responsibility had forced him to consider the system carefully, and he had chosen one which had not been subject to any of the fighting that seemed to be afflicting parts of the Former Imperium, and one which was likely to remain neutral. They would be able to get commercial liners back to their own territories.

"What do you intend to do then Captain, if one may ask, and it is not subject to operational security?"

He hesitated, and then said gently, "I do not know, my Lady. Everyone asks that of me at the moment, and I do not know."

A look of genuine concern crossed her face, as she poured the remainder of the white wine into both their glasses. The bucket and ice clinked as the empty bottle was returned. "It is very difficult for you, one is sure." She took a deep breath, and calculating green eyes met his blank brown ones. "May one make a suggestion?"

Is *this* why I'm here, he wondered.

"Of course, my Lady."

"House Towers is one of the territories that lies in the Core, getting close to the edge of the Mid-Sectors. We only have six systems, but my dear father, Erik Towers, has become one of the richest House Lords in the surrounding sectors. Despite that, ones' self has made her own money, with no help from her father, by trading and investing wisely in a wide number of businesses. My influence and interests expand far beyond the borders of House Towers, and notwithstanding the current upheavals, providing House Towers survives, my industries and commercial interests should hopefully continue to prosper in some form or another. They are wide and varied; one has spread one's risk widely. But there is one more type of investment one has been considering of late, and one feels you may be interested. There seems like no better time to make the proposition."

She paused, to assess his reaction, of which there was none. Inside, privately, James Gavain had thought this was to lead to yet another offer to become a part of the private House Armies, but the introduction had intrigued him, despite himself.

"Please continue, my Lady," was all he said, but she smiled like a shark. He jacked into the system quickly, and in the space of a nano-second had downloaded a full bio on Lady Sophia Towers, and a separate one of

House Towers. He would re-read it slowly in the days ahead, but that nano-second was enough to radically alter his opinion of her. She was graceful, pleasant, and gracious, but had numerous commercial interests as she claimed, and in business had a reputation for being a prospector, a predator and prudent in different situations.

"One looks at the state of the galaxy, and the disruption afflicting much of the Former Empire. It is pulling itself apart. There is conflict and hardship everywhere, and one does not discount the distressing nature of the situation we all find ourselves in. And yet, this presents an opportunity to those willing to take advantage of it. We all must survive, dear Captain, yourself as well as oneself. The Interstellar Merchants Guild has been acting as the commercial bondsman since before the Red Imperium, and has once again proclaimed itself neutral. This is good, as it gives one hope that we will emerge from this strife one day and not all people have lost their senses. But some have, and these people create conflict, and these people, my dear Captain, suddenly find themselves in need of military resource they do not have. The IMG, Captain Gavain, is posting new contracts on a daily basis for military personnel and equipment."

"All of this I know," he said softly, by way of encouraging her to get to the point.

"My point, Captain," as if she had read his mind, "is that this is a good time for a new venture in the military arena. One does not propose that you join House Towers; instead, one suggests that she invests some of her hard earned capital in a new business, one which you run for her. A military business, Captain, a mercenary business."

"I will admit," he said slowly into the sudden silence, "mercenary employment was one of the options I was considering. But why should I need your help to do this? I have this ship, a crew of thousands of people, some of whom may want to do it, but some of whom may not. Why would you be interested, and why should I?"

She clapped her hands together delightedly. "An excellent couple of questions, Captain. You do indeed bring to the table, so to speak, the ship, the contacts within the Imperial military, and the personnel to make the business viable. What you do not have, Captain, is the means to fund such a venture continuously, the business expertise to make it commercially viable, advertise, find new contracts - and to provide continuous repairs should you need it. One knows you have recently refitted, but one also guesses that this service may not be available in future - or maybe it will, one does not know. But it is the money and the experience one can give you, Captain, and a base of operations should you require it in House Towers."

"I would not want to become part of the House Army," he said quickly and sharply.

"You would not," she said equally as fast. "One is not her father, and Erik Towers is the Lord of House Towers. One is completely separate from him, and would resist any attempt of his to use you - without a suitable contract, of course," she smiled. "My own landholding has a commercial shipyards, and this is one of my own businesses. Even the repairs would be done as a transaction between two commercial organisations - at favourable rates, of course." She winked at him.

He looked blankly at her, his mind whirring. He had not truly made his mind up to become a mercenary, but Harley Andersson's words had affected his thoughts, and he had found himself thinking more and more of the mercenary life. It was preferable to becoming a House vassal. He had not put any thought into money, or how to survive as a business, and from what he had just read about House Lady Sophia, she certainly had the knowledge.

"You do not have to make your mind up now, Captain," she smiled. "All one asks is that you consider it carefully, and perhaps provide a decision before we reach the destination where you will off-load all of us inconsiderate nobles. It would be a true partnership, a business, and as many or as little of your command staff could be a part of it as you wish. Like any business, one would seek to grow it as well, so you would have my attention and time. One will write and send a proposal to you later tonight; please read it at your leisure. If your decision is not to proceed, well -" she smiled and opened her hands expressively "- there is no harm done in the consideration."

He was still for some time, then eventually, he inclined his head slowly. "Very well, my Lady, send the proposal through. I will think on it, my word as an officer." He coughed gently and stood. "I must go to the bridge to relieve Commander De Graaf."

"Of course, my dear Captain. Good day to you, my man."

*

StarCom Chief of Station Fuller sat in his office atop the HyperPulse Communications Generator. He could feel the throb of it through the floor beneath his feet as it sent its last messages, and if he crossed to the window he could see down into the Hall of the Generator and look upon a part of the machine.

To call it a machine was to understate its importance to him. He had spent all of his life working in HPCG stations across the Core, and a fairly large proportion of it as Chief of this station on St Thomas. St Thomas was one of three inhabited planets within the Exeter System, a part of the newly independent nation of Weiberg.

Chief of Station Fuller sniffed, closing down the datasphere as his emotions overcame him. The old man loved his work, believed passionately in what he did as one of the guardians of the knowledge that kept the galaxy talking to each other. He believed in what President Nielsen had said, that in these times of strife, they had an even more important role to play in keeping the parties of the galaxy in touch with one another. He had accepted the new white and regal blue robes of the StarCom Federation with almost as much pride as he had taken the white of the old StarCom Network under the Red Imperium.

He stood up from the desk, and crossed to the window. Below him the part of the generator that he could see was ringed with flashing blue lights, beating with a deep thrum in time to the resonations he could feel through the floor as the mighty pulses were sent upwards. The generator transmitted a pure column of energy into the sky, far beyond the atmosphere of the planet, to the array that floated in space in a geosynchronous orbit with St Thomas. The array constantly ripped a hole in space-time, in time with the beat of the generator, to allow the pulse of coded data to flit through to another solar system at an unbelievable and unimaginable speed.

He pressed both hands against the glass of the window. He would have to apply for another station, but if any vacancies existed he would be lucky to get one he liked. He cursed House Weiberg, and their new Weiberg nation, and the self-proclaimed King Ibbe Weiberg for his decision to reject StarCom's offer to continue to run their interstellar communications.

He had received the communication from StarCom HQ on Earth with shock. Once the last messages had been sent, he was to enter the Armageddon Code, and blow the HPCG station to smithereens. Even now, the emergency lander shuttle would be prepped, waiting for him and his station crew to complete the last sending sequence. The fledgling nation of Weiberg had politely refused to pay StarCom for its services, and so those services were being withdrawn. Permanently.

He swallowed, his throat dry as he watched the sending mast suddenly deactivate. That was it; the last of the messages. The generator began to cycle down before his eyes, and it was as if he was watching the end of his own life.

He felt tears well up in his eyes.

He was still watching the generator cycle down when suddenly the red alert panels began to flash. The entire Hall of the Generator was bathed in a ruddy red glow, as if it had suddenly bled upon the metal decking.

Chief of Station Fuller jacked into the datasphere, and screamed across the network <What's happening?>

<We're under attack, Chief,> one of his subordinates, the Head of Security, was calling back. Every StarCom station had a small security force, more to deter thieves and petty vandalism than anything else.

<Under attack? What? But – from who?>

<Weiberg commandos have scaled the facility walls - > the Head of Security transmitted a brief image across the datasphere, a couple of live seconds through his eyes as he faced a power-armoured figure, firing his own handlaser ineffectively at its armour as the hulking soldier stomped forward and opened fire with a rotary cannon. The cannon was designed as anti-vehicle rather than anti-personnel, and the Head of Security stood no chance.

The Chief of Station's training jumped to the fore. There was still time – his priority was to safeguard the knowledge of how the HPCG worked, and to prevent the facility falling into hostile hands.

The mainframe computer was located deep below the generator, but he had a direct link to it through its firewalls over the datasphere. He knew that word of what had happened here would get to StarCom – every facility was watched by members of the StarCom Central Intelligence Department for just such an eventuality, usually a very boring duty for them he was given to understand. Not today, obviously, he thought, as he prepared to send the Armageddon Code. There were several layers of checkpoints and sequences to go through before he could fully activate it.

There was a boom from outside, and another one, and then he felt the building rock. He saw and heard the metal all around him shudder and creak. There was a louder explosion, far too close, and so loud that he wondered what in Earth's name could cause it. He worked even harder and faster, desperate to get the Armageddon Code into the system.

Weiberg wanted the HPCG facility for itself, that much was certain. They were not going to pay for a service, and so-called King Ibbe had made the decision to take them by force.

His office was bathed in an orange and yellow light, the window and its glass blew in, he smelt the fierce vaporisation of air and felt the searing heat. He was so shocked he paused in entering the Armageddon Code, and turned and stared.

The explosion had ripped open the Hall of the Generator in one corner. There had been several floors and offices beyond it, but the battlewalker that now peeled the walls apart as if it were opening a tin can had literally blown a path all the way through the facility once the commando insertion had been detected. Chief of Station Fuller had no way of knowing that this was the back-up plan, to prevent him entering the Armageddon Code that Weiberg knew StarCom used in such situations.

The ten-metre tall monstrosity that was the AH-9 *Aztec Warrior*-class medium battlewalker, a missile-launcher in the shape of crest on the cockpit and a left-hand extendible power-axe giving it a distinctive look, ploughed through into the Hall below. The right arm came up, the barrel of a plasmacannon aiming directly at the office of the Chief of Station.

"No no no no –" he screamed, seconds before superheated plasma burning as fierce as a sun ploughed through the entire office, melting and incinerating everything in its path, including him.

He did not finish sending the Armageddon Code, and the HPCG station was captured with its function, if not its outer shell, intact.

*

De Graaf groaned as he woke up. The lights in his small officer's quarters had gone onto full, and they blinded him. His head was throbbing.

He rolled out of bed, his still-booted feet kicking empty bottles skittering across the floor. He groaned aloud, waiting for the room to stop spinning.

"What?" he muttered, words slurring.

His internal modem was requesting a link-up. There was a message waiting.

He groaned again, and reached over to the bed-side table. He found the dermajector, rolled up a sleeve on his shirt, and pressed it to the skin. With a hiss it dumped a vast amount of drugs into his system; the hangover would be gone shortly, and his brain would start functioning normally.

He logged on, jacking only partially into the datasphere. The message was from Captain Gavain, the cold bastard. It was a summons to a meeting in half an hour, all the command staff, in the ready room.

He was not due on duty for another five hours yet.

He stood up awkwardly, and made his way to the showerhead, hopefully to rid himself of the smell of alcohol before the meeting.

Gavain looked up as Commander Lucas De Graaf entered the ready room. He stared at the handsome man, reflecting not for the first time that he had the same good looks as Commodore Harley Andersson.

"Sit, Commander," he said shortly, indicating a spare chair at the table. Major Andryukhin and Lieutenant-Commander Kavanagh were present.

"Apologies for calling this on such short notice," he said, not sounding sorry at all, "but I've reached a decision. The nature of it, however, demands that I tell you .... and, actually, I ask you to join me in it."

He saw Ulrik and Jules exchange a glance at the unusual phrasing.

He explained quickly about House Lady Sophia Towers' offer.

"Frikking hell," Andryukhin said, "and you intend to take her up on it?"

Captain Gavain actually felt his heart beat faster as he said it aloud. "Yes," he said simply. "I think it is the best thing for me, and for us, to do. If we were to do this, each one of us would have an equal say with Lady Towers as to what contracts we took as mercs or not. What do you say?

I've decided to do it, and as my friends," here he glanced at De Graaf, including him charitably in the phrase, "I want your opinion, and your agreement to it – if we are to do it together."

Lieutenant-Commander Julia Kavanagh did not have to think about it for long. It was typical of James to surprise them with this, but then they had all been thinking about their future for some time. To become a mercenary was something she had considered, and she had liked the freedom they would have under this arrangement. Above and beyond that, she trusted James Gavain with her life.

"Yes," she said simply. "I think it's perhaps our best option. I wouldn't want to go to one of the Houses anyway, not at the moment, and StarCom's out."

"Bloody hell yes," Major Ulrik Andryukhin sat there, arms crossed, brow furrowed, initially outraged at the suggestion. He too had thought about becoming a mercenary, just as he had thought about becoming a pirate, or joining a House. None of those options had seemed likely to him. He had thought about leaving and going his own way, but he could not do that, not to his people or especially to Jules, or even Jamie. Lucas De Graaf he could not care less about.

"Let's frikking do it," he said, thumping the table in his exuberance. "I don't see what else we can do, eh?"

"Commander?" Captain Gavain looked at Lucas De Graaf.

De Graaf sat there. His head had cleared, but the feelings of being lost and alone had not. He was alone in the galaxy, he knew, with no Praetorians to be a part of. He had thought of leaving, joining the StarCom Federation, but there was something of President Nielsen that reminded him of the False Emperor. He did not particularly care for these people around him, although Julia seemed the closest to a friend he had on the ship, and that was not saying much. He did not particularly want to go into business with them, be it as a mercenary or any other venture. Then, the thought occurred to him that he could go along with it, and then leave whenever he wanted to if a better opportunity came along.

"Yes," he said, nodding in agreement. "Why not?"

"Looks like we're mercenaries then," Captain James Gavain gave a rare smile, leaning back in his chair. He actually felt a small feeling of elation. The months of feeling lost, of watching his life fall apart around him, would actually begin to serve a purpose. All of a sudden, there was a future, and it was theirs.

"What are we calling ourselves?" Julia Kavanagh asked.

Major Ulrik Andryukhin's response was predictably vulgar.

"It's a good point though," said Commander De Graaf, not really interested in the discussion. "We need a name."

"Gavain's frikking Guerillas."

"We'll think of one," said James Gavain confidently. "Until then, we have something more important to think about. What of the crew? We can hardly be mercenaries without taking the crew along with us."

"A vote?" Andryukhin said, as they had covered this ground before. "A fucking stupid idea. We're still ex-military."

"But they should have a choice, Rik," Jules Kavanagh pointed out.

"Why? Smack 'em round the head and tell 'em."

"No," Gavain waved his hands curtly. "We will allow anyone who wants to leave to do so, when we dispose ourselves of the House Lords we have down below. Every crew member has the option. Technically, each one of them needs a contract, or so Sophia Towers tells me."

"Really?" Ulrik sounded incredulous.

"This isn't the Praetorians," Gavain said, "And you had better get used to it."

"You're looking forward to this, aren't you James?" Kavanagh asked.

He actually laughed out loud before he nodded. "It's good to know what we're going to do," he said. "Wish I'd had this discussion with Lady Sophia earlier."

"Ah," said Ulrik, "we should have known. How intimate –" he stopped when Kavanagh dug him in the ribs.

"That's all then," Gavain waved them away. "Dismissed, all."

*

Rear-Admiral Adare unstrapped himself from the jumpseat, and deactivated the suppression field that was holding him in place. He saw the frown on Special Agent La Rue's face, and saw her gesture a command at the two Marines who followed him literally everywhere. He had tried speaking to them when the Special Agent was not present, but they never responded. He was beginning to think that they were drones, without vocalisers.

He glanced back at them, and said, "What do you think I'm going to do, open the airlock? We're on a shuttle in the middle of space, where am I going to go?"

He then ignored the entire trio, and made his way to the cabin of the lander shuttle. He stared through at the front viewport at the sight beyond. The curvature of Uranus could just about be seen, and in the distance, one of the four gigantic Uranian shipyards.

By far the largest object, and not just because it was closest, was the behemoth that was the dreadnought *SFSS Thor's Hammer.*

She was built along standard Imperial lines, with a heavy, boxy aft where the majority of the engines were housed, with the two long extensions jutting out from the main body at angles underneath the hull, but with a third riding like a crest along top. The midsection bulked out somewhat, and then it tapered to the bulbous head. As a dreadnought she had power and capabilities far beyond even the largest battlecruiser, and was worth four or five of any other ship. She could level a city in minutes, and was capable of facing down even the weaponry on a starbase or space station. The T-class dreadnought was a battle winner, and was unmatched throughout the Former Empire.

"Impressive bitch, isn't she?" Admiral Adare said sarcastically, to hide his joy at the sight of his new starship. He rubbed at the trimmed growth of his square, black beard as he thought of how much his life had changed in just a few short months.

"Yes, Admiral," Special Agent La Rue remarked neutrally. "Let's make sure you earn the right to keep her."

Rear-Admiral Adare strode confidently onto the bridge of the *SFSS Thor's Hammer*. All Imperial bridges were designed in the same way, with the pits, the walkway in-between and the command dais at the rear, but this was the largest bridge he had ever seen.

Even his two Marine shadows did not bother him, as irksome as he found it to have an armed guard wherever he went. Even when he slept, one of them stood watch in his room. President Nielsen was not taking any chances with the Praetorians who had supported the False Emperor until they had proven themselves.

"You have been given this ship as a chance to prove yourself," Special Agent La Rue had said as they had docked half an hour ago. "We believe you have the capabilities and the strategic mind to manage her correctly. But you still have to earn our trust, and you will be watched constantly, as well as having your loyalties tested at every opportunity."

He had no loyalty to the StarCom Federation, or President Nielsen, but he wore their uniform and felt nothing whilst he was in command of this beauty. He crossed the bridge from the turbolift, mounting the command dais and passing by the command stations without even acknowledging the crew. He was not here to be their friend, he was here to earn his freedom.

A man stood up slowly from the command chair. He wore the insignia - which was still Imperial, Adare noted - of a Commodore. Everything about the small man was self-contained, but his eyes betrayed him, and they shone with hatred.

"This is Commodore Enrique Pacheco, temporary captain of the *Thor's Hammer*," said Special Agent Caterina La Rue. "He has commanded the *Hammer* since the ship was almost destroyed in the Battle of Mars - originally, you fought on different sides, Admiral Adare."

Rear-Admiral Adare strode up to Commodore Pacheco. Pacheco

hesitated far too long, and then saluted. Adare was cognisant of the fact that he was replacing the Admiral who had commanded this ship during the Battle of Mars, and Pacheco would no doubt greatly resent that. The *Thor's Hammer* had received an extensive refit, having been badly damaged during the conflict and losing the majority of its crew. It had led the assault on Starbase 1, and had opened the way for the ground forces to penetrate Mars' defences, but the previous Admiral, whilst a hero to the rebel Praetorians at least, had died in the attempt.

"At ease," he commanded. He did not care particularly how Commodore Pacheco felt.

"And this is Commander Zehra Sahin, also transferred like you - but not with your particular background," Special Agent La Rue stated. "She was a former member of the loyalist Praetorians who joined the rebellion, but her ship has been abandoned as it was too far beyond repair."

"The loyalist Praetorians were those who remained true to the second Emperor," Rear-Admiral Adare pointed out bluntly. He watched both officers of his command staff rankle.

"History will say otherwise," Special Agent La Rue commented, ignoring the icy atmosphere. "Finally, we have Lieutenant-Colonel Iyan Lamans, commander of the Marines on-board."

"Admiral," the Marine Lieutenant-Colonel gave nothing away.

"All of these people can be trusted, and have decided of their own volition to join StarCom," La Rue continued. "They have been fully briefed on your background, Rear-Admiral Adare."

"I expected no less," Adare waved Commodore Pacheco out of the way, and sat in his command chair. He was not going to let the theatrics spoil his enjoyment of having the mastery of this ship.

He jacked into the datasphere, and read for himself the status of the ship. It had a full crew, a full complement of fighters, and all of its ground forces at maximum capacity. Everything was ready for them to carry out their duty in the name of the StarCom Federation, whatever that may be.

Chapter VII

Scanners in the Parowa System detected the incoming signature of a jump. The electromagnetic disturbance was located first, and it was identified in seconds that the ship or ships were jumping in at one of the authorised and designated points in-system. It was however an unscheduled jump.

Two defensive frigates belonging to House Zielinski that were on patrol at the jump point immediately changed course, zeroing in towards the incoming jump co-ordinates. The ship or ships would be defenceless when they first emerged from the warp.

Infra-red scanners mounted on the static drone probes picked up the heat signature next, and they determined that it was one lone ship, but from the size of it, it was either a large transporter or one of the type-III cargo-freighters, or a battleship. The frigates of House Zielinski went to red alert from amber.

With a burst of white light, the terminus point for the warp jump opened. The starship appeared, elongated but visually snapping back into its proper dimensions as it translated successfully from hyperspace. The shockwaves from the sheer energy release could be detected easily from the planet Parowa Czwarty, the fourth planet in the solar system, despite its distance from the designated jump-point.

The *ISS Vindicator*, complete with Imperial Eagle proudly displayed upon its flanks and its prow, blazed into existence. It was challenged immediately. The commanders of the frigates knew they had only a handful of seconds before the mighty battlecruiser could go operational and would cease to be defenceless.

The Captain of the *Vindicator* replied immediately, System Command digested his message, and the frigate commanders were to their great relief ordered to stand down.

It took over an hour for this Captain Gavain's request to filter through and reply to come back from the Solar Chancellor's office. All the House nobles were off-planet and out-system. The Solar Chancellor herself was greatly intrigued by their presence, but granted the *Vindicator* permission to approach Parowa Czwarty.

It took nearly four hours for the battlecruiser to near a reasonable distance from Parowa Czwarty, and even then it was not allowed into direct orbit to keep its formidable weaponry out of range of the planetary surface.

The *Vindicator* released one of its landers, which sped towards the capital of House Zielinski.

Captain Gavain pulled his cold-weather gear closer around his neck as the exit from the lander snapped open. The blast doors retracted into the flooring in a split second, and the ramp had been thrown out as if it were a projectile from a cannon; the landers were designed for the rapid deployment of a military force, after all.

The locals were a bit shocked by their entrance to the commercial star port, he could tell. They had been offered a landing berth at the military port, but he had refused - he had no intention to stay on-planet longer than he had to, he had explained.

He pulled the oxygenator down over his mouth, and fixed the protective visor into place over his eyes. The ramp was already slick with a thin covering of snow. The temperature inside the lander dropped rapidly. Apart from a small portion of the northern hemisphere, which was largely deep ocean, Parowa Czwarty was a frozen planet. The population dwelt mainly on the second continent, the southern continent being mainly too mountainous and far too cold for humans to survive comfortably.

Borgs could have managed it he thought to himself, but House Zielinski was predominately unaugmented human, with humanist leanings so strong that they did not even allow gene modifications. This meant their external technology had to do all the survival for them, especially in such an inhospitable environment as Parowa Czwarty.

It was a long time since he had taken planetfall, and the first time in months had to be a frozen mudball like this, he thought uncharitably.

His boots crunched across the snow as he approached the Solar Chancellor and her armed escort of a squad of soldiers. He had no doubt that there were even more secreted away across the starport, just in case. These were dangerous times.

Even with the cold-weather gear he could feel the coldness of the environment setting his teeth on edge. He glanced at Lady Sophia Towers, who did not appear to notice the cold in her typically ostentatious baaka fur thermal trousers and jacket. Behind him marched Major Andryukhin and Corporal Naomi Calaman, his adjutant, in full Imperial Marine power armour.

The Solar Chancellor stood outside a small vehicle, engine running and repulsor lifters blowing snow-clouds into the air. The snow was so heavy, it was almost impossible to make out the shape of the star port buildings, even though they were no more than five hundred metres away from this landing pad. Landing lights flickered along in a long linear line, disappearing into the white out and then reappearing as they came back from the unseen edges.

"Captain Gavain!" Solar Chancellor Kowalczyk shouted out across the storm. It was impossible to make out her features beyond the oxygenator mask. Oxygen did exist on Parowa Czwarty, but in such low levels that although it was breathable, prolonged exposure to the atmosphere could damage human lungs and lead to a slow, painful death. If hypothermia did not bring death first, Gavain thought. "A pleasure to meet you, Captain!"

"Hail in the name of the *True* Emperor," he greeted as standard, thinking to himself that already that was a bit of an anachronism. He noted that the Solar Chancellor did not reply.

"House Lady Sophia Towers, it's good to see you again," Solar Chancellor Kowalczyk changed her attention. "Will you be wanting to check on your business interests here?"

"Yes, but only briefly, as one is sure my dear Captain explained we are in rather of a hurry, Lina."

"Of course!" Chancellor Kowalczyk shouted. "Captain, your message said that you would be disembarking a number of House Lords here?"

"Yes, they are onboard," he indicated the lander behind him. "Send some of your transports into the hold, we'll leave it open. Get them off my ship."

Even behind the visor he could see the shock in the eyes of the Solar Chancellor.

"The Captain means to say that we wish to conclude our business, and the Lords and Ladies are in such a hurry, they cannot wait to continue on their journey," House Lady Sophia Towers put her arm through the Captain's, and gently led him towards the vehicle. "Come, Captain."

Captain Gavain sat in the office, staring out of the window at the vicious snowstorm beyond. He could not even see the lander, although he was assured by Lady Sophia that this particular office overlooked their landing pad.

Major Andryukhin and Corporal Calaman stood at ease behind them, still suited in their power armour although they had at least removed their helmets. Iced water ran in rivulets down the sculpted plates of the armour, to drip on the lush carpets.

Gavain was removing his protective gloves and throwing them on the desk in front of them in disgust when a side door opened, and a nervous clerk entered. His formal shirt bore his name-badge, 'Downs', on the right breast above the symbol of the Interstellar Merchants Guild, a five-pointed gold star with the letters IMG below. The star had once stood on the breast of an Imperial Eagle, but following the fall of the Imperium, the Head of the IMG had ordered it removed.

"At last," said Captain Gavain as Senior Clerk Downs sat on the other side of the desk, suspensor seat taking his considerable weight with a groan of the motors. He noticed that the clerk was staring with some trepidation at the two power armoured Marines by the main door.

"I am Senior Clerk Victor Downs, of the Gdanskal City First

Commercial Starport branch of the Interstellar Merchants Guild," he said with an attempt at grandness, badly spoilt by the shaking voice as his eyes flicked several times to the weaponry the Marines were carrying openly.

"It is nice to see you again, Senior Clerk. One trusts the family is well?" Lady Sophia Towers asked.

"Y - yes indeed, my Lady, very kind of you to ask. I have prepared all your usual reports and downloads, but I can run through any of them with you right now if you wish?"

"In a short while, certainly," Lady Towers said with a pleased look on her face. "However, we are here to discuss a particular business matter first, so we do not detain these colleagues of mine longer than we have to. One sent it through to you as soon as we entered the system. One trusts you received it?"

"Ah, yes, ah -" the Senior Clerk's hands quickly flicked through a holographic display in front of him, until he reached the document he wanted. He tapped its image in thin air, and the document enlarged in front of his unaugmented eyes. " - yes, er, the new business set up for a venture you wish to call 'The Vindicator Mercenary Corporation'." He seemed to regain some composure, and he gave Lady Sophia and Captain Gavain a shy smile. "It's certainly an interesting asset list you're opening with."

"Yes, yes," said Captain Gavain. He was feeling out of his depth already, a state he was not accustomed to, and that was making him very edgy and more short than normal. "Can we get to the point, please?"

"Of course," the Senior Clerk swallowed. "The Articles of Association are very much the standard, and list Captain James Gavain -" he looked at the Captain, who nodded once, "- and yourself Lady Sophia as the two Directors of Company. The Associate Directors are listed as a Commander Lucas De Graaf, Lieutenant-Commander Julia Kavanagh, and a Major Ulrik Andryukhin."

"Pleased to make your frikking acquaintance," the Major commented dryly from behind. Despite himself, Gavain was amused to see the Senior Clerk swallow audibly once again.

He stammered through some more details, and then added, "any legal documents need both Director's signatures, or one Director's signature and two Associate Directors signatures as stipulated in your documentation, my Lady. Do you have the genetic identifiers for me?"

Captain Gavain handed over a case of samplers, which contained the genetic information for his command staff and Lady Sophia.

"Excellent. The company is fully registered -" and with a flourish, the Senior Clerk pressed a holographic button in front of him above the documentation "- as of now. On the next HPCG upload, it will be communicated to all of the Guild mainframes across the galaxy, which should be within the next twenty-four hours. Here are your letters of marque."

Captain Gavain accepted the datapad, which had a copy of his letter of marque. It was this that he prized above all else from today. The letter of marque was the sign that a mercenary or a privateer had been officially registered, and conferred upon them all prisoner-of-war status if captured. Without it, they would be seen as pirates, subject to summary execution under Imperial Decree. This did not stop some Houses from executing mercenaries as well, even before the fall of the Empire, but he felt the extra protection was worthwhile, and besides which, it made him and the Vindicator Mercenary Corporation legitimate.

"One trusts you will register us on the notice-boards for all military and mercenary contracts, as instructed?" Lady Sophia asked.

"Of course, my Lady. The Mercenary Bonding Office is an old service of the IMG, but it has been rather active of late. By the time you return to your ship, there should be a full download of available contracts for you to peruse. You can indicate an interest in those and wait for acceptance, or they can respond to your advertisements and contact you directly. For any contract pending, you will have to pay a bond into the MBO against poor or unsatisfactory performance, as the customer places the full contract value against that bond. There are a number of conditions I suggest you read."

"We know how it works," said Captain Gavain. "What are you doing with my advertisement for more crew?"

"Ah, yes, er, Captain, the advertisement is going into the gazette tomorrow. There are a number of adverts requesting applications from ex-Praetorian Guard, are you sure you don't want to widen your criteria so that –"

"No," Captain Gavain said curtly. "Near two hundred of my crew decided not to join the Company, so they must be replaced with other Praetorians."

"Ah, I, er, see. Of course, Captain." Senior Clerk Downs looked to Lady Sophia for help.

"Thank you, Captain," she said graciously. "Would you like to return to the lander whilst you wait? Oneself and the Senior Clerk have other business matters to discuss. One's holdings in House Zielinski territories and beyond, one is sure you understand?"

"Yes," Gavain snapped, glad to be leaving the office. He stood up abruptly. "I'll see you on the lander, my Lady."

He turned and left, seeking the safety of his ship as soon as possible.

*

President Rebecca Nielsen entered the Golden Room, resplendent in her new robes of office as the leader of the StarCom Federation. She even had a staff of office for ceremonial occasions, which was currently carried by a small robotic drone hovering along a couple of metres behind her.

The Golden Room lived up to its name, being primarily coloured in gold, brown-yellows and deep yellows for relief. The only other colours came from the paintings and the sculptures from the second millennium, arrayed around the large circular room in a vast number of alcoves, the continuous line of which was broken only by the grand, ornate, golden door that allowed entrance and exit from the audience chamber.

The room itself was located deep in the heart of the Palace of Communications, the central hub of all of the StarCom Federation's activities for centuries. The Palace itself was located on a large continent on Earth, an unimaginably large complex almost the size of a city that had been built on the ruins of a former, much older, bombed out metropolis once known as St Petersburg.

She swept to the head of the circular table in the centre of the room, the table itself designed for a much larger crowd than this. In the old StarCom Network, every decision was reached by committee. With the strength of her grasp in the new StarCom Federation, every decision was to be made by her, and occasionally a small circle of trusted advisors.

The three sat in the room were among that small trusted conclave. There was the dark face of her spy chief, the Director of the Central Intelligence Department, Malika Chbihi, typically serious with a furious frown on her face. The new Commander-In-Chief, Jaiden Ryan of the StarCom Federation Army, who in bringing the force out into the open and setting up the service had combined both the land army and the navy into one combined organisation. He was jovial, but dangerous, and had displayed little compunction in disposing himself of his political adversaries.

Finally there was her Vice-President, a woman by the name of Giovanna Pereyra, almost as equally as ruthless as the C-I-C, but exceptionally loyal to Rebecca Nielsen.

She sat down in the suspensor seat, and the drone tapped the staff three times to signal she was about to speak.

"You all know what this is about," she said coldly. "The StarCom Federation has to grow beyond this one system. We will conquer where we have no reason to, apart from our own self-defence. We also have various attacks on our assets, which must be defended as a point of honour. I want you all to be clear on that. Jaiden, our current dispositions and the first phase of our invasion plans?"

C-I-C Jaiden Ryan was running to fat, almost inexcusable with modern medical treatments. He leaned his heavy bulk forwards, using his connection to the datapshere to call up a table of organisation. It focused in on the lists as he spoke, with slowly spinning representations of each ship as he spoke.

"We have re-organised into five fleets of ships-of-the-line, four offensive and one reserve, with another three transportation fleets for the ground forces. There are also a number of unattached units ready for miscellaneous duties. The Federal Guard is the new unit assigned to protection of the home system. The re-organisation is now complete, and we are fully operational.

"First, Second, Third and Fourth Fleets consist of ex-Praetorians, whilst Fifth Fleet - in reserve - are a mix of the forces we built up before the Fall of the Empire. Sixth, Seventh and Eighth are the transportation fleets."

He then called up a holo-map in the minds of his colleagues. The map zeroed in on the targets as he spoke. It sped first to the Sol System.

"All the fleets are currently in the Sol System. At least until the conclusion of the first phase, we will leave Fifth Fleet here in the Sol System for defensive purposes and to support any unforeseen problems. We may then rotate fleets depending on damage assessments and to build up veterancy and experience.

"The first phase of the overall plan consists of taking the systems closest to Sol. For this phase, codenamed Operation Fortress, First, Second and Fourth will be the vanguard of Operation Fortress, supported by Sixth and Seventh transportation fleets for ground invasion. I have assigned targets and the division of the fleets thusly."

Arrows appeared on the three dimensional map, showing where the various elements of each fleet would attack first. "The assaults will be simultaneous, a blitzkrieg assault similar to that currently being employed by the upstart nation of Amiens. There will be three waves, each wave heading further out sequentially before we pause to consolidate our expected gains. The first wave takes Rigel Kentaurus, Barnard's Star, Wolf 359, Sirius, Ross 154, Epsilon Eridani, Ramas, Aegypta, Harrenfall, and Fomalhaut."

Malika Chbihi interrupted at this point, a furious frown on her face. "Barnard's Star and Wolf 359 are former outposts, with Praetorian-manned facilities. They may surrender or come over, so assault may not be necessary, but our intelligence in this area is thin. We will be taking the entire territories of two Houses - Tremane and Hannover - and half the territory of House Ymar, in Ramas, Aegypta and Harrenfall."

"House Ymar may respond in force, which is why they receive a significantly larger proportion of the fleet than is necessary to take Aegypta," Jaiden Ryan pointed out. "If all goes according to plan, they will be wiped out by the leap-frog of the second wave four days later."

"As long as you are prepared," was President Nielsen's only comment.

"Tremane and Hannover will not be easy, so do not discount them," Malika Chbihi responded, "but we have significant intelligence on all of them, and propaganda prepared to explain our invasion of their territories. House Ymar, on the other hand, have provided us with a perfect and real excuse."

"The theft of our assets - nine HPCG stations and one stargate," President Nielsen nodded. Her voice hardened. "This concerns me more, people. I want to know what the plans are to punish those who have defied us."

Vice-President Pereyra spoke up at this point, her angelic and soft tones being very misleading in terms of the true nature underneath. "To date, five Houses have openly defied us, although I'm sure there will be more -"

"- another fifteen are considering it, as far as we know," Chbihi interrupted.

" - which is all the more reason to respond harshly now, to deter the others," the Vice-President continued. "We still obtain a great amount of information from decoding supposed ciphered communications, I am sure. In any case, the five who have seized our assets consist of House Ymar, House Van Hausenhof, House Schmidt, House Nelson and House Weiberg."

"This is a direct challenge against my ascension speech," President Nielsen was seeing this as a personal slight. "I want all of them dealt with. What are your plans, Commander-In-Chief."

"House Ymar will be dealt with by the first and second waves of Operation Fortress, and House Schmidt by the second and third waves. Within two weeks, those Houses will no longer exist. Third Fleet and Eighth Fleet are at our disposal to punish the other Houses." Here he glanced at Malika Chbihi, who took up the plan.

"President, our assessment of House Van Hausenhof is that they are too far away for us to reach easily without extending our lines unnecessarily, at least until the completion of Operation Fortress. They are in a war with Cervantia, so we propose to give House Cervantes monies and support in their war, and use the trade as a way to make an ally of Cervantia. It allows us to ignore their territories and concentrate in other areas."

President Nielsen was not impressed, but as the debate began between the four, she was eventually persuaded of the necessity. "But," she said, "I want to know about the newly-founded states of Nelsonia and Weiberg?"

"Nelsonia is weak, of three systems and no real military, and lies within two jumps of Sol," Commander-In-Chief Ryan replied. "Weiberg is only seven systems, lies within one jump, and both can be conquered in a rolling campaign over the two weeks it takes to complete the first phase of Operation Fortress. We can take Weiberg and Nelsonia by dividing Third and Eighth Fleets. My tacticians and strategists estimate this should be feasible, and we do have Fifth Fleet in reserve, although I would prefer to task them to any problems we find in the first phase of Operation Fortress."

"Hmmm," President Nielsen looked at all of them. "I'm still unhappy about Van Hausenhof. Will Nelsonia and Weiberg be taken and held?"

"Yes," the Commander-In-Chief nodded. "We will hold the territory, but we will need to adjust the second phase of the invasion plans to bring us closer to both or our supply lines will be extended. I have allowed for that flexibility, though. These are interesting times, madam President."

"Excellent." President Nielsen said, her eyes resting on the territories of House Nelson and Weiberg. "I want the punishment of both nations to be severe, a warning to the others that defy me," she said.

"How severe?" the Commander-In-Chief asked.

"The razing of several large cities should be enough," she replied casually.

Chapter VIII

The *Vindicator* completed its jump into the Blackheath System, coalescing back into realspace. Almost immediately, it began to broadcast its Identity Friend or Foe signature, and instantly the defensive forces in the Blackheath System stood down. The *Vindicator* was expected.

Already the Imperial Star Ship moniker had been dropped from the *Vindicator*'s electronic IFF systems, and the hull paint had been altered at one of their layovers. Instead of 'ISS', it now bore the simple prefix of 'SS', to indicate that it was a private ship. The Imperial had already been scrubbed from its name, and to those on board it had been an emotive moment when it was removed.

The *Vindicator* began to move in-system, heading for the seventh planet in the solar system. From the jump-point they had used, the journey would take little over an hour.

The Blackheath System was the primary solar system of six inhabited systems within the holding of House Towers. A binary star system, with some twenty-one planets and countless moons and planetoids within its boundary, as well as three large asteroid fields, the Blackheath System was large and sprawling, and was the source of House Towers' riches.

The first three planets were too close to Blackheath Primary, the fiercer sun of the two. They were blasted, heated, fiery balls of waste, only the third and largest of the trio - aptly named Dante - being far enough away to be mined for the precious metals it carried in abundance.

Then came the two gas planets, Yin and Yang, with the awesomely complex and advanced mining station in orbit around the first gas planet. The Yin mining station was there to support operations not just on Dante, but in the Goldfields asteroid field that ringed the fierce burning star of Blackheath Primary. The gravitational pull of the larger Yang would cause major gas bursts around Yin, radioactive pulses more devastating than nuclear explosions that would occasionally cut the Yin mining station off from external contact for days or weeks at a time.

Beyond the Goldfields asteroid field was the first heavily colonised planet in the system, Tahrir, which was also the personal fiefdom of Lady Sophia Towers. Well-populated, heavy in industry, Tahrir also had a lively tourist industry - at least before the fall of the Red Imperium.

After Tahrir was the second colonised planet, the seat of House Towers' power, the planet of Alwathbah. Heavily commercial, rich, the hub of trade for a number of sectors, the gigantic planet was largely temperate and close to 'normal' for humans to live on in almost all respects.

Further out from Alwathbah were another two colonised planets, the worlds of October and November. Smaller than the other two, they had benefited historically from their proximity to Alwathbah and Tahrir in economic terms. November was the primary military base for House Towers. The Blackheath stargate, monitored and staffed by StarCom operatives, was located out in deep space, but was closest to the orbital paths of October and November.

The Silverfields asteroid field separated the initial part of the solar system. There were a number of gas giants - including Titan, whose rings were also mined under the support of the orbiting Vulcan mining station, a much smaller affair than Yin - and smaller gas worlds, leading to the sun of Blackheath Secondary. Weaker than Primary, Secondary was nevertheless locked in a loving, revolving embrace with its sister.

Orbiting Secondary were two more gas planets, until the inhabited worlds of Omaha and Utah. The first worlds in the system to be colonised, they were still heavily populated. Both were famous for their illicit underworld and organised crime. The Bronzefields asteroid field lay beyond, a recognised haven for smugglers and pirates, tolerated at times by House Towers and cracked down upon at others. Some said the crime gangs and the smugglers were tacitly encouraged and involved with the senior members of the House.

The *Vindicator* had jumped in at a jump-point between Tahrir and Alwathbah. It took a little over an hour for it to reach its first destination in the system. As soon as the *Vindicator* neared the blue, green and white of Alwathbah, at the appropriate point it launched a lander.

The lander came in low, anti-air batteries tracking it automatically even though the targeting systems were in passive mode. The laser targeters were inactive, but even in passive mode, the computer systems were more than capable of operating under visuals only.

The lander flew over the megapolis that was the capital city of Alwathbah and the entire holding of House Towers, Tiananmen. Tiananmen was built in a valley, nestling not just in the crux between the two giant mountain ranges either side but up the steep slopes as well. Lady Sophia Towers looked out of the lander's open blast shutters, and felt the welcoming warm feeling of coming home.

The Sky Keep was the palace of Lord Erik Towers, her father. It was a mighty construct, a circular building with numerous crenallations and battlements above, domed spires and towers, which floated on huge suspensor fields above the megapolis of Tiananmen. On special occasions it would be lowered down into the docking collar deep below, on days of public holiday or celebration, but the majority of the Standard year it rested on its cushion of highly powered repulsor beams. At second dawn and final dusk during summer, when the dust particles were heavy in the air, it was possible to see the lines of the repulsor beams and the suspension field glittering in an amazing light show high above the city.

The lander came in and halted above the enlarged landing pad the jutted out from one wing of the Sky Keep, its own repulsors flaring as it slowly lowered itself down into place. The disembarkation ramps of the lander lowered at the same time as a massive door in the palace retracted downwards.

House Lady Sophia Towers led Captain James Gavain down the ramp, his small honour guard of power-armoured marines following at a respectful distance with arms at port. The party coming to meet them also had its own small honour guard of House Towers soldiers, in their emerald green ceremonial armour, white feathers in long linear plumes flowing from the crests of their helmets.

Lady Sophia glided gently across the short distance from the ramp to the approaching welcoming party, enjoying the crisp smell of the air. It was autumn on Alwathbah, the temperature becoming chillier, only one sun in the sky and that a fading orange as the short night-time approached.

"Father," she smiled gently in greeting. Theirs had never been an overtly warm relationship; Erik Towers had been raising an heir, not a daughter.

His greying hair, lined face, and stern demeanour all added to the reputation of the man as a hard master. He was a hard-line humanist, to such an extent that rather than have corrective surgery for his degenerative disease, he preferred to withstand the pain and the suffering and rode around in a droidchair. His hatred of borg-life was so well-known that his first born son had been one of the first False Emperor had arrested to ensure his continuing loyalty, and the various pogroms against humanists had only served to harden that hatred into an all-consuming fury. Jared Towers had died in the False Emperor's cells, and then Sophia had been taken as hostage. It was shortly after this that Erik Towers had joined the Revolutionary Council, allying himself with some of the borgs he hated to rid himself of the greatest borgite of all - the False Emperor.

Sophia had not seen her father in nearly two years, and all he said was, "Sophia. You survived then." There was a not a 'good to see you', an expression of personal relief, a sign of love. She had grown up this way, but it never ceased to hurt.

Sophia looked at her father, and in that instant, she was reminded of her father's disappointment in her. Jared had always been the favourite, and his death had put her next in line for the seat of House Towers. The bitterness Erik Towers carried within him led him to resent his daughter, refuse the genetic modification, re-grown legs or cybernetic implants that would allow him to walk again, and made him hate everything Imperial or remotely connected to the Red Empire.

"Sophia," her second brother, Luke, glanced once at his father then stepped forwards and embraced her in a large hug. Luke was a bear of a man, and it was like being wrapped in a warm blanket. "It's so good to see you back again, alive. I've been so worried about you these last couple of years. I feared you would go the same way as Jared."

"One sometimes thought the same," she said to her younger half-brother. They loved each other, despite their separate upbringings and lack of common interests. She had been brought up in the Imperial Academy on Mars, he had been educated at home on Alwathbah. She was a successful and graceful business woman, he was the brute who led the House Towers army as its High General. Lord Luke wore the ceremonial uniform to match his honour guard, but with a number of medals pinned to the chest and the double-star on the epaulettes that denoted his supreme rank, whilst Sophia had never even been considered for such a role and had made her own way in life. As a female, Erik Towers had been tolerant of her and dismissive, as a male, Luke had been encouraged and supported.

"We have much to discuss," Lord Senator Erik Towers interrupted, his face thunderous. He was looking at Sophia, absent-mindedly touching the preserved flower he always wore in his lapel. The flower had been a last gift from Sophia's mother to her father before she died in childbirth. "Is this who I think it is?" he looked directly at James Gavain.

Lady Sophia was about to speak, but Captain James Gavain had stepped forwards and extended a hand. "House Lord Senator Erik, hail in the name of the true Emperor," and even as he said the words Sophia cringed.

"An Imperial and a borg," Lord Erik Towers sneered. Sophia knew instantly it was a mistake to have brought the Captain. "Sophia, what is the meaning of this?"

"One did send a message," she said calmly, although inside she felt the usual resignation when she knew a confrontation with her father was about to take place. "The VMC venture one has embarked upon."

"You neglected to mention that your new pet mercenaries were cyborg Praetorians!" Erik Towers ground out. "How could you do this, Sophia? I want that abomination off my planet and out of my territory." He had not even looked at the Captain, who withdrew his hand.

"I am only here to escort Lady Sophia to the surface," he said calmly.

"It's probably best if you left," said Lord Luke quietly. He did not share the extreme humanist view that his father did, but all the same he was still viewed as a humanist rather than a free-thinker like Sophia.

Lady Sophia turned to Captain Gavain. "Captain, perhaps you had best return to the *Vindicator* and make way to my landholding."

"I said, out of my territory, Sophia!"

"He is welcome on Tahrir," she snapped back, before stepping closer to

James Gavain. She whispered, "I'm sorry," her strong Imperial accent and received pronunciation dropping in that moment.

Startled, Gavain merely nodded. "Yes, my lady."

"We will speak soon," she said loudly, as Gavain and his honour guard walked back towards the ramp. She turned back to the argument she knew was inevitable.

Captain James Gavain sat in his ready room, several hours later, still fuming about his reception on Alwathbah. His normally unruffled nature had been deeply offended by the reaction of House Lord Erik Towers. It was not helped by his own mistrust and dislike of the pure humanistic viewpoint that Erik Towers obviously held, and his personal reservations about unaugmented humans. He reflected that there could have been a very nasty incident if Major Andryukhin, with his extreme borgite views, had been present to witness the exchange.

He had not encountered many humanists in his career in the Praetorians. Every member of the Praetorian Guard was a borgite, bred in vats for a life of service in the elite Imperial military. He had always thought of himself as a free-thinker rather than a borgite, but the experience on Alwathbah with Erik Towers had reminded him yet again that he was probably more borgite than he thought. They were so inferior, these unaugmented humans, and to meet a humanist that detested him for being a cyborg just made him view the unaugmented even less favourably. Lady Sophia Towers was not a humanist, by any means, but even she was a step into the alien being unaugmented herself. Expediency and lack of option had led to his formation of the Vindicator Mercenary Corporation with her, and he had thought that he could ignore the fact that she was unaugmented human.

The reaction of her family made her wonder if he had made a horrendous mistake.

He shook himself, reflecting that it was now too late. He had to forge a future for himself and his crew.

His dormant connection to the datasphere provided a constant update of their position in orbit above Tahrir, Lady Sophia's planet and landholding. They had to take a job and leave as soon as possible, he resolved. He did not want to stay in-system any longer than necessary.

There had been a number of respondents to their advert, placed when they had been in the Parowa System, for replacement crew. Not that many had decided to leave the *Vindicator,* for which he was thankful, and there was still more than enough crew for the ship to operate effectively and efficiently. He was surprised at the hundreds of people who had already replied.

He sighed, and decided he would hand over the responsibilities for crew replacement to Lieutenant-Commander Kavanagh. She tended to have a better judgement of people than he did, he was fully aware, and there were that many it was difficult to decide. He realised he had subconsciously filtered out every single unaugmented human from the applications, and had preferred ex-Praetorians where they had applied. His original advert in the gazette had specified ex-Praetorians only, but obviously the economic situation out there was so dire that many had ignored the stipulations and decided to apply regardless.

It made sense to employ Praetorians as much as possible, he had decided. The truth was they would have to employ some non-Praetorians eventually, but the order of preference should be Praetorian, cyborg and then human. He was in no mood to have an unaugmented on his ship in anything other than an extremely junior role, and preferably not at all.

He had a sneaking suspicion that this was his own prejudice and reaction to Erik Towers, so he would ask Julia to provide a second opinion.

He supposed it should be Commander De Graaf doing the sift and filtering, but he had some unexplained reservations about the man. He was undoubtedly capable, but in the last four months, he had made little attempt to get along with the command staff or the crew. Gavain had been surprised when De Graaf had decided to join the VMC venture.

He accessed the data-feed from the download of Tahrir's datapshere, and reviewed the three new contract offers placed on the Mercenary Bonding Office's notice-boards of the Interstellar Merchants Guild. Of the three, there was one in particular that had taken his attention.

The nation of Cervantia was at war with House Van Hausenhof. House Cervantes had declared its independence, and immediately began its campaign against the neighbouring territory. The contract was a raiding strike on a Cervantian convoy route, many of the details being withheld until contract acceptance, but the MBO's threat and risk assessment was within the parameters that Captain Gavain viewed as acceptable. It had the added benefit that he would be striking back against House Cervantes and causing some pain, extracting some revenge for their attempt to seize his ship, although the potential pay-off was so good that was only a minor point in the contract's favour.

The Mercenary Bonding Office contract only required a small bond from himself, a mere two million Imperial Crowns, which was quite low in relative terms for such contracts his research indicated. Sophia's start-up money would cover that. The payout terms were between ten and twenty million Imperial Crowns, depending on the damage inflicted, the defence encountered, and which particular convoy along the route the mercenaries and their employers agreed upon, plus prize rights. Taking prizes meant that the Vindicator Mercenary Corporation could keep any assets or equipment they captured during the raid – the primary objective was to disrupt or destroy the convoys.

He decided to accept the contract; in order to do so, it required either his and Lady Sophia's signature, or his and two of his command staff. It would be better to have Lady Sophia's while they were in-system and orbiting around her landholding, he decided. He hoped Lady Sophia had finished her argument with her father, because he sent a mental command to communications to patch him through back to the Sky Palace on Alwathbah.

*

Admiral Adare sat on the bridge of the dreadnought *SFSS Thor's Hammer*. Despite his resentment at his current position, he was secretly delighted at the command. Being strong-armed into the StarCom Federation's Armed Forces was humiliating enough, but it was better than being airlocked and the compensation of command of such a powerful and beautiful vessel went some way towards mitigating that humiliation.

<Rear-Admiral,> the thought flicked into his mind across the datasphere, placed there by Commodore Pacheco. The Commodore was marching along the command dais. <There is a priority one communication coming in from Head Quarters, your eyes only.>

Adare saw one of the two nameless marine keepers behind him lean down and whisper to Special Agent La Rue, obviously translating what had just been sent in machine-code across the intranet.

"My eyes too, Admiral," she said quietly in spoken speech.

<Provide a download for the Special Agent,> he commanded, even as he accessed the orders.

He read them with interest, the contents of the data package burning itself into his mind in seconds. At last, he thought, some real action. Orders from the President herself.

They had assembled in orbit around Pluto, with the great armada that was Third Fleet. They had not been told what the plans were for them, but they had watched with some jealousy as the other fleets had jumped out of the Sol System some hours before, heading for destinations as yet unknown. Doubtless all would become clear shortly.

Their orders were surprising, to say the least. They were to jump straight away to an uninhabited system, recharge to full capacity, and then jump into their target system at a pre-arranged time. The figurative clock was already ticking. The mission was to punish, then take and hold. As a Rear-Admiral, he would have full command of a large squadron responsible for taking one entire system.

<Prepare for jump to these co-ordinates,> he ordered.

*

The woman moved with the travelator droid as it followed its pre-programmed path across the starport concourse, inertia slightly throwing the crowd of people to one side as it turned a sharp bend around the raised landing pad. There was a strong smell of burnt ozone in the air, the metallic hull of the gigantic passenger liner above them ticking as it cooled, even this long after atmospheric re-entry. The droid ran smoothly across the even metacrete flooring, the passengers stood in neat rows within the tight confines of their individually assigned berths, complete with their own hand-holds.

She looked up at the clear blue sky overhead. Exeter's capital planet, also named Exeter, was a high-gravity planet, quite dry in this region of the largest of the five continents. Heavily industrial, besides being the capital, the planet Exeter was also the backbone of the Weiberg nation's manufacturing and production facility, and provided the driver for a large proportion of its economy. The air was dry, the heat from the sun strong, and there was a sulphurous tang to the atmosphere. The ground shook briefly, throwing the passengers around; whether it was a starship lifting off, or one of the many daily earthquakes, it was impossible to tell.

The woman was smartly dressed, in a modern inner-Core style suit, a loose jacket with Nehru collar and sharply creased trousers made of lightweight synthesised material, a wide-sash belt tied loosely at the front bearing the symbol of some corporation. In this heat it was the most sensible thing for someone to wear. A single band of wrap-around dark sunglasses hid her eyes. A small droid-case, presumably carrying her essentials for the visit, lay at her feet with its tiny repulsor deactivated.

The woman wore a friendly, easy-going smile, obviously enjoying the ride. Long blond hair waved gently in the draft created by the travelator's movement, the harsh sun shining off its perfectly presented cut as the vehicle swished into the main terminal.

She removed her sun-glasses as the travelator droid continued down the terminal, heading towards the immigration post. The Weiberg Nation was effectively on high alert, the seven inhabited systems under its control all on lock-down with martial law, and travel limited only to those with security-checked passports. Their leader, King Ibbe Weiberg, explained it as a precaution considering current galactic events; the rumour boards on the global dataspheres all across the Weiberg Nation claimed it was for fear of StarCom reprisals following the aggressive seizing of the HPCG Stations.

The travelator came to a halt, and the passengers disembarked. The starport was relatively quiet for such a major thoroughfare, but the queues were still large due to the lack of open gates in immigration post. The droid-case lifted up and hovered along behind her.

Eventually the woman reached the head of the queue.

"Next." The immigration official, old and obviously extremely bored, stared obviously and rudely at her before speaking. The woman pretended not to notice.

"Normal or augmented?" he grunted from under his cap. The question in itself spoke volumes, and would instantly have offended any borgite, and maybe even a neutral, free-thinking borg.

"I'm normal," she said, obviously not one to take offence at the phrasing.

"Your passport, then," he said. She handed over a small electronic card, and he inserted it into a reader on his belt.

"What is your name?" the immigration official asked.

The woman told him. He nodded as the name came through on his display from the immigration checks.

"Where are you from?" he asked.

"I'm from Maceron, in the Sennora System," she said pleasantly.

"Purpose of visit?"

"I'm here on business for the Tallox Corporation, to try and obtain a chemicals export licence and inspect local facilities."

He hesitated. "Your visa checks out," he nodded.

He pressed a holographic pad on the display projected in front of his podium, and a special mounting for the checking apparatus descended from the ceiling of the gate doorway. If she had been a borg, a different set of checks would have been needed.

"You know the drill," he assumed.

The woman moved forwards, allowing the apparatus to take a retinal scan, fingerprint, DNA sample and hair sample.

"Send the case through the scanner-hole and step through the gateway. Anything to declare?" he asked. The droid-case lifted up and drifted through into the scanner.

"No," the woman replied. The immigration official examined the scan of the case, the computer already telling him that there was nothing except clothes and a non-lethal datapad contained inside.

"Your visa is for seven days," he said. "Do you understand that if you do not present yourself for departure within one day's expiry of this date, you will be listed as an illegal immigrant. You will be actively searched for by the Enforcers, detained, and unless there is a reasonable and proven excuse for non-presentation, incarcerated for up to one year before being subject to forced deportation?"

"Yes, I do," the woman replied.

"Welcome to Exeter. Enjoy your stay. Next."

It took another forty minutes for her to negotiate the terminal and the main hall, before reaching the main exit. She emerged into the capital city, past the heavily armed soldiers in front of the reinforced glass front. The droidcar sent to pick her up was parked very close to a stationary repulsortank.

The droidcar was a luxury model, one that would not seem out of place used by a mid- or high-level executive. On the spare seat in the enclosed passenger compartment, was a datacard. As the droid-case hovered to a rest, she pressed a button on the holographic screen which popped up in front of her to start the ignition and set the car off on its pre-programmed path. She then waved the screen away as the windows darkened.

The droidcar's passenger compartment had four seats, two to a row and each row facing each other. She lifted the droid-case up onto the seat opposite, and clicked it open. Neatly pressed clothes were displayed, with a datapad tucked in at the side. It was exactly what the scanner in the starport had seen.

Her hand hit the disguised recess panel inside. The image of the clothes and the datapad shimmered, and then disappeared, revealing the true contents. Various pieces of equipment lay inside - even those unfamiliar with the equipment's nature would recognise some of the explosives, and the broken down elements of weaponry. She plugged the datacard left for her on the seat into the special reader in the roof of her case.

A beam shot into her eyes, a HRV beam designed to pass the information directly onto her retinas. In seconds she had absorbed the information, receiving the next stage of her mission. She now knew who her target was.

She closed the case down, clicking its special locks shut expertly and with familiarity. With a quick check to ensure that the glass was still darkened, she then began the transformation.

Her body shifted, the shoulders widening, her facial features cracking and then reforming, hair shortening to almost skin-cut and changing colour from blond to a grey-peppered black, eyes turning from blue to brown, nose elongating and widening slightly, skin tone changing from soft white to a shiny black, arms and legs thickening with muscle, hands and feet enlarging. His breathing pattern had changed, his posture had altered, his voice would be deeper, and even his mannerisms would be different.

The cybernetic biomorph had special implants that even the technology of the starport's immigration post could not detect. The Faceless were far too advanced to get caught out by even the most modern commercially-available technology in the galaxy.

The Faceless assassin had his, her or its target, and nothing or no-one would be successful in preventing the murder.

*

Lady Sophia Towers sat with what remained of her family at the dinner table. Her own mother was long dead, and Erik Towers' second wife had divorced him. That left Erik Towers himself, her, and her half-brother Luke. Their servants had retreated at the terse command of her father, and then the meal had largely been eaten in silence. The harsh words following her arrival had only escalated, despite Luke's attempts to calm the situation.

She wondered idly if the furious silence indicated the end of the matter, or whether like the storms that battered Tiananmen relentlessly, this was merely the calm in the eye of the storm and the thunder was about to begin again. With their father, one never knew.

A servant entered quietly, his face apprehensive. Their father looked up.

"I said no interruptions." His tone was level, but his eyes betrayed his simmering anger.

"Begging your pardon my lord, an urgent communication for Lady Sophia is awaiting."

"It must be business," she said. "One had better take it." She turned to the servant. "But ask for text only, one cannot interrupt the scintillating and entertaining meal." she ordered.

"Yes, my Lady." The servant left to retrieve the message and convert it onto a datapad.

"I see your sarcasm has not improved," Erik Towers growled, before returning to his meal in silence.

The servant returned just as they were finishing, and passed a datapad to Sophia. She read it quickly. There was a foreword from Captain James Gavain, explaining his reasoning, and then a contract underneath from the Mercenary Bonding Office.

She looked up thoughtfully, staring out of the ceiling window as she considered. They were dining in one of the private rooms, in the upper levels of the floating Sky Keep. The reinforced metaglass windows wrapped around the majority of the room, the ceiling also constructed of the clear glass to provide an outstanding view of the surroundings. She could see the higher skyscrapers of Tiananmen, pointing up from the city proper, a multitude of vehicles swirling around the upper levels.

It was probably best for the VMC to leave, and besides, they needed to start generating income. She would have to bow to Gavain's judgement in this. She quickly wrote a short message wishing him luck, and suggested the use of the Blackheath Stargate to speed him to the location and to conserve jump charge. She tapped in the code and pressed her finger to the reader, electronically signing the contract document and handing it back to the servant. "Thank you," she said politely.

Her brother Luke tucked his eating wand into its holder. "Is business going well, Sophia?" he asked.

"Yes and no," she replied honestly. "One's various interests have suffered from one's imprisonment; however, the majority of one's senior executives are chosen for their capability and have done their best in the circumstances. The dissolution of the Empire is destroying the macro-economy; some markets are doing better than others. Everything is in a state of flux."

Lord Senator Erik Towers leaned back in his droidchair, and folded his arms. Whatever his relationship with his daughter, he respected her intelligence and assessment. "Agreed, Sophia. But we have more to worry about than the economy. Let us talk of the future."

He summoned the servants and they cleared the table. The three Towers family members were silent until they were once again left alone in the room, around the circular table.

"Your arrival is timely Sophia," Erik Towers said. A holoprojector built into the table suddenly flared into life, displaying a holomap of the colonised galaxy. As he spoke it zoomed in on the immediate territory of House Towers.

"The galaxy is falling apart, and Houses are seceding rapidly. Wars have already broken out between various houses. StarCom has amassed a massive army, mainly of ex-Praetorians, and although we are distant from Sol, I still consider them to be perhaps our greatest threat. I do not trust President Nielsen. Do you agree, Luke?"

"You know my thoughts on this, father," Luke nodded. "That's my assessment too. Everyone in the Core has reason to fear this StarCom Federation. Nielsen's ambition looks out, not within, the Sol System."

Lady Sophia kept her eyes on the starmap. The six inhabited systems of House Towers were displayed, the territory when combined forming a three-dimensional comma, the tail pointing towards Sol. Blackheath, the strongest of the six systems, sat close to the tail, with only the much smaller predominately agricultural system of Hothe actually in the tail. The other four systems consisted of the vast manufacturing bases of Ardposs and Siluru, the largely uninhabited but heavily militarised system of Fort Bastion, and finally Fellstar, a system overly rich in precious minerals and metals. There were a number of uninhabited systems in between which technically fell into House Towers territory and were policed to greater or lesser extents by the House military and automated drones.

"One leaves such matters to you," said Lady Sophia.

"You are the heir to House Towers," Lord Erik snapped. "It is time you took an interest, Sophia."

"If one had not been languishing in the prisons of Saturn's moons one would be more up to date," Sophia responded mildly.

"Stop baiting our father, Sophia," Luke interrupted. "You have always taken an interest. Father, please continue. Sophia needs to know this."

Erik's eyebrows were so close together they were virtually one, but after a long pause, his characteristic scowl lightened slightly and he leaned back in his chair again, head coming up slightly as he realised that Sophia had been deliberately taunting him.

"That was below you, Sophia," he commented. "You have always been very politically aware." He held up a hand to forestall her as she opened her mouth. "Enough." He pointed at the map. "I have a decision to make, and I want your opinion. As heir, and considering my health, you will have to live with this decision. Count yourself lucky I am asking your counsel and hold your tongue until you have something useful to say, woman.

"We have three options, as I see it." Erik continued. "We can delay making a choice, but not for long. Our first option is to declare House Towers independent. This brings a whole host of problems, and potentially makes us a target." Two territories began to flash on the map, that of Houses Obamu and Jorgensson.

"Obamu and Jorgensson have long coveted our territory for its abundant resources," Lord Luke said. "Either would most likely consider us a target, especially considering our history during the days of Empire. We could stand against either, but a prolonged period of warfare would drastically weaken us, and cut off nearly forty percent of our local trade routes. If StarCom does begin to expand, we could be in their invasion path and have to consider them the greater threat."

"One agrees that StarCom is a threat, but do you have additional intelligence to indicate an immediate threat?" Sophia asked.

"Yes," Luke nodded. "Several of the StarCom Central Intelligence Department operatives have been exposed, and we are tracking many more. I believe we have some penetration of our own intelligence service, and definitely in our military. The scale of interest suggests we are of note to the Commies. In Sol, they have amassed some eight fleets of ex-Praetorian ships, some of which no less than a couple of days ago began jumping out-system and have not surfaced in any inhabited system. Their fleets are on the move. They are about to begin an invasion of neighbouring systems, and will most likely be successful. They have threatened retaliation for seizure of StarCom assets, HPCGs and stargates, and are likely to use this as an excuse for aggression. We are in the Core, and only about a month and a half out from this new Federation."

"That is serious," Sophia nodded. "But could we stand against the StarCom Federation and eight fleets?"

"Not eight, definitely not," Luke shrugged, "but what will StarCom tactics be? Invade slow, or fast? Take and consolidate in strength, or divide forces and hit multiple targets? Perhaps we could take on part of a fleet, but even then success would not be guaranteed against Praetorian ships and our losses would be high, and we could not guarantee full protection of all our systems."

"Our second option is to become a protectorate of the StarCom Federation," Erik Towers stated. "We do not know how likely that it is to happen, but I suspect that even if Nielsen considered the idea, as territories fell all around us and we became isolated, eventually we would become a part of the Federation in more than just name."

"No," Sophia shook her head. "There are too many variables and uncertainties to be seriously considered. Besides, we have escaped the False Emperor after years of struggle and pain, why would we swap such a dictator for another?"

"My assessment as well, daughter. This leaves us with the third option, and perhaps a surprising one." Instantly Sophia realised this was her father's preferred choice. The starmap began to glow with different House territories than before. "The third way is an alliance with some of our neighbours. There is strength in unity."

Lady Sophia leaned forwards in interest. House Jorgensson had faded to black, but House Obamu was still glowing, its territory flashing on and off. House Zupanic was also varying between highlight and dark. House Claes, House Galetti, and House Lapointe, were solid blocks of colour.

"There have been some initial discussions whilst you were away, and before the Empire fell, discussions of the utmost secrecy," Erik Towers continued. "We are thinking of allying ourselves, beyond just a military pact, but into a new nation. The two Houses flashing on and off have been approached, and terms are being discussed, but we are not certain they will join. This is our third option, Sophia. What do you think?"

Sophia was taken aback. She did not think her father had the vision or the willingness to see such an alternative as a possibility. Once again, she was reminded that despite his many faults and his declining health, Erik Towers was not a fool and was still a very sharp political operator.

Her mind kicked into gear however, and she evaluated it as she would any other important decision, by picking it apart and considering every angle. Her brother and her father watched her, waiting for her to speak.

Eventually she said, "Even without Zupanic or Obamu, the nation would be one of the strongest power blocks in the Core. We would be the Corewards version of the new OutWorlds Alliance. Zupanic is a leviathan, of seventeen inhabited systems, and with it we would stretch into the Mid-Sectors. We would be a threat the StarCom Federation could not ignore, but would not take lightly. It may be the best option we have, depending on how it would work. How did you convince Zupanic - or Obamu - to consider this?"

"Obamu have been approached by Claes and Galetti initially, and then latterly Zupanic. They were handled carefully," Luke replied for her father, "We've kept very much out of their initial discussions, although our presence in the new state worries them greatly. Moafa Obamu is a man of reason, for all his cunning and viciousness, and he sees the advantage in this. I think he will put aside his enmity for us, as he fears the StarCom Federation as well. House Jorgensson were also approached, but have flatly refused upon learning of our involvement. That was when Zupanic envoys came to us."

"House Lord Ramicek Zupanic learnt of the talks we were having," Lord Erik Towers said quietly. "He has proposed joining the new nation we are forging, and further - he suggests marriage to seal it."

"Marriage?" Sophia had a sudden flash of insight.

"His son Micalek Zupanic, due to inherit the Household after Ramicek," Luke said quietly.

"To me?" Sophia asked, her Imperial accent dropping.

"Yes," Erik Towers replied.

"One would need to consider," she said eventually.

"Well, consider quickly," Erik Towers suddenly snapped. "Zupanic joining the nation would make it unbelievably powerful, and give us an upper hand in the new government being suggested."

"One will consider quickly," Sophia spoke coolly, "but you realise, they are only after our resources, our people and our House military?"

"Of course they are, " Luke said. "But inter-house marriage has always consisted of such reasons. Please consider, Sophia."

"You too?" she asked, eyebrows raised. She then sighed deeply. "One can see the sense in such an arrangement, but please, let one think on it."

"N -" Erik began.

"Yes, sister, of course," Luke leaned across to put one hand on hers, and then shot a glance at his father.

"Would the terms of marriage allow Zupanic to inherit all House Towers territory?" Sophia asked, with another flash of insight.

"No," Erik Towers shook his head. "Luke would be named heir to House Towers territory. There is no other alternative, Sophia, I will not allow our landholding to be taken from us by politics rather than by force. Ramicek Zupanic accepts this."

No wonder you favour this, Sophia thought to herself. It seemed her father's uneasy relationship with her had come to a head, and this alliance provided him with the perfect excuse to break the line of inheritance.

Seeing the explosion that was about to occur, Luke spoke quickly. "The discussions with all the Houses are still ongoing. There is a secret summit being called for two weeks time, where we all meet to hammer out the terms of a constitution, and to decide if we are really going to do this. We may name the nation after the world where we are meeting, if the constitution is signed – The Levitican Union. We want you to come to the Leviticus summit, Sophia."

"To meet one's new husband?"

"No, as a Lady of House Towers, with the right to speak and to be a part of making history!" Erik Towers roared, slapping his hand on the table. "Cease your petulance, Sophia!"

"Father," Luke said quietly. He turned to Sophia, "It has been suggested that the new constitution allows for a rotating leadership, with a government or council consisting of House representatives. The House of the elected leader would have no representatives, but carry the casting vote in case of a tie. Each house would have their own portfolio of responsibility – military defence, economic affairs, that sort of thing. It's the initial positioning that's causing the major problem now, amidst a myriad of small niggling points."

"This is all very advanced and it sounds agreed," Sophia said quietly.

"Your marriage is not," Luke said. "It's been made clear to Ramicek and his son Micalek that the choice is yours. But the marriage would give us the chance of a casting vote should we ever need it, considering our close ties with House Lapointe."

Sophia Towers stood. "One needs to reflect on this," she said. "Please excuse me."

"Yes," Luke said, while their father sat and glowered angrily at her. "I will come and see you later, so we can have a proper catch-up on things."

"Thank you, brother," Sophia said, and with a last hostile look at her father, swept from the room, well aware that she had been completely outmanoeuvred by her own family, and also aware that it was probably the best hope for her House's survival.

The battlecruiser *SS Vindicator* fired the last of its manoeuvring thrusters, halting its forward motion and lining up with the portal of the Blackheath Stargate simultaneously. For a long period of time, nothing happened, and all was motionless.

Suddenly the massive stargate burst into life, power crackling around its eight launching pylons. The stargate was big, a huge ring with its circumference so large and the radius so wide that it could easily accommodate upwards of ten ships, and the Blackheath Stargate was one of the more average-sized designs.

The energy crackling along the pylons suddenly linked together in gigantic arcs, exploding the warp field that had been generated. The entire region of space flashed, a bubble of energy flowing out and capturing the

Vindicator. For a moment it was held static in real-space, and then with another flash, the *Vindicator* translated into warp-space, and was catapulted out of the system. A stargate could throw a spaceship far across the galaxy, up to fifteen or twenty times the jump that even a military-grade ship could make.

To the crew on the *Vindicator* the journey took nearly two and a half weeks in jumpspace, but in real-time they emerged almost seconds later on the far side of System K-3459. The system was uninhabited, consisting of a number of gas giants and planets and one brilliant, over-hot sun that was nearing collapse.

The *Vindicator* took nearly a day and a half to traverse the system, and when it rounded the sun to line up with the jump-points on the far side of the system, it fired its engines to give it forward thrust.

The spaceship's running lights winked out, its chameleonic field activating. Its shape shimmered, and then the *Vindicator* disappeared, stealthily invisible even to the naked eye. A special low-level inhibitor field prevented any stray energy signatures from giving away its position, and the powerful drives were deactivated.

Running silent, it ghosted in silently towards the three designated jump-points in the system, evading detection by all the remote drones that watched for ingress and egress from the jump points. They were deep in Cervantian space, and they were waiting for the next supply convoy to jump in.

Chapter IX

King Ibbe Weiberg stood within the safety cordon of the protective force field, the voice microphones picking up his words as his speech was thrown across the crowds in the square before him, and transmitted across all of the Weiberg Nation.

The safety cordon was wide, a rectangular box of energy that covered the stage to protect against would-be assassins in the crowd. It was near invisible, but every so often it would glisten or shine, a rippling in the air like the surface of water under a breeze. He and his entire family stood within, a number of aides, his Prime Minister, the Field Marshal of his armed forces, his Defence Secretary, and a small honour guard of four armed soldiers, wearing ceremonial uniform without armour. With the exception of the guard, they all stood behind his podium, listening and clapping at the appropriate moments in his speech.

He felt completely safe, despite his deliberate pillaging of the StarCom hyperpulse communications generators and stargate. He had security forces out in the crowd, armed soldiers on visible display and aerospace units ready to scramble at a moment's notice. He felt completely invulnerable.

He was wrong.

The Faceless assassin had killed one of his aides this morning, and taken his place. He stood within the safety cordon. Apart from the Field Marshals handgun, and the four assault rifles carried at port arms position by the four soldiers, the assassin had no other threats within the safety cordon. As a security feature, it could only be deactivated from inside. No-one could get in - which meant all the armed forces and security were locked out.

The contract said it had to be a highly visible assassination, and it would be. The assassin's internal chronometer clicked onto the target time for the murder, and without even missing a beat, the Faceless assassin calmly moved into action.

He stepped forward out of line, raising both arms up and to the side. His hands transformed, becoming organic barrels. Two precise shots rang out, the laser beams scything through two of the guards. He shifted aim, and the other two guards were falling to the floor, their heads neatly burnt away by the over-powered weaponry. A fifth of a second had passed.

He brought his left elbow back, a huge blade extending out and stabbing into the Field Marshal. It slid into his chest, piercing his heart with pin-point precision. Even as it withdrew, the assassin's right arm was firing into the people on his right. Just over half a second had elapsed.

In one point six seconds, every person on the stage was either dead or grievously wounded, with the exception of the King. Ibbe Weiberg was still turning round as the assassin calmly walked forwards, barrels changing into two long swords.

He paused for one second to allow the cameras to capture the image, with the King facing him, mouth beginning to open. He crossed the blades and rested the King's neck between them at the far end. Then he snapped his arms to either side, the blades scissoring cleanly through King Ibbe's neck and decapitating him in a burst of arterial blood.

Shoving the body aside, drenched in blood, the assassin spoke into the microphone on the podium.

"In the name of the StarCom Federation. Seizure of StarCom assets is an act of aggression, and will be punished."

Even as the tens of thousands in the square beyond were screaming out, the assassin let off the fast-flowing smoke grenades. In scant moments the entire security cordon had filled with the thick smoke, special particles within the fog preventing any specialised scanning equipment from penetrating the fog and discerning what was about to occur within. In the smoke, working by feel only, the Faceless assassin tipped a dissolving acid over the dead body of one of the other aides. In seconds the aide had been completely eaten, and a special suction device had removed the last traces. The assassin lay down in the aides place, his body changing into that of the dissolved, female aide.

Some members of the armed forces were gathered outside when the security cordon suddenly went down. Alert for the assassin as the smoke cleared, when it had finally dissipated, they found nothing but corpses and wounded. The alarm was sounded, but the police had their own problems with the crowd beginning to riot.

In the confusion it took slightly longer for the medical teams to arrive. They found three people still alive, and air-lifted them to hospital. A short while later, one of the three would disappear as the Faceless made her escape.

<Hyperspace exit in ten seconds,> the warning came from the helm.

Rear-Admiral Silus Adare released combat drugs into his system, artificially heightening his awareness. They were running a couple of seconds too early, his internal chronometer told him, but he quickly evaluated the strategic situation and decided it was of no importance.

<Commodore Pacheco has tactical command of the ship,> he announced. He would direct the vanguard squadron in the initial phase of the assault, one of two squadrons which were jumping in on the Exeter System. Their part in the invasion was moments away from beginning. At this precise time, StarCom Federation fleets would be jumping in to their selected targets, a mass co-ordinated attack according to the overall

master-plan.

Special Agent La Rue and his two marine escorts were watching him as he called up a strategic map display in front of him, from which he would direct his squadron.

<Translation in three .... two ..... one ..... exit!>

The dreadnought *SFSS Thor's Hammer* ploughed into real-space, bursting into the Exeter System with a flash of light. They were coming in hot, as close to the gravity well of the capital planet of Exeter as they could safely get. They were on the other side of the planet from the protective starbase, but the defensive forces had forewarning of their arrival and were already moving into position.

Admiral Adare evaluated the overall theatre of war in less than a second. All of his ships exited almost simultaneously, but he knew there would have been at least a three-minute warning of their incoming jump through magnetic distortions and heat signatures. The *Thor's Hammer* was in the lead of the V-formation, as the ship most capable of soaking up the heaviest damage. The battlecruisers *SFSS Revenging Angel* and *Veritable* were in the second line and set slightly back from the *Thor's Hammer,* followed by the two strike cruisers *Snake-Eyes* and *Serendipity,* then the destroyers *SFSS Underworld* and *Ubermacht.* The frigates *SFSS Nero* and *Orion* were in the furthermost arms, and the star-carrier *Queen of Egypt* nestled within the inverted V-formation, creating a diamond shape with the *Thor, Angel and Veritable* near the head.

The enemy ships arrayed against them began to fire. There were any number of ships in-system, but only thirteen of them were military, and only six were in orbit around Exeter. Adare calculated that the initial wave of reinforcements on their way were only thirty-nine minutes away from effective firing range, but the six Weiberg ships were hopelessly outgunned and outclassed against the ten ex-Praetorian starships. He had expected heavier initial resistance - the Weibergers were obviously far too complacent in their own perceived safety and had been unprepared and not expecting a full assault.

As predicted, the majority targeted the *Thor's Hammer,* but their firing discipline was poor, Adare noted. Of the six ships, two began firing on the *Revenging Angel,* before their leader realised the mistake and re-tasked them onto the *Thor.* Despite his considerable begrudging hatred of his current situation, press-ganged into service for the Federation, Adare felt the thrill of command, his role in this conflict, and the blood-rushing call of sheer aggressive combat.

He listened to the damage report as the *Thor* came under fire.

<Twenty-two seconds to weapons hot,> Commander Sahin reported. <Shields begin power-up in one minute fifteen. Sixteen second cycle-time expected.>

Adare watched as the *Queen of Egypt* launched its fighters, which were thrown out of their launch tubes by mechanically operated catapults. Ordinary magnetic rails could not operate this close after a warp translation, the energy fields necessitating the complete shut-down of all vulnerable systems. The fighters and bombers would form a protective screen around as much of the squadron as possible, sometimes sacrificing themselves in order to distract and protect the unshielded ships.

Mentally he assigned all the enemy ships name-tags, choosing the colour red and a number. Red-One was the heaviest Weiberger ship out there, a battlecruiser. It was old and ancient, like much of the Weiberg fleet, an antiquated model long discontinued by the shipbuilders Drax Naval Architects. It had been retro-fitted with updated weaponry, and they were beginning to cause damage to the *Thor's Hammer.*

Explosions roared around its entire forward hull and underhull, making it appear that it had a fiery red-orange crown, as torpedoes found their mark. It was impossible to miss, the distance was so close in nautical terms. The Weibergers had come to the limits of extended range for their turbolasers, but were moving in closer. The battlecruiser designated Red One opened up with its full array of weaponry first, having moved in to close range on the defenceless StarCom squadron.

Adare directed the destroyers to hang back with the frigates, but began to pull the cruisers forwards. By the time Commander Sahin called across the datasphere, <Weapons hot>, the cruisers were in a line with the *Thor,* facing the shattered zig-zag line of the Weibergers.

<All ships fire at will,> Adare ordered. <Target selection Red One.>

Commodore Pachenco began to turn the dreadnought, presenting the starboard side of the *Thor,* aware that even the tough hull of the super-ship was taking too much damage. It had the advantage of also bringing more of its weaponry to bear.

In the first thirty seconds after translation, all the Praetorian ships were returning fire, still unshielded but no longer defenceless. Red One took a battering in the first exchange, shields flaring and then failing in under twenty seconds as the combined firepower of the ex-Praetorian StarCom Federation starships turned into a sustained barrage. When they failed the torpedoes launched, and by the time the squadron's shields were starting gear up, Red One began to break apart in a series of explosions that lasted for minutes afterwards.

"An outstanding performance, Admiral," Special Agent La Rue commented.

"I'm working," he snapped. "No distractions." He returned his attention to the strategic battlemap, and ordered <Frigates and strike cruisers to sweep forwards above the enemy line, targets Red Three and Four. *Hammer, Angel, Veritable* to target Red Two. Destroyers to remain at

long-range, supporting fire onto Red Five and Six. *Queen* to target Red Three.>

If his plan worked, they would eliminate the enemy squadron utterly within a very short period of time.

Special Agent La Rue clapped her hands slowly, almost mockingly. "Very well done, Admiral Adare. If you keep this up, you will soon have your freedom onboard unrestricted."

He turned a cold gaze onto her. "I feel honoured to have you as my own personal cheerleader," he said levelly.

Despite his sarcasm, he was pleased. His new squadron had performed admirably well. They had made very short work of the enemy. Red Two had been the first to fall, followed by a lucky shot made by the destroyer *Ubermacht* on Red Six which had taken penetrated right through its aft quarters and triggered a full meltdown of the primary engines. The frigate *Orion* had taken a pounding, but the reinforced assault frigate had withstood the damage, as all the frigates and strike cruisers had scissored back and forth over the enemy zig-zag line.

Instead of turning into the planet, following the destruction of the six Weiberger ships, the *Orion* had remained behind to play mop-up with the *Queen*, whilst the remaining members of Adare's squadron had turned to face the enemy. Rather than consolidate position and attack as one, the enemy commanders made their other great tactical mistake, coming in at Adare's ships in two waves. Perhaps they had been concerned about trying to prevent a possible assault on the planet by the StarCom ships. Their concern had led them to rush in, if that were the case, and in so doing they had lost the battle.

<All hands, well done,> Rear-Admiral Adare announced on the ship-wide datasphere. <We are over twenty minutes ahead of schedule.>

The starbase was still on the far side of the planet. It was ultra-modern, an updated weapons platform which even his ships would find difficult to assault. However, the plan was for the second squadron of military transporters to jump in-system in twenty minutes time, and land their marines. With heavy naval support taking out the majority of land targets on this side of the planet, eventually they would make their way around to the other hemisphere, and take the space-lift up into the starbase to assault and take it from the inside, with no need for a naval engagement on the fortified structure.

"What are your plans now, Rear-Admiral?" La Rue asked.

"We will begin eliminating ground forces and land-based orbital guns ahead of the transporter squadron's arrival," he replied.

"Can I make a suggestion?"

"Are you my tactical advisor now?"

"Oh, your wit is cutting, Silus," she said. "The city of Exeter."

Silus Adare knew what she was telling him to do. "Are you concerned I had forgotten?" he asked. "That I am too squeamish for such a task? That I will disobey mission orders?"

"I am merely reminding you of your duty and your orders, Rear-Admiral."

"There is no need. In the name of the StarCom Federation," he spoke with no hint of regret, and no internal feelings of shame, horror or reluctance, "I will order the complete razing of the capital city Exeter Alpha."

The Faceless assassin was now a thick-set, heavy, burly, sweaty transport driver. The hover-truck was huge, and it was carrying a large cargo of meat for an out-of-town distributor. The cover story would be perfect - the assassin had only killed the driver a couple of hours earlier - and the official documentation the driver carried would be enough to see the assassin safely out of the city of Exeter Alpha city. The meat consignment was for Exeter Beta, but it would never arrive. The assassin would go into hiding, lie low for a couple of weeks, and then leave the way he came in; on a passenger liner at a starport, in another disguise. Personas would be changed regularly, to ensure there was no trail behind the Faceless.

It was nearing mid-day, but the sun was currently obscured, hidden by the dense white clouds overhead. Small patches of blue shone through the atmosphere in some places. The meteorologists on the datasphere were predicting a rainstorm later this evening.

He leaned back in the cab of the hover-truck, raising two hammy hands behind his shaven head. The cab was currently droid-controlled and cruising at a slow forty-two kilometres per hour in the middle lanes. The main traffic way for hover vehicles was lit by floating lights and transponders, to ensure traffic stayed in line.

The datasphere was awash with the news that King Ibbe had been killed. Reports had begun to come through that there was some kind of naval engagement overhead, which piqued the assassin's interest. It would not be the first time he had been on a mission to assassinate a head of state, just as an invasion got under way. From what he had seen of the Weiberg Nation, they bred incompetents, so their military was probably already breaking apart. Someone may have shown some sense though, because the reports on the intraplanetary datasphere were quickly silenced and deleted. The Faceless assassin was not concerned in the slightest whatever the truth was.

The Faceless was staring at the data-display on the seat next to him, which was currently showing the driver's holographic face and confirmation of the travel-plan to the city of Exeter Beta, when the clouds above and behind suddenly split asunder. The assassin caught it in the rear display, showing what was happening behind the vehicle.

A gigantic laser beam was stabbing down from the sky, having vaporised and punctured the clouds over the main part of the city. It roared down through the atmosphere, like a bolt of lightning ten times more bright, a hundred times more noisy, and a thousand times more destructive. It blasted into the city of Exeter Alpha, devastating a tower block. The block was struck almost directly, blowing inside out, shattering apart at the top and collapsing in on itself at the bottom.

The Faceless assassin had been in war-zones as well. He had never seen a city assaulted before, but he had seen holo-vids, and he had been on ground zero when a starship in orbit had begun a terrifying orbital bombardment. He could only guess that the StarCom Federation was really intent on sending a very strong message about people who took their HPCG stations and facilities.

He disengaged the droid-cab, even as the second, third, and then in rapid succession fourth, fifth, sixth and seventh laser beams stabbed down from the sky. He was in a large heavily reinforced hover-truck. He used it to dive down, shouldering aside a couple of smaller vehicles with heavy metallic crunches and showers of sparks, emerging out of the middle lane and into the clear space between the differently-moving tiers of traffic. Then he hit accelerate, rapidly gunning the engine and heading for the city limits, even as the first torpedoes began their deathly whistling descents into the city.

Packed with nanobot technology, the deadly warheads exploded, and he was glad he could not see the results. The nanobots would multiply rapidly, eating and consuming everything in their path, from building material to people. Other torpedoes carried thermonuclear warheads, and mushroom-clouds began to blossom around the city.

After several heart-stopping minutes, the hover-truck approached the city limits and crashed through the unmanned barriers with no problem. At this point a number of other vehicles were behind and before him, panicking people struggling to get out of the city as fast as they could. Just as many more would die in the crush to escape, as they would under the guns of the starships overhead. A series of deep-throated roars evidenced that PACs - Particle Acceleration Cannons - had been deployed, their disruptive particle beams perfect for wide-area effect devastation on the sort of scale required, rather than the pin-point accuracy of a turbolaser.

Speeding away from the already-devastated and suffering city, still under relentless bombardment, the Faceless assassin reflected that this had been a most interesting day, after all. He wondered how long it would be until the contracts against the StarCom Federation started coming in.

The dissolution of the Empire was going to be most profitable, he thought, as he watched the city burn in the glow of nuclear fire.

*

"The translation into realspace is complete, Captain," his helmsman, Serena Sanchez, shouted across the small bridge.

Captain Rodrigues Cesare stood up, leaving his command chair, and clapped his hands. "Well, people," he announced. "We're here at K-3459. Our lay-over is supposed to be twenty-nine hours - is that right, Chief?"

The woman nicknamed Chief, Holly Cheung, was the only non-Cervantian national aboard the *SS Featherlight*. "That's right, Captain, we'll be at full jump capacity again in twenty-eight hours and fifty-two minutes."

"You a borgite, Chief?" Captain Cesare joked. He was a big, broad man, with a full beard and messy, thinning hair. Rejuvenation treatments had recently removed the lines and the grey from his face, and his brown eyes sparkled with mischief.

"Not one of those filthy augments, Cap," Chief Engineer Cheung slapped back at him.

"Thought I had a traitor on-board," he chuckled. "Right, people, wait for the order from our escort, and then let's move this bucket out of the jump-point. I assume our escort have arrived?"

"Yeah, sir," called out the green, rookie navigation officer, Juan Ramirez, who on the small bridge of the *Featherlight* also doubled as the scanners operator. The *Featherlight* was a large Type-II Arbus Commercial Corporation Marbella-class cargo-freighter, carrying nine freighter-tanks in its transport bays. It was run on a crew of no more than thirty-six people, with the majority of the systems automated despite its relatively large size. Vast parts of the ship did not even carry oxygen.

"Good news then," Cesare resumed his seat. "Give me a shout when our lords and masters say we can move."

"You wouldn't say that if we were under attack, senor," Serena Sanchez laughed.

Captain Cesare snorted. A small holographic display, a miniature version projected out of the arm of his chair, showed the position of the convoy. The convoy was large, fourteen civilian ships - all manner of transporters, including two very large military transporters with full lander complements, a couple of liners, numerous freighters, even a fully laden mining ship - and four frigates in escort.

"We're deep inside Cervantian territory," he said. "Who do you think is going to attack us here? House Van Hausenhof?" He snorted again.

Captain James Gavain reflected on the information that House Van

Hausenhof had given him. It had been considerably incorrect. The convoys jumping in at K-3459 were supposed to be no more than eight civilian ships, and two military escort frigates, sometimes one. This convoy was double the size, and there were four Cervantian ships-of-the-line out there, not including the two armed military transporters. The frigates were in a defensive pattern around the convoy.

<Threat assessment on the frigates,> he demanded across the datasphere.

Sub-Lt Woolfe responded as the Data-Tac Officer in charge. <Three Cervantes Military CM-4 defence frigates, and one Hunter-Class Nihima Corp assault frigate. The Hunter-Class is only five years old, and capable of inflicting some damage. The CM-4s will have to work together to be effective, and were designed to operate within small-unit tactics. The most significant single threat present. The two military transporters are Cervantes Military CM-T6s, and have significant anti-aircraft power, but limited ship-to-ship capability. They can still inflict damage, and may be fully laden with Cervantian soldiers and equipment.> The Data-Tac Officer Woolfe uploaded his assessment schematics even as he spoke across the datasphere, the entire commentary taking less than a half-second.

<Do we attack, sir?> Commander De Graaf asked.

<Opinions?> Gavain asked.

<The intel from Van Hausenhof was incorrect. We can disrupt the convoy, but we will take greater damage than the simulations predicted,> De Graaf replied. <I counsel against .... but, a Praetorian V-Class is more than a match for all four frigates, and the two transporters. The difficult part will be ensuring the convoy does not escape. If they have any jump charge left, and have not come in empty, they will jump out before we can interdict.>

Gavain hid his surprise behind his typically blank demeanour. He was surprised at the quick, speedy and concise response from De Graaf. He realised he had come to discount the Commander and his performance perhaps a little too much recently.

<However,> Julia Kavanagh said, <The pay-off will be greater. This is closer to the twenty million Imperial Crowns promised by House Van Hausenhof.>

<Frikking do it!> Major Andryukhin said across the link, from down in the launch bays. <Jamie, work your magic and re-task us – let's take these Cervantian bastards and give them some frikking pay-back!>

<We attack,> Gavain said after a moment's pause. He selected his targets on the strategic map, gave his orders at the speed of thought, and fed additional data through to Tactical. <Bring us round to this heading, and wait for my mark.>

The fourteen civilian ships were arranged in a linear pattern, spaced relatively tightly in a standard armed convoy formation. The intention was for the armed escorts to be able to provide the maximum all round cover. They were heading out close to the contested border with the new, humanist nation of Van Hausenhof, and even though they were fairly distant they were observing the strict regulations laid down by the Cervantian military for armed escort missions.

The civilian ships, on their way to the front line, were formed up in four lines of three ships each, with the two military transporterships out on a spur at the front. The escorting frigates were in a diamond-box shape holding pattern, one on top and one below, one to port and one to starboard, at roughly the middle of the convoy lines, all perfectly equidistant from another. It afforded the military ships the maximum possible fields of fire considering their numbers.

Their discipline was good; with only a few very minor variations due to the vagaries of warp travel, the convoy was roughly in the places they were supposed to be, and the civilian ships were already manoeuvring into their correct holding patterns. The adjustments were minimal. The escorting frigates had jumped in precisely where they needed to be.

Even though they were maintaining strict convoy formation, none of them were attempting to raise their shields. They felt safe. The frigates and the military transporters were conducting aggressive, active scans of the surrounding spatial area, but were detecting nothing.

The *SS Vindicator* ghosted in silently towards the convoy, its chameleonic fields the best in the galaxy. Special dampeners were hiding their engine signature, were very minimal anyway, the *Vindicator* battlecruiser relying on its forward momentum and manoeuvring thrusters to adjust its heading. Long minutes dragged by as its heading changed, to bring it level with the convoy's four armed frigates. It was coming in at an angle, completely invisible to the naked eye, leaving no electronic or mechanical signature, running silent and nothing more than a barely perceptible blur in the blackness of space, on a level with the port escort frigate and heading to overshoot it, its prow's heading adjusting so it was pointing directly at the *CMSS Apollo*, the Hunter-Class assault frigate.

The superb technology of the Praetorian battlecruiser allowed it to get incredibly close in naval terms to the convoy.

Despite himself, Commander De Graaf felt his chest tighten. He knew intelligently that the *Vindicator* could do this, but nevertheless the mission parameters had changed drastically. He did not like the lack of planning – but he guessed he would finally get to see this fantastic leadership that the others spoke of Gavain as possessing.

He could barely believe that Captain Gavain was taking them in this close to the convoy. He kept waiting for the order to come, for Gavain to give his command to launch the overly ambitious, multi-target assault, but the word was not given.

He gripped the arms of his chair tighter. The *Vindicator* had rotated on its linear axis to bring full starboard weaponry to bear on the nearest escort frigate, designated target alpha, and had almost passed the half-way mark where all of its starboard weaponry had clear fields of fire on the enemy ship.

He kept an eye on the passive scan read-outs. The frigates had their anti-electronic warfare systems activated, as standard on a warship, but the data-viruses and malware that the *Vindicator* carried could in theory rip through them, especially when the ships had communications open and shields down. Then it would depend on the anti-virus checkers' efficiency. The civilian ships did not stand a chance.

"Erm, Captain?" Juan Ramirez called out.

"Yes?" Captain Rodrigues Cesare replied.

"I think there may be something out there ...."

"What!" Cesare was on his feet immediately. "Don't be stupid, boy - the escort would have picked it up." He was crossing to the junior rookie's console, which on the small bridge did not take long. He leant over him. "Show me."

"I was bored, so I was using the scanners .... and look ...."

Cesare took one proper look at the read-outs and paled. By pure chance, their mainframe computer had detected random radiation emissions in space, interpreted them as unusual, and then when Juan Ramirez had focused infra-red and magnetic scanners, they had uncovered the massive, hidden starship that was virtually on top of them.

"Fucking he -" Cesare began, hand already reaching for the emergency command that would transmit the scan read-outs to the rest of the convoy, but it was already too late.

<All hands ......> Gavain's mental command went out across the entire ship, <Mark!>

The chameleonic fields rippled as the torpedoes streaked out of multiple launch tubes at once, heading in multiple directions for multiple targets. Nanoseconds later they failed and dispersed rapidly, the fully glory of the ex-Praetorian *SS Vindicator* being revealed like a shark suddenly appearing in a school of fish as the starboard weaponry fired in a blistering broadside of unbelievable firepower, upper hull and lower hull weaponry that were on-target joining in as the *Vindicator* unleashed its full terrible capability.

The entire convoy was caught completely unawares.

The *Vindicator* could not miss. Their range-finders, targeting computers and weaponry operators, although under battle-conditions, were actively engaged, and had pre-selected their targets. They had been tracking their targets all the while.

In seconds the laser weaponry, area-effect particle cannon and close-range disruptor beams had crashed into the escort frigate designated target alpha, followed by the slower-moving but still lightning fast projectiles from the magnetic accelerators. Its entire upper hull was struck square on, the naked, unshielded metal hull visibly rupturing, rippling and being wrecked by the terrible onslaught it suffered in the first moment of the engagement.

Torpedoes slammed into the softened targets, nuclear explosions blossoming briefly as they punched into the superstructure. Three penetrated the infrastructure, diving deep into the escort frigate and mortally crippling it. Lights went off all across the ship, and in that instant it had lost a vast majority of its ability to function and to fight.

At roughly the same time the fore-launched torpedoes smashed into the unprotected hull of target beta, the *CMS Apollo* assault frigate. They had different warheads, nanobot warheads designed to eat into hulls. A much more deadly cargo followed behind, strikepods carrying power-armoured marines that ploughed into the enemy ship at the weakened target points.

At the same time as the strikepods were hitting home, the *Vindicator*'s electronic warfare was beginning to cause massive problems convoy wide. The entire convoy was linked by its own datasphere, which by its nature was open and unrestricted. Aggressive algorithms, borne on carrier-waves which penetrated the datasphere, were unleashed into the intranet. Initially carried in by hidden Trojan programmes, all manner of data-viruses and other military-grade malware burned into the convoy's interlinked computers. The primary target was target beta, and it was the first to suffer ship-wide shutdowns. Anti-virus programmes tried to compensate, but the Praetorian technology was the best in the galaxy, battering through the firewalls and protective systems with ease.

Other targets were the civilian ships, those that the *Vindicator* could reach easily and were not protected by the sheer physical bulk of the other ships closest to the battlecruiser. Lasers and some torpedoes slammed into engines, warp nacelles and bridges, the layouts of the civilian ships already pre-assessed and the desired targets on each pin-pointed. In that first salvo, fully nine of the fourteen civilian ships were targeted, and no less than four were crippled with their unshielded engines destroyed or damaged, suffering power loss even as the command bridges of three others blew out with direct hits.

<First heading change on my mark,> Captain Gavain ordered, feeling the responsiveness of helmsman Lieutenant Vries and his two Sub-Lieutenants - the redundancies who supported her in her function as the chief pilot of the starship - <Mark!>

<Aye, sir,> Vries acknowledged the order, even as the starship was already turning.

The *Vindicator* had fired again and then once again on target alpha, a series of broadsides that was more peppered as the various weaponry types fired at their own cycle rates. The CM-4 frigate, already irreparably damaged by the first salvo, went nova as the engines entered forced meltdown and then blew out as several laserbeams and then a final heavy slug from a MAC utterly destroyed it.

The frigate was catastrophically breaking up - with almost total loss of life bar a handful of the crew, it would later be realised - as the *Vindicator* began turning. It was pumping secondary fire into the nine unarmed civilian ships in its firing range, doing a fantastic job of causing yet more destruction to the convoy, as it began to accelerate. It fired some weaponry into the ailing *CMSS Apollo*, targeting weaponry systems only, but then it began to swing back out from the convoy again. The *Apollo*, an assault frigate respectable for its class, had been caught unawares and with damage sustained and under severe electronic attack could only fire a small portion of its comparatively light weaponry on the *Vindicator*.

Apparently the *Vindicator* was swinging away from the convoy. Targets gamma and delta were the two military transporters. Target delta, the furthest of the two targets and previously protected by the bulk of the convoy from the *Vindicator's* position, received the heaviest portion of the long-range broadside as the *Vindicator* sped to the front of the convoy, swinging back in and twisting slightly, engines kicking in to full power from cold-start in less than twenty seconds. Target gamma received torpedoes with nanobot warheads, with more marine strikepods striking in afterwards.

CMSS Apollo had already been boarded, and the first boarders were landing on the military transporter *CMSS Titan of Stars*, target gamma. The *Vindicator* fired strikepod after strikepod from its starboard assault launchers, carrying their cargoes of power-armoured marines into the military transporter. The viruses which had been targeted for the *Apollo* and the *Titan of Stars* were specially encoded to shut down the oxygen supply on the two ships, to open certain airlocks and close certain blast doors, trying to flush naval crew and soldiers out of the ship before they could pose a threat to the marines that were boarding them.

On board the *Featherlight*, Captain Cesare watched the horror unfolding upon the convoy with sheer disbelief. The battlecruiser was a behemoth, and it had caused untold damage. It had used the element of surprise to its fullest extent.

"Engine Propulsors are destroyed!" Chief Cheung was crying out. "We can't go anywhere. The mainframe's completely incapacitated - some kind of data-virus, it came across on the datapshere -"

"Get it back up and running! We need it!" shouted Cesare, losing his entire cool.

"I can't!" Chief Cheung cried back. "We're fucked!"

Serena Sanchez grabbed Cesare forcibly by both arms, having abandoned her station. "We can't pilot the ship, we have no main computer systems, we're dead in the water," she said. "Think, Rodrigues."

His heart felt like it had stopped. He stared at Serena, not understanding.

She slapped him, hard.

"Abandon ship," she whispered.

"Abandon ship," he croaked, then louder, "Abandon Ship! The order is given - abandon ship!"

Major Ulrik Andryukhin's mental link to his power-armoured suit's special on-board computer mainframe warned him that the way to the primary target was not clear. <Nine frikking hostiles, Sergeant,> he indicated.

<Aye, sir,> Sergeant Jack Inman, the leader of his command squad, responded. He selected Corporal Calaman, Andryukhin's adjutant, and one other, giving them a quick command. The ten man squad of power-armoured marines had halted temporarily.

Suddenly the androgynous forms of the three selected marines dived around the corner of the corridor, showing agility the suits did not look like they were capable of. Andryukhin watched in his normal vision as the corridor he and the six others stood in was bathed in a series of light-flashes, heavy weapons fire. The wall of the right-angle bend nearby was peppered with projectile spatter, and at one point something pinged off Andryukhin's armour, even his enhanced reflexes too slow to avoid it.

Eventually it all went quiet.

He marched around the corner. The hostiles were dead on the floor, the end of the corridor bathed in blood spatter and scorched corpses. <Congratulations,> he said. He went past the three who had taken the last siege point, and broadcast to his command squad, <We have the primary target in sight. Breaching team.>

As two members of his squad jogged forwards, each with special packs of breaching plates loaded into their leg-mounted carriers under the armour plating, Andryukin checked the mission chronometer.

They had boarded the strikepods onboard the *Vindicator*. The nanobot torpedoes and the strikepods had been fired at the same time. The torpedoes accelerated faster than the strikepods, and had slammed into their targets to soften the hull of target beta, the *Apollo*. Andryukhin's strikepod, a special vehicle designed to carry power-armoured marines at extremely high speeds to their landing areas - be it the hull of a starship or a planetary surface - had been specifically targeted at an area near the bridge of the *Apollo*.

The *Apollo*'s bridge was well protected, some six decks down at the top-fore area of the assault frigate, and protected by no less than three thick blast walls. The nanobots softened the target, but Andryukhin would not forget the sickening crunch as the strikepod had smashed through the first two decks and into the initial blast wall at an angle.

The breaching plates were in place, and his two marines had retreated to a safe area. The breaching plates were designed to direct their blast in a particular direction.

It had taken only a short time to make their way through service ducts to the deck level of the bridge, their biggest delay being caused when the navvies on board realised they had been breached and had closed the third blast wall ingress points. That had taken precious time to burn through.

Andryukhin gave the command to breach the bridge, and with a bang, the thick blast doors on the bridge blew open.

He ran through the breach into the bridge. Laser fire struck towards him, and for moments, all was chaos as his squad followed him into the hail of small-arms fire. The Cervantian navy had their own version of power-armoured marines, and although vastly inferior to Praetorian technology, they could nevertheless cause some damage.

Explosions lit off all around Andryukhin as he began to fire his rotary cannon, the backlight of fire casting him in demonic light as his multi-round anti-personnel short-range missile launcher threw projectiles forwards. Consoles, stations and people disappeared in vast sheets of flame and fire as the missiles spread out in their pre-programmed pattern.

He stalked forwards, even as a marine staggered out of the inferno before him. His right-arm power-claw grasped the marine's head, and with a groan of servos, after a scant second of resistance ripped it away from the shoulders.

Corporal Calaman used her twin-linked shoulder pulse-lasers to pin-point the body of the captain of the ship, a House Cervantes Commander, and with a series of rapid-fire scorching blasts his charred body was thrown back into and over his command chair.

Sergeant Jack Inman swung around Andryukhin, his heavy chemical flamer firing bursts into the lower command pit. Using the optics within his suit, he used his left-mounted rotary cannon to clear out shrieking targets within the flames.

Eventually, the bridge fell silent, when the Vindicator Marines ceased firing.

<Losses> Andryukhin ordered.

Sergeant Inman paused. <We lost one,> he said. <Ship-wide, two fatalities, two immobile casualties, nine walking-fighting casualties sustained.>

<Overall SitRep?>

<Fierce resistance in the engine room. Marine barracks nearing full clearance. Mainframe computer room seized before we took the bridge. Bridge secure, Major,> Sergeant Inman finished.

<Shut down all systems on this bloody ship, stop it dead in the water and close down all fucking weapons control,> Major Andryukhin ordered. <Order the remaining ship's crew to surrender, and promise them life if they do so.>

<Aye, sir.>

<Corporal,> he said to Naomi Calaman, <Signal *Vindicator* that we have taken the *Apollo* bridge and it can now be considered neutralised.>

<Assessment?> Gavain asked De Graaf and Kavanagh on their private channel.

Commander Lucas De Graaf was amazed. Whatever his private doubts about Captain Gavain's prowess as a leader and his strategic and tactical acumen, it had just been completely dispelled. For the first time in a very long period of his life, ever since the Dissolution Order, he felt an old emotion, that of elation, one of victory, one of winning and success. And he had been part of it, he reflected. His own assessment had been to proceed with the attack, but it had been bravado, for image, and he had thought that eventually they would sustain so much damage they would have to retreat with only some partial success. This had been a near-complete victory.

He double-checked to be sure, before he said <Targets epsilon and zeta are in a fighting retreat.> The last two remaining escort frigates were indeed moving away, although zeta was badly damaged. They were protecting three civilian freighters, and the mining ship. <Zeta and the mining ship have sustained serious damage and will fall behind,> he continued. <They are in complete rout, we can take them if you wish, sir.>

<Damage Report?> Gavain demanded.

The damage report was given; although the *Vindicator* had taken some return fire, it was minimal, at least until the fight had begun in earnest to fore starboard of the main convoy, once the *Vindicator* had looped around the head of the fore segment of the formation. Their shields had taken most of the damage the two escort frigates and target delta could throw at them.

A couple of lucky shots had landed amidships underhull, and on the rear once the battlecruiser had turned to focus heavy fire on the unboarded military transporter to rip it to pieces, but apart from that the *Vindicator* had emerged relatively unscathed. No naval fatalities, and although extremely heavy resistance had been encountered aboard the military transporter *Titan of Stars*, Vindicator Marine fatalities stood at eleven.

The first escort frigate lay in pieces, and the second military transporter was dead in the water, powerless and shaking itself apart as its superstructure was ripped piece from piece by the forces of catastrophic decompression. It would be a slow death for that ship.

Life-pods were scattered out across the entire area. The humane part of Gavain had made it clear that life-pods were not a target, but inevitably some had been caught in the cross-fire. Such were the fortunes of war.

<Commander De Graaf,> Captain Gavain ordered, <Take command. I want that mining ship taken out as a priority, and the frigate as a secondary. Lieutenant-Commander Kavanagh, you're in charge of assessing the convoy and selecting destruction patterns. We have to be in a position to jump out-system with our prizes no less than fifteen minutes after the first enemy ship leaves this system. Carry on, people.>

Commander De Graaf felt his chest swell with pride at being given the command, under the eyes of the silent Captain Gavain, as he went about the mopping-up of the enemy.

The door to his private ready room swished open, and Lieutenant-Commander Julia Kavanagh entered. She was positively beaming, virtually bouncing across the carpet to his desk.

"We've entered hyperspace, Jamie," she said.

"Good," he acknowledged with a curt nod of his head. He stopped looking at the display in front of him, and glanced up at her. "Lucas did well," he commented.

Julia hesitated, before deciding credit was due where it was due, despite her own reservations about the man. "He did, yeah," she nodded. "We all did. That was fantastic, Jamie. If the Praetorians still existed, that would be an engagement to go down in hist –"

"It was an attack on a convoy," James said quietly. "For money. Not wanting to burst your bubble Jules, but we committed murder for our own monetary gain."

Julia Kavanagh pulled out the suspensor-chair and sat down. "Are you having doubts about what we're doing, Jamie?"

There was a long pause. "No," he lied. "We are committed. But we must remember what we do and why."

He could see his long-time friend saw through the lie, but also saw that she knew now was not the time. "If you ever want to talk about it," she said, leaning forwards through the holodisplay and laying a hand on his. "But, just remember - there was a purpose. We took a contract, yes, to help ourselves by helping the nation of Hausenhof and House Van Hausenhof against Cervantia and House Cervantes. Who were owed a reckoning from us anyway."

"True," Gavain nodded.

"What's the final outcome?" she asked, noting the contents of the holodisplay as she pulled back from it.

"The full twenty million Imperial Crowns," Gavain replied. "Plus prize rights, and maybe a bonus for the number of kills. We can either sell or keep the frigate *Apollo,* transporter *Titan of Stars,* and of course the *Featherlight.* I suspect Hausenhof will want the contents of both, but the contract was clear - full prize rights, starships and their contracts. I need a full stock-take of both before I can confirm value, but that will have to wait until we are in a safe system. And most of it I am not minded to sell."

Julia Kavanagh nodded. Although fighting had been fierce upon the *Titan of Stars,* as it had been fully loaded with Cervantian soldiers, the majority had been incapacitated or killed by the effects of the deadly data-viruses upon their mainframe computers, opening airlocks, decompressing entire sections, and de-oxygenating entire decks. Over ten thousand Cervantian dead or dispossessed, sent off floating in emergency life support pods. The transporter itself was carrying all manner of amour, vehicles, and weaponry, including battlewalkers - none of it to Praetorian standard of course, being primarily Cervantian, neutral or allied-Cervantes made, but all of it useful to somebody nonetheless.

The bigger surprise had been the contents of the freighter *Featherlight,* which after scanning James Gavain had ordered be boarded and taken with them when they jumped out-system. It's nine cargo-pods had been full of a mixed bag of shipping, as such freighters usually were, but two of the cargo-pods were full of vital equipment, power sources and charging chambers for starship engine drives, jump initiation capacitors and warp accelerators, enough to keep an entire fleet running. The Vindicator Mercenary Corporation would not have a replacements problem for a very, very long time, decades into the future.

The final Cervantian losses, besides the three captured starships, consisted of two other escort frigates, the mining ship, a military transporter, and seven civilian ships, all totally destroyed or damaged beyond conceivable repair. Crews had been given permission to vacate their ships and take their chances in life-pods before the *Vindicator* had utterly destroyed their host vessels.

"We must have significantly aided the Hausenhof war effort today," Kavanagh commented.

"Yes," was Gavain's only comment. Even Julia found it impossible to read his reaction.

Chapter X

Captain James Gavain sat behind the desk in his private ready room, looking out of the unshielded floor-to-ceiling window at the vast upper hemisphere of Parowa Czwarty. They had returned to the Parowa System, part of the still neutral and undeclared House Zielinski, partly because it was within a double-jump range after their last lay-over to fully recharge the captured starships, and because they had to pick up new crew.

His connection to the datasphere had overlaid an image on the upper hemisphere, with a number of dots showing the current locations of his crew. He had granted permission for shore-leave, although he had little interest in such a thing himself. Roughly a quarter of the crew had already gone down to the planet surface, although two thirds had elected not to at all - ex-Praetorians were born in space, lived in space, and many like him found a planetary atmosphere disconcerting.

He was the only member of the command crew on the *Vindicator*. Both Major Andryukhin and Commander De Graaf had taken the opportunity of shore-leave, and Lieutenant-Commander Kavanagh had decided to do the same, although technically she was still on duty at the moment. She was currently with Senior Clerk Downs, overseeing the selection and enlistment of the crew who would eventually be posted on the *Apollo*, *Featherlight* and *Titan of Stars*. There were not enough applications to provide full complements, but the ships would at least be fully functional - although they still needed repair.

<Captain Gavain,> Lieutenant Forrest, the Senior Communications Officer, hailed him on the private channel, <The uplink from Parowa Czwarty is now established.>

<It has been Praetorian encoded?>

<Of course, Captain.>

<Well done, Lieutenant.> Gavain felt her log-off from the private channel, and as he rotated in his chair, the holoprojection suite in front of him activated. A full-size image flickered into being before his desk, that of a man probably in his early hundreds although as ever with rejuvenation treatments it was difficult to ascertain. "Ambassador Grunehaube, Captain Gavain, Vindicator Mercenary Corporation."

The image of Ambassador Grunehaube straightened, receiving a securely-encoded image of Captain Gavain in his own office, down on the surface of Parowa Czwarty. The comms link had been encoded by Praetorian technology, making it extremely hard to break into. Gavain suspected that with the Dissolution Order, Praetorian technology would soon be leaking onto the black market and into the new state militaries sooner rather than later, so he had ordered his comms officers to generate new coding algorithms, and abandon the pre-programmed Praetorian sequencing that had previously been the norm.

"Captain Gavain, I am pleasured to make your acquaintance. I spoke with your Lieutenant-Commander Kavanagh – I am disappointed I could not meet you in person too."

Gavain had reviewed the public data on Ambassador Grunehaube before agreeing to the request for a private discussion. He was an ambassador for House Van Hausenhof, with a very distant blood link to the House many generations ago, had been resident on Parowa Czwarty for six years, and like the majority of the new Hausenhof nation, and was a pure-bred humanist in his views. Married, with three children and a fourth on the way, he was a largely unremarkable character.

His status as an ambassador, especially considering the admittedly distant familial link to the ruling Van Hausenhof family, probably meant he was also a member of the House intelligence services. Gavain was given to understand that most ambassadors were either spies, or were aware to some limited degree of their home nation's clandestine activities in the region they were stationed too.

"My duties prevent my presence on-planet," Gavain shrugged. "How may I assist you, Ambassador?"

"I was told you were straight to the point, Captain," Grunehaube smiled an ingratiating smile that also looked utterly false. "Firstly, let me congratulate you on your recent mission for us in System K-3459. The file was passed to me by Hausenhof Military Command. A most impressive contract completion, indeed."

Gavain said nothing, merely regarding the Ambassador with an impassive stare, allowing the silence to force the man to continue speaking.

"So," the Ambassador rubbed his hands together uneasily as no reply was forthcoming, "we have transferred the full contract funds into your accounts, and have released your bond at the MBO of the Interstellar Merchants Guild."

Gavain still remained silent, awaiting the next comment.

"So, ah, there is a small matter of the prizes you took," the ambassador continued. Gavain knew this would be coming. "Although the contract stated that all the prizes were yours, we would be most interested in obtaining the contents of the military transporter, and perhaps some of the engine drives and similar space-faring equipment you took on the *Featherlight*. Do you think we could make a deal here, Captain? We would be willing to pay."

Captain James Gavain did not even consider. "No, Ambassador. The VMC has need of it. My decision is final. If that is all, or was there something else to discuss?"

"Oh." Grunehaube looked non-plussed for a moment, as if he was replaying the conversation in his head. He shook that slicked-back haired head rapidly, and then opened his arms wide after another nervous hand-rub. "Well actually, there is another matter, Captain."

"Yes?"

"We did consider asking if you would like to be put on retainer by House Van Hausenhof, a regular payment if you will, to join our military forces as a privateering company. Whilst you were in transit, we did have a conversation with Sophia Towers by hyperpulse, and she assured us you would not be interested in such an option. Is this the case?"

"Yes."

"OK," another hand-rub, "that being the situation, we were nevertheless impressed by your actions in K-3459, and we would like to offer you another contract. On very favourable terms, but perhaps more high-risk."

Captain Gavain had not been expecting that. He leaned forwards slightly despite himself, leaning his elbows on the desk. "I am listening, Ambassador Grunehaube. Speak."

"Your action in K-3459 has assisted in creating a weakness in the Cervantian front, one we intend to exploit. We are planning a deep-strike into a certain system within Cervantian territory, not just a strike but an invasion to take and hold the system. The system is still heavily defended, but our droid armies will of course be more than adequate to the challenge."

Captain Gavain had mentally called up a map of the Cervantian / Hausenhof front, and was reviewing the destinations of the convoys that had been pulled from the captured ships' computers. He could narrow it down to two likely systems.

"However, within this system there is a highly secret military research installation, on the far side of a planet which is also used as a military base for Cervantian ground forces. We want a full data-dump of that installations computer core. Your mission would be to jump into the system once our invasion has been launched, which should hopefully draw away the starships defending the planet, although we expect there would still be some naval presence left to defend. A ground assault would be necessary, a quick insertion and withdrawal. We believe that in the event of enemy forces landing on the planet, the standing orders are to wipe the core, and we want to prevent this. We want that information."

Captain Gavain had narrowed it down to one system. "If I agree to accept this contract and assault the Santiago System –" he read the reaction of Grunehaube and knew he had guessed correctly "- what are the contract terms, when do I get the full mission details and intel, and why are you not using your own special forces to take the installation?"

"Ah, well," Ambassador Grunehaube stammered, "contract terms are twenty million Imperial Crowns, payable just for when you jump in-system, and a further thirty million Crowns if you are successful and payable on information transfer, with a ten million bond from yourselves. Full details and intelligence will be released on contract acceptance, although I will transfer as much non-classified information prior to signature as I can if you confirm your interest, Captain?"

"Why not your own forces?"

Grunehaube seemed to become more hardened all of a sudden. "Captain, although we recognise your ability, the mission is very high-risk. We want the information, but cannot risk a droid control-ship in orbit around the planet. We suspect that the naval forces, which are considerable, will be drawn to the main focus of our attack - however, we cannot guarantee that all of the navy will be re-directed to our invasion point, and of course some elements will remain in defence. There is no guarantee as to the resistance you will face on-planet, either. Running silent with Praetorian technology, you would have a massive advantage over even our own special forces combat droids, and you have proven your ability to handle unexpected and unforeseen events, which is definitely what this contract calls for."

"So you use us on the basis we are disposable?"

"You are mercenaries, Captain," Ambassador Grunehaube said.

James Gavain looked away for a moment, then snapped his eyes back. "My crew are on three day's worth of downtime. I will review other contracts, and give you an answer. Is three days acceptable?"

"If you pay for a stargate out of Parowa, yes. We are on a deadline, Captain. Could you give me an answer by tomorrow?"

"If you pay for the stargate, you will have my answer tomorrow."

The Ambassador actually laughed. "Done, Captain. Who thought Praetorians could learn to negotiate?"

"Send me the details you can, Ambassador. Gavain, out."

*

Sophia Towers stood on the gantry of one of the open decks of the *TwSS First Ship*, the House barge that was always used to convey the members of House Towers nobility across the stars. She was staring out into hyperspace, eyes following the red-purple-orange swirls of the unreality out there beyond the windows as it sped in transit towards their ultimate destination.

She could not see the shapes of the military escort, although she knew that on translation back into realspace they would also materialise with three escort frigates and two battlecruisers. It was rare for the noble barge to carry more than one House Towers noble, but to be carrying all three from the first and ruling branch of the family called for heavier escort than normal, particularly with the events currently unfolding in the colonised galaxy.

She heard the footsteps ringing on the metal gangway, suspended high above the throbbing jump initiation capacitor nacelle, and her eyes flicked in the glass to see the reflection of her brother Luke approaching steadily.

"Sophia," he said quietly, "there are much nicer places on this ship to watch hyper-space from."

"One knows, Luke, one just ......"

"... wished to be alone," Luke nodded understandingly, gently placing a brotherly arm around her shoulders with a tenderness that belied his great, muscled bulk. The majority of the *First Ship* was full not of crewmembers, but various attendants and court regulars, all of whom were constantly engaged in ceaseless and Machiavellian attempts to ingratiate themselves with the ruling family. They relentlessly prowled the public and more common areas of the ship; down here in the open cavern of the port nacelle, the only people were far below, and were ordinary crewmen.

"And if I were to guess what you were thinking about, I would say its father and the Union? And Micalek Zupanic."

She sighed. "Yes, my brother."

"And your thoughts are?"

"One is angry she was not given more of a choice. The negotiations are already fairly advanced. Father could have mentioned this much earlier."

"You were imprisoned by the False Emperor, Sophia."

"Messages were still being sent to me."

"You could have been tortured and killed like Jared, and given up all the information you held before your death," Luke pointed out. He turned Sophia gently, holding her hand. "I was scared for you, Sophia. The False Emperor was even madder towards the end, and he was indiscriminate in selecting his victims, be they planets or single, house nobles. We were told you were safe and unharmed, but we knew that could change in an instant, and you were after all a hostage. Father was planning for the dissolution of the Empire long before it started to happen, as it is now. As much as you dislike him, at least respect him for his foresight and his wisdom in keeping you safe by keeping the knowledge of the proposed Union from you."

Sophia sighed again. "You are ever the peacemaker between us, Luke. One would be lost without you."

"So tell your brother what you are planning to do."

Sophia felt drained. She was under intense emotional pressure, and she could not accept what she was about to say. Perhaps saying it aloud would help.

"There is no real choice for me," she said quietly. "The alliance, this Levitican Union, must be formed. One must marry Micalek Zupanic, and join our houses together. It is part of the glue that the Union will be formed by."

"Yes," Luke nodded slowly. "I am sorry. I know how much you have always valued your independence. When we were younger, you always swore you would never be put in this position in the name of the House."

"But one is older, and one likes to think, wiser."

"You are that, sister." Luke hugged her, then released her. "Thank you. It is our best hope. You know the StarCom Federation has begun its invasion of neighbouring systems?"

"One does. Their lightning attack belies belief. One never believed President Nielsen would be so daring, so far-reaching in her ambition."

"She is. Emperor curse her stars."

"Ironically, her unveiling of power will probably force more Houses to band together for defence, much as we are about to. This Micalek Zupanic, what do you know of him?"

"A little," Luke admitted. "Not much of it very encouraging, I must admit."

"He is known as the Butcher of Balthazar. A ruthless man, much like his father, but perhaps even more dangerous. Some of it may just be propaganda, the Zupanics like to control their public images as do we all one supposes. Married twice, Luke - twice! The first wife died in mysterious circumstances, the second divorced following their abortive attempt to form an alliance with House Jorgensson. It was shortly after their Imperial-sanctioned intra-House War that Micalek earned his name as the Butcher."

"The rumours of his behaviour are even worse," Luke Towers stated. "I promise you, Sophia. Having got you back from the False Emperor, if anything happens to you at Micalek's hand, the Zupanics will regret it deeply, union or no."

"One can look after herself, Luke," Sophia smiled weakly, "but thank you, all the same. It means much to me."

They stood there for some time, silently regarding hyperspace flash by, brother and sister staring forwards into the future.

*

Ulrik Andryukhin was walking up the street of Gdanskal City on Parowa Czwarty. He could feel the effects of the alcohol, but was far from drunk, partly thanks he suspected in his slightly inebriated state to his enhanced marine physiology. Naomi Calaman, Jack Inman, his second-in-command Marine Captain Adeoye, and a number of other marines they had picked up along the way during the course of the drunken tour of the backstreets of Gdanskal were all happily enjoying their shore-leave.

"Where the frig next?" he asked, gazing up in wonder at the flashing lights of the hover vehicles overhead.

"It's snowing," Adeoye hiccoughed.

"It's always fricking snowing here," Andryukhin slurred. "Where the hell next, people?"

"There!" Calaman pointed. "Looks like our sort of bar."

It was called the Cavern. For some reason, it made Ulrik think of Julia Kavanagh. Cavern. Kavanagh. God he missed her, but she would be on shore-leave tomorrow he hoped, as soon as she was done with the hiring of the new crew.

"Let's go!" Ulrik punched the air.

They made an unsteady line towards the flashing neon lights of the Cavern, the downmarket holographic display sign fizzing and blurring as the snow poured through it. They emerged through the heat curtain in the doorway, laughing at the bouncer droids on the door, and stared around them as water began to drip around their booted feet.

The Cavern was large, and dark, and full of people. Heavy repetitive music blared in the foreground, coming from a caged off stage with a live band. There were a lot of people in the club, and smoke filled the air. The dance floor was heaving, and the equally large relaxation area around the three main bars were full of people shouting, enjoying themselves and generally forgetting the details of their lives for a couple of hours.

"Whose round is it?" Ulrik demanded.

"Yours!" Calaman laughed. "You always ask when it's your turn, sir."

"Fuckin' hell," he swore. "Fuck me, it is. C'mon then, who's having what?"

They were making their way to the bar, when Ulrik suddenly spotted someone. "Frigging hell," he swore again.

"What?" Captain Adeoye asked.

"Lucas De Graaf is over there. Fuck, is it too late to go?" Even as he said it, Ulrik realised that even though he was on shore-leave, it was not appropriate for him to speak like that in front of his marines. Calaman, his adjutant, knew what he really thought of De Graaf, but he tended not to share his feelings on the matter despite his often outwardly-seeming inappropriateness and relaxed, informal nature with his soldiers.

Ulrik saw something else, too. Despite himself, he felt himself suddenly sober up. "Naomi, you get these and I'll pay you back later, yeah. I'll be with you shortly."

"Yeah, sure, where ya going Major - oh ....." Calaman trailed off as Ulrik headed in a direct line for Lucas De Graaf.

He tapped the Commander on the shoulder. "Lucas," he said softly, then much more strongly, "Lucas!"

The Commander raised his head up from the row of empty glasses in front of him, staring unknowingly at Ulrik. The Major watched the recognition settle in with Lucas, although that took a long number of seconds. The Commander actually snarled.

"Oh, it's you," he sneered. "Wha' you wan'?"

"You're drunk, Lucas. Not just drunk, you're paralytic. Let me get you a cab back to your quarters." He took De Graaf by the arm.

Lucas shrugged it off heavily, his arm swinging wide and smashing into two customers on the other side of him. "Gerrof me!" he roared. "'ve alwa' hated you!"

"That might be true –" Ulrik ground out.

"Hey." A deep voice rumbled. "What do you think you doing, man." A large, burly city worker had turned and grabbed De Graaf by the front of his uniform. De Graaf was so drunk he did not even seem to know what was happening.

"Leave him be," Ulrik warned.

"This is nothing to do with you, fricker," the man said. His nose was squashed flat. He did not look unaccustomed to fighting. His biceps were as large as some men's necks, but he was still smaller than Ulrik's super-enhanced physique. "This borg, this metalfreak fricker owes me a drink."

"Na I don' –" De Graaf slurred.

"Metalfreak?" Ulrik questioned.

"Yeah, a fucking borgite metalfreak, just like you." The freighter worker turned back. "Listen, jack-head, I want me drink!"

"I said, leave him be. He's on my crew, you un-augmented piece of throwback human fleshed shit," Ulrik said, resting a hand on the man's arm.

"Fuck you," the man said. "Boys?"

Ulrik suddenly found himself facing another five men. The six of them were all big, out-of-town spacers he guessed. Freighter workers maybe, judging by their clothes.

"Backing off now, you metal borgite jack-head metalfreak of a fucker? Leave us to it," the freighter man said. He turned back, and slapped De Graaf around the face. De Graaf slid off his chair slowly, smashing the glasses on his way down to the floor.

Ulrik knew that the rest of the marines he had entered with had abandoned their attempts to get served, and were coming up behind him. However much he disliked Lucas De Graaf, no-one was striking someone from the *Vindicator* and getting away with it, much less insulting him or anyone for being a cyborg. He was also a marine, a super-enhanced Praetorian with unbelievable fighting skills. He knew his biggest challenge would be to stop himself from killing the fucker in front of him.

Before De Graaf had hit the floor, Ulrik's right fist had connected with the freighter worker's jaw.

Ulrik opened his eyes slowly. He could still feel the cold metal of the dermajector against his neck before it was removed. The drugs coursed around his system, and in a few seconds, he was fully awake. His system had powered up fully, and he was alert to attack. He sat upright, arms rising.

"Hey, hey!" the medic called out, startled as she jumped back, hands in the air.

"Major!" a familiar voice snapped.

Ulrik assessed the situation immediately. He was in an open holding pen, a local enforcer station prison cell if he was any judge. He had seen them on the HRV. The medic was hurrying out of the cell door. Two grim enforcers in full protective armour and pull-down visored helmets stood either side of Lieutenant-Commander Kavanagh, who herself stood with arms crossed, legs in a braced stance, and jaw very heavily set.

"Oh god," Ulrik groaned, lifting a hand to the back of his head. His internal chronometer told him he had been out for about six hours. The enforcers had been called, and because the marines had made short work of the freighter workers, they had stunned him and most of his fellow comrades.

"No, worse," Lieutenant-Commander Kavanagh said drily. "Jamie Gavain is very angry with you, Rik. Which is nothing .... compared to me."

*

Adare sat in his private ready room. Marine 1 and Marine 2, his personal bodyguard and executioners should he ever betray the StarCom Federation, stood by the door impassively, not speaking and not moving.

"Do you two ever do anything more than stare at me?" he asked. At the expected lack of answer, he grunted, and rubbed a hand over his unshaven face, running it up and over his buzz-cut hair. "You two bore me," he taunted, before straightening his hated white and regal blue StarCom Federation uniform and returning his attention to the mental imagery the datasphere was creating in front of him.

He was looking at pictures of the destruction of Exeter Alpha, trying to decide if he felt anything. He was not surprised to find he did not. As his own psychological profile stated, he had strong sociopathic tendencies bordering on the psychopathic. The loss of life did not concern him in the slightest.

What rankled was that he had not done this in the name of Emperor, as a member of the Praetorian Guard. He had committed this act in the name of the StarCom Federation, a strong message to all who defied President Nielsen's declaration on the protection of StarCom assets the galaxy over.

Yes, he decided, the only feeling he had in relation to the razing of Exeter Alpha was extreme irritation he had done it in the name of the Federation. What were his choices though? If he left the Federation service - assuming he could successfully escape Agent La Rue and tweedle-dum and tweedle-dee - where would he go? He would forever be a fugitive, hunted by the Federation to the ends of the galaxy. Perhaps he would be killed by a Faceless, much as the once-King Ibbe had been so publicly assassinated.

No, his only choice was to stay where he was, and watch for the opportunity to make his escape. He would not be held in servitude against his will. In the meantime he would have to serve the Federation, no matter how grudgingly.

The door chimed, but instead of the person requesting permission to enter, Special Agent Caterina La Rue simply swept in.

"It is considered polite to knock at the commanding officer's door," Rear-Admiral Adare commented.

"I am not in the military chain of command," La Rue replied. "Congratulations, Silus, President Nielsen has issued commendations on the first actions of Operation Fortress. You have been named in despatches following the battle around Exeter - and of course, the razing of Exeter Alpha."

"I am honoured," he said neutrally.

La Rue laughed. "I'm sure you're not, but no matter." She crossed the ready room, and sat disrespectfully on the edge of his desk. "There are new orders, Silus. They are about to be issued, but I thought you would like to know in advance."

Adare thought back to the Red Imperium. Although he had supported the Second Emperor, he knew there had been many detractors who resisted the dictatorship, but for all the Emperor had been reviled as an authoritarian leader, he had never let his secret services conduct his military affairs for him. He supposed he was not the only Praetorian Guard member press-ganged into service for President Nielsen, and that was the reason why. She had an army and a navy she could not trust. No wonder she was so often portrayed as paranoid; perhaps she had reason to be.

"We missed the second wave of Operation Fortress, but we do have a target in the third wave, although it is something of a special mission."

"What would that be?" Rear-Admiral Adare leaned back in his chair, putting his hands behind his head.

"Your squadron is to jump ahead of the third wave, to strike a particular target. You will join with Admiral Haas' squadron, rendezvousing at an uninhabited star system just prior to the final jump to the target. Do you know him? Admiral Haas?"

"Besides being the officer-in-command of StarCom's Third Fleet?" he asked.

"Less of the sarcasm please, Silus."

He held La Rue's gaze for a moment. "Presumably he is a trusted officer, as he willingly joined the Federation. He was a traitor Praetorian, fighting on the side of the rebels, formerly of the Praetorian Guards Eighth Fleet. Heinrich Haas has a long and distinguished service career, blemished only by his treachery."

"You will get along famously, then," Agent La Rue laughed. "He will be the senior officer in this special strike, of course."

"What is the target?" Adare asked.

"I believe you may know of it. Please, tell me what you know, in fact. The target is the Janus Shipyards."

Silus Adare's eyes opened wide for a moment, unable to contain his surprise. "That is some way beyond the third wave's target zone," he said, "but I see why the Federation wants it. Janus Shipyards holds the largest stockpile of ex-Praetorian Guard weaponry outside of Sol - and of course, most of that went walkabout when the assaulting fleets dispersed following the Dissolution Order. The Shipyards is, or was, commanded by Commodore Harley Andersson."

"It still is. We believe Janus Shipyards is still almost fully provisioned. We need Janus Shipyards, not just for the weaponry and resources, but as a forward operating base for the galactic eastern sectors push."

"It will also be suicide, even for -" Silus quickly accessed the datasphere records, checking the Tables of Organisation for 2nd Main Squadron commanded by Admiral Haas "- twenty-two ships. The Janus Shipyards are very heavily defended, automated systems as well as starships, and the entire system is locked-down. We are not talking standard defences here either, but Praetorian Guard. We will be detected on entry. Losses will be high."

"Ah, well, there we will have an advantage. It will be a wonderful surprise, to work in our favour. But even then, high losses are acceptable. Prepare yourself, Rear-Admiral. There will be sacrifices in the name of the StarCom Federation, as well as glory."

Special Agent La Rue smiled her more usual humourless smile, stood, and left the room.

*

<Come,> Captain Gavain said.

Commander De Graaf entered. Gavain watched him stride up to the desk, and salute, an old-fashioned Praetorian right hand slam to the left breast then out.

Gavain un-jacked, feeling the comforting warm glow of the many data-streams being constantly fed to him by the starship receding.

"Sit, Commander," he said, gesturing at the suspensor-chair. Lucas De Graaf somewhat nervously took the seat.

"I understand you were in this bar or club, the Cavern, when the fight happened."

He watched Commander De Graaf's reaction with interest, hiding it behind his usual neutral face. Guilt, he read, along with fear.

"Yes, sir, I was. I wasn't one of those arrested, Captain, but I was there."

"What did you see?" Gavain pressed.

De Graaf stammered. "I thought you had already disciplined –"

"Yes, but I am interested in what you saw?"

"Well," De Graaf began. Gavain listened as De Graaf spoke, all the while not believing a word of it. It confirmed to him that De Graaf, despite being in the bar before Andryukhin and his cronies arrived, had no idea what had occurred. A fight, enforcers called out, and he had not a clue.

"Major Andryukhin's behaviour was disgraceful," Gavain commented when De Graaf finally stuttered to silence. "As the senior officer involved, he will bear the brunt of the disciplinary punishment. Although you were present, I have not received a single report that you were involved in any way, Lucas."

"Yes, sir. That's correct, sir."

"Good." Captain Gavain steepled his hands in front of his face. His eyes had gone from their normal steely grey to an ice blue, a sign to those who knew him that he was incredibly angry. Lucas De Graaf, he realised, despite being on the ship for nearly seven months, did not know him at all, nor Gavain him.

"Commander De Graaf, you are to take the *Featherlight*, the *Apollo*, and the *Titan of Stars* back to the Blackheath System, for repair and refit at Lady Sophia's shipyards around Tahrir."

Lucas De Graaf looked incredibly surprised. "Sir?" he asked.

"You will have overall command over the three ships whilst the *Vindicator* carries out House Van Hausenhof's contract in the Santiago System. This is important, Commander De Graaf. I want those three ships fully functional as soon as possible. I am considering giving you or Lieutenant-Commander Kavanagh permanent command of the *Apollo* frigate, although I realise the military transporter *Titan* is more befitting your rank. Would you be interested in the opportunity before Jules?"

"I - I would, I think, sir, but I never really considered –"

"Either is only a possibility. It will depend on your performance from this point on, Lucas."

"Yes, sir."

"You leave at the first opportunity, as soon as the new crews are aboard. You must make the new crews bond, and whilst the ships are refitted, promote in them a sense of belonging to the Vindicator Mercenary Corporation. You will find it a challenge, but personnel management is an area you sorely need to develop in. Dismissed, Commander."

"Sir." Lucas De Graaf stood, and walked towards the door.

The doors were just begging to open, when Gavain called out "Commander?"

"Sir?"

Gavain looked up from his holo-display slowly, piercing De Graaf with a stare that could burn through a starship hull. "No drinking whilst you are in command of the *Apollo*. You have an opportunity to prove to me your capabilities and your professionalism – take it."

Julia Kavanagh emerged from the particle shower, listening to its gentle hum as it cycled down. She preferred the old fashioned water showers, but there was absolutely no chance of having one of those on a starship. Even the gyms only held zero-gravity rooms to swim in, not the old fashioned water-filled pools.

Naked she left the shower head. At the moment her small but private cabin was laid out in its bedroom arrangement. The bedroom would descend on top of the living room, the table and the two-seater couch currently recessed into the floor. She rolled onto the bed, and punched the naked male figure under the covers playfully.

"Hey!" Ulrik Andryukhin opened his eyes slowly.

"You're lucky that's how I'm waking you, after your performance yesterday."

"What about my performance last night?"

Julia laughed, watching the smile light across Ulrik's face. "Five out of ten," she said.

"Six, at least, surely?"

"Captain Gavain is going to have you so tired on the disciplinary detail you'll be lucky to manage a two tonight. What's he got you doing, by the way?"

Ulrik Andryukhin groaned. "Teaching the new marines who landed yesterday the code of conduct for Imperial Officers and Crew."

Kavanagh laughed again. "Trust Jamie. The punishment fits the crime."

"He needs to find his sense of humour again," Andryukhin groaned.

"Well, he had to promise to leave Parowa Czwarty immediately in exchange for your release, and post a bond – or bribe I suppose you could call it – to have you, Jack, Naomi and all the others released. I think in this instance he's entitled to have a sense of humour failure."

"Don't you think he's been more bloody serious than normal recently? He's not been as much of a laugh for the past couple of weeks - months, maybe," Ulrik complained. He rolled over in the bed, and wrapped one insanely massive arm around the thin, lithe figure of Julia Kavanagh. He kissed her gently on the cheek, a side of him many would have doubted existed.

"He has a lot of responsibility," Julia said. "Since the Dissolution Order, he's trying to look after all of us, find us all a future. Of course he's going to be more focused and serious than ever."

"I suppose," grumbled Ulrik. "But I want my friend back."

"Oh, grow up," Jules slapped him on one large pectoral muscle. "He's fine. Give him a while to get used to it. I guess we all need some time to get used to our new lives, he isn't the only one."

"At least most of us aren't turning to drink," Ulrik commented darkly.

"Are you still blaming Lucas De Graaf for the arrests?" Julia Kavanagh stiffened, suddenly not playing any more. Ulrik seemed to sense it, and pulled away, sitting up in bed.

"Well, if it hadn't been for him Jules," he said.

"Leave it, Rik. You're responsible for your own actions. Just as Lucas is his."

"It's getting beyond a joke. He was completely fucking out of it. I'm of a mind to go up to Jamie's fricking office and tell him exactly what Lucas De Graaf was like in the Cavern."

"I think Jamie probably knows," Julia Kavanagh said quietly. "Give him credit. He doesn't appear to take notice, but perhaps he has always known. I heard on the grapevine that De Graaf had been summoned to a meeting at seven Standard this morning."

"What about?"

"Jamie probably won't pick him up on how he's been turning up drunk for shifts and all the rest, if he knows, but I'm willing to bet he'll make a point on his state in the Cavern. Knowing Jamie, it will be a direct, short, sharp warning, but he'll make Lucas think. He'll shake him up a little. De Graaf will either have to pull up, or ship out, I'm guessing."

"If you say so," Ulrik shrugged non-commitedly. "Personally, I don't care. Lucas should be shoved out of the nearest airlock." He stood up, perfect musculature brilliantly highlighted in the glow from the starlight of the cabin window. "Time for me to go and teach the newbies."

"Uh-huh," Julia Kavanagh reached out an arm and pulled him gently back to the bed. "You haven't finished making up to me, lover boy."

Chapter XI

Commodore Harley Andersson strode across the command centre of the massive starbase that was the Janus Shipyards, red alert warnings blaring out across the entire asteroid-hidden station.

<Report!> he demanded as he entered the control pit in the centre of the circular ComCen. It was arranged in tiered rows of three different levels, the lowest level at the centre being the area where the majority of the command functions were arrayed. Deep in the huge asteroid the Janus Shipyards was hidden within, the imagination could almost sense the thousands of tons of rock above them all.

<We have numerous gravity distortions forming, magnetic resonance hits and infra-red heat signatures. There is a major incursion into the Andes System underway, Commodore,> Commander O'Connor stated matter-of-factly, as if he was reporting on a solar storm.

<Show me a tactical projection,> Andersson commanded, as he came up level with his two senior officers, Commander Jonathan O'Connor and Marine Colonel Petra Raimes.

The centre of the control pit was a holo-tank, and it threw up a tactical display showing the entirety of the Andes System. It focused in on a narrower selection of the system, highlighting the position of the Janus Shipyards, their numerous and untold defences, and a vast array of numbered dots showing the locations of the incoming starship translation points. The terminus points actually overlapped, there were that many of them, and they were all arranged in a hemisphere around the current mouth of the Janus Shipyards, at quite a wide range out, beyond the range weaponry systems mounted on the base.

<We're estimating between twenty and twenty-five incoming starships,> Commander O'Connor said.

<We must assume this is hostile,> Marine Colonel Raimes opined. She was as ever in her power armour, helmet clipped to the belt at her waist, severe buzz-cut blonde hair framing the furious look on her fiercely grimacing face.

<I concur> Commodore Andersson stated. <It cannot be anything else, the numbers are too great. This is a hostile incursion.>

<Who?> asked Colonel Raimes.

<It can only be StarCom, considering what we already know.>

<Orders, Commodore?> Commander O'Connor asked.

<You both know> Andersson said grimly. <Activate the emergency plan. Now.>

They each had their role in the emergency plan, and only certain members of staff throughout the base knew what it was in order to keep its existence secret.

Commodore Andersson was to supervise the defence of the starbase, commanding not only its base defences, but the automated drones that peppered the system. Working quickly he ordered the tactical teams to pull the drones in on suicide missions, to explode close to the incoming starships. He had no worries about leaving the system undefended after the drones had been used up. He also had a number of starships at his disposal, which would run out and harass the enemy, although some were tasked to supporting Commander O'Connor.

Commander O'Connor was in charge of co-ordinating the complete evacuation of the starbase. The crew of the Janus Shipyards had been practicing emergency evacuation for months now, and as the call was issued, the entire starbase jumped to the order, heading for the multitude of warp-capable escape ships that even now would be slipping their moorings, ready to blast out of the currently-camouflaged entrance maw of the shipyards.

Andersson was keeping a track of all of this through his link to the datasphere, and although it took no greater processing time, he instinctively could not help but be more aware of the actions of Marine Colonel Raimes.

She had sent a coded order to the most trusted of her marines, some of whom were always stationed on rotation at strategically important points throughout the starbase. Colonel Raimes herself affixed her visored helmet as she stalked towards the bank of communications stations, up on the first tier of decking.

She strode directly up to Comms Lieutenant Ideyoshu, who remained completely unaware of the marine commander's presence behind him. The power-claw on Colonel Raimes' left hand smashed through his backbone, pulverising the chest cavity on its exit and severing the spinal cord on its way. As blood exploded around the screaming comms officers, Raimes was explaining to them on the open channel, <Lieutenant Ideyoshu was a StarCom spy. He has been feeding them information on our dispositions.>

It had all been falsified information, Commodore Andersson knew, and specially crafted by Commander O'Connor who displayed a gift for counter-espionage Andersson had never suspected he possessed. Ideyoshu was not the only member of StarCom's Central Intelligence Department aboard. Currently, all across the starbase, each one of the CID members was being terminated with extreme prejudice by Raimes' marines.

Andersson had known this attack was coming, and he was more than fully prepared. He might have to give up his beloved shipyards, but the trap he had laid would more than compensate him for his loss.

"This is not going well," Special Agent La Rue commented.

"Blame Admiral Haas," Silus Adare spat out vehemently. "What happened to your 'surprise', Agent?"

There was the sound of distant explosions, a series of torpedoes tracking up the hull of the dreadnought *Thor's Hammer.* On the datasphere, Adare read that the damage report stated that up to three decks had just been opened up to the void, with some loss of life.

<Shields, Commodore Pacheco!> Adare demanded.

<Twenty seconds, sir.>

<Patch me through to Admiral Haas, now,> Adare ordered his Comms Lieutenant. "Caterina," he drew out her name, "answer me. Your surprise?"

"It would appear to have failed," Agent La Rue responded finally. "We had agents in deep-cover aboard the Janus Shipyards. They had fed us the codes to by-pass the firewalls. The entire Andes System should have been defenceless."

Adare used his internal modem to look out through the *Thor's* forward viewer cameras, and watched the sheer volume of enemy fire coming in at them. The automated drones that literally covered the entire system were homing in on them, turned into lethal mines, and stealthed gun platforms were not in the positions they should have been, well within range of the StarCom fleet, and they were exacting a heavy toll. The tactical map showed a number of enemy starships active in the theatre, hammering away at the Federation ships with ferocity. Damages were already running high.

"It doesn't look very defenceless to me," he commented, as the signal came through that he had connected to Admiral Haas across the inter-ship datasphere. He felt that he only had a small portion of Haas's attention, the rest of being directed towards his other captains and doubtless his desperate attempts to regain control of this operation.

<Admiral Haas, what are your orders?> Adare asked.

<Stand fast, Admiral. Once ships are shielded they are to advance. Task fifty percent of your squadron on the enemy ships, the rest to join my squadron in assaulting the starbase. This will be bloody, Adare.>

<Yes, Admiral Haas,> Adare replied, signing off electronically.

Shields were coming up all across his squadron, and he tasked certain ships under his command to target the enemy craft that were running interference. The rest, including the *Thor's Hammer,* he ordered forwards with Admiral Haas's squadron, to plough into the Janus Shipyards.

Even as he was giving the order, the chameleonic fields around the Janus Shipyard rippled and disintegrated, and the escape ships roared out. The sheer volume of the transporters, freighters, and military craft surprised him. Their intelligence was drastically incorrect, he realised.

Even as the *Thor* powered forwards, main drive engines thrumming with the strain of propulsion, the flotilla of ships began to jump, heading in all sorts of different directions to maximise their chances of escape post-jump.

Commodore Harley Andersson ran down the corridor, an umbilical cord that connected his designated starship with the interior of the Janus Shipyards. He crossed into the airlock, the last one to do so, glad despite himself to see the outstretched hand of Colonel Raimes grasping him and forcing him through the inner lock door.

It snap-cycled shut with force enough to cut through titanium, and with explosive detonations, the umbilical cord was blasted off the starship.

<All aboard?> he asked Raimes.

<Aye, sir.> the Colonel replied. <We're the last to go.>

<To the bridge,> he commanded.

They took the nearest turbolift to the bridge. The three minutes of the journey seemed to be the longest of his life, but eventually, the doors swished open and they were pounding down the corridor to the bridge. He emerged onto his own personal flagship's bridge.

<Commodore on deck,> Captain Danae Markos announced. <Command is yours, Commodore.>

<You have the ship, Captain. Get us out of here,> Commodore Andersson replied. He stormed across to the secondary command seat, and called up the strategic map.

There had been some casualties, but a large number of his crew had escaped in their myriad of transports. Him and their small group of ships were the last to leave the shipyards, powering away as fast as their propulsors could manage. They were exiting not through the mouth, but through the emergency upper tunnel, and the gambit worked. He watched on the map as they blasted away from the Shipyards, successfully avoiding the StarCom Federation fleet.

<Warp fields are ready, Captain,> the helmsman finally said.

<Course plotted,> the navigations officer added.

<Jump!> Captain Markos ordered.

Rear-Admiral Adare was uncharacteristically silent. At the last moment, and to Admiral Haas's increasingly loud demands to know what the hell he was doing, Adare had ordered his squadron to back away at full speed from the Janus Shipyards.

His foresight had shortly been proven. As 2nd Main Squadron continued to move ever closer the Shipyards, the shielding around the massive power cores began to drop. They were going into full meltdown, and their impending catastrophic shut-down and enforced over-heating had been carefully disguised.

Minutes later they blew, the Shipyards, whatever remained of its stores that had not been taken aboard the numerous escaping starships, and the entire asteroid sequentially, dramatically and enormously blowing itself apart. Shields flared as they fought off the energy of the explosion, felt even this far out, and then in the aftermath, they had to deal with the bounding rocks and debris blasted out by the unimaginably huge detonation. It was like watching a vid of a planet-cracker in operation, in the olden days before such weaponry was outlawed by Imperial Decree.

Three of Haas's twelve ships were caught and destroyed in the detonation, and more were damaged, some shields failing and hulls rippling under the onslaught of the explosion. Out of Adare's squadron, the *Snake-Eyes* strikecruiser was too slow to escape the danger zone, and it sustained massive ship-wide damage. He knew just looking at the badly limping ship that it would have to be sent back to Sol for repair and refit. His entire 5th Rearguard Squadron would require damage repairs before they could be considered fully operational and ready for duty again, including his own *Thor's Hammer*.

He ignored the look on Special Agent La Rue's face, although not being a major supporter of the Federation, he found he could not care less over what had happened. Nevertheless he ordered a link to be made to Admiral Haas.

There had been a total loss of four ships, and a further two so severely damaged they would be sent back to Sol and could no longer be considered operational. Their mission objectives were not only unachieved, they had been spectacularly denied. This was a defeat of untold parallel in the fledgling StarCom Federation military record.

<Admiral Haas,> Rear-Admiral Adare said when he was finally connected. <Congratulations on making history – for all the wrong reasons.>

*

Lady Sophia Towers sat next to her father, at his right hand, her brother Luke at his left. Their luxury landercraft was being escorted by a full wing of starfighters, a lander in front and a lander behind, all carrying elite House Guardsmen.

After jumping into the Newchrist System, they had punched through the atmosphere of the planet Leviticus. Leviticus was currently in the ownership of House Claes, chosen because of its location almost central to the proposed combined territories of all the Houses if there was a unification of their landholdings.

"One has never done this before," Sophia Towers commented. "Have you?"

"I have in combat training," Luke said.

"Perhaps there is a parallel."

The planet of Leviticus was predominately an oceanic world, with two small continents making up less than eight percent of the landmass excluding the polar caps. Its population existed under the waves, at varying levels within the vast planet-wide ocean.

"Quiet!" Erik Towers snapped. "That's both of you. Remember who we are."

Sophia just raised her eyebrows at her brother, who pointedly gestured with his eye-sight. Sophia turned her head just in time to see the ocean surface rushing towards the lander's forward viewscreen, and then with massive splash, shock carefully managed by the hypersensitive inertial dampeners, the three landers and their wing of escorting starfighters ploughed into the deep blue of the ocean.

Sophia Towers stepped out onto the red carpet that had been draped across the metal decking of the underwater hanger. Rivulets of water were still streaming down the lander's flanks, and the metal was hissing, creaking and cracking. It would require a full service before launching again as atmospheric re-entry followed by the shocking cold of an oceanic dive, whilst being within the design tolerances of some modern spacecraft, was not recommended regularly for those not especially engineered for such an operation.

Sophia and Luke maintained their respective positions slightly behind Erik Towers' humming, hovering droidchair as it advanced across the carpet. Their honour guard of marching House soldiery began to hold back as they approached their welcoming committee.

She recognised all the various House Lords and Ladies of the proposed members of the Union. Not only had she read up to date biographies and intelligence on every single one of them, she had grown up knowing who they were, even though some she had never even met. The history of the occasion began to strike her for the very first time.

"Lord Erik Towers," an extremely tall man, elegant almost with a delicate, skeletal frame opened his arms welcomingly as if to hug the chair-bound ogre that was her father. His ostentatious robes had sleeves so wide and long that they draped almost to his knees, a stiffened collar rising high above his head. "Welcome to Leviticus, and Levitican Megapolis."

"Lord Brin Claes, may I present once again my son Luke, and my daughter Sophia."

"Ah, Lady Sophia, you have grown so much since one last saw you."

"One was five years old, Lord Claes," Sophia nodded. She had to desperately try not to let her eyes stray, towards the people she had really been brought here to meet.

They went through the introductions, and inevitably, the people she both wanted and dreaded talking to were left to last. She met the leaders of Houses Galetti and House Lapointe, and their associated senior family members. House Obamu's Lord Moafa Obamu looked every inch the cunning Machiavellian politician he had been made out to be, with his long fingernails, shaped eye brows, tattoos, open hairless chest and fantastically expensive jewellery, some of it most likely worth more than most cities and bought in centuries of blood. His family was not much more to her liking.

"Luke, Sophia, allow one to introduce House Lord Ramicek Zupanic," House Lord Brin Claes, acting as the host, said, "One believes only your father has had the pleasure?"

"That is the truth of it," Lord Luke said, striding forwards confidently and grasping the hand of Lord Ramicek. He was tall, wide, and strong, of a similar build to Luke himself. He wore a military dress uniform, in sharp contrast to the decidedly opulent but nonetheless civilised clothing the other Houses were wearing - although admittedly with the possible exception of House Obamu.

Sophia could see the two men sizing each other up in that handshake, and a part of her wanted to either laugh or cry at the ridiculous machismo of the little scene. They both held the gaze slightly longer than necessary, before Luke nodded respectfully and stepped back, allowing the Lord Ramicek to shift his attention to Sophia.

He had a heavy localised accent that underlay his Mid-Sectors twang. "Lady Sophia. Allow me to introduce my family." He seemed to sense her nervousness, she knew - mentally she slapped herself, reminding herself that she was successful businesswoman in her own right, as well as the heir to the House Towers seat and lands.

She was introduced to his current wife, the Lady Wyn. She was not of Zupanic blood line, Sophia knew, but instead a minor former house that had been annexed into Zupanic territory. Her apparent timidity surprised Sophia, as Lady Wyn was supposedly the head of Zupanic's intelligence services, and she was rumoured to be every bit as ruthless as the rest of the family.

The four youngest sons were introduced, in ascending age order, and the two daughters. The Zupanic looks ran strong in all of them. Finally, the very last to be introduced was Micalek Zupanic.

"Lady Sophia," Micalek Zupanic strode forwards. She knew of his reputation, was aware of his moniker as the Butcher of Balthazar, and everything he was capable of and was rumoured to have done. Despite all this, she knew that he was extremely attractive. He was therefore even more dangerous to her than she thought, she realised.

He bowed in front of her, before taking her hand and kissing it.

Devilish eyes alive with the promise of something forbidden sparkled at her. "You are even more beautiful than I was led to believe."

"You flatter oneself," she commented quietly.

"We will have to find time to talk, my Lady," he said.

"Yes," said Lady Sophia, "We most certainly will, my Lord."

The devilish eyes were matched by the hellishly knowing smile, she found.

*

<Mount up!> Major Andryukhin ordered. The heavy vehicles were already loaded aboard the strikepods, but the specially-selected foot soldiers he had chosen for this mission had been allowed the maximum amount of freedom before being cramped into the fast-attack pods.

Major Andryukhin was the last to enter his strikepod, the ingress hatch poking up through the floor of the mustering hall. As he quickly made his way to his seat past the marines strapping themselves into the passenger berths, he knew that far below his feet, the strikepod was dangling above a magnetically charged tunnel that led to a closed blast door, which when open would expose them to the void of space beyond.

He strapped himself into the leading jump-seat, ordering Jack Inman to sort out the two marines who were straggling. Eventually every Marine was in place.

Jacked into the datasphere, he said to the mission controller up on the bridge of the *Vindicator*, <Strikepod One ready to launch.>

<All pods ready for launch, Major,> came the confirmation. <There will be a one-second warning before firing.>

<Standard procedure, mission control,> he said to the Sub-Lieutenant. <Load us into the firing chambers, and patch me through to the mainframe.>

<Aye, sir,> the Sub-Lieutenant replied.

The strikepod was lowered by a combination of sequential force fields and mechanical weight-bearing arms through the floor of the mustering hall, the breach doors closing rapidly. Mission control gave him confirmation moments later that the strikepod was now fully locked into the firing chamber.

Major Andryukhin was concentrating on the feed from the mainframe datasphere. The *Vindicator* had jumped into the Santiago System some four days before, out on the fringes of the solar system and well beyond any possible sensor readings, along with a major battle-group of Van Hausenhof naval starships. They had all gone to running silent and had ghosted in-system, the *Vindicator* parting company with the starships at the given point. Even the *Vindicator*'s systems had lost the traces of the invasion force as the distance had grown too great.

The *Vindicator* had maintained position for a given time, nearly twenty hours, and then moved closer to the target planetoid. It was a small planet, but heavily defended with no less than eight Cervantian ships, covering every approach.

As the *Vindicator* coasted ever closer to the planetoid Angelo, the battle began in earnest further in system. The Van Hausenhof plan was simple but effective; their droid control-ships, the large transporters which carried and controlled the droid armies of Van Hausenhof, began to jump in-system. Even as the Cervantian ships were reacting and drawing close to the target zone where the control-ships' incoming jump signatures were near the fourth planet, the camouflaged naval ships already in system caught them completely unawares.

The battle was raging, Andryukhin knew, but he was somewhat disappointed to realise that he could no longer watch it on long-range scopes. The planet Angelo was now between them and the battle, which also meant they could not be detected by the majority of the Cervantian ships present in-system.

The *Vindicator* had also been on the receiving end of another stroke of luck. Six of the eight ships around Angelo had sped away, heading further in-system, leaving only two destroyers, both of which had last been seen disappearing around the curvature of the planetoid. Major Andryukhin knew he would have orbital support for a large part of this mission.

The *SS Vindicator* was fast approaching the point where it could no longer avoid the planetary scanners on Angelo.

<Good luck, Major,> Captain Gavain suddenly said on the private command channel. <Any second now.>

<Thanks, Jamie,> Andryukhin replied. <See you in twenty minutes or less.>

<We better had, Major,> the voice of Lieutenant-Commander Kavanagh popped into his head.

<Mark!> Mission control suddenly announced.

A second later the blast doors had opened, the magnetic coils throbbed powerfully once, and the strikepod was thrown out of the *Vindicator*'s belly like a foreign body being vomited from a person's stomach.

Andryukhin's connection to the ship was violently severed, but internal safeties prevented any feedback or damage. The inertial dampeners protected him from the bone-crushing g-forces the strikepod was being subjected to as it rocketed at speeds nearing a warhead-tipped projectile's capabilities towards the surface of Angelo. It flashed through atmospheric re-entry, barely slowing as its own engines kicked in and it actually began to accelerate towards the target on the planet far below.

In the thirty-four second journey to the planetary surface, Major

Andryukhin found himself thinking of Commander De Graaf for some reason. He could not have been more pleased when Gavain had told him that De Graaf had been sent away on a repair mission with the captured ships. Jules had been convinced it was a punishment. Ulrik fervently hoped that Gavain would consider promoting Julia, or even better, permanently throwing De Graaf out of the VMC.

<Impact in ten seconds,> he warned the strikepod crew. He knew that in the three other strikepods, similar warnings would be given by the section leaders. The strikepod's limited computer systems showed him that far above, the *Vindicator* was in the process of disengaging its chameleonic fields, which in any case would have been disrupted by the strikepod launches, ready to support the ground forces in their lightning assault. Similarly, the two landers which would pick them and their strikepods up post-mission were just speeding away from the battlecruiser, chasing after them on their much slower four and a half minute descent.

A pin-point accurate turbolaser beam flashed down between the strikepods, followed by another and then another, as the communications array on the installation on the planet's surface was blown to smithereens. The Cervantian forces inside the installation would have no communications to the two destroyers on the other side of the planet, no hope of calling for assistance.

<We have no more than fifteen minutes to achieve our objective,> Andryukhin said to his marines. <Three seconds. Emperor's blessings be on us all.>

The strikepod slammed into the ground, smashing through into the western wing of the installation. No sooner had it landed than the inner skin was peeling away, the outer blast shielding explosively blowing away. The interior of the strikepod was revealed, and Andryukhin violently pushed himself out of the jump-seat and onto the exit ramp that had suddenly appeared in front of him.

His power armour suit was already painting targets, and through his cybernetic connection he was portioning them out to his squad. The missile launcher mounted on his right shoulder zeroed in on the nearest gun turret, hi-ex warheads flying out and striking home in a fireball.

The four squads each of ten marines were disembarking rapidly from the hissing strikepod. The planetoid had no breathable atmosphere, no heat, a very limited weather system, and extremely light gravity, but their power suits allowed the squad to move easily and paint their targets in seconds. Oxygen was streaming out of the ruptured inner wall of the installation where the strikepod had purposefully penetrated its thick metacrete, and flashing lights inside the building complex spoke of the emergency its staff were facing.

<Major, eight battlewalkers moving on our position,> Captain Adeoye

from strikepod three called out over their battle-net. <They must have already been out on patrol.>

<Squadron One, move in to support Pod Two,> Andryukhin ordered.

From larger, cavernous entrances in the strikepod, huge shapes were already moving. A massive armoured leg, more than twice the height of a genetically-engineered marine, slammed into the dust, shimmering in the planetoid Angelo's starry night.

The form of an Imp-XXXI *Executioner,* a brand new Super-Heavy Assault battlewalker, emerged from the strikepod. A monster even in its class, it was heavily armoured and was a walking fortress, at nearly twelve metres tall one of the largest walkers manufactured in the old Red Imperium. A sister machine exited a second holding bay, an Imp-XXVII *Katyusha* Heavy Support battlewalker and two Imp-XXIV Medium Combat *Revenant*s following behind. They were already firing, heavy weaponry lighting the entire base complex as they targeted the battlewalkers they could see.

Andryukhin ignored the blast of weapons fire coming back, and ordered his squads into the depths of the base complex.

Captain Adeoye watched as the Cervantian CMBWv8 *Mace,* a Medium Combat battlewalker, reversed away from the advancing squadron of ex-Praetorian Guard vehicles. His squad were in cover, blazing away ineffectually at the *Mace.*

The VMC *Executioner* strode directly towards the *Mace,* its energy shields flaring as contact was made with the Cervantian *Mace* battlewalker. The left arm blazed, a power sword energising. With a massive flash, it plunged through the *Mace's* shields and directly into the cockpit. The Cervantian battlewalker staggered backwards, shields down.

<Advance!> Adeoye ordered two of his Marines. They broke cover.

He stood and began to run towards the *Mace.* His reinforced legs powered him forwards, and with a leap he was up on one knee, then with another leap he had reached the rupture in the cockpit. Even as the *Executioner* was shifting targets, he was using his power claw to rip into the cockpit. His rotary cannon fired, filling the interior with lethal projectiles. The two-man crew of the *Mace* did not stand a chance.

Him and his two Marines had jumped clear of the *Mace,* even as it fell backwards.

Adeoye landed neatly on his feet, running back between the legs of his friendly *Executioner.*

<You are welcome, Captain,> Marine 1st Lieutenant Zuo Li-Chan said, her voice carried on the battle-net from the lead *Executioner.*

Captain Adeoye quickly assessed the situation. Pod Two had come under heavy fire from eight battlewalkers, and they had been relatively out in the open, their mission being to hold the large central courtyard for the landers, when they arrived. It was even more important to resolve this situation quickly, as the landers were only minutes away. The Vindicator Mercenary Corporation had brought ten battlewalkers with them.

Pod Three had landed in the barracks, and was making very short work of the local Cervantian soldiers, who had largely been caught still in the process of scrambling to readiness following the Van Hausenhof invasion further in-system. Pod Four had landed in the main vehicle hangars, and had successfully disabled all the vehicles within the hangar. They were now moving on to their secondary targets, a general sweep into the main complex buildings, on a vector which would secure Pod One team's exit from the depths of the installation.

They were progressing quickly – Major Andryukhin was already ahead of schedule.

The remaining three Cervantian battlewalkers were retreating from the field, beyond the installation walls, as the two Vindicator Friederich-class landers came in, engines and repulsors flaring as they decelerated rapidly.

Docking clamps extended from their underbellies, their armoured hides easily soaking up what little fire was coming from the base and the retreating Cervantian military. The clamps attached to the downed strikepods, lifting them up and pulling them into safe flight positions, ready for the return back to the *Vindicator.*

<Major,> Captain Adeoye reported, eight minutes into the assault. <The perimeter is secure. Landers have collected the pods. Your exit corridor through the complex will be ready in less than one minute.>

<Good work. We're breaching the central mainframe room now,> Major Andryukhin replied.

Major Andryukhin led his squad back up the main corridor to their exit point. Sergeant Jack Inman was just behind him, carrying the secure data unit on his right arm that held the information they had transferred from the isolated mainframe computer of the installation.

"Get me the Captain!" he vocalised to Corporal Calaman, running alongside him. As they progressed up the corridor, the elements of the various squads that had taken up position along their exit route joined their retreat. It was a perfect operation so far, only the Cervantian battlewalkers proving to be the unexpected hitch in the plan.

Calaman's booster pack patched him into the *Vindicator,* high above them.

<Captain,> Major Andryukhin was not even panting as he ran, <we have the cargo. We'll be leaving approximately two minutes thirty ahead of schedule.>

<Good news, Major. We have company up here.> Gavain data-spat a

quick burst of information; the *Vindicator* had been detected by one of the destroyers, that had crested the horizon. It had signalled its other comrade, and both were now forming up, doubtless preparing to pound the battlecruiser with their long-range weaponry.

<What you fricking doing, Jamie,> Andryukhin laughed, <trust you stargazers to fuck up a wonderfully executed plan.>

The *Vindicator* coasted in close to the atmosphere of the planetoid, virtually kissing its upper reaches. Forward shields were flaring, as the two Cervantian destroyers pummelled it from afar. Some shots had gotten through, and the *Vindicator* was beginning to take damage.

The landers came into dock at a roaring speed, perhaps not as fast as the strikepods they carried had left the mothership, but it still required special purpose-built force fields to prevent them charging into the innards of the battlecruiser and causing great damage.

The *Vindicator* entered a running pursuit, speeding away at maximum from the planetoid Angelo, mission accomplished. As soon as they were out of the gravity well of the planet, the *Vindicator* engaged its structural integrity field, ignited the jump initiation capacitors, and in a flash of light made the transit into hyperspace.

Chapter XII

House Lord Senator Erik Towers was tired. His health was suffering, and was beginning to move beyond even the powers of modern medicine to remedy. The day had already been long, with audience after meeting, whispered conversations amidst celebrations both public and private, before they had re-convened for another night of discussions. Now, as it approached Imperial Standard midnight, after the sixth hour of deliberations, he was finding it difficult to pay attention.

He had passed most of the negotiations over to Luke and Sophia, although he listened. House Towers had already achieved most of what he wanted in any case. He was pleased at how well Sophia had comported herself during these negotiations, although he could never show that pride to her. She was everything that Luke was not, but her capabilities were so far in excess of even his own that Erik felt sure the only way to prevent her over-reaching herself was to keep the usual distance he maintained in his relationship with her. Besides, after decades of estrangement, he did not know how to make their relationship anything else.

There had been a fifteen minute recess to read the latest Union Charter. They had been arguing over the minutiae for some time now, and he saw no point in taking the discussions any further.

A bell chimed, as the chronometer struck midnight.

"Let us reconvene," House Lord Senator Brin Claes clapped his hands, summoning the House Lords and Ladies back to the large, circular table. The flags of each House were laid out across the expensive, veneered nahalwood surface, at the positions laid out for each House member.

"Ladies and gentlemen," Lord Claes stated. "Are we ready to vote?"

There were some murmurs of assent.

"Then please, let us vote."

Erik reached forwards, and pressed the 'aye' holographic button hovering in front of him. Luke and Sophia did likewise.

Brin Claes, standing at the head of the table, began to smile widely. "We are in agreement," he said, unable to hide the relief from his voice. "Ladies and gentlemen, here, at this hour, the Levitican Union is born."

It seemed an appropriate moment for a round of clapping. Servants appeared, handing out glasses of Fomalhaut champagne. Wiping some tiredness from his eyes, Lord Claes then called for the next phase of the meeting, the election of the first leader, and appointment of the cabinet.

Lord Claes supped from his fluted glass, and then carefully laid it on the table at the point when the room had naturally fallen silent, able to speak without raising his voice over the servants and the chattering between the lords and ladies.

"We have five ministries, one of which will each go to a House in the new oligarchy," the skeletal House Lord Senator. "We have all named our first and second preferences. All we have to decide now is who the new leader of the Union will be, for this historic first term of four years. It will then be up to each individual house to name their own chosen representative for ministry. Every house is eligible, but we cannot vote for ourselves. Are we ready to begin the first round of voting?" He waited whilst everyone nodded confirmation.

Holographic black screens appeared in front of the small visual displays projected for each House Lord or Lady Senator, enough to allow the members of each House around the table the privacy to cast their votes in secrecy. The computer would not record who cast which vote - every House had ensured their own security experts had examined the purpose-built software.

"Cast your votes," Lord Claes sat in his chair whilst he cast his vote.

Erik leaned forwards, and tapped the air where the display-button for House Zupanic was located. He had warned Luke and Sophia beforehand that this was all part of their secret deal. Whilst he waited for the results Lord Erik reflected that every person in this room had been cutting their own secret deals. Now was the moment of truth.

The results flashed up on a display hovering in the centre of the circular table. House Claes and House Galetti had one vote, which was predictable, each voting for the other he guessed. House Towers had two votes, which would be Zupanic and their old friends, the Lapointes. But Erik felt his colour rising, as House Zupanic had also received two votes. One was his, and the other had to be House Obamu.

All the House nobility were looking around at each other, but Erik was boring a hard stare into Ramicek Zupanic. The man was the very picture of a statesman, sure of himself and an accomplished politician. He shrugged ever so slightly, but Erik did not believe the gesture of innocence. He began to feel uneasy, suspecting a plot behind this voting.

Lord Claes stood. "Houses Obamu and Lapointe are removed from the nomination for not receiving a single vote. A second round of voting, with votes on the four remaining Houses eligible, is to begin. All six Houses, cast your votes, now." He stood again.

Erik reached forwards, his hand hesitating over House Zupanic. He was not sure, but he had to follow through on the deal, even if Ramicek had outmanoeuvred him.

The results flashed up again when the voting was complete.

Erik resisted the urge to grind his teeth, his anger rising even further. At the least he expected exactly the same votes. However, out of the six votes, House Claes had one, House Towers still had two, and someone had switched to give House Zupanic three. He looked right at Lord Brin Claes, who was smiling.

Not the least bit disappointed, he rose again. "House Claes is removed from the nomination for not receiving a single vote. House Galetti is removed for being last. Only House Towers and House Zupanic remain nominated. Cast your votes now."

Erik had no other option but to vote for Zupanic, there not being another candidate to vote for, although he was allowed to abstain. Brin Claes and Ramicek Zupanic must have agreed to some form of pact, he decided. He would spend hours tonight trying to work out the voting, and not getting his sleep he knew.

The results were displayed, and Luke put a warning hand on his forearm to prevent the explosion.

Lord Brin stood. "One abstention, House Towers with two, and House Zupanic with three. The decision is made, and the Union has spoken. May I present Lord Ramicek Zupanic, the first Principal of the Levitican Union."

Lord Erik Towers forced himself to sit there as Lord Ramicek Zupanic stood and gave a relatively short acceptance speech. He was to play it back to himself later, listening to every word in detail, but at the time, Erik did not take much of it in. He had wanted to be Principal, but he was not.

Eventually Ramicek finished his speech, and Lord Claes took centre-stage once more. "According to the agreement we have signed and ratified, with the election of Ramicek, House Zupanic are now debarred from running one of the five ministries. According to our first and second choices, each House now has a ministry to control. Please name your elected Minister." Here Lord Brin Claes smiled. "House Claes selected the Ministry of Justice. One nominates oneself as the Minister."

House Obamu had selected the Ministry of Foreign Relations as its first choice, and Moafa Obamu had also nominated himself. Lady Aria Galetti had also chosen herself for the Ministry of Domestic Affairs. The ailing Lady Elouise Lapointe suggested her daughter, Lady Monique Lapointe, as the Minister for the Ministry of Economic Affairs and Trade.

Swallowing his disappointment, Lord Erik Towers said clearly and concisely, "House Towers nominates Lord Luke Towers as the Minister for the Ministry of Military Defence."

Luke leant towards his father and whispered, "we still have what will most likely be the most powerful ministry in the oligarchy, after the Principal, father."

"It is not enough," he hissed.

The historic meeting was called to an end, allowing the various members to retire to their bedchambers before beginning the new round of celebrations and discussions tomorrow. Erik Towers was for once glad he was confined to his droidchair, as if he could have walked, it would have been obvious from a stiff marching stamp how displeased he was.

Lady Sophia Towers strolled through the gardens, enjoying the moment's peace. A pair of guards followed behind her at a respectful distance but even their presence did not spoil her stolen moment of relaxation.

The curvature of the underwater dome rose sharply on one side of the perimeter of the gardens, rising up above and over her head. It was possible to see aquatic creatures through the clear metaglass, of a myriad number of shapes and sizes. Up near the top of the dome, Levitican Megapolis was currently close to the surface of the ocean. The massive mega-city could detach itself and float around the oceans, rising or falling to different depths, a legacy of its origins as a fishing facility. In modern times the Megapolis was nearly fifteen times bigger than it was originally designed to be, a triumph of Imperial engineering.

There was a gentle simulated breeze in the gardens. It felt like being outside, on a temperate and beautiful wood-covered pleasure planet. Birds fluttered in the transplanted trees, and insects buzzed in the pathways border hedges and from flower to flower. The gardens ran for nearly a kilometre long and two kilometres wide. A small slow-moving droidcar would come to pick them up, if she did not fancy the walk back to the entranceway to the restricted-access park.

"My lady," one of her guards warned.

She turned to face him, but saw the reason for his comment. A droidcar was approaching, decelerating, and as it came to a rest above the perfect section of lawn beyond the small courtyard she had reached, the figure of Micalek Zupanic jumped lightly to the ground. She sighed, feeling that her moment of respite from the politics and her immediate situation was abruptly called to an end.

Her long, elegant dress swirled in the gentle breeze as Micalek approached. He wore the Zupanic military house uniform, which would soon be replaced by a new Levitican Union uniform, she supposed. It was part of the terms of the Unification Charter.

"Lord Micalek," she greeted him with a nod.

"My lady Sophia," he bowed and kissed her hand once again. The devilish eyes twinkled at her, and despite herself, she felt a warm glow beginning as he looked at her. "I thought I might join you for a walk in the gardens. We have not had a chance to speak alone so far. I thought you might be avoiding me?" he added playfully.

"One merely finds oneself with so many demands on her time," Lady Sophia replied with a grace only made possible by her training in the Imperial Academy. "Please, walk with me, Lord Micalek."

She had a role to play, and besides which, she found herself drawn to the incredibly handsome man. It was dangerous though, she reminded herself, thinking of the reputation he carried and the entire arranged marriage being one merely for political advantage. She placed her arm through his, and enjoyed his open surprise, which was followed almost moments later by that killer smile.

"Call me Micalek in private, please," he said, startling green eyes wide and close to hers as he turned his head.

"Then call me Sophia," she replied. They walked for a while in the silence, half-awkward at the situation, half-considering their positions.

"How do you feel it has gone?" Micalek asked, choosing a safe topic.

"Well, we have reached agreement .... union ...." Sophia deliberately lingered on the word. She would play this game, she decided, unsure whether she was only playing or whether she meant the attempt at flirtation. "So it has been most productive."

"Many things will come to pass from yesterday," Micalek said. His jack-booted feet crunched in the light gravel heavily as they walked. "I think your father did not appreciate my father being elected as the first Principal, however."

"House Towers plays a long game," Sophia commented. Then she relented. "Although one suspects you are right. My father has a legendary temper, as one is sure you are aware. He coveted the position of Principal. Myself and Luke are not as concerned. Speaking of position, you are aware of course that my brother is to be named heir to House Towers, and one is being stripped -" she stressed the word again "- of the position?"

Micalek laughed a strangely alluring laugh. He had a goatee, thin and square, and his left hand rubbed it before he answered a gesture of self-reassurance. "I was made aware of that. Your father made it clear in the negotiations we held in secret. My House would not gain the mastery of your territory under any circumstances, nor you ours."

"My father was counting on your support in the elections."

"Which he received, Sophia."

"An impartial observer could wonder how your father became elected, in that case."

"One of your allies in House Lapointe or House Claes did not support you, at least as far as the election was concerned. I'm sure as matters proceed that may change."

"We shall see," Sophia said neutrally.

"I had expected that Lord Erik would decide to claim the Ministry of Military Defence for himself, rather than give it to your brother Lord Luke."

"He has no interest in military affairs particularly, Luke is far the better strategist," Sophia nodded. "If it had been my father that became Principal, Zupanic had Military Defence listed as their first choice. Would it have been you, or your father, who would have been Minister?"

"We never discussed it," Micalek replied. Sophia believed his outright lie as much as her own obscuring of the truth. They were sparring with each other, flirting with the power of their positions as much as any other potential fiancés would with their affections. Such was the nature of a political marriage, she supposed.

"The Butcher of Balthazar could have made a good job in the position, controlling the combined House Armies of six nations," Sophia deliberately dropped the mantle on his shoulders.

"Perhaps the Butcher could," Micalek winced. "Sophia, I hate that moniker. It was placed on me by our enemies, and is not the full story. Perhaps one day I will tell you the truth of it."

"Very well," she nodded. She smiled suddenly, and saw a faint answering smile from him, realising she had crossed some unknown line. "What of the marriage? What do you hope for from it?"

"An alliance of our Houses, a solidifying of the Levitican Union in more than just name," he promptly replied. Then he sensed the change in her attitude, smiled wider, and said, "and a beautiful, intelligent, successful, and very formidable wife, my Lady."

"We shall just have to see," she said, and they walked in silence for a while longer, eventually discussing smaller, more neutral matters. The conversation only became serious at one point, when Micalek enquired as to what her imprisonment under the false Emperor had been like. She told him the truth, the painful moments as well as the points of relief, but living with the fear of the constant knowledge that your death could rest on a madman's whim was not an easy point to convey.

"Will you be residing on Levitican Megapolis for long, Sophia?" he asked at one point.

"No, not much longer," she replied. "My brother will of course stay with the other Ministers and their Ministries, as the government is established. As soon as the declaration is made to the galaxy, one will be leaving. One has her businesses and interests to attend to. And your own plans?"

"That is a shame, I had hoped for longer. I would arrange to visit you within the month, if that is acceptable? We should get to know each other. There is much to discuss, in practical terms of course."

Sophia was not sure she liked the sound of that. "Of course there is Micalek, but be warned, one has her own ideas as to practicalities." She changed subject back quickly. "What are your own plans?"

"The same as yours. I will be leaving after the declaration with my mother and the rest of my brood. I have to hand control of our military over to your brother. It will not take long."

"Then perhaps you can visit my own world of Tahrir, and we can discuss the particulars of the marriage. It will make the negotiations of the

Unification Charter appear Childs-play, one warns you now," she added playfully.

He laughed again. "I have no doubt it will, my lady. Just remember, you have your own reputation as I have mine. There is an element of truth in them, to be sure, but they are not the whole truth." He stopped, and turned to face her. "Please just remember that it is important we find our own truth. We are two individual people, as well as representatives and pawns in the plans of our Houses."

Sophia thought she understood, and nodded gracefully to him. They said their goodbyes, and he left to return to his droidcar, she graciously refusing his offer to take her back to the entranceway to the gardens.

As the droidcar lifted off and scooted away, she reflected that their brief meeting had given her much to think about in relation to Micalek Zupanic.

It was only later on reviewing her guards' scans that she realised that Micalek was an augmented - the very minor tell-tale traces of his high-grade cybernetic implants gave him away. That was a carefully concealed secret. She was aware that the officially free-thinking House Zupanic consisted of both humanist and borgite elements, a legacy of its combative and successful history of conquering neighbouring houses over the centuries, but she doubted her father knew of the borg nature of the man he had betrothed her to.

Considering Lord Erik's hatred of the borg, she found it a most delicious irony.

*

Lucas De Graaf sat in his private cabin aboard the *SS Apollo*. The Cervantian-made captured assault frigate was in dry-dock at the shipyards above Lady Sophia's landhold planet of Tahrir, in the Towers' capital system of Blackheath. Held stationary by powerful forcefields and hard, physical mechanical arms, its repair and refit was calculated to be another four days. Regardless of that, his orders were to remain in the Blackheath System, until either Captain Gavain returned or he received rendezvous orders.

He liked the captain's cabin on the *Apollo*, he decided, as he stood at the large observation window. In the dry-dock berth of the shipyards, he had a wonderful view of the planet Tahrir, and could see the multitude of small spacecraft and droid-controlled repair barges as they shuttled back and forth from the berth's single reinforced repair pylon, a large extension a quarter again as big as a battlecruiser.

Thoughtfully, he turned away from the window, and his eyes fell on the desk he had moved into the spacious, luxurious cabin. It still had the previous occupant's paintings and decorations within it, as he had decided he quite liked the ostentatious taste of former captain of the *Apollo.*

Upon the desk rested a bottle of real whiskey, unopened.

There was little to do on the *Apollo* when it was in dry-dock. He had refused the crew shore-leave, insisting that they be ready to leave the shipyard at a moment's notice. Much of his time had been taken up overseeing the training of the new crew. He had found it difficult at first, but found that because they all came from different ships and backgrounds, it had been easier for his training regimens to take effect.

All in all, he thought, he rather enjoyed having his own command.

It was strange on reflection, as he suddenly realised how concerned Gavain, Kavanagh and maybe even Andryukhin had been over his behaviour when he joined the *Vindicator* from the *Retribution* after the Battle of Mars. He had kept to himself, making no real attempt to integrate as he descended further and further into alcoholism.

He stepped closer to the desk, and rested his hands on the bottle.

In the last fortnight, as he had worked on bringing his crew together, he had begun to see the truth of James Gavain's words; "You will find it a challenge, but personnel management is an area you sorely need to develop in." They had stung at the time, but he knew Gavain was right, and in addition to that, now he had his own command, he appreciated how much integration and moral of his crew mattered.

James Gavain's other words also stung at the time. "No drinking whilst you are in command of the *Apollo.* You have an opportunity to prove to me your capabilities and your professionalism - take it."

Lucas De Graaf had found himself enjoying the command of the *Apollo,* and suddenly, with the freedom had come the realisation that he had allowed the Dissolution Order and its destruction of his former life to ruin his present existence. The drink had been in control of him. Suddenly, there was a future, with the Vindicator Mercenary Corporation, and he had been too blind - or blind-drunk - to see it.

He picked up the bottle, and with a smile on his face, pushed it into the disintegrator chute. He would see the ship's doctor in confidence later tonight after his shift, he decided, and ask for drugs to help. No more drink, he told himself.

All of a sudden, the ship went to amber alert. "What?" he said aloud. "We're in dry-dock, how can we be on amber?" He jacked straight into the datasphere, and felt the glow as he joined the ship's hive-mind consciousness.

<Commander De Graaf,> his second-in-command, an acting Lieutenant-Commander Ffion Wybeck. <Your presence is required on the bridge.>

<SitRep,> he ordered, already having exited his cabin and heading down the corridor to the bridge.

<The House Towers forces here in Blackheath have gone to red alert,> Wybeck said. <We're patched into their military comms systems. They have detected an incoming jump signature, a terminus point large enough to indicate several starships inbound.>

<What's the reason for the alarm?> he asked. Blackheath was a busy trading system, the largest in Towers territory and also it's richest. That meant a large amount of interstellar shipping.

<They are not coming in at one of the designated jump-points, and the Interstellar Merchants Guild has no scheduled trade vessels logged for jump for another two point two hours, sir.>

<Serious,> Commander De Graaf said on the private channel, as he emerged onto the frigates small bridge. <You were right to sound the alarm. There's not much we can do in dry-dock, but all hands had better be ready. Signal the *Titan of Stars* and the *Featherlight* to be prepared for anything.>

He sat in the command chair, and quickly accessed the tactical map. The developing terminus point was between the planet Tahrir and the capital of Alwathbah. House Towers military ships were scrambling, but the potential enemy ships would be fully translated by then.

<What do you think, sir?> Lieutenant-Commander Wybeck asked. A former Praetorian, he found himself getting along with her very well, and he knew that she was desperate to prove herself.

<It could be pirates, an emergency unscheduled jump by a trading convoy, or the start of another House invasion. No other jump signatures reported?> he asked of scanners.

<No, sir,> was the answer.

<Then we wait,> he shrugged.

Out in the depths of space, there was a sudden flash as the starships exited the terminus point and left hyperspace, translating fully into realspace. Their forms were unnaturally extended, so blurred they would hurt the naked eye, before they snapped back into their real dimensions. The true nature of the starships were revealed, and the House military in-system began to scream warnings at each other over their comm-nets, their commanders panicking as they saw what had just landed in their defensive zone.

They were unmistakably Praetorian in origin, with the standard long construction, boxy afts and extended nacelles to either side. Energy still crackled around them as the jump capacitors cycled down and the structural integrity fields dispersed. Whatever speed they had entered hyperspace at must have been great, as on their exit they were travelling at the very limits of safe exit velocity, which only added to the House Towers military alarm.

<Ex-Praetorian,> said Lieutenant-Commander Wybeck. <They could be a StarCom Federation raiding party, or pirates?>

<There is something not right about this,> Commander De Graaf said. <Their formation is all wrong for an attack. IFF readings?>

The scanners Sub-Lieutenant answered quickly, <No readings, Commander.>

Identify Friend or Foe was the electronic tag most starships emitted to identify themselves. If IFF was switched off or not transmitting, they were doing their best to avoid being identified.

<Match ship dimensions and emissions to the profile log,> Lt-Cmdr Wybeck ordered. They had downloaded the *Vindicator*'s tactical data files to the *Apollo,* so it had complete access to the entire Praetorian Guard historical data, accurate up to the Dissolution Order. They would begin searching every metre of the ships for any identifying repairs or known distinctive features, and analyse the full spectrum of electronic readings, engine emissions, and aggressive scans to hopefully identify them.

The ships were still coming in fast, headings adjusting directly for Tahrir. De Graaf briefly thought about requesting detachment from the shipyard, even though it would take too long to properly disengage and in less than fifteen minutes at this rate the interlopers would be within striking distance of the planet. The House military would have to deal with this. In addition, the strike force could tear the *Apollo* apart, and his first priority was to protect the *Titan of Stars* and *Featherlight.*

<Comms, request disengagement from the shipyard. Order the *Titan* and *Featherlight* to do the same,> he ordered. Even if they came under fire, he would have to protect the Vindicator Mercenary Corporation assets first.

<ID on one - no two, of the ships. Their comms are coming back up.>

<Feed it through,> De Graaf ordered, and then gasped as they were identified on his tactical display.

<Cancel my previous order,> he demanded. <Patch me through to House Towers military command immediately, and hail the battlecruiser directly. We have to stop this, now.>

Commodore Harley Andersson sat in the command chair of the *ISS Remembrance*, the R-class battlecruiser that had been permanently assigned to the Janus Shipyards as his own flagship.

The tactical display showed his small squadron of ships, those that he had escaped with from the Janus base in the Andes System, or determined beforehand they should rendezvous with after that escape.

A Praetorian M-class military super-transporter led the way, a behemoth still unmatched by most intergalactic standards, the *ISS*

Monstrosity. By its side but slightly behind, was the military type-IV cargo-freighter *ISS Hannoverian*, fully loaded with sixteen armoured and shielded cargo-tanks carried on its spine, and a type-III cargo-freighter, the *Deliverance*.

The *Remembrance* battlecruiser rode slightly above it, the star-carrier *Quintessential* in the same position below. Two strikecruisers, the *Sorceror* and the *Solace* carried the wings of the convoy, and nearly at the rear rode the destroyer *Undefeatable*. Lastly there was an interdictor, the *ISS Kinslayer*.

<We have to get through to someone, before the firing starts,> Commander O'Connor looked tense, breaking off from his communication with the House Towers military. They were having none of his protestations.

<Hail from the *SS Apollo*,> his comms officer suddenly said.

Commodore Andersson located the *SS Apollo* on his three-dimensional map, noting that it was relatively close by, in a shipyard in orbit around the planet Tahrir. <I'll take it,> he told O'Connor, <Carry on.>

A holographic image of a man in ex-Praetorian Guard uniform appeared before Commodore Andersson. <Commander De Graaf, *SS Apollo*, Vindicator Mercenary Corporation. Hello, Commodore. It is you after all.>

<Commander,> Andersson felt a surge of relief. <We're here to find you. Last time I saw you, you were on the *Vindicator* with Jamie. Where is he? Where's the *Vindicator*.>

<You're here to find me?>

<The *Vindicator*, then. Janus Shipyards was attacked, and Jamie had kept me up to date with what he was doing. I did say I may come join him – well here I am.>

Commander De Graaf appeared momentarily non-plussed. <Jumping in with nine ships, Commodore ->

<No time, Commander. What can you do to call off the House Towers navy? They will be firing on me shortly, and after coming all this way, I don't want to have to jump out again. Not if you're here.>

<We're trying to contact their military command, but the in-system comms network has gone crazy since your arrival. We're having problems getting through to the right people.>

Andersson glanced at O'Connor, who was furiously trying to convince holograph of a man in a local admiral's uniform that they were not hostile. <We'll tell their senior officer to contact you directly, do you think he'll listen?>

<I don't know,> said De Graaf, <but we can try ....>

Chapter XIII

The ocean of Leviticus swirled above his head. They were at the very apex of the dome, in a specially cleared courtyard. There was a small crowd in front of the stage, consisting mainly of the local nobility, the servants and attendants who had accompanied the House members on their journey to Leviticus, those ambassadors present in the Megapolis, and some of the local upper class. Security was being provided by a combination of the House soldiery who had escorted their Lords and Ladies to the Megapolis.

Lady Sophia stood on the left-hand side of her father, Luke in his customary position on his right. She kept her green eyes resolutely forward, resisting the urge to screw them shut in the harsh lighting the holo-camera team were casting on the entire stage. A display hovering above their heads showed the images that the cams were picking up, although they were not recording yet.

Without thinking of it, her eyes strayed to the depiction on the display of Lord Micalek, resplendent in his military-cut uniform. She could not be sure, but it looked as if he were staring back at her.

His father, the Lord Principal Ramicek Zupanic, stood centre-stage. His wife Wyn was at his side, but as the time neared, she left him without any gesture of affection or words of encouragement to rejoin her large family at the far end of the line of House nobles.

Only one news crew had been allowed to be present, and that was the local one belonging to House Claes. The StarCom News Media, although they would receive a live feed which they would then broadcast across the galaxy, had not been invited.

Finally, the director raised his hand, three fingers extended. "Lord Principal, we'll be live in ..... three .... two ..... one .... live!"

"Citizens of Houses Claes, Lapointe, Galetti, Obamu, Towers, and Zupanic," the Lord Principal began. "I address you all in particular, as much as I address every person in the colonised galaxy. You see behind me and before you -" he gestured and turned to both sides "- the assembled Lords and Ladies of our six great Houses. We all have a message of great historical import to convey to you all.

"We speak to you from the planet Leviticus, in the Newchrist System, in what will soon become known as the former Claes territory. It was three days ago, that House Claes, Lapointe, Galetti, Obamu, Towers and Zupanic, completed months of careful negotiations which resulted in the signature of the Leviticus Unification Charter. The purpose of the Unification Charter is to join all our Houses together into one, great, powerful Union.

"Today, citizens, you now know that you are each and every one of you, members of the Levitican Union.

"The Union is so much more than just an agreement. It is not a mutual defence pact, a trading treaty, a monetary union or a trading bloc. It is all of those things and more. The intention was to create a new nation, our six Houses putting aside our differences whatever they may be, to join together in the hope of finding a new future; a phoenix to arise from the ashes of the old Red Imperium.

"We will be one nation. We will be releasing full details of the Unification Charter following this broadcast, and we strongly advise you all to read it. The Charter is our new constitution, my people.

"The Levitican Union has a role for each one of our Houses, and shortly each House will introduce themselves and their Ministry in the new government shortly. However, very briefly, let me tell you now that we have allowed for a new ultimate leader of the Union to be elected by House vote once every four years. I have the great honour and privilege to be elected the first leader of the Levitican Union."

Here Ramicek bowed deeply. When he straightened, he continued, "I am the Levitican Union's new head of state, the first Lord Principal. The seat of my government, of your government, of *our* government, will be and always will be here in Levitican Megapolis, on Leviticus. We have chosen this place not only because we signed the Charter in its environs, but because it is the place most equidistant to all our former House territories.

"As part of the Levitican Union, we will join all our militaries together under the control of Lord Minister Luke Towers. Our relationships with our neighbours both near and far, with all bodies external to our new, great nation, will be overseen by Lord Minister Moafa Obamu. Our justice system, our enforcers, and our law-making will be overseen by Lord Minister Brin Claes. Our domestic affairs, a wide remit including education, welfare, infrastructure, our solar administrator civil service, will be run by Lady Minister Aria Galetti. Our economic affairs, our trading, our banking system and our government treasury will be overseen by Lady Minister Monique Lapointe.

"The Levitican Union will span sixty-nine inhabited star systems, across the Core and the Mid-Sectors. We reassure the people of the colonised galaxy that we have no hostile intentions to any of our neighbours, and that we wish merely for peaceful co-existence and to provide a light in the darkness that seems to have befallen much of the galaxy following the dissolution of the Red Imperium. We wish to ensure that our citizens at least are spared the suffering that much of our neighbours have succumbed to, a suffering that was not supposed to be following the death of the False Emperor."

Lady Sophia managed to resist the urge to smile. She had to stand in admiration of Lord Principal Ramicek. His comment 'spared the suffering that much of our neighbours have succumbed to' was general enough to be read as a statement of distress over the dissolution of the Red Empire, but could nevertheless be taken as a direct reference to the rapidly expanding StarCom Federation.

"Now, my citizens, let me hand the stage over to your former House leaders." Ramicek stepped back after he introduced Lord Minister Brin Claes.

Lady Sophia did not have to force herself to pay attention to the speeches, but she knew that within a couple of hours of the end of the conference, she would be leaving Leviticus to return to her own landholding of Tahrir back in the Blackheath System. She could not wait to escape this politicking.

*

The shuttle came into dock slowly, Captain James Gavain displaying his usual, impassive, stony, ice-cold demeanour despite the tremendous excitement he felt inside. Out of the corner of his eye, he caught Lt-Cmdr Julia Kavanagh smirking as she looked at him. He felt sure she knew what he was really looking forward to.

De Graaf had shuttled across from the *Apollo*. He now stood in the line behind Jamie. His right to be present was due to his current position as a director of the Vindicator Mercenary Corporation. Gavain wished he had discovered De Graaf's drinking problem before he had made him a member of the executive of the company; but then, he also firmly believed that everyone deserved a second chance, and so he given Lucas De Graaf the short, sharp shock he needed and the opportunity to make amends and change the direction of his life.

From the reports he had received from the *Apollo*'s doctor, Commander De Graaf appeared to be making every effort to take the chance. The doctor also added that there was a significant danger of relapse. Jamie resolved he would seek counsel from Harley on the subject, his advice on whether the risk was too great to leave De Graaf in a position of command.

The shuttle clunked into place with a hollow, metallic thump. After a moment the airlock chamber began to cycle.

Major Ulrik Andryukhin stood on the other side of Jules. Jamie noticed that they were stood very close together, almost touching in fact. He did not say anything. They were not in the Praetorians now, and although everyone on-board knew about their relationship, even before the rebellion no-one had said a thing. Fraternisation was strictly prohibited in the old Praetorian Guard, but it was one of the rules that the more lenient captains ignored. Jamie reflected that De Graaf was one of those who would probably have had the two thrown in the brig.

Openly displayed relationships between staff and crew were just one of the many minor, subtle changes that Jamie had begun noticing of late.

The airlock completed its cycle, and with an almost soundless expiration of air the door swished open.

"Jamie," Commodore Harley Andersson stepped through the airlock, hands and arms open slightly. Jamie smiled, feeling his heart leap once again.

"Harley, it's good to see you. I heard that you had quite a journey to get to us."

Harley Andersson laughed. "Indeed I have Jamie. Allow me to introduce my command crew."

They exchanged pleasantries, and introduced each other's staff. There were other shuttles en route to the *Vindicator*, carrying the command personnel from the other starships that Harley had brought with him when he escaped from the Janus Shipyards.

"We're breaking out the real food, and clearing out one of the conference rooms so we can have a bit of a celebration and welcoming to all your squadron later," Lieutenant-Commander Kavanagh had said excitedly as she spoke to Commodore Andersson.

"Maybe not my squadron," Commodore Andersson had said, glancing at Jamie. Eventually, he pulled Jamie to one side, and suggested that they leave their two command crews to mingle whilst they had a private chat.

Captain James Gavain and Commodore Harley Andersson sat in the captains private cabin. It was large, but Spartan, as was typical Jamie. He sat in a seat at the small circular table, a cup of real coffee in his hand, whilst Harley leaned his chair back against the wall behind him.

"At least you gave them a bloody nose," James was saying. "Did you ID any of the ships?"

"We managed to identify some," Harley nodded. "And then when we fully reviewed the communications intercepts later, we were able to crack in to some of the non-data channels and work out a bit more about who they were."

"Such as who?"

"Admiral Heinrich Haas appeared to be in command," Andersson raised his eyebrows, "the traitorous bastard that went over to the StarCom Federation almost before President Nielsen asked for volunteers. We're not sure, but we think that the other dreadnought was commanded by Silus Adare."

"I'm not familiar with him," Jamie shook his head.

"He's as nasty a piece of work as Haas is a Commie-lover. He supported the False Emperor during the war, and was actually listed as captured and incarcerated on the Saturn moon prisons. The fact that he has ended up in command of a starship for the StarCom Federation Armed Forces suggests he sold out to them. This definitely surprises me, having read his psych-profile."

"How up to date is your archive and intel?" Jamie asked.

"As up-to-date as it can be, following the chaos after the Dissolution Order," Commodore Andersson shrugged. "I'll have new copies uploaded to you as soon as I return to the *Remembrance*."

"Thank you," Jamie took a sip of his steaming hot coffee. "At least you escaped Janus to tell me the tale. Nine ships, too."

"We rendezvoused out-system, but there were many more starships that weren't ships-of-the-line in the Andes System when the StarCom Federation attacked. They all had orders to get as far away from the Core as possible, trust me. And of course, now they are all yours." Harley waited for a reaction from Jamie, and when he did not get one, merely shook his head and chuckled.

Inside, he felt shocked. Eventually he put his head to one side, and merely said, "All mine, Harley?"

"Yes, Jamie, they are all yours. With the fleet you're amassing, we'll have to start calling you Admiral."

"I can't –"

"Yes, you can," Harley suddenly leaned forwards, his face sharpening. "When you came to Janus Shipyards for refit, I may have been joking at the time about coming to join you if you went mercenary, but later on I realised I hadn't been. I either move with the future or become a thing of the past, Jamie, its adapt or die time. You seem to be doing rather well for yourself, here in the Blackheath System with your mercenary company, so I want to join. And I bring you six ships-of-the-line and three support ships as my joining gift. Seriously, it's not as if Praetorian High Command are going to ask for them back, no-one's stopping me handing them over to you – take them. And let me and the people out there have a new future."

Jamie was silent while he thought. Harley waited patiently. Eventually Jamie took yet another sip of coffee, and then said, "The VMC is set up in a very particular way. I'm a Director, as is Lady Sophia Towers. Commander De Graaf, Jules and Ulrik are all Associate Directors. Perhaps we could have you made an Associate Director, but I would have to speak to Lady Sophia."

Harley Andersson only laughed. "That's your only concern? Jamie, I don't care. Rank, position or title, all I want is a home and somewhere to belong. I belong with you."

There was a long silence between them, each holding the others gaze.

"Good," said Jamie quietly. "I'm glad you came to find me."

Harley smiled. "So we're in?"

Jamie just nodded his head.

"Excellent."

"All your crew must have a vote before they sign the contract," Jamie said.

"There's a contract?"

"Yes."

"I guess that's commercial life, then. So be it," Harley nodded.

"And I do want you as an Associate Director, but I must speak to Lady Sophia first. She's due in-system in the next seventy-two hours."

"I'll be glad to help in any way I can," Andersson said. "Jamie, there are over ten thousand of us out there. My primary concern is the people I rescued from the Janus Shipyards, and making sure they have a future. You seem to have grasped the future, so here we are. Everything else is secondary."

"I only grasped it based on your advice. You gave me the push I needed to make the leap."

Harley Andersson smiled. There was a look in his eyes, and James Gavain returned it. James had never thought that today would even come, had never even dreamed it were possible. He reflected once again that life was entirely unpredictable.

"Lady Sophia is going to be surprised when she lands in-system," Gavain commented.

"I bet she will be," Harley Andersson nodded. "Is it likely that House Towers is going to be a problem over our presence?"

"There is a possibility, but you know that technically we now reside in the Levitican Union? Besides which, Lady Sophia seems to be perfectly capable of withstanding her father. If he wants your - well, our - ships, she will stop him. She's a brilliant businesswomen - the Vindicator Mercenary Corporation would not exist if it were not for her." Jamie drained his coffee, and stood to make a new one from his old fashioned cafettiere. He had recently grown to have a dislike for the molecular-materialised version from the simulator.

"As long as you are confident," Andersson said. "I've brought more than just crew and starships. House Towers - sorry, the Levitican Union - will definitely want what we're carrying."

"Meant to ask what was in the cargo-freighters," Jamie said with his typical brusqueness.

"I have Praetorian-grade supplies, raw moleculisation blocks, and constructor machinery with two industrial-grade fabricators, both space-capable. A third armoury fabricator - you will never run short of weaponry replacements again. There's spare jump initiation capacitors and fuel for the main drive engines." Harley hesitated, then said slowly, temptingly, "the *Hannoverian* is carrying a full suite of accelerated-growth biovats with cybernetic infusers and educational downloads, for the production of new Praetorian cyborgs. I have medical specialists and trainers, the best the Shipyards carried."

Jamie was staggered, despite himself. "Outside of Sol, that is probably one of the largest treasure troves in the Core."

"We can manufacture our own replacement Praetorians, built to order, no more recruitment on the open market for you," Harley confirmed. "Refit of the starships will never be an issue, nor will supply. It will only be the time to manufacture. We could even build our own starships."

"We will have to arrange for a permanent base for it all," said Gavain, his mind racing.

"We don't want to be carrying it around with us, no," Andersson agreed.

"I will speak to Lady Sophia. She's a very accomplished businesswoman - I am sure she will have ideas and know how to arrange that for us. Money is not something the VMC is short of just at this moment."

"Business is good then?"

"We have completed two contracts, high payout." James had sat down again with his steaming brew. "What's the complement on the super-transporter *Monstrosity*?"

"It's at two-thirds load of Marines," said Commodore Andersson. "But with full loads of equipment and vehicles."

James nodded. He knew the statistics for the load-out on the M-class super-transporters. It was an invasion force. He could take a planet. His mind raced ahead - with the sudden size of the Vindicator Mercenary Corporation, he could take on contracts to invade and hold entire solar systems. The power he held was immense. The costs of running it all would be similarly high - he desperately needed to speak to Lady Sophia, he decided. He felt almost out of his depth.

"I wouldn't worry, Jamie," said Harley gently. "The responsibility is huge, but think of all you can do."

Jamie explained that he would have to wait for Lady Sophia to return to the Blackheath System before he started planning anything, and confessed about his need for her guidance in this.

"I'm glad to see you are accepting advice," nodded Harley. "This is new for all of us, I suppose. However, if I'm understanding your arrangement with Lady Sophia correctly, there is something you have to organise quickly and it is within your realm of expertise."

"That is?"

"The new command structure," said Harley. "I wanted to spend some time .... just with you, if you see what I mean, but its perhaps just as important to sort this out now. Not all the ships I brought have commanding officers of sufficient skill, or full command crews, some are under-crewed, some ships need repair. We were running for our lives from the StarCom Federation. We need to arrange the new command structure as soon as possible."

Jamie knew that Harley was right. Despite the burning of his own feelings, he nodded and pulled a data-pad from his uniform belt to make the necessary notes.

James Gavain stepped aboard the *TwSS First Ship*. Being entirely used to military ships, he found the sheer ostentatiousness of the House Towers barge completely alien. Everywhere he looked the riches of House Towers were on display. Even the uniforms of the attendants who met him and led him through to Lady Sophia's private chambers were grand. He had never been on a starship that had carpet on every deck in his life.

The House Towers family had returned to the Blackheath System on schedule. Apparently, Lord Erik had been virtually apoplectic when he discovered that he had the equivalent of a Praetorian Guard battlegroup residing in the system, and had predictably demanded that it be de-powered and turned over to him. In the message Lady Sophia had sent him, she had been unable to hide her glee as she described their argument, and how she had forcefully reminded Lord Erik that this was a private business venture of her own. Lord Erik had apparently demanded that the ships leave his system, and Sophia had pointed out that whilst they remained in orbit around Tahrir, they were in her landholding, and she would do as she pleased.

Even the air was scented with a mixture of rich spices, creating a fragrance he found somewhat uncomfortable. The attendants appeared to be fully familiar with it however.

Lord Erik had been left on the capital of Alwathbah, although Gavain reflected that strictly speaking it was no longer the capital as the week-old Levitican Union was now centred on the planet Leviticus. Part of him wanted to question Lady Sophia on her thoughts as to the entire Union - and more to the point, why she had not mentioned it to him - but ultimately he supposed it was not his concern. She was a business partner, not his House ruler.

He was made to wait outside the door to her private chambers for a minute or two, before he was permitted entrance.

"James Gavain," she clapped her hands excitedly as he entered. "All of you leave," she demanded of the various people fussing around her. As soon as they had exited and the doors to her amazingly large private chambers had closed, she stepped forwards and very formally bowed to him, then shook his hand. "You have been a very busy individual, haven't you, Captain Gavain?" she teased.

"Admiral Gavain," he corrected sternly. "There have been a lot of changes in your absence," he conceded.

"It was worth it to annoy one's father," she laughed, leading him by the hand to a luxuriant sofa. She sat on a three-seater placed at right-angles to his, and crossed her legs, leaning in to him with one arm relaxing over the back. "We have much to discuss one thinks. Seventy million turnover in one month exceeds projections, very well done. If only all one's business ventures showed that percentage of success. With all the recent changes in the Vindicator Mercenary Corporation, the value of the assets in the business has also just gone through the proverbial roof."

"All the changes meet with your approval?" Gavain asked.

"Operational matters are your concern, the finances are mine," Lady Sophia said. "All one would ask is that if we ever make an acquisition which costs, you consult me first. Accepting assets offered for free, or taken in conflict, is another matter entirely. All one would counsel against is growing too fast too quickly, James. One has seen many businesses that expand far too rapidly - without the proper foundations and preparations such ventures usually fail spectacularly."

"Understood," Gavain acknowledged.

"So you are an Admiral, now?" Lady Sophia asked playfully.

"The changes have necessitated a significant re-organisation in command structure," Gavain replied. "Commodore Harley Andersson has brought some command staff with him - but I am having to reorganise them and my own. There will be movement in ranks throughout the VM Corporation."

"Movement and progression is good for your staff, it is highly motivating," Lady Sophia nodded. "On the subject of Commodore Harley Andersson ..... your request for him to be made an Associate Director ....?"

"Yes?" Gavain said simply.

"In theory one agrees, conditional on meeting him oneself of course. As a friend of yours - and clearly as a close friend, one who would bring half an army to your side - one is sure he will be more than acceptable. It is clear how much you hold him in high regard."

"Harley has been one of the guiding lights of my former career in the Praetorians," Jamie felt distinctly uncomfortable. "He has been a mentor to me. He is a close friend, my Lady, as you say. A very close friend." He hesitated.

Lady Sophia smiled a small, perhaps sad smile. "One understands, James. One is not blind."

"Good, my Lady, as long as we understand each other."

"We certainly do. It is no concern of mine. Now I believe there was another matter you wished to discuss with me?"

"The manifest provided to you was not complete," James said, watching Lady Sophia's face darken. He explained quickly that he had applied the principal of operational security, being unwilling to transmit the full details of the contents of the cargo-freighters on even a Praetorian-encoded communication channel. He explained about the facilities they were carrying that could manufacture new cyborg Praetorians, and the special manufactory equipment for Praetorian re-supply and refit, and how it must never appear on any public listing or valuation of their assets. "It is too much of a target and temptation," he said. "We keep it secret and safe. In the wrong hands, these sectors could suddenly face a new Praetorian army, and that is not to be allowed. May I ask you to keep it even from your father?"

Lady Sophia's face lightened. "One understands your reasoning," she said, "and of course one agrees. Excuse one's initial reaction, but one dislikes having business partners keep her in the dark. One understands the need for secrecy, and also has her own reasons for wanting to keep this secret - the Levitican Union is yet a new, young nation, and much remains to be understood about the political currents and direction we are yet to take."

"Good," Gavain nodded sharply. "The existence of the facilities raises another problem for us."

"Where do we put them," Lady Sophia said.

"Yes," Gavain nodded again.

"Well, one did offer you a landholding on Tahrir ....." she trailed off, "You're getting better, Capt - sorry, Admiral. You walked into this room always intending to walk away with new land on Tahrir, did you not?"

Gavain gave a rare smile. He merely inclined his head in affirmation.

"The Vindicator Mercenary Corporation will pay one the appropriate value of the land, according to current market value," Lady Sophia said without missing a beat. "We can take it from the company one set up to manage all of one's property on Tahrir. Is that sufficient?"

"Yes," Gavain said. "I would ask your advice on how best to construct the facility, considering the need for secrecy. Harley can handle the actual construction, but we may need some equipment. Will you be in-system for some time, my Lady?"

"For the immediate future, yes," she nodded. "How much land do you need?"

"There must be an underground facility, which eventually we will reinforce against orbital bombardment. It will be a joint warehouse, bioartification and production manufactory, and database server house. Above ground will be the training facilities and visible warehouses to allay suspicion under a chameleonic field. We wish it to be the new home for the Vindicator Mercenary Corporation."

"Something very expensive then," said Lady Sophia. "The profit you have made even in this extra-ordinary month will not cover that.

Remember, with your increased size have also come increased overheads. All these people will need paying, Jamie."

"We will build it quickly. Perhaps rather than outright purchase of the land, some form of mortgage and loan? The banks of House Towers, or even the Interstellar Merchants Guild, should not have any issue about lending to us with our asset base."

"You are learning very fast, Admiral Gavain," Lady Sophia smiled widely, laughing and clapping her hands. "One will offer an interest-free payment schedule for the value of the land, then, to avoid the need for costly banking loans."

"Then all that remains is to chose the location," James Gavain said.

"Oh, one already knows just the place," Lady Sophia replied.

Admiral James Gavain entered the room, Lady Sophia walking alongside him. The room had been rented in a hotel's large conference centre, the hotel located near the starport on the planet Tahrir's largest city of Tahrcity.

Everyone around the circular table stood as they entered, giving the Praetorian right hand to left breast clenched salute. The new senior staff of the Vindicator Mercenary Corporation had all assembled here in this hotel room, which had been carefully swept for bugs and listening devices. The hotel staff had not been too pleased about the sudden invasion of nearly a hundred armed Marines, who insisted on providing highly visible security, but a word from Lady Sophia to the manager had resolved any issue. Gavain learnt later that she owned the hotel.

"Staff," Admiral Gavain said as he approached the head of the table, "be seated."

They all sat, and he could feel the nervous anticipation in the room. He introduced Lady Sophia to those who did not know her, and then said, "welcome to the first General Meeting of the Vindicator Mercenary Corporation. It would appear we have grown so large we now require one." There was polite laughter around the table.

"To business," he said with typical brusqueness. The lights abruptly dimmed, and a large holoprojection kicked into life, centred on the middle of the table. It showed the new organisational structure.

"First, congratulations to Commodore Harley Andersson on being made Associate Director of the Corporation. The Commodore will be the senior commanding officer in charge of the new Base Tahrir, which I will cover in a moment. Congratulations are also due to Jonathan O'Connor, promoted to Captain, Julia Kavanagh, promoted to Commander, Wolfgang Meier, my former senior tactical officer, promoted to Lieutenant-Commander, and Ulrik Andryukhin, promoted to Lieutenant-General and command of the entire Marine forces."

There was a polite round of applause. "Captain O'Connor takes command of the vacancy aboard the star-carrier *Quintessential*, Lieutenant-Commander Meier has the *Kinslayer*, and Commander Kavanagh takes the *Sorceror* strikecruiser." His eyes tracked to Major Andryukhin. His displeasure at the prospect of being separated from Julia was plain to see, but they were both also very pleased at their new positions, he knew.

James Gavain stared out at the people assembled around him, seeing both faces old and new, mostly new he reflected. They would have to be welded into a new unit, and fast. "In terms of operations, the plan is this. The *Solace*, *Apollo* and *Kinslayer* all require repair, not including our supporting ships. The remaining ships-of-the-line will jump to this uninhabited system –" a starmap suddenly appeared, showing the location they were to jump to " – for two weeks of intensive training. We need to become accustomed to working together, people. When we're not fighting, or travelling to a fight, we will be training, so get used to the idea. In two weeks time we will take on our first contract as a new squadron, which will be covered after the intel briefing. The three cargo-freighters, once they are emptied, the frigate and the *Solace* will take on convoy contracts for the immediate future, and provide us with a regular income, which will hopefully fund Base Tahrir."

The map changed, and a representation of the planet Tahrir appeared, revolving slowly in real-time. It became overlaid with digital markers, highlighting the major cities and points of interest. The planet suddenly zoomed in, close to the southern hemisphere on the second of the four continents. A mountainous region was revealed, with graphics displaying the heavy all-year round snowfall. It was fairly isolated with the nearest city, which was small by the standards of Tahrir, over seven hundred kilometres away.

"This is where we will construct Base Tahrir," said Admiral Gavain. He went into some of the detail of the construction, the purpose of the base, and what they would accomplish there. He concluded with the comment, "the only possible delays in construction will be our success in taking and completing contracts, to provide the required funds. On that subject, I will pass over to Captain O'Connor, who will provide our intelligence briefing on the current state of the galaxy."

Captain O'Connor stood. Gavain found he quite liked the man, and was aware that Harley Andersson had picked up on his feeling. O'Connor was also very capable; in fact, he was the sort of person Gavain wished he had been assigned instead of Commander De Graaf, back in the days before Dissolution. Jonathan O'Connor had also taken on the mantle of the chief intelligence officer, on Harley's insistence, as he showed some considerable flair for the position.

Gavain also noticed the interest from Lady Sophia. He supposed this part of the briefing would be useful to her, beyond the requirements of her position as Director of the VMC.

The holo-map widened suddenly, becoming a coloured three-dimensional depiction of the colonised galaxy. The changes from the last time Jamie had viewed such a map were startling.

The StarCom Federation had swallowed several independent Houses, and had increased its territory in five waves of attacks and invasions. Their sudden blitzkrieg seemed to have ceased, as they must now be consolidating their holds on the conquered territory. They had expanded rapidly in every direction from the Sol System. The only breaks in their almost even advance from Earth were where they had conducted so-called 'punishment invasions', targeting specific nations which had defied their control of the HPCG and stargate assets. The conclusion was simple; the Federation had the means to continue expansion, although at a slower rate than their initial advance, but considering their aggression against Houses and nations which had not even offered defiance it suggested that their intentions were after all to build a new empire. The StarCom Federation had the largest collection of ex-Praetorian starships in the galaxy, and the considerably vast manufacturing capabilities to make many, many more. There were already a vast number of contracts appearing with the Mercenary Bonding Office targeted either directly or indirectly against the StarCom Federation, and there would probably be many, many more.

Next O'Connor moved on to the three states of Korhonen, Cervantia, and Hausenhof, all of which were big enough to provide the Federation a severe headache if they wanted to intercede, unless they concentrated their fleets, which with current dispersal and tactics looked unlikely. The war between Cervantia and Hausenhof was still raging, and until this week Hausenhof had been making major inroads into Cervantia, despite tacit StarCom aid and assistance. The new Arch-Chancellor Lucija Korhonen had launched her armies at the rear of the Hausenhof line, and their advance had stalled. Cervantia and Korhonen would most likely crush Hausenhof between them, and yet, they did not seem to be working together. There were similarly a vast number of contracts being offered by Cervantia and Hausenhof, although Korhonen appeared significantly uninterested in mercenary support.

Gavain interrupted at this point to mention that the Hausenhof nation through Ambassador Grunehaube had approached him on the matter of a retainer fee, and that they could get very regular work through the former House.

There was all number of minor Houses between the three warring nations, and the location of the new Levitican Union. So far there had been no contracts offered, and Commander Kavanagh took the opportunity to ask Lady Sophia if that would change, to the great laughter of the assembled senior staff. She politely refused to comment, citing conflict of interest. The Levitican Union was huge, was O'Connor's assessment, by its sheer size unlikely to attract the interest of the StarCom Federation juggernaut if it ever reached that far. Much as they were likely to avoid the major nations of Cervantia, Korhonen and Hausenhof, the Levitican Union was simply too big for them to assault without significant and damaging losses.

The map shifted rapidly. The Republic of Varrental was in a similar position as the Levitican Union, large and potentially in the path of any StarCom Federation advance, but also perhaps too big for them to handle. They were suffering heavy piracy on their merchant vessels, consisting of some ex-Praetorian units gone rogue, and were offering a number of contracts to hunt them down. They were on the other side of the Core from the VMC's current location, but if operating in that area, could provide active secondary contracts if needed.

A truce had been called between the Houses of Solomon and Kzarjic, but both were now offering privateering contracts. Both also had a number of ex-Praetorian forces complementing their navies. The outlook was for hostilities to break out again.

In the Mid-Sectors, the nation of Amiens under Archon Jacques Devereux was advancing in its blitzkrieg invasion, perhaps less rapidly than President Nielsen and her StarCom Federation were and on a much smaller scale, but with no less effectiveness or success. A number of Houses were offering very attractive contracts. The OutWorlds Alliance, right on the Boundary and Frontier, whilst also very large seemed to be mostly peaceable and uninterested in war. There was some hope for the future perhaps, after all.

There were a large number of new Houses declaring independence. The Red Empire was truly dead, Gavain reflected. There were shifting trade alliances, mutual defence pacts, and all sorts of treaties being formed constantly. Of note, however, were a couple of the new nations. In the Mid-Sectors, the two Houses of Zhou and Zheng had formed the Zhou-Zheng Compact. They had both instantly taken the opportunity to settle a very old historical score with the independent nation of a single local House, and all were posting frequently on the Mercenary Bonding Office's notice boards.

More amazingly, a relatively unknown General in the armies of a House towards the Boundary had staged a revolution, murdered the majority of its noble family, conducted a purge of the upper classes, and had promptly engaged in a war with a neighbouring House in the space of a few weeks. The nation of the Helvanna Dominion, named after the planet the General had come from, was fighting that and a nascent civil war in his own territory.

Captain O'Connor sat down, and Admiral Gavain continued with a small word of thanks.

"We have accepted not one, but two new contracts," he said. "Hausenhof offered us a retainer fee, which I refused. However, they are keen to continue some form of business relationship with us, so we have accepted an armed convoy contract. Upon repair and emptying of the cargo-freighters, the *Apollo*, *Solace*, and the freighters *Featherlight* and *Deliverance* will join Hausenhof convoys, escorting and carrying supplies to their front-line.

"The remainder of us will be training for a very specific mission. The contract is on behalf of the Amiens. The Archon Devereaux was advertising for a number of mercenary units to take on an assault in his name - they have been bogged down in the system of Petersburg, and are in danger of losing the entire flank against the House of Ilyvan. Whilst Amiens have diverted away from Ilyvan territory, if they lose the system or even become committed they have exposed their fleets forward of this position to counter-attack. Our mission will be to break the deadlock in Petersburg System, assist in conquering it, and hold in concert with Amiens forces for a further period of two weeks until they have stabilised the system.

"Amiens wanted a number of merc units to support their action in the Petersburg System. I have spoken to their Ambassador here, and with the new size and strength of the Vindicator Mercenary Corporation, we can take on the whole contract. The pay-off will in total be two hundred and twenty million Imperial Crowns."

There was silence in the conference room as everyone swallowed the large value of the contract.

"There will be bonus pay-outs dependent on our effectiveness in the system. Strategy and tactics are to be of our own devising; Amiens will furnish us with accurate dispositions of the Ilyvan forces before we jump in. Our own aim, people, will be to maximise the pay-out by destroying as much of the Ilyvan defences as possible. There could be another hundred million Imperial Crowns on top of the initial payment depending on our performance. This is a very ambitious contract for us to take, but we are capable of completing it successfully.

Let me explain the plan."

*

Silus Adare pushed off from the wall, sweat droplets flying out from his body. He was alone in the zero-gravity swim room of one of the *Thor's Hammers* gymnasiums, and had turned the heat up to almost unbearable levels to make his work-out even more strenuous. Specialised particles had been released into the air to create resistance, making it difficult for him to swim against them. His implants told him that his heart-rate was up above normal levels, and his muscles were suffering oxygen deprivation. More implants had kicked in to ensure that he could continue to function.

It was the only place he could be truly alone, he had discovered. His two bodyguards, Dum and Dee as he had nicknamed them, would not enter the zero-g swim room in those conditions. They remained outside the room, content merely to watch him through the clear reinforced windows.

Special Agent La Rue and the two marines were a constant reminder that despite his position in the StarCom Federation, his loyalties were not trusted. It was wise of them, he knew, as he had no loyalty to the Federation. He resented his enforced servitude to their cause, such as it was. He also knew there was no alternative for him but to play the cards fate had dealt him.

He thought of escape sometimes, but there was nowhere to escape to. The only escape he could ever have was in here, and that made him angry.

He slammed into the wall opposite, brought his legs around, and kicked off again.

Admiral Haas remained in command of 2nd Main Squadron, 3rd Fleet, but Agent La Rue had informed him that High Command had seriously considered removing him following the disaster at the Janus Shipyards. It rankled considerably that he obtained more of his information through Special Agent La Rue than he did through the normal chain-of-command.

Slam, contact, kick and push, reach and pull, and he was flying off again in a new direction.

Adare had lost one of his ships at the Janus Debacle. He had lost ships before, although not often. He blamed the Admiral of 2nd Main Squadron, although apparently his own actions at the Shipyard had been recognised by High Command. Agent La Rue had informed Adare that he was being considered for promotion.

Slam, contact, kick and push, reach and pull.

He did not care for promotion. He did not want a career with the StarCom Federation. He would take the first opportunity to leave, if such an opportunity ever presented itself. He doubted it greatly, however. His eyes tracked downwards. Dum had his back to the window, but Dee was watching his movements avidly.

Slam, contact - but he did not kick, hands grasping suddenly for the railing that ran around the gym. The door had cycled open below him, and someone was entering. Dum and Dee were both suddenly watching, but as the door cycled shut, they seemed to assess the person entering and lost interest.

"Admiral Adare," the man called up. "Would you mind if I joined you?"

"Whatever you wish," Adare shrugged, and then kicked off. He had no interest in any further conversation.

Marine Lieutenant-Colonel Iyan Lamans climbed up to a level equal to Adare's and then he kicked away from the wall.

For a couple of lengths they crossed each other, roughly in the middle of the swim room. Adare paid little attention. The Lieutenant-Colonel and he had formed an adequate working relationship, but so far the Marines on the *Thor's Hammer* had seen little action so Adare had nothing to judge Lamans on. He knew the Lieutenant-Colonel's service record, but Adare preferred to make his own assessments on his crew.

"This was the only way we could have a private conversation," Lamans suddenly said as they swept past each other.

Adare heard the words, and continued to swim without any outwards reaction. Dum and Dee were not really paying that much attention at all.

The next time they swam past each other, both going much slower, Adare said, "What do you wish to have a private conversation about?"

"Not everybody aboard the *Thor's Hammer* wants to serve the StarCom Federation - there are more of us than you think," Lt-Colonel Lamans replied.

Adare thought quickly in the next break before they crossed each other's paths again. This could so easily be a trap, he thought. It could be a set-up by Special Agent La Rue. Then again, such a set-up was so unnecessary - she knew his exact thoughts on his position, he knew.

"How can I know I can trust you?" Adare asked.

"You can't."

"So what do you want from me?" Adare replied.

"Nothing yet. Just to let you know that there are some of us who have no loyalty to the Federation." On the next pass-by, Lamans continued, "If you ever want to do something about it, there are those of us willing to stand by you, and who will assist in whatever you decide to do about it."

"How many of you?"

"Enough."

"Why come to me?"

"You're obviously not trusted because of your loyalty to the last Emperor."

Adare was out of speaking range, so on his return he said, "You supported the first Emperor, me the second. Why would you trust in me?"

"The old Empire is dead. We would seem to be in the same boat, Silus Adare. I have no desire to serve the StarCom Federation. Whatever one's views on the Emperors, they were better than President Nielsen."

"So why did you join?" Adare asked.

A minute or two later, when the head of the marines on-board had swam back in hearing range, Lamans said, "Commodore Pacheco and

Commander Sahin both wished to join. Pacheco has many contacts in StarCom. There were more staff who wished to join the Federation than not, and I did not see any alternative. If I had spoken out, I would have ended up in the Saturnian moon prisons. And out of an airlock, most likely."

"Yes," Adare thought back to the scene he had witnessed on his prison-moon.

"Commander Sahin is with us now," Lamans continued. "She hated what we did to Exeter Alpha. It was the reason many of us turned against the False Emperor. She knows you were under orders to obliterate the city. It spoke too much of the old Emperor's style. Sahin is not the only one, either."

Adare felt it best not to say that he had not felt any regret or apprehension at ordering the city's destruction. There may well be an opportunity here to gain some support, should he ever decide to move against the StarCom Federation.

"Where do we go from here?" he asked when he was able to.

"For now, nowhere, we gain more support," Lt-Col Lamans said. "And wait for an opportunity."

"An opportunity to do what?"

"Leave the StarCom Federation, of course," Lt-Col Lamans said. "Or did you want to carry on serving them, Admiral?"

"Of course not." Adare snorted.

"And everyone knows it," Lamans nodded as he swam past. "This is why we've come to you, Admiral."

Chapter XIV

President Rebeccah Nielsen was relaxing in her own private chambers. Technically, the entire Palace of Communications on Earth belonged to her, as did the entire StarCom Federation. The newly-christened Presidential Chambers had been renovated and re-made to her precise instructions.

Occupying the top floor of the central spire, it was incredibly spacious. She lived in a luxury that many in the galaxy could only dream of. Her portrait hung from the walls, of a size equal to the new statues displaying the symbol of the StarCom Federation. The statues were made of pure silver with solid blocks of gold running through them depicting the planet Earth, a laurel wreath around the globe. The Red Eagle of the Imperium had long since been disposed of.

The roof of the part of the chamber she sat in was open, but as a precaution against any assassins, a force field flickered along the sky occasionally. The chamber was nicknamed the gardens, but in reality it consisted of a swimming pool the size of a football pitch, with clear, specially filtered water rippling in a simulated breeze. The entire chamber was heated and lightened with artificial sun, this being the winter season on the Earth continent the Palace of Communications was located on.

She was draped out on a suspended lounger, wearing a light-weight but astoundingly expensive swimming costume. As the galaxy burned in her name, two well-muscled, blond, mostly naked men fed her food and saw to her every need. It was no accident there were a number of bed-chambers leading off the gardens.

Above the swimming pool, a holographic map rotated. It showed the new boundaries of the StarCom Federation, and was replete with digital graphics providing real-time information of minerals being mined, money flowing across the systems, population increases and decreases, and all manner of other statistics she viewed as important. Her new StarCom Federation was growing rapidly, and she would see the galaxy bend its knee to her. In the space of a couple of months, the blitzkrieg the Commander-In-Chief Jaiden Ryan had overseen in her name had sent the armies and navies of StarCom out across the galaxy, and brought more and more territory under her control.

The nine invasion waves of Operation Fortress had come to an end, and C-i-C Ryan was pressurising her to take her time and consolidate the gains they had already made. Jaiden Ryan had overseen one of the most successful large-scale military operations in history, perhaps on a par with the Battle of Mars. However, she felt the hunger, the growing power she craved. The Houses newly freed from the yoke of the Emperors and their

Imperium were forming their own nations rapidly. Each was reliant on her stargates for long-distance interstellar travel, and definitely on her Hyperpulse Communications Generators to conduct all communications, whether it be personal or matters of state. Without the HPCGs, the Interstellar Merchant Guild would be handicapped, and the economies of these new states would fail rapidly.

Still, the ones that defied her stuck in her craw. She would never, ever accept such defiance.

She suddenly heard footsteps on the marble flooring. Her eyes narrowed in anger.

"I did not want to be disturbed!" she snapped.

"My apologies, President," came the voice she instantly recognised as belonging to Malika Chbihi. "This is a matter of some urgency, however."

"Go," Rebeccah Nielsen dismissed the two male servants. They hurried from the gardens, and in short order she was alone with her spy chief. She swung her legs off the lounger and sat up, draping a towel across her shoulders before standing and walking across to a small table where a jug of iced orange juice resided.

"Malika," she addressed her dark-skinned spy chief, "you have never interrupted me before without reason. This must be important. I hope you are not about to spoil my very good mood."

"Sadly, I am, my President," the Director of the StarCom Central Intelligence Department said. "You recall that we have recently penetrated the upper echelons of the OutWorlds Alliance military?"

"Ah, yes," said President Nielsen. "This is the so-called First Lord Yassin Al-Zuhairi's fiefdom, out on the Boundary and the Frontier. It's a fairly large state, but much too distant for me to be interested in. You recall my comments on your report, I presume?"

Malika Chbihi ignored the unsubtle rebuke. "You may suddenly be interested in the OutWorlds Alliance, President. My operatives are telling me that their military have begun moving into certain positions."

"They are preparing to launch an assault on a neighbouring house or territory, then?" President Nielsen asked. "Such a thing is very commonplace nowadays, it seems. The galaxy is at war, if you had not noticed."

"Not in this instance, President. My analysts, and Commander-In-Chief Ryan's, agree on the assessment. There can be no doubt as to their intention. They are preparing to seize all of the HPCG stations and stargates in their territory."

President Nielsen slammed her glass of orange juice down onto the table. "How dare Yassin do this!" she roared. "There can be no doubt?"

"No doubt," Director Chbihi averted her eyes.

Nielsen ranted, "Do they learn nothing? Have they not seen what I have done to those nations that defy me? I warned all of them that to seize StarCom assets was to be taken as an act of war."

"Many of the nations that stole our assets initially have either returned them, or fallen to our invasion forces, or been assassinated. My assessment of the situation," Director Chbihi said, "Is that First Lord Al-Zuhairi feels safe in taking this course of action. The OutWorlds Alliance lies on the very Frontier, so they are remote enough that we cannot possibly provide any military action against him beyond a long-range strike. Commander-In-Chief Ryan suggests this is not practicable, considering the current consolidation of gains in Operation Fortress."

"Ryan needs to learn his place, and become more daring," Nielsen snapped. "This is intolerable. Put the stations on high alert, and authorise the use of Armageddon Codes as soon as we see any sign of hostile action from the OutWorlds Alliance."

Director Chbihi suddenly tensed. A cyborg, she was currently jacked in to the Palace's isolated datasphere. She looked up slowly. "I am sorry, President Nielsen. It is too late. The StarCom News Media are already carrying reports that the OutWorlds Alliance has begun to strike against our assets."

Without saying a word, Nielsen jacked into the datasphere. As the swirl of data swallowed her mind whole, she dialled directly into the StarCom News Media central core. The news reports coming in showed stargates surrounded by OWA special forces, HPCGs exploding as they came under assault. SCNM broadcasters and journalists were being arrested, and reports were already dying out as the OWA fell under a blanket of silence.

"I will deal with Al-Zuhairi, if Commander-In-Chief Ryan and your intelligence services cannot," President Nielsen ground out, knuckles turning white where she gripped the edge of the table.

The two servants re-entered the gardens, and crossed silently to President Nielsen's side at the pool. Director Chbihi had left, and after a short while, they had been summoned back by the President.

She was obviously still angry, but somewhat calmer. Both of the servants knelt to either side of her.

The first one opened his mouth to speak, to ask what she desired, but the second one suddenly held up his hand in front of the first servant's face. There was a flash, and the almost-naked male froze in place, eyes wide open, unblinking.

President Nielsen was not concerned at all, having become used to seeing this sort of thing, although she was still a little surprised.

The second servant's form shifted, the bones crunching out of place, eye colour changing, size and shape becoming something other. In a matter of moments, the Faceless was revealed in its all-black ensemble, crouching by her side. It was completely genderless, even featureless, nothing but black oily skin shining in the artificial light, with no eyes, no distinguishing marks, a mouth that only appeared when it spoke.

"You've been quicker in responding than normal," President Nielsen said.

"We expected you to contact the intermediary," the Faceless said. "I was on hand."

Nielsen just nodded, sitting back up. The Faceless stood over her, and she felt the need to get to her own feet. She had sent a message to a back-door program in the datasphere. It connected to a person, she knew, although she had no idea who that intermediary was. The person carried the message out of the Palace of Communications, linking back into the general planetary datasphere to transmit it onwards, probably through any number of cut-outs and diversions, to the Faceless. At least that was what she had been told, and she very much doubted that was even the entirety of the truth of the small part she had been informed of. Such a data transfer, even through a person, was supposed to be impossible through the security systems of the Palace. Then again, the Faceless were masters at the impossible.

"Why did you expect it?" she asked.

"The Faceless have always kept abreast of events in the galaxy," said the thing. "We know what happens, everywhere. We suspected your likely reaction to the OutWorlds Alliance seizure of StarCom assets."

"I have only just been informed by my own Director of intelligence," Nielsen protested. "How could you know?"

"We are the Faceless."

President Nielsen exhaled heavily. "It is of no matter. You are correct, of course. I want Yassin Al-Zuhairi assassinated, publicly. Very, very publicly. The message is to be - do not defy the StarCom Federation."

"It is understood, President Nielsen. We have prepared." The voice was strangely child-like, almost angelic, and all the more chilling for what it said in such a tone. "Yassin Al-Zuhairi can be dead in ten days time." The thing then told her the contract cost.

"That is extortionate," she exclaimed.

"Al-Zuhairi is extremely well-prepared," the thing said.

"Very well. It will be paid," said Nielsen. "How could you prepare a cost so quickly, and plan everything?"

"The Faceless do not tend to inform customers of our methods," the thing said. "However, we wish it to be known to you that we prepare for all eventualities, and all contracts, based on a probability calculated from extrapolation of real-time political events, both macro and micro."

President Nielsen blinked rapidly as she assessed what had been said to her. "Was that a threat? Are you saying that you have such a plan for me?"

"That is why you pay us an insurance premium to prevent us completing a contract against you, President Nielsen," the Faceless said. She was uncomfortably aware that she was stood facing an assassin who could kill her in an eye-blink. "Such are the dangers of employing assassins. When you bring the Faceless into play you adjust the rules, and allow your enemies permission to employ the same tactics."

The Faceless began to morph back into the male serving figure it had assumed before. The other manservant began to stir. As it morphed, with eye-stretching and mind-bending contortions, it spoke one final time.

"You have enemies, President Nielsen, and we have made our plans should your insurance payments prove to be ... unprofitable."

Suddenly President Nielsen felt scared, for the first time since the revolution.

Commander-In-Chief Jaiden Ryan entered the President's Golden Room, the meeting place where the leaders and the main players of the StarCom Federation assembled to discuss the plans of the nation. By now, news of the President's fury had spread throughout the Palace, and he did not view the summons as something necessarily positive considering the day's events.

He was all the more disconcerted to see the Vice-President Pereyra leaving as he entered, a shadowed look in her eyes. As Giovanna Pereyra passed by him, she refused to meet his questioning gaze.

The doors shut behind him, and he walked up to his usual place at the table. The room was darkened, the main light coming from the holoprojection in the centre of the room. President Nielsen sat at the head of the table, a stern look on her face, resplendent in her robes of office. The droid that carried her staff of office hovered behind her, the pure gold long-handled sceptre topped with the symbol of the SCF above a cross-piece panel emblazoned with her name.

"President Nielsen," said Commander-In-Chief Ryan. "You summoned me?"

"Yes," she said. "Sit."

He did as he was commanded, eyes taking in the holo-map displayed by the projector. As with all holo-maps, it projected its image directly into his eyes, an optical illusion making every observer think that it actually hovered in the centre of the room.

He recognised the strategic map, primarily because it had been drawn up in his office with his advisors. The StarCom Federation lay in the centre of it. It showed the future dispositions of his armed forces, in preparation for the next waves of leap-frogging invasions that would further expand the borders of the Federation. It had been drawn up over a number of painstaking days and weeks, and made a number of assumptions about the state of their already-conquered territory, and their targets defences and positions.

It was codenamed Operation Storm, and it was every bit as ambitious as Operation Fortress. He had some misgivings about it, but the orders from President Nielsen had been clear. The overall strategy was much the same as before, consisting of a number of waves that would progressively expand further out into the galaxy and take a large percentage of the Core of the colonised galaxy. He was limited by his own forces however, and the damage they had sustained during Operation Fortress, so whereas Fortress had been a blanket, almost-even levelled expansion, Storm expanded out in four directions, and then swept in curves to isolate whole houses in salients. Director Chbihi and Vice-President Pereyra had made a number of deals with certain territories, allowing them to be ignored - whole regions as space, such as Cervantia, Korhonen and Hausenhof, would not be in the path of the invasion.

"Jaiden Ryan," President Nielsen continued. "You have done a very impressive job. But I must require more of you. I want Operation Storm launched immediately."

Ryan blinked. There was a long, drawn-out silence between them.

"President Nielsen," he said, "When you say immediately -"

"Now," Nielsen said.

"That is just not possible, or wise if I may be so bold," Ryan said. "Our forces are not in their correct staging areas. Whilst we could move the main offensive elements into position, we would expose ourselves considerably within the territory we have already taken. A number of my ships and land forces are still heavily engaged with resistance elements, particularly further out towards our borders -"

"But we have the situations under control within our conquered territory," Nielsen said.

"In the main, yes, but -"

"Then how long will it take to move the fleets to the Operation Storm staging areas?" President Nielsen asked.

Ryan sighed and leant forwards, jacking into the local data-core to manipulate the map and plans, overlaying current positions and calculating the period of time. While he worked, he said, "At the moment, we could completely one hundred per cent pacify the conquered systems within the two month window we allowed between Operations Fortress and Storm. By launching Operation Storm now, we extend that pacification period to between six months and a year on current estimations, and of course increase our own casualties exponentially and reduce our own effectiveness overall and in the long-term."

"That is acceptable to me," said President Nielsen. "I will repeat my question only once, Commander-In-Chief. How long will it be until you can have my ships in the Operation Storm staging areas?"

"Fifteen days until they are all in position and ready to go, assuming we have clean disengagements from current operating theatres," said Ryan.

President Nielsen smiled darkly. "Excellent, Jaiden - make it so. Sixteen days from now, we launch Operation Storm."

Jaiden Ryan sighed heavily. "President, please, if I may. The Federal Guard can be bolstered with the first elements of the new 9th Fleet we are building, and those few ex-Praetorian ships that have joined us and the conquered house units that have defected. We limit our future operations by launching Storm too early. We will also face heavier resistance during Operation Storm. The fleets need time to recuperate. We will also begin stretching our supply lines before we have the infrastructure in place to support extended ops. I would strongly counsel against this."

"Your objections are noted, Commander-In-Chief. But this can, and will, be done. I will have no more from you. You have your orders, now see to them. You are dismissed, Jaiden."

He could see she would brook no more argument. He stood, bowed, and then turned and walked towards the door stiff-backed.

His forces could do this, he knew, but they would severely damage their capabilities in the future. They would also begin coming up against ex-Praetorian ships, not House army vessels, and that would increase losses.

He would not compare her to a great leader, he thought to himself, but the historical precedents were there. Napoleon over-reached himself going into Russia. Hitler did the same. The English Empire grew too large to operate. The American nation over-reached itself with the Asian wars. The dictator Perepolous did much the same when he faced the father of the first Emperor.

The parallels were there with history, and President Nielsen was beginning to resemble Napoleon, Hitler, and Perepolous more than he cared for.

*

Lady Sophia stood on the observation balcony of the low-flying shuttle. It skimmed at a safe height above the agricultural fields of Tahrir. The managing director of one of her companies was explaining in excruciating boring detail about the new techniques they were employing to increase yield.

Four starfighters kept level with the slow-moving shuttle, engines straining at what to them was relatively low speed. In the modern galaxy, nowhere was safe, she reflected. As the colonies of man tore themselves apart, she could not even go on a tour of her own planet without an armed escort. She had almost been safer as a prisoner of the False Emperor, and certainly had more freedom.

"My lady," one of her attendants called her attention. The managing director, who also had a boring, monotonous single-toned voice, stopped speaking at the interruption.

"Yes, Sarah?" she asked.

"A Priority Alpha message has been received at the HPCG station in Tahrcity," the attendant Sarah said. "They have re-routed it here for you."

"Thank you, Sarah. One's excuses, but a Priority Alpha must be important," she said with no small amount of relief to the balding managing director. She listened patiently to his polite but disappointed protestations that it was not an issue, and then retired to the communications suite on the shuttle to take the message.

The room was sealed to ensure her privacy, and when satisfied she was secure, she keyed in a personal code and followed the various security procedures installed in the hardware. A display informed her that the message was a simple one-way recording, with an origination from the city Savrecik, on the planet Zupanica.

A message from the capital of House Zupanic could only mean one thing. The Lord Principal Ramicek was reigning on the planet Leviticus, and only Lord Micalek could wish to contact her. Despite herself, her heartbeat increased slightly.

She activated the recording, and a holographic image of Lord Micalek Zupanic sprang into being. It was full-size, and it was as if he were in the room.

"Lady Sophia," he began, "I hope this message finds you well, and that you have had a safe and uneventful journey back to the Blackheath System and Tahrir. I have sent a separate message to your father, Lord Erik, but wished to record a personal one for yourself.

"Mine own father, our new Lord Principal, has directed me to proceed with the marriage between myself and you as soon as possible. It was in the terms of the secret agreement between our two great houses. We must announce our marriage immediately; however, let me assure you that I have insisted to my father that this is something we do together.

"I must also admit, I also wish to spend some time with my new wife to be. After all, we do not really know each other. I have a few minor matters to attend to here, delegation of my responsibilities mostly, and then I will immediately leave for the Blackheath System if you agree to it? I could be with you within the week, as we will only be recharging once. We can make the announcement to the Levitican Union together, hand in hand, if that pleases you? Please let me know your thoughts before I depart.

"I look forward to seeing you, Lady Sophia, and hope you agree with my reasoning. I would plan to stay with you for some months before I have to return, all being well. All the best to you, my Lady, and awaiting your gracious response." He nodded, and the image winked out.

Lady Sophia leaned back in her chair. It was all happening so fast. She took a couple of minutes to compose herself, and then not without some excitement, leaned forwards to activate the cameras for her return message.

She told him to come to Tahrir.

*

The *Vindicator* translated back into realspace, exiting its hyperspace jump and flowing through the terminus point smoothly. The automated defence systems bristling within the system read its IFF signatures, and deactivated. The *Vindicator* was expected.

The battlecruiser coasted away from the designated jump zone, gliding in towards the starbase. It was still showing signs of damage, although there were signs of repair all over its outer hull, and indeed there were still repair barges flitting around its skin. It had been captured in the Amiens assault on this system.

The *Vindicator* cruised to a stop, and held position.

James Gavain sat in his private ready room, waiting for comms Lieutenant Forrest to confirm across the datasphere that connection with the starbase had been made. Eventually, she said, <Connection established, Admiral.>

He activated the channel, and before his eyes, a holographic image of a tall man, also seated behind a desk, appeared in the middle of the ready room.

"I am Admiral D'Souza," the man introduced himself with a sharp nod. He had sharp features, a large, blunt nose, and piercing eyes. He wore a dark grey uniform, and a full military cap of outrageous proportions. House military uniform varied widely, in colour, style and cut, the galaxy over.

Gavain straightened his own uniform. It was still in Praetorian black and red colours, but now over the left breast and on the right shoulder it carried the label 'VMC', with *Vindicator* written underneath. Across his back a large black 'V' had been stitched into the uniform, to further differentiate it from Praetorian uniform - but otherwise it was the same. His own short-brimmed flat cap lay on the desk before him. "Admiral Gavain," he introduced himself in turn.

"You're younger than I thought," D'Souza said. It was possible to see the doubt in his eyes. "Where is the rest of your fleet of ships?" he asked. "We were expecting many more than just the *Vindicator*."

"Moving into position," Admiral Gavain replied.

D'Souza waited, and when it became apparent he was going to get no more than that, he continued, "Well, that's your concern, I'm sure, but next time please make sure we're kept up to date on what is coming in and out-system, Admiral."

"Yes," was Gavain's only comment. In truth, his units were still training together, although they would shortly be jumping by stargate to an uninhabited system within a half-jump of House Ilyvan and the target system of Petersburg. The training appeared to be progressing well, and although there was still much more to do, he was pleased at how well his senior staff were operating together.

"Are you still on target for the start-date of your contract?" asked Admiral D'Souza.

"We are," Gavain nodded. "Do you have the intel?"

"Certainly," Admiral D'Souza confirmed. He signalled to someone off-camera. "We're transmitting it now. Essentially, the situation in the Petersburg System is unchanged. Five inhabited planets, two in the same region of space, three in another. We have captured two of the five; at the other end of the system and on the other side of the sun, we are having difficulty however. It has ground down into a stalemate. We have a planet each, and fight over the one in the middle. Our navies can no longer engage each other, and ground forces are locked in tight. I cannot divert Amiens forces to the system, and indeed, I need those ground forces on Peters IV released from action as soon as possible."

"All of this is understood," said Admiral Gavain. "The stalemate on Peters IV and Peters III will be over four days from now, Admiral D'Souza."

"I certainly hope so," said D'Souza. "You realise that is of utmost importance that the enemy naval forces do not escape? They have been using the Petersburg System to sporadically jump out and raid our supply lines to the front? We cannot have them loose behind our lines."

"They will not escape, Admiral."

"It was not a condition of your contract, but –"

"- it was one of the bonusable payments," Admiral Gavain continued. "My plan allows for this."

"Will you share those plans with me?"

"No," Admiral Gavain shook his head. "Operational Security, Admiral, I am sure you understand."

"I do have five ships-of-the-line around Peters IV and III, and another two on Peters IX and X," Admiral D'Souza pressed. "We can assist you if it is required. As much as mercenaries are disposable, I would rather the objectives were met successfully, Admiral."

"We will achieve the objectives. Thank you for the information,

Admiral D'Souza. Gavain out."

*

First Lord Yassin Al-Zuhairi raised his hand into the air, and waved at the assembled crowds. Local enforcers and some of the OutWorlds Alliance soldiery were holding them back at the force-field barrier, tens of thousands facing the long parade ground. Beyond it lay the high walls of the Great Citadel.

As the crowd roared approval, he turned and looked at his wife with love in his eyes. It was all carefully captured by the holo-cameras. The StarCom News Media, so prevalent across the galaxy, was not allowed anywhere within OutWorlds Alliance territory. First Lord Al-Zuhairi had made sure of that when he took the stargates and the HPCG stations. Every trace of the StarCom Federation was being eradicated within the borders of his frontier-nation.

He and his wife smiled for the holo-cameras, before beginning their walk across the parade ground. The huge walls of the Great Citadel, the seat of government and also the palace of House Al-Zuhairi, were lined with row upon row of gigantic battlewalkers.

The local house-produced battlewalkers stood at the back, huge and imposing. A-Zu Industries had produced most of them, but there a number manufactured by the neutral inter-galactic corporations that had made a fortune selling them to the houses.

In front of them, stood the ex-Praetorian battlewalkers. The OutWorlds Alliance had been successful in attracting many of the Praetorian Guard who had been dispossessed following the Dissolution Order. They were painted in OutWorlds Alliance colours, the dusty-orange yellow that also matched the general landscape of the capital planet Zaharra.

First Lord Yassin Al-Zuhairi and his retinue walked along the line of ex-Praetorian battlewalkers, the vicious war machines that ruled the planetary battlefield. It was all carefully stage-managed, the images and the entire event today intended to portray the new-found power of the OutWorlds Alliance, its defiance of the events sweeping the galaxy and the aggression of the StarCom Federation following the seizure of its assets.

First Lord Al-Zuhairi looked up at the imposing shapes of the battlewalkers as they passed them. There were a number of different models. At the appropriate place, he stopped at the foot of a gigantic twelve-metre tall Imp-XXXI *Executioner*. At rest, the Super-Heavy Assault-class battlewalker resembled a giant, the cockpit hidden behind heavy armour plating, the shoulders rising up above the point where a head would have been on a humanoid. The power sword blade extending from its left arm reached almost to the floor, the metal inert and unenergised.

The huge double-barrel of the twin-magnetic acceleration cannon on its right arm pointed down towards the ground on the other side.

He turned towards the cameras following them, placing an arm around his wife. This was one of the important shots in the carefully choreographed display, he knew, a shot that would be produced as a still in future propaganda and in recruitment posters.

The battlewalker behind him suddenly moved. It had been running its engines on cold, but with a noisy hum they suddenly activated. Actuators whirred as the arms came up, and lights flashed all across its chest.

Yassin Al-Zuhairi turned and looked round in surprise, wondering what was happening. His eyes opened wide as he saw the twin-cannons on the machine's right arms swivelling to point down at him, his wife, and their retinue. There was a growing hum, rings of light and deep blue sparks inside each dark, deadly barrel.

The loudspeakers on the vehicle activated. "In the name of the StarCom Federation," blasted out across the parade ground, "seizure of StarCom assets is an act of aggression, and will be punished."

The twin cannons, designed to propel metal slugs into enemy battlewalkers and break through siege-walls, clunked and loaded. Yassin Al-Zuhairi was releasing his wife just as they fired at ridiculously short range, the projectiles flashing across the short distance to plough with earth-shaking force into the hardened metacrete of the parade ground.

Chief Amab Al-Zuhairi had a hand over his mouth, stroking his short grey beard as he calmly walked through the corridor deep inside the Great Citadel. He approached the door with the power-armoured and very alert OutWorlds Alliance soldiers stood outside. He gave the password, submitted his personal code into a reader, and passed the DNA-sampling. He was allowed entrance into the private chambers of the First Lord.

"What news?" First Lord Yassin Al-Zuhairi demanded of his uncle. His wife was in tears, surrounded by some of his daughters and his sons. Other members of the large Al-Zuhairi clan were arranged around the room, some with angry looks on their faces, some with surprise.

"The assassin has escaped," Amab said. A number of the family members shouted and roared at him, and eventually he had to hold his hands up for silence. "The smoke grenades discharged by the battlewalker covered his escape. We found two of the three crew inside the battlewalker dead - we assumed it was the commander of the walker who pulled the triggers. We raided his quarters five minutes ago - the commander is dead. Whoever was in that battlewalker, was an imposter."

Yassin strode up to Amab, and placed a hand around the back of his neck. "Uncle," he said, "where did the assassin go?"

"Deep scans have shown us that he transformed in the smoke caused by the grenades," Amab said quietly. "He became one of the soldiers on patrol at the feet of the battlewalkers, and then slipped away in the confusion."

"Transformed?" Yassin asked, and then suddenly his confusion cleared. "The Faceless," he whispered.

"We believe it was a Faceless assassin," Amab confirmed.

"President Nielsen and the StarCom Federation go too far!" Yassin Al-Zuhairi snapped. He clenched his fists angrily. "What of my double and my wife's double? Were there any survivors at all?"

Amab shook his head. "The cannons are battlefield artillery weapons," he said gently. "There were no survivors, none at all, Yassin. We cannot even identify body parts, they were liquefied in the impact of the projectiles."

"Those doubles were virtually a part of my family," Yassin ground out. "They may as well have killed me for the pain they have caused me."

"I know, Yassin," Amab said gently. As Chief of the Al-Zuhairi intelligence services, he had been the person who had first suggested the creation and grooming of the two doubles, over thirty years ago. "We have of course stopped the images going out across the galaxy, but someone defied the edict. The Faceless, or StarCom agents, must have had their own cameras in the crowd. It hit interstellar news about thirty minutes ago."

Yassin slammed a fist into his other hand. "In that case, we cannot hide here in the Citadel any longer," he said. "We must put the lie to our deaths."

"I agree," Amab said. "But remember that the damage is done. As far as the galaxy is concerned, the StarCom Federation has struck at the heart of the OutWorlds Alliance, with impunity. This is a public relations disaster, and has cost us much honour."

"Then we strike back," said Al-Zuhairi.

"How?" Chief Amab asked. "We are on the frontier, and they lie many, many, many light-years away at the core."

"The way they struck at me," said the First Lord. He looked deep into Chief Amab's eyes. "Uncle, find me the Faceless. President Nielsen will learn that those who use assassins, can be killed by assassins."

Chapter XV

The *Thor's Hammer* dreadnought coasted gently in space, one of many StarCom Federation starships currently in the Emriss System. Emriss had been part of House Alsopp, one of eight systems which had been struck by elements of the Third Fleet in the first wave of Operation Storm. Every system in House Alsopp had fallen under the shadow of StarCom.

The *Thor's Hammer* fired one precise blast down towards the planet surface, in support of its ground forces. The Marines had landed over an hour ago, and occasionally they called in for orbital support.

"Another superb, flawless action on your part, Admiral," Special Agent Caterina La Rue said. She stood by his side, his two bodyguards at rest behind her.

Admiral Adare shrugged. "This has been too easy," he said, "they did not have any real chance of resisting. How was it done?" he asked.

"How was what done?" La Rue countered.

"The introduction of the data-viruses into the intra-system datasphere, and the complete debilitation of all House military forces," Admiral Adare said. He watched a real-time visual of the planet Emriss Beta, a super-hot world whose surface burned in continent-wide fire storms wherever it faced the sun. The cities on Emriss Beta actually moved at a slow crawl, to keep them permanently in the dark side of the planet.

His entire squadron had jumped into the system at multiple points, having been told to expect light resistance, but not having been informed as to why. House Alsopp was hardly an easy house to assault, and Emriss was known to be a virtual fortress of a system.

When they had emerged into the solar system, every single automated drone, gunship, starbase and naval ship had been completely deactivated, fully dead in the water. The planetary defences were down. The enemy had no communications capability whatsoever. Damage to enemy naval assets was kept to a minimum, the StarCom Federation intending to capture as many of the enemy ships as possible. Adare still had his Marines engaged in heavy boarding actions amongst those ships seen as desirable, whilst military transporters had jumped in-system to disgorge vast amounts of landing forces.

It was the most surreal battle he had ever engaged in, and in practice, was beginning to amount to little more than a brutal slaughter.

"What makes you think I would know," Agent La Rue toyed with him. "And are you sure it was a data-virus?"

Adare snorted. "What else could cause the complete collapse of every computer in this forsaken system? What was it, and how was it introduced? Surely someone as highly placed in the CID as you are would be informed."

La Rue was enjoying her superiority, he could tell. She could not resist telling him. "The data-virus is newly engineered, developed by our lab technicians back on Earth. It was based on a combination of Praetorian and StarCom algorithmic code, and was introduced through various back-doors into the House computer system. The same scenes are probably being played out not just across House Alsopp's territory, but in most systems struck by the first wave of Operation Storm."

"What sort of back-door?" Adare pressed. "The penetration of the enemy virtual defences is almost absolute. I have never seen its like before."

La Rue hesitated, then leaned down and whispered in his ear, "We transmitted it through the Hyper-Pulse Communications Generators. The back-door was the very system that supported the infrastructure between the House computer systems, planet-to-planet, in the first place. It took barely seconds to take them down."

Adare raised his eyebrows in surprise, and was silent for a moment whilst he thought.

"Was this wise?" he eventually asked.

"Wise in what way, Admiral?" La Rue replied.

"HPCG stations have never been used in electronic warfare before," he said. "To do such a thing completely undermines the unwritten trust between StarCom and the Houses it serves. Imperial Decree stated that use of HPCGs to disseminate electronic viruses and conduct virtual war would be considered to be on the same level as Weapons of Planetary Destruction and Weapons of Solar Destruction."

"Imperial Decree no longer matters, Admiral."

"What of the trust of the other Houses and their new nations?"

La Rue paused, and he saw that she recognised he had a point, so he pressed it.

"The nations and the Houses out there will not trust our continued control of the HPCGs, not if we use them to assist our invasions. This will guarantee more seizures of your network, not less."

La Rue shrugged, which in itself was unusual for her. "Ours is not to question the StarCom Federation leadership," she said.

Adare suspected that would be the closest he would ever get to an overt criticism of StarCom's tactics from his Special Agent.

*

Lord Minister Luke Towers sighed and leaned forwards, rubbing his eyes, with his elbows on the table. The Council session had lasted most of the day, and the various Lord Ministers of the Levitican Union were returning from their latest fifteen-minute recess. He had spent those fifteen minutes furiously consulting with his advisors.

Every Ministry consisted of a mix of all six Houses in the oligarchy. This led to its own problems, with cultural misunderstandings being just the least of the new rivalries that were springing up amongst their young civil service. As Lord Minister of Military Defence, his 'civil servants' consisted of a mix of the former Solar Administrators and their staff, and senior members of each House military. The antagonism between the two functions was palpable.

Council meetings, held twice a week, were sometimes productive but only in small doses. Every decision made on every motion tabled, or topic debated, were subject to the minutest of scrutiny by every Lord Minister and the Lord Principal. The Levitican Union was making decisions, and were changing things rapidly, but the pace of change was almost as strong as the wills of the various factions to ensure their House did not suffer. The politics was mind-bending.

He almost wished their father had put Lady Sophia into this position. He was a High General, a man of the armies and of the navies, and his baptism in House Towers court politics had not prepared him for this. Sophia was much more of a natural choice for the Council, but he suspected their father's blind prejudice against Sophia had forced him into the wrong decision, and not for the first time either.

He leaned back in his chair, and took the steaming coffee being offered by the servant. The last of the servants were retreating from the Council Chamber, so they could be left to discuss matters in private. The Council Chamber was near the top of the dome of Leviticus Megapolis, and the Megapolis had risen in the waters so that the sun shone through the scant metres of water above them. It created a pleasing, reassuring ripple effect inside the clear-ceilinged chamber room, soothing and enough to make those that were tired even drowsier.

"Session called to order," Lord Principal Ramicek announced, as they were finally left alone again. Everything they were saying was being recorded, for transmission back to their respective homes, and each Lord or Lady in the room was sat in front of a special suite of equipment inlaid into the top of the specially-designed six-sided table, which would allow them to communicate with the advisors and ministers in their various Ministries.

"We proceed onto the subject of the StarCom Federation, and our response," the Lord Principal said. "We have all read Lord Luke's briefing notes, I assume. Lord Minister, if you would like to summarise for us?"

Lord Minister Luke cleared his throat. "The StarCom Federation's latest recommencement of their advance has taken many houses, nations and analysts by surprise. Whilst the reconfiguring of their fleet positions was noted, there were very few signs that they were about to re-start their invasion of the Core. We believe this phase is codenamed Operation Storm. It is a bold and perhaps foolhardy move, stretching their military resources at a time when they have not fully pacified or consolidated the many territorial gains they made during Operation Fortress.

"Notwithstanding this, they have altered tactics. Whereas Operation Fortress consisted of a number of waves, spreading out rapidly and constantly from the Sol System, resulting in an almost even circumference of territory, Operation Storm appears to be much more selective. They are channelling their forces in a number of various directions. Whether they are keeping to the blitzkrieg, leap-frogging wave tactic is yet to be seen, but some of their naval assets have not appeared in this first wave, so my analysts are predicting that we are about to see some variation of their wave tactic, perhaps one specifically focused in the directions they have already taken. We should know within the next couple of days, if and when these missing naval assets began to strike their target systems.

"More concerning is a new weapon that they are employing. We have received intelligence, sourced from House Alsopp territory that indicates StarCom are actually using their HPCG stations to disseminate debilitating data-viruses into local system-wide dataspheres and intranets. Such an act is of course completely heinous, and strikes at the principles of interstellar communication that StarCom was originally developed to protect. The StarCom Federation is something completely different under President Nielsen, so it would appear the sacred covenant between the Houses and StarCom in relation to interstellar communications is now well and truly dead."

He finished speaking, taking a sip of his drink, and the Lord Principal took this opportunity to ask a question. "Have we been able to analyse the source-code of the data-virus?" he asked.

Lord Luke knew that the information had been obtained by his wife, the shadowy Lady Wyn, who appeared to be running the intelligence services for the Levitican Union. The question was more showboating for the Council. "We have," he nodded, "we can probably develop defences, but as we do, StarCom will also enhance the code."

"What is the scale of our risk of susceptibility to these new military viruses?" asked Lord Minister Brin Claes.

"It works by spreading across the data gateways between planetary dataspheres," said Lord Luke. "Introduced by the HPCG stations, its penetration is absolute and almost instantaneous. It has to make the jump into military systems, but judging by its initial success, the viruses are very effective and can penetrate our defences with ease. At the moment.

"The principalities of Towers, Claes, Galetti and Lapointe have differing infrastructures than those of Obamu or Zupanic," he continued. "The gateways themselves are heavily monitored, and have emergency cut-outs that could in a nano-second sever the connections between data-spheres. This has the additional problem that communications suddenly become impeded, although military networks in all but Lapointe would be intact. Obamu and Zupanic have no such cut-offs, being of older, outmoded virtual-software architecture."

"So our risk is considerable," Lady Minister Lapointe said sharply. Monique Lapointe was an intimidating woman, with a direct manner and an icy gaze. "We cannot afford such interruption to our trade, let alone to our military forces I would assume?"

"If we are to be a target of the StarCom Federation," Lord Luke pointed out.

"Is that likely, according to your analysts?" Lord Obamu asked in his thick accent.

"Potentially, yes. We are on the possible path of one of the arms of the invasion, if it stretches as far in scope as Operation Fortress did. There are no guarantees however, and our own military strength is hardly inconsiderable - providing we are successful in resisting the new data-viruses."

"We must take steps to limit the effectiveness of the data-viruses, and their possible dissemination," Lord Principal Ramicek Zupanic said. "What do you think of the suggestions in Lord Minister Luke's report, my Council?"

"Upgrading the architecture of the Zupanic and Obamu networks is impossible," said Lady Minister Lapointe. "We cannot afford it."

"And logistically, we could not do it in time," added Lady Minister Galetti, of the Ministry of Domestic Affairs. "It would take several years to complete the upgrades, and I'd suggest we do not have that luxury."

"I would agree," Lord Principal Ramicek said.

"The effectiveness of introducing system-wide shut-downs is in doubt," Lady Minister Galetti continued, referring to the second option in Lord Luke's report. "If we cannot introduce the cut-outs on the gateways in time, we cannot protect against the one or two second warning we may or may not have if StarCom launches the data-viruses through the HPCGs."

"How likely is the third option?" asked Lord Minister Brin Claes.

"We could develop an effective firewall solution in time," Lord Luke repeated his earlier comments, "but we cannot predict the mutations and enhancements that StarCom would enable the viruses with. We can't rely on the third option," he added reluctantly, leaving only two options left.

"The fifth option of doing nothing is not something I favour," Lord Principal Ramicek said. There were a number of assents around the table. "That leaves us with the fourth option," he continued.

The tension in the air around the table could almost be tasted on the tongue. Eventually, Moafa Obamu said, "If our only option is to seize the HPCG stations, then we must."

Lord Luke closed his eyes, and spoke. "If we take the HPCG stations and the stargates that belong to StarCom Federation, we will provoke their ire. We make invasion more likely, not less, although I will admit that part of the reason for the existence of the Levitican Union is defence against President Nielsen precisely because we knew we would eventually face their armed forces. Taking the StarCom assets will prevent delivery of the data-viruses, at least in such a devastating way as occurred with House Alsopp, and increases the chances of our firewall programmes resisting the infections."

"However, it is our only viable option of defence," Lord Minister Obamu said. "Short of deactivating every solar data network in the entire Union."

"An action which would destroy our economy," added Lady Minister Lapointe.

"Lord Minister Luke, you appear uncomfortable with the option," Lord Principal Ramicek observed.

"Indeed I am, Lord Principal. Where StarCom invasion is only a possibility, taking their HPCG stations will be an act of war. Even if they do not launch a full-scale invasion of the Union, look at their recent actions in the OutWorlds Alliance. Where they cannot take nations by force, they kill their leaders with assassins."

"Fear for our lives should not prevent us from protecting our people," said Lady Minister Galetti.

"I was not suggesting that," said Lord Luke.

"So what would you suggest?" asked Lord Minister Brin.

He took a deep breath, but was beaten by Lord Principal Ramicek, who said "I would suggest that we formulate the plans for the seizure of the HPCG stations, but we do not act on them just yet. We must draw a line, a point beyond which the StarCom threat, if their invasion forces reach towards us, must not be allowed to cross. Once they pass that point, we take their HPCG stations and stargates, on the basis that we are within striking range of their armies. What do you think, Council?"

There were a number of opinions. Despite feeling very uncomfortable with the idea of provoking the Federation, no matter how close they got to the borders of the Levitican Union, Lord Luke could see the sense in the alternative suggestion. He wondered if Ramicek had intended this all along, if Brin Claes had deliberately provided the opening for Ramicek to make the suggestion. He rubbed his eyes again; that was ridiculous, the politics of the Union was making him paranoid.

"The motion will be tabled," Lord Principal Ramicek called an end to the debate. "A vote. We have five options on the table, Council, the fifth best in my opinion being seizure of the StarCom assets triggered by the renewed StarCom Federation crossing a particular interstellar line. Please vote now."

Lord Luke hesitated, and then very reluctantly struck the representation of a button on his display that would cast his vote for the fourth option.

Lord Principal Ramicek grunted with small amusement. "Lords and Ladies," he said, "it would appear that we have reached a very rare, unanimous decision. The fourth option it is.

"Lord Minister Luke, at the next meeting you will present your proposals for the position of the trigger line."

With that, the Lord Principal moved on to the next subject, and the recorders entered the vote into the minutes and it became a matter of record.

*

Admiral D'Souza was being escorted through the *SS Vindicator* by two Marines, and their Major Adeoye who was apparently new in his position. The commander of the VMC marine forces, a man bearing the rank of Lieutenant-General, had returned from the surface of the planet Peters IV, and had met them on the bridge. His power-armour bore all the marks of battle, with burns and a painful looking dent in the centre of his chest piece.

"Here we go," said the man introduced as Lieutenant-General Andryukhin. He stepped into the private ready room with Admiral D'Souza, and the doors closed behind them.

Admiral Gavain stood as his client walked towards him. He gave an Imperial salute, which Admiral D'Souza declined to return. He was the customer, after all, and he was also a member of the nation state of Amiens. He did not follow the Red Imperium's doctrine after all.

"Admiral," Gavain said, seating himself in time with D'Souza. Andryukhin remained standing, adopting an at-ease position without being told to. "Your presence here was unnecessary."

"On the contrary, Admiral," D'Souza shook his head. He was used to the short, almost abrupt way that the mercenary spoke. "I see it as very necessary. You and your forces have performed exceptionally well, far beyond what was called for. I have already recommended, and it has been confirmed, that not only are we releasing the full payment to yourself inclusive of maximum bonus, but we are also giving you an additional fifty million for exceptional performance. In one day, you have cured a major headache for us here in the Petersburg System."

Gavain merely nodded, whilst the hulking brute of Andryukhin grinned mirthlessly. There was a ruthless look in his eyes, D'Souza decided. The man was probably still high on combat drugs.

He had already reviewed the reports of the mercenary actions here in Petersburg. They had brought their strikecruiser and destroyer into the system early, jumping in under cover of the sun and then running around to take up position close to the planet Peters IV, where the fighting was ground based and the limited naval forces of Amiens and House Ilyvan sheltered from each other, unable to contest the orbital space. One of their battlecruisers had likewise jumped in system, and taken up position nearby the uncontested Peters III.

At a predetermined time, all but one of the rest of the mercenary ships-of-the-line had jumped into the space equidistant from Peters III and IV. The House Ilyvan ships around Peters III had been on a wider patrol, so were quicker to respond, but one of the two ships around IV had also moved towards the incoming jump signatures.

It proved fatal, a brilliant trap. The star-carrier and the other battlecruiser had moved towards Peters IV, again pursued by all but one of the defenders around Peters III. At this point, the trap was sprung, and their interdictorship jumped in at the pre-determined co-ordinates.

Interdictors were often the same size of destroyers, although lighter armed, trading armour for offensive capability. Their main purpose was to generate massive gravitational distortions on the scale of solar bodies, preventing enemy ships from jumping out-system.

The battlecruiser around Peters III engaged its target, and the strikecruiser and destroyer around Peters IV engaged theirs. All enemy forces in-system were now engaged, and unable to withdraw or jump away, as they were all within range of heavy gravitational distortions, either naturally caused by the planets or artificially by the interdictor.

Predictably, the House Ilyvan strikecruiser around Peters IV was the first to be destroyed. As it was breaking apart spectacularly, the VMC strikecruiser was already powering towards the battle in the middle of space, even as the gigantic military transporter *Monstrosity* was jumping in. It launched its multitude of landers and then later strikepods, conveying a major Marine assault force down to pre-determined targets on the planetary surface. The House Ilyvan forces, although greatly outnumbering the marines, were no match for the surprise attack.

The battlecruiser around Peters III was the next to be successful in destroying its foe, a hopelessly outclassed frigate. A smaller military transporter, Cervantian in design and not ex-Praetorian, had then jumped in-system, disgorging its contents towards the surface. House Ilyvan forces were much lighter on Peters III, and they were also unprepared for the lightning-fast orbital assault.

The battle in the depths of space was over shortly, one of the House Ilyvan ships offering surrender. The mercenaries had not only secured the single remaining survivor, but then turned back to Peters III and IV and commenced blistering orbital bombardments.

Three hours after they had launched the assault, they had removed the Ilyvan defences and ensured that the system was now totally in Amiens control, bar some small pockets of resistance on Peters IV.

"Rather than have the additional fifty million, I would rather have the Ilyvan ship that surrendered," Admiral Gavain said.

"Well, prize rights were not included in the contract," Admiral D'Souza shook his head, "and Amiens needs the ship ourselves. When will you release it to us?"

"General Andryukhin, see to it," Gavain ordered.

"Yes, sir," the Lieutenant-General gave the Imperial salute again, then marched away to deal with the order.

"What were your losses?" Admiral D'Souza asked, crossing his legs and leaning to one side as he spoke.

"Acceptable," Gavain said, and then he obviously relented. "Eighty-one fatalities amongst the Marines, sixty-three navvies. Casualties were much higher amongst the ground forces, but we borg recover quickly."

"Outstanding," De Souza commented.

"We are Praetorian," was all Gavain said. "Is there anything else, Admiral?"

"Well, yes, actually," Admiral D'Souza said. "Allow me to explain, Mr. Gavain. Many in the Amiens Armed Forces High Command felt that we were taking a major risk by placing this entire operation in the hands of one mercenary unit. There are some large merc units out there in the galaxy, of course, some decades or even centuries old. But we felt no one unit could successfully complete this contract. That you have proven yourselves in such a way has greatly impressed us."

Gavain remained completely impassive. Unusually he seemed to sense something was required of him, so he said, "Thank you."

"Amiens would be interested in offering you a permanent contract, more than just a privateering contract, but a permanent position in –"

Admiral Gavain had closed his eyes and was holding up a hand, and D'Souza fell silent.

"Admiral," Gavain said. "In the months since the Dissolution Order was signed and sealed, ending my Imperial military service and Praetorian involvement in the rebellion, I have been variously offered positions, homes, and service, by the Weiberg Nation, Cervantia, Hausenhof, and now you. I will give you the same answer I gave them."

D'Souza was surprised. He did not think that the taciturn Gavain was capable of such a lengthy, explicit response.

"The Vindicator Mercenary Corporation whilst for hire, will never become a permanent vassal of any House, nation or state. I am building a future for my soldiers here, Admiral, giving them a purpose where there was nothing but the Dissolution Order to deal with. We were bred for war, and it is all we know, all we have to trade. We are free, Admiral, and whilst we will fight for money, we will not fight for a nation's imagined honour. The only nation I would ever fight for again selflessly, out of patriotism, without any wish for recompense, is the Red Imperium under the one True Emperor."

"I ..... see," said Admiral D'Souza, momentarily non-plussed.

"That being said, however, we will consider further contracts with Amiens should you wish to offer them, maybe on a long-term basis. We are currently doing something similar with Hausenhof. But we chose the contracts, and will not do it on any form of retainer. Nor will we be subsumed into your nations military, Admiral."

"I understand," Admiral D'Souza nodded his head. He uncrossed his legs and stood. He found himself somewhat angry at his treatment, and despite his admiration for all that Gavain had accomplished, he found the man's lack of manners appalling. It would only be later when he digested the words that he would understand some of what the ex-Praetorians he had contracted must be feeling, considering they were bred to serve the Imperium and the Imperium only. "I take my leave of you, Admiral Gavain."

Gavain stood, and to D'Souza's surprise offered a hand. "A pleasure, Admiral," he said.

Gavain sat back in his chair after Admiral D'Souza left, closing his eyes. He realised he had gone too far. He had much to learn about negotiations he decided, knowing that Lady Sophia would have handled that much better. His attempt at the handshake had been a poor attempt to recover from his gaffe.

Sighing heavily, reflecting that although he was learning fast he still had a lot to learn about the ways of the colonised galaxy, he jacked into the datasphere and gave the order for all his ships to jump out-system as soon as the entire group was assembled and ready. He would leave it to his captains and commanders to organise between them.

*

Commodore Harley Andersson stood in the central courtyard, hands on hips, legs in a wide stance, surveying the construction work going on all around him with a broad grin on his face. It was going very well and better than the plan, he knew.

He always had been good at construction projects, as well as siege warfare, and the chance to bring his skills to the fore for the VMC excited him. It was an intellectual challenge, and gave him pride to see his meticulous plans coming to fruition.

They had levelled a shelf into the mountain using a constructoship hired from one of Lady Sophia's mining companies. The base was being constructed in as much secrecy as possible, but such a highly-visible activity was unavoidable. Nonetheless, the media had been prevented from reporting the activity, the constructoship was hired through a number of proxy companies, and the location of the base was remote enough that it did not attract any attention beyond perhaps a few of the very distant villages, hundreds of kilometres away who saw the ship fly overhead.

The only other thing the villagers may have noticed may have been the days of sudden shuttle traffic, but the landers came in on different vectors and usually at night, engines silenced as much as possible to allow quiet delivery of their payloads.

The shelf created, Andersson had engaged the next stage of the project. He had brought a large number of constructowalkers from the Janus Shipyards, with modular attachments that could be swapped out for any number of different construction duties. Some had been tasked with building the reinforced base walls, printed up by the large prefabrication units that literally manufactured any building material or semi-completed component. The gigantic walls were slotted in place, and then more added, reinforcing the thickness. Special metallic plates would be added later for additional security.

Other constructowalkers, and special multi-directional boring-vehicles, burrowed deep into the mountain. The majority of the base would be underground, and work was progressing quickly. It had taken two weeks, but eventually the entire structure of the underground warren had been hollowed out. Reinforcement and wall-linings had been added to the higher underground levels, but they had rushed to put the inner walls in at the very lowest level of the structure, and for good reason.

Low-level buildings had been constructed on the artificial plateaux, and the first furnishings had been manuprinted for the interiors. The upper level of the base was nowhere near complete, but at least the shells of all the surface buildings were in place.

Most importantly of all, the power generators had been delivered and assembled, and located underground in the very lowest level of the structure, in the huge hall that had been completed ahead of plan. The power generators had been connected through special drone-created tunnels to the field initiators that had been located in special housings on the surface.

Commodore Andersson, in his special anti-weather jumpsuit, cocked his head to one side as the local, isolated datasphere demanded his attention. The base's independent intranet had only been activated hours before.

He jacked in, and said, <Andersson.>

<Commodore, we are ready to activate the field initiators on your command.>

Behind his oxygenator, which had a visor to protect his eyes, Andersson's grin widened considerably. His thermal jumpsuit hood was moulded around the oxygenator, so that no single part of his skin was exposed to the cold. They were in the southern hemisphere of the planet Tahrir. The southern hemisphere was mountainous, and exceptionally cold, never rising above zero temperatures. It was almost permanently dark, at the utmost only receiving six standard hours of daylight per standard day, and for a number of months, being completely without natural light in perpetual night.

<Activate the field initiators,> he ordered.

He raised his right hand, and tapped his forearm. An implant in the forearm activated, and a small, personal viewscreen flickered into existence. It was showing a live feed from a satellite above the southern hemisphere. The satellite net had been carefully manipulated on Lady Sophia's order, so that construction of the base would not be recorded anywhere, but nevertheless it still showed the plateau and the buildings that had been constructed on zoom. Especially for today's events, its highly paid and bought operator had zeroed in on the base. The live feed allowed him to stare at the base; it was almost surreal to see himself standing out in the open, a tiny, ant-like figure on the magnification provided.

He raised his hand and waved at the sky, then laughed.

<Chameleonic field activation in three .... two .... one .... we are go,> the voice on the datasphere said.

Andersson looked up, and the very air above the base began to flicker and distort. It was like being underwater and staring upwards at the surface as it grew in intensity, and then suddenly, the distortion stopped as if nothing had ever happened.

He looked down at the viewscreen. All the satellite could see was the mountain as it had been before. The Commodore cycled through the various views, running a check to ensure that the base was completely undetectable from the surface. The power generators, although deep underground, were heavily muffled and shielded. There was no trace of the VMC's Base Tahrir.

<All of you, congratulations,> he said proudly. <It's worked first time.>

There was a small cheer across the datasphere, a wave of happiness as all the people jacked in felt the same joy as he did at a job well done.

They would continue to build now under the permanent secrecy of the chameleonic field, checking regularly as more and more of the base came on-line to make sure that not a single emission or trace of their presence was escaping the protective umbrella above their heads.

His next priority was to ensure that the science levels were built and constructed. He had to get the accelerated-growth biovats, cybernetic infusers and data-cores containing the genetic information safely into the base. The landers would begin bringing down the remainder of the equipment in a couple of hours, fully emptying the *Hannoverian* of all its highly precious cargo.

Andersson looked up again, and gazed at the stars through the transparent roof above.

Chapter XVI

Commander-In-Chief Jaiden Ryan sat in his office in the Palace of Communications on Earth, resting his face in one hand as he stared at the data before him. It was late at night and he was tired, and he was seriously considering leaving it until tomorrow and going to bed.

He shook his head, stood, and crossed over to the simulator. He dialled in a super-strong coffee, hit the activation button, and waited for it to materialise inside the cup he had placed into the unit. The simulator hummed as it manufactured the coffee, and when he pulled it from the unit, he smiled as he smelt its artificial aroma.

It was probably a hang-over from his early days in the military, before he had joined the old Star Communications Network. Synthesised food and drink was the best way to run an army and a navy, and real food and real drink did not taste the same to him anymore. He liked synthesised food, perhaps a little too much and too often, because it reminded him of his past and his roots.

He crossed back to his desk and sat his considerable, plump backside down. The spacious office was low-lit, but he resisted the urge to up the lighting level. He could see the glow of the data better. He rubbed his eyes. He must be due another visit to have regenerative treatment on his eye-balls, his sight was starting to suffer.

The data before him was a listing of the new assets and units captured during Operation Fortress. Although not comparable to the Praetorian ships, battlewalkers and military vehicles he had under his command, it would nevertheless increase the size of the StarCom Federation Armed Forces. The majority had been placed into the Federal Guard, and were now redeployed across the conquered territory. He was organising some units into the skeleton of a new 9th and 10th Fleet, but getting the mix right was very difficult.

It did not help that the Federal Guard, designed to hold the territory they had taken, was now heavily overstretched with the launching of Operation Storm two months early.

There was a bleep at his door, and computerised voice told him who was outside. He checked his chronometer, surprised at receiving a visitor this late. "Enter," he said, wearily getting to his feet to welcome the guest.

Vice-President Giovanna Pereyra strode confidently into his lushly-carpeted office, gliding serenely across to his desk. He bowed first, in deference to her higher rank and position in the hierarchy.

"Vice-President," he said. "It is late, but you're welcome. Please, take a seat. How can I help you?"

Giovanna Pereyra crossed her legs, and her deep, brown eyes were framed with gentle laughter lines as she stared at him, with an innocence that was completely misleading. She had not risen to be the Vice-President through being gentle and kind. She had a strong ruthless streak in her. Then again, so did Jaiden Ryan.

"I wished to have a private discussion with you," she said. "There is not much time these days for us to talk."

"We are all busy," said Ryan, taking the hint and activating the electronic counter-measures. Various fields and security devices activated all across his office, and eventually, he nodded at Pereyra when it was all fully active.

"Tell me of our current dispositions and status," she asked, referring to the Armed Forces.

Taking a deep breath, Jaiden Ryan launched into a summary of what was currently happening out in the galaxy. He spoke at length about the measures he was going to, in order to reorganise the reserve forces to hold their captured territory, and the insurgencies they were encountering in the captured solar systems as the main forces of the SCFAF had moved on in the invasions of Operation Storm.

"You are very concerned, aren't you, Jaiden," the Vice-President said gently.

He hesitated, and then decided there was no harm in the truth. "I most certainly am. I advised President Nielsen against launching Operation Storm. I felt it a mistake, and unnecessary. Her ambition and impatience may - well, no, has - imperilled some of our operations in territory already captured. We are increasing the risk of a severe military defeat during Operation Storm, on the scale of the Janus Shipyards debacle, or maybe worse."

Vice-President Pereyra hesitated, in a very carefully controlled and stage-managed manner, then said pointedly, "President Nielsen is showing a number of grievous errors in judgement, I am sure we can both agree."

Jaiden Ryan recognised the tone, and being used to the political currents of the old Red Empire and the new StarCom Federation, instantly recognised the criticism for what it was. He was being tested. He had never heard of Pereyra either openly or privately criticising Rebeccah Nielsen before.

"I have said as much to her," he repeated. This could either be a test of his loyalty instigated by Nielsen, or the Vice-President jockeying for position and seeking support.

"Can you think of any other areas where she has shown lack of judgement?" Pereyra asked. "Perhaps areas where you have not shown your dissatisfaction?"

"Vice-President," he said, "I am a simple, straightforward man.

Anything I say to you is something I would say openly to President Nielsen."

Pereyra raised her hands. "I understand that, Commander-In-Chief."

"In that case, yes, there are numerous areas. The use of the Faceless to assassinate political leaders we cannot reach is one thing, but to use them - without my knowledge, I hasten to add - to assist military operations is quite another. Leaving aside the whole question of what to do about those nations that seize our assets, I am not sure assassination was the answer."

"Personally, I am not sure that threatening nations which took our assets was such a clever idea in the first place," Vice-President Pereyra said smoothly, offering an opinion to encourage him. "There are always other alternatives. We are pursuing an agenda of aggressive expansion, only marginally under the pretence of protecting assets. Look at what the Interstellar Merchants Guild have done - they have proven there is another way."

Ryan kept his eyes locked on Pereyra's. "Military tactics and strategy is my purview," he said smoothly, "Larger strategic and political direction is outside of my remit."

"Although of course you have an opinion," Pereyra said. He nodded slowly. "Staying on the military tactics then, using the HPCGs to disseminate battle-grade viruses into our target systems? What do you think of that, Commander-In-Chief?"

"A huge mistake, maybe our greatest," he said without hesitation. "Utilising the HPCGs to spread viruses undermines one of the basic tenets of trust in the old Star Communications Network. Rather than encouraging nations and Houses to allow us to continue providing their communications services, they will now go to greater lengths to seize our installations. Coupled with our obvious plans to aggressively expand, they have no reason to trust us at all."

"I agree," said the Vice-President. "We have made a grievous error in judgement. May I confide in you, Commander-In-Chief?"

"Of course."

"When we first agreed to form the StarCom Federation, I believed it was the best thing we could do in the collapse of the Red Imperium. I believed Rebeccah Nielsen was the best person to lead us out of the darkness. I felt she would bring light to the cataclysm that was coming following the death of the False Emperor. She did many great things during the rebellion.

"However, since then she has become more and more power-mad. Myself, you, Chbihi, anyone in the senior echelon of the Federation, we have no say anymore. We've always had a military, admittedly a clandestine one. Strengthening it seemed wise. Operation Fortress, whilst far-reaching, appeared sensible to a degree, although I had my doubts.

Sadly, I have come to the conclusion that there will be no end to this. Operation Storm will be followed by another, and another. Emperor help us when the factories are on-line and at full production again, because then our military might will become unstoppable. President Nielsen has lost her way.

"Maybe she always planned this. Maybe I never saw it. But she is trying to build a new Empire out of the blood of the citizens of the galaxy. She has authorised the destruction of entire cities in blood-baths the like of which the False Emperor used to engage in. I have seen new instructions as well, ones that I do not believe have been issued to you yet."

"What instructions, Giovanna?" Commander-In-Chief Ryan asked.

"She intends to authorise and instruct the use of WPD's," said Giovanna quietly.

"Destroy entire planets?"

"Yes. I believe she is now reaching the level of insanity of the False Emperor, Commander-In-Chief." He saw the true horror on her face as she said, "We have deposed the False Emperor, and put a new one in his place."

*

The starship jumped into the Blackheath System. The Zupanic noble barge was being escorted by four defensive frigates, although it was a sign of the way the new Levitican Union was working that not one of the frigates came from the same founding House. Lord Luke Towers was very speedily integrating the militaries.

The *LSS Divine Right* had been repainted in the new Levitican Union colours, and the symbol of the Union was emblazoned across its flanks and blunt-nosed prow. The new flag consisted of an emerald green field overlaid with a black hexagon, divided into six triangles, with the previous symbol of each House picked out in a simple white outline.

The *Divine Right* and its escort floated in towards the planet Alwathbah, bearing Lord Micalek towards his soon-to-be fiancé, Lady Sophia.

The Sky Keep had been lowered from its position hovering above the city of Tiananmen, docking in the gigantic holding ports, making it merge into one with the city. The giant squares to all sides of the landed Sky Keep were full to capacity, soldiers and enforcers keeping the crowd in order. Giant holographic images of Lord Erik Towers, Lady Sophia Towers, and Lord Micalek Zupanic stood above the crowds, which were roaring their adulation.

The images eventually winked out, fizzing and fading as they were deactivated. The figures of all three, as tall as battlewalkers, disappeared, leaving after-images on the eyes of the tens of thousands staring up at them.

On the north balcony of the Sky Keep, the three nobles re-entered the private drawing room, and two servants closed the rolling balcony doors. The drawing room was full, of holo-camera crews deactivating their equipment, servants, court attendants from both Houses, and members of the upper class. It was as private as the private drawing room was going to be.

"So, it is done," Lord Erik Towers growled in his gravelly voice, "the announcement has been made."

"The entire Levitican Union knows now, Lord," Lord Micalek nodded. He kept his back straight, every movement carefully controlled, betraying his military background. He wore the standard Zupanic uniform.

Lady Sophia found it interesting. His manner of speech, his body language, his entire bearing was completely different in public than it was in private. She had only spent two occasions in his company on their own - and even then with bodyguards in shouting distance - but both times he had displayed more personality, and she found him attractive. In public, and she counted this as public, he was much more distant and very different. She saw how he had earned his reputation.

"I still feel aggrieved over what happened in the election of the Council," Lord Erik Towers said. "Your father did not renege on the terms of our deal, which is why I have honoured it, but I expect to see him complying with the spirit of the terms in future, not just the letter. Am I understood, Lord Micalek?"

"I believe I understand, Lord Erik," Micalek nodded again.

"Very well," Erik Towers acknowledged the comment. He heightened the hovering height of his droid-chair, and turned to Lady Sophia.

"Daughter, the entire galaxy knows that you are to marry Lord Micalek. On behalf of House Towers, I thank you for seeing this through."

Lady Sophia was greatly taken aback. She blinked several times. To receive praise from her father was so rare she could not even remember the last time he had said such a thing. "Th - thank you, father," she stammered in surprise.

Lord Erik Towers motored his droid-chair around to face Lord Micalek again. "We may not always see eye-to-eye, but she is my daughter," he said. "She *will* be looked after when she moves residence to your landholding, Lord Micalek, terms of our pact, existence of the Union, or not."

"Of course, Lord Erik," Micalek betrayed nothing of his own feeling in being threatened in such an open, overt and public manner.

"Good," Lord Erik replied. "The marriage is set for six Imperial Standard months from now. In one month, I will make the announcement that Luke has been named my heir-apparent, and that Sophia is no longer in line to my seat of power. The political capital in the delay of the second announcement will be useful in this initial phase of the Levitican Union, I am sure."

"It is as we agreed," said Lord Micalek. He reached out a hand, and took Lady Sophia's in his. "If we may take our leave, Lord Erik."

"Yes," Lord Erik granted the permission. "Remember, both of you - no off-spring until after the wedding."

"Father!" Lady Sophia was scandalised. Her father merely laughed at the look on Lord Micalek's face, and waved them both away.

With her arm linked through Micalek's, they left the private drawing room, bodyguards falling in a short distance behind. In the Sky Keep in theory they should be safe enough, but many House Lords and Ladies over the last few centuries had discovered to their fatal surprise that nothing could be taken for granted. The Imperium may be dead, but the homicidal tendencies amongst its ruling classes appeared no less violent in the aftermath.

They were walking down the long gallery, the faces of previous Lords and Ladies of House Towers staring down upon them. Their feet, his jack-booted and hers in elegant high-heels, stepped upon the floor almost naturally in rhythm. He did not move away from her, and she did not move away from him.

"I'm glad that's over," Lord Micalek said after a moment or two of comfortable silence.

"Which do you speak of? One's father's points on the pact between our houses, or his ribald comment at the end?" Sophia teased.

He squeezed her arm gently. "The public speaking, I meant. Although you do have a point, Sophia."

"You always seem so confident in public," she said, surprised. "Well, confident in general, if one tells the truth."

"Which just goes to prove appearances can be misleading," he replied.

"One looks forward to getting know you better," she said, seriously.

"The marriage feels artificial in many ways," Micalek said, "and I suspect your reaction to it was the same as mine when my father told me, but after meeting you Lady Sophia, I have to say I feel much the same way." Then he looked at her and smiled that devilish, heart-stopping smile.

She felt her cheeks redden slightly, and they carried on walking.

*

President Nielsen sat in her private office, reading through an intelligence report that the Director of the Central Intelligence Department, Malika

Chbihi, had just brought to her in person. It made for disturbing reading, but it was unsubstantiated.

She had rung for her main meal of the day to be delivered, and when the door chimed, she assumed this was it. She had a representative from the Interstellar Merchants Guild coming to see her in two hours, but she intended to be fully fed before she had to listen to his boring excuses again.

The door opened, and indeed, a servant was entering with a droid hovering behind him carrying a tray upon which her steaming meal was resting.

"Put it just here," she indicated, blanking the data-slate screen to protect its contents, and reaching into a drawer for her own personal eating wand. She heard the tray being placed on the table as she found it in the drawer, but when she sat back up the servant had disappeared.

A member of the Faceless stood before her.

"We hope you enjoy your meal, Madam President," the genderless Faceless acolyte said.

Her heart rate was racing. "I think I may pass on a meal delivered by an assassin," she said, with a calm tone that she really did not feel at all.

"That may well be wise, Madam President," the Faceless replied. Its blank, featureless face seemed to be staring at her more intently than usual. Normally she could not tell the difference between the various agents that visited her, but something about this one told her it was not one of her usual contacts.

She was feeling very, very afraid.

"I did not call for a visit from the Faceless," she said. "Why are you here?"

"I came to a deliver a message," it said.

"What message would this be?"

"You currently pay insurance to us, to prevent us from taking out a contract on your life," the Faceless said. "I am here to tell you that the insurance value has been reviewed, assessed as no longer adequate, and we have revoked the protected-status on your life. We have received a higher bid on your life, President Nielsen."

"What?" she stammered. Her voice was incredibly high. "I pay you enough to purchase a small solar system. What do you mean, a higher bid?"

"Someone is willing to pay a very large amount of money to see you dead, President Nielsen."

"Who?"

"We do not reveal our clients."

"I'll pay more," she said desperately.

The Faceless suddenly said nothing.

"I'll pay you a lot more," she said. "Name your price."

The Faceless cocked his head to one side, and named the price.

"But that is extortionate!" she exclaimed.

"Then we will accept the contract on your life," the Faceless replied. "President Nielsen, we have received a great many contract enquiries against you. Up until now, your insurance payment has ensured we will not take them. We have re-assessed the risk, and decided you need to pay us more. You have many enemies. Pay us, or we accept the contract."

"I will pay you," she said. "Is this every year?"

"Every two months," the Faceless corrected. It ignored her pained look. "The next time we cancel the insurance contract, we will simply let it lapse, and you will know that your life is back on the market."

"You cannot do this," she whispered.

"We can, and we will. If you do not like the position you are in, you should not create so many enemies for yourself, President Nielsen."

"You never took a contract out on either of the Emperors!" she objected. "They were always immune and insured!"

"You are not an Emperor," it replied coldly.

*

Every planet the galaxy over operated to Imperial Standard time, a centuries-long standing tradition based on one of the very first Imperial Decrees. There may be certain practical exceptions where a dual-time chronology was utilised, such as on heavily agricultural worlds where localised seasons and times based on the planet's rotation had to be taken into account, but as far as possible Imperial Standard time in terms of twenty-four hour days and three-hundred-sixty-five days a year applied. It was important for human biology and physiology to keep to the timings it had been genetically programmed to abide by.

This meant that when the Council was called to an emergency session at just before 02:30 hours, the Lord Ministers of the Levitican Union were all in bed asleep. To their credit, and aware that it must be something extremely urgent to be woken that early in the morning, they were all assembled in the Council Chamber in very short order. Lord Minister Luke and Lord Principal Ramicek were the last two of the hegemony of ruling Houses to enter.

"We're all very, very tired," Lord Minister Obamu snapped, "this must be important, or –" he stopped at seeing the look on the faces of the young Luke and the much older, but no less concerned Ramicek. As the Lord Principal took his seat at the head of the table, Lord Minister Luke did not sit, but quickly pressed a couple of buttons on his console and began to pace around the circular table. He had been so tense since he had found out about an hour ago, he could not sit now.

"Lord Minister Luke, explain, if you please," Lord Principal Ramicek said, as a holo-map sprang into being above the centre of the table.

All the ministers assembled could read it perfectly well, and understand the import of what it was presenting to them.

"At midnight Imperial Standard Time, the armed forces of the StarCom Federation jumped into numerous systems, a third wave under Operation Storm. It reached further than our analysts predicted," Lord Minister Luke said. His voice was hoarse as he spoke, his throat dry. "We drew a line across the galaxy here, Ministers, the line at which we said we would take action if the Commies crossed it.

"Tonight, they crossed the line."

"How reliable is the information?" was the first thing Lord Minister Obamu asked. "How do we know this?"

"I have the information from over eleven separate sources," Lord Minister Luke said. "House military ships that jumped out after failing to resist the invasion forces, and civilian trading ships, have spread the word of the StarCom Federation's latest activity. The word is already spreading across the galaxy via the free and the StarCom HPCGs. Even the StarCom News Media is carrying the story, it cannot be hidden, or denied."

"I will remind the Council we took a vote," Lord Principal Ramicek said. "Once StarCom crossed that line, we said we would take certain action of our own. In the interests of fairness, now that day is finally here, I will give anyone who wishes to a chance to raise an objection, and they will be heard. StarCom are likely to offer us war, or an assassin each, after all."

He waited, and there was no sound apart from Lord Luke's boots pacing on the rich carpet underfoot. No-one said a word. The decision had been made.

After a long minute's silence, with everyone looking at each other, Lord Principal Ramicek said, "Let the record show there was no dissent of opinion. Lord Minister Luke, explain the plan to us, please. I assume you have prepared for this, based on our previous vote?"

"I have, Lord Principal," Luke Towers said, "although I had hoped this day would not come." He bent over the controls at his seat, and the holo-map changed to show a strategic three-dimensional map of the Levitican Union, overlaid with numerous graphics. As he spoke, it automatically highlighted the small graphical icons he wished it to.

"We are ready to launch the operation to seize all StarCom Federation Hyper-Pulse Communication Generators and stargates within Levitican Union territory," Lord Luke said. "Ground units have received special training, and have been practicing, in preparation for assaulting each and every HPCG in our land. At a given signal, they can all launch the attack. The signals will be staggered, travelling as they must through the HPCGs, and masked underneath regular mercantile comms traffic.

"Similarly in relation to the three stargates in our territory, naval and marine units are ready to launch. Again, the method of getting the go-order to them will be the same. At precisely 07:13 today, simultaneously, every single unit will attack and seize their targets. I am predicting eighty-five to ninety percent success rates, excluding the stargates. By 08:00 we should already be receiving a decent picture here on Leviticus of what the actual success rate has been."

"The success rate seems high," said Lord Moafa Obamu. "How certain are you, Lord Minister?"

"A cross-House team of analysts has provided me with the figure," Luke replied. "Our military's integration is almost complete, on paper at least, and that includes all the support functions. I believe it to be accurate."

"What are the redundancy plans in case of failure?" Lord Principal Ramicek asked.

"Failure overall is unlikely," Luke replied. "Failure at certain target sites is a certainty. Where that happens, we flatten the facility concerned, and take prisoners where we are able to. It may give us a bargaining chip with StarCom, but primarily it will give us a source of information to interrogate."

"And what of the long-term plans to deal with StarCom Federation reprisals?" asked Lord Brin Claes.

"We can only guess at their response. We are now within a couple of standard-days long-distance jumping range of their warships, although their more modern stargates can always reach us. The Union's military will remain on high-alert, ready for surprise attacks. I have reinforced key, strategic systems. I find it much more likely that assassination will be the favoured response."

"Our personal security has been heightened? I've not noticed any difference," said Lord Claes.

"It will be effective as soon as we leave this room," Luke replied. "We must all restrict our travel and movements as a precaution. Public events will be limited for those of us in the Council - there will be remotely recorded interviews only."

"I'm more interested in the key strategic systems," said Lord Minister Moafa Obamu. "Which ones are these, pray tell?"

Here it comes, thought Lord Luke. He manipulated the holo-map, and a number of systems were highlighted.

"Our forces are concentrated in the systems of Svenge-Talia, Fort Bastion, Blackheath, Newchrist, and Cannai." In other words, a system each for House Obamu, Galetti and Claes, and two for Towers, with no heavy concentrations for Lapointe or Zupanic. "This is not to say we have left other systems undefended, of course, as it accounts for roughly seventy percent of our ships-of-the-line, and we have numerous reserve forces spread out across the rest of –"

"What was the thinking behind the selection?" Lady Monique Lapointe asked, her eyes narrowed.

"Blackheath and Cannai are economic power-houses, driving forces behind our economies, with a great number of static defences. Newchrist is home to the planet Leviticus, and has to be defended purely as it is the seat and namesake of our nation. Fortifications are currently underway. Svenge-Talia and Fort Bastion as they are both militarised systems, easy to defend, and battle-groups launched from those two positions can reach between them all but the furthest reaches of Zupanic territory within a minimum of five to seven jumps."

"There are other systems that could be viewed equally as valid," the Lord Principal said neutrally. "There are fortified systems in Zupanic and Lapointe, after all."

"And other systems are just as economically important as Blackheath and Cannai," said Lady Minister Lapointe.

Ramicek thinks this is deliberate, thought Luke. He resisted the urge to sigh, as he tried to explain that it was easier to attack a nation than to defend it, as the defenders must spread their forces thinly and react to incursions, whereas StarCom was making good use of pin-pointing their attacks, no doubt with the advantage of the intelligence garnered from cracking messages transmitted over their HPCGs. His strategy was based on delivering overwhelming force to wherever StarCom Federation forces landed.

He hoped it would be enough, should they decide to retaliate in arms with starships delivering death from orbit, rather than with a shadowy figure's knife in the dark.

*

StarCom Chief of Station Adrian Aldris was relatively new to the Blackheath System. He was of a senior grade, but he had been put in-station less than a year before the Battle of Mars. He was approaching middle-age, at one hundred and sixty-four years of life, and he liked the quiet life. He had seen it as a furtherance of his career to accept the promotion and command a Stargate, but nowadays all he could think of was the garden in the private grounds of his last posting, a large HPCG station on the warm, sunny world of Sanctuary.

He did not like the way that the once peaceful, neutral organisation he had joined as a young adept third-class had turned into the Federation, an aggressive, war-mongering, power-hungry, territory-stealing dictatorship.

He was unhappy, and he toyed with the idea of tendering his resignation, serving the one-year notice period, and then disappearing off to some backwater world unlikely to be touched by war.

He sipped at his morning orange juice, not sure that there was anywhere peaceful in the galaxy any more. There were some pockets of peace, but everything was so unsure. He could not remember a time like it. Actually, he thought, that's not true. When the Second Emperor, or the False Emperor depending on your viewpoint, had taken the throne from the First or the True, there had been a long period of uncertainty and strife, but the warfare had not been as wide-spread as it was nowadays.

Chief of Station Adrian Aldris carried his cool glass of real orange juice - his one self-permitted luxury - to his command seat in the middle of the ComCen. The Command Centre of the Blackheath Stargate was situated atop the huge ring-shaped structure, the eight elongated launching pylons currently dormant. He had a superb view out of the main viewing window from his seat, staring at the distant planets of October and November, which on their current orbital paths were coming around to the point closest to the stargate installation. The Silverfields asteroid field was the constant view, a wonderful vista of rocks hanging suspended in the middle of the binary star system.

Today the view was somewhat spoilt by the Union starship rapidly nearing the stargate's maw. The frigate was an assault frigate, designed for operating stealthily and individually, rather than as part of a larger unit of ships-of-the-line.

He sat in his command seat, eating the synthesised toast. His staff knew better than to interrupt him. He always allowed them the first few minutes of his presence to carry on with their duties uninterrupted. He ran a very relaxed station.

Eventually, at 07:10, he asked his second-in-command for a report on the days upcoming activities.

He read the report carefully. There had been an unusual request from the new, infant Levitican Union military for a Code Red use of the stargate, which meant House priority over any and all commercial traffic. The terminus they had to program in was on the far-side of the former Zupanic territory. He wondered what had caused the panic. It was probably another incident of piracy, most likely, another activity which was rapidly increasing within the colonised galaxy.

"Chief," his scanners officer called out, "it looks like the frigate is experiencing a problem."

"What sort of problem?" he asked.

"They've lost all power. They're floating dead in space."

He raised his head, frowning. "Is there any sign of external damage?" he asked, concerned about the integrity of the Blackheath Stargate. "Are they about to lose containment on their main drives?"

"No, Chief," his scanners officer replied. "It looks like they're launching life-pods though."

He sighed. It looked like an end to his uneventful day. "I suppose we had better get ready to take them in," he ordered. "Keep an eye on that frigate, and be ready to raise our shields should it look like it's about to blow. Otherwise, we'd better take in the lifepods."

The time was 07:13.

Inside the lifepods, all was silent. The Levitican Union marines, in their power armour and ready for battle, maintained absolute discipline. The frigate they had been launched from was far from dead. Many of the lifepods were actually empty, to make it look as if the entire crew was abandoning the frigate.

The lifepods rocked when they were captured by the force field beams projected out from the habitable sections of the stargate, dragging the escape vehicles in towards small external airlocks.

The marines readied their weapons.

"Chief?"

"Yes?"

"We've just received a coded signal from HPCG Station Three on Alwathbah, on the StarCom back-channels."

He sighed. What had happened to his quiet day? Back-channels were used between StarCom installations, and were never opened up to House or private communications use.

"What sort of distress signal?" he asked. "Decode it."

"It's .... oh my Emperor .... it's an Omega Signal, Chief."

Omega Signals had been instituted decades ago, but had become more increasingly used nowadays. It was a sign that the StarCom installation was under attack, and in imminent danger of falling under superior firepower.

"Sir .... I'm receiving another from Alwathbah Station Two .... Tahrir Station One ..... October .... November ..... more .... they're all under attack, Chief!"

Chief Adrian Aldris hesitated for a number of vital seconds, and they would be the seconds that counted. In that time, his brain absorbed the information, realised that they were under attack, and whilst he dithered, the lifepods were docked at the various airlocks.

By the time it had occurred to him to order the lifepods to be repelled away from the Blackheath Stargate, it was too late. The Levitican Union had gained access to his installation. Even as his shaking hands were tapping out the sequence to activate the Armageddon Code, the Union marines stormed the Command Centre, and it was all over.

Chapter XVII

Admiral Gavain stood with his new Commander on the flagship *Vindicator*. Now that Commander De Graaf had command of the destroyer *Undefeatable*, and Commander Kavanagh had the strikecruiser *Sorceror*, he had been forced to select a new Commander to be his second-in-command. His flag officer was one of the newly hired personnel, but she had performed admirably well in the Petersburg contract. He had high hopes for Commander Saifa Al-Malli.

Part of him missed his old command crew, not that he would ever show it of course. Despite this, he seemed to be developing a decent working relationship with Saifa, who had been wandering the colonised galaxy ever since the Battle of Mars, finally ending up on Parowa Czwarty and taking the decision that the mercenary life was the only way forwards for her skills. She had previous command experience too, aboard a battlecruiser which had been sold to the OutWorlds Alliance in the early days of the Dissolution Order.

She had certainly performed well in their latest exercise. He had taken a backseat, conducting computer-generated enemies against all the VMC ships not currently out on the convoy contract for Hausenhof. He had won, but he had been pleased to see that it had been a more taxing victory than normal.

Gavain was watching the replay, listening to Commander Al-Malli explain what she would have done differently as the recording progressed. All the other ships had stood down.

They were currently in the uninhabited system of SD4-M2, within what had been House Towers territory. It was off the trade routes, and was virtually guaranteed to be unused by anyone except maybe smugglers taking the long route around the galaxy.

It was actually colonisable, which made it all the more surprising it had never been colonised. Expansionism had died a death in the Red Imperium many years ago, especially in the Core. The system was quite large, a triple star-system, with numerous asteroid fields, gas planets and moons. The marines were currently on one of the planets, engaging in a major simulated warfare exercise organised and conducted with glee by Lieutenant-General Andryukhin. He was like a child with a new toy.

The size of his command staggered Gavain if he stopped to think about it. He had over sixteen thousand Imperial Marines assigned to his naval units, thirteen thousand of them to the two specialised troop-carriers *Monstrosity* and *Titan*. There was another thousand back at Tahrir Base, assisting with the construction. He had over ten thousand Imperial Navvies, and another two thousand assisting in the Base construction.

Tahrir Base itself had a permanent staff of eight hundred, some non-combatants but still former members of the Praetorian Guard, such as the doctors and scientists in charge of the accelerated growth bio vats.

Soon, he knew, Tahrir Base would be fully functional, and the Vindicator Mercenary Corporation would begin growing its own cyborgs, synthesised from Praetorian genetic stock. They would never reach maximum capacity, as there would be enough to create a new army within a year, and he knew his limits.

It amazed Gavain how much things had changed. He felt like he had purpose. He had a new direction. Although it had been perhaps nine months since the fall of the Empire in real-time, when he accounted for the transit-time, biologically to him the Battle of Mars was over two years ago. He had done well for himself, he knew, especially at his relatively young age.

<Commander,> Comms Lieutenant Forrest addressed him, <We are receiving a hyper-pulse message, from Commodore Andersson, Priority Alpha.>

Priority Alpha, Gavain thought, they were expensive. He then had one of those moments where you look at yourself, and laugh. He truly was turning into a mercenary, concerned only for the coin.

More to the point, what could be so urgent it would require a Priority Alpha? <Private channel, Lieutenant Forrest.> He would take it in his minds-eye, not requiring a holograph or privacy to receive the transmission whilst jacked into the datasphere. Commander Al-Malli went respectfully silent, then returned to her seat in the captain's chair, leaving him whilst he received the message.

A mental image appeared to him of Commodore Andersson. Once again, James Gavain was reminded of why he liked the man so much, but there was something in Harley's posture that betrayed his agitation. The message he had to deliver was seriously unsettling.

Gavain listened, and then closed down the private channel.

With his usual composure, he walked across the bridge and sat in the flag commander's chair. <I want a conference with all senior staff in-system, now,> he demanded.

It took the talented Lieutenant Forrest barely two minutes to organise, with General Andryukhin being the last of the holographic figures to appear in the centre of the bridge of the *Vindicator*. All the bridge crew had fallen silent, and Gavain had been steadfastedly ignoring the questioning look on Commander Al-Malli's face.

Andryukhin was obviously in the field, crouched down as if he were inside a *King Cobra* HAPC. His helmet had been removed inside the oxygenated atmosphere of the armoured personnel carrier, but he had the wild look in his eyes that said he had been fighting. The other holograms depicted Captain Markos of the *Remembrance*, old but experienced and very, very capable, Captain O'Connor of the *Quintessential*, young and no less capable, Commander Kavanagh looking comfortable in her new position in charge of the *Sorceror*, Commander De Graaf of the *Undefeatable*, sober and with a light in his eyes that showed his renewed purpose in life, and Lieutenant-Commander Meier of the *Kinslayer*, the man who had been his former senior tactical officer on the *Vindicator* and seemed to be showing every sign of justifying Gavain's faith in his abilities. The Captain and the Commander of the *Monstrosity* and the *Titan of Stars* transporters were present too, both comrades of Andersson from the Imperial days.

<Late as ever, General> Gavain said.

"It's better late than frickin' dead, Jamie," Andryukhin said, one of the few that were on first-name terms with Gavain nowadays. The mouth on his holographic image moved, but in reality, he was jacked into the system-wide datasphere too, so it was a computer-generated fantasy.

Gavain did not react to the comment. Instead, he merely launched straight into the point of his message, with typical brusqueness.

<I have received a Priority Alpha message from Commodore Andersson, informing me of a worrying event that took place shortly after 07:00 hours this morning. The Levitican Union has captured all StarCom Federation HPCGs and stargates in their territory. It is bound to force a response.>

"What sort of response?" Lieutenant-General Andryukhin interrupted. He was also probably one of the few who would dare.

"It will be either an invasion by force, or multiple assassinations of their leadership," Captain Danae Markos said. Raven-haired, broad-faced and confident, she was a very outspoken person. "They use no other tactics."

<It is impossible to predict, but neither presents us with an acceptable outcome,> Gavain spoke.

"How so?" Andryukhin asked.

"Rik," Commander Kavanagh interrupted, "it's obvious, use your head. An assassination could result in us losing Lady Sophia, as she is bound to be a target. That's one of our company directors."

"An insult that cannot be ignored," Captain Markos slammed a fist into the seat of the chair she was sat upon.

<Perhaps not,> Gavain said. Only his longer-term friends really took the import of that simple sentence. <But it is nevertheless not to be wished for.>

"The other alternative is an invasion, and the Blackheath System is a prime target," said Commander Kavanagh.

"Meaning we may lose Tahrir Base," said Captain O'Connor. "I told Harley we shouldn't be placing the base there, but he wouldn't listen."

<For future reference, Captain, you should also voice such concerns

with me, I was unaware of your thoughts,> Gavain said calmly. <That applies to all of you. I have always run a command where all can voice their opinions. But my final word applies.> He was silent a moment. <Tahrir Base, whilst far from being fully functional, has no defences as yet beyond physical walls and an operational chameleonic field. It is still under construction, and contains all of the specialist equipment from Janus Shipyards. In retrospect, it may have been a poor decision to unload the *Hannoverian* before the base was able to defend itself.>

"Bullshit. We couldn't have predicted this. What are the Loonies thinking," Andryukhin exclaimed.

"Loonies?" Kavanagh questioned.

"Levitican Union. L-Union. L-Uni. Loonie. The troopers are calling them that," he said.

<Loonies or not, they have done it,> said Admiral Gavain. <I find it highly unlikely that under a StarCom Federation incursion, the Commies would allow us to continue using Tahrir Base and the Blackheath System. They are more likely to seize all of our assets.>

"Under either alternative, what are our options?" asked Captain Markos.

<Captain O'Connor, myself and you will prepare a plan for either eventuality. In an assassination attempt, we respond with force, unpaid, to avenge our director's death. We assault various key StarCom Federation systems in retaliation, and relocate away towards the Frontier. Perhaps the OutWorlds Alliance.

<If there is an invasion, we have a decision to face. Our only concern is Tahrir Base. My initial thought is that we run an emergency evacuation, unpaid of course, perhaps an assault after the main StarCom forces have moved on from Blackheath. Alternatively, we evacuate the base now, but we have no way of knowing how much time we have, or even if it will be necessary.>

"The first option," said Ulrik promptly.

"What about taking a contract with the Levitican Union?" asked Captain O'Connor. "They are after all a very strong nation. It was the whole point of the creation of the Union. The chances of success must be high - the SCF cannot divert that many resources towards the Union without harming their activities elsewhere."

"Which makes assassination much more likely," Commander Kavanagh pointed out.

"Or a punishment raid, although they are not using tactics like that - yet," said O'Connor.

"Is the Levitican Union posting merc contracts?" asked Kavanagh.

<I will find out. The *Vindicator* will be jumping to Blackheath for me to have a discussion with Lady Sophia,> said Gavain. <Although she does

not know it yet. It is an option – but all of you should be aware of the conditions of the creation of the Vindicator Mercenary Corporation.

<I said to Lady Sophia that we would be business partners. We would not and could never be a part of their House military. That stands equally for the Levitican Union as a whole. We cannot show partisanship to any political entity – we are mercenaries, people. We do not take sides in the secession of the Empire.>

"We are against the StarCom Federation," said Andryukhin. "Unless you're saying we would take a contract even from them?"

<No,> Gavain shook his head. <They are the one exception. President Nielsen and the StarCom organisation cannot be trusted. They are not forgiven for the Dissolution Order and the events after the fall of the Red Imperium.>

"So why not take a contract from the Levitican Union. We already have a base there," Captain O'Connor shrugged.

<I take your points,> Gavain nodded his head, after a moment. <But I am still against contracting with the Levitican Union, when we have a Director in their nobility and a base in their territory.>

"It depends on the money, Jamie," said Andryukhin quietly.

<True. But my decision is all but made. I have ordered the ships we have on the convoy contract to complete their last run, and make their way here. O'Connor, prepare your scenarios and present plans to me upon my return. You may consult with whomever you wish. The *Vindicator* will be jumping out immediately for Blackheath. Lieutenant-General Andryukhin you have overall command, but I want our marines onboard the transporters today. Captain Markos, you have operational naval command. Praetorian rules, people.

<Admiral Gavain out.>

*

"This is insufferable," President Nielsen hissed, her rage having taken her beyond mere shouting, and into a voice-trembling growl of pure red emotion.

Inside her office, stood before her like old-fashioned schoolchildren dragged before their teacher, Commander-In-Chief Ryan, Director Chbihi, and Vice-President Pereyra, were motionless on the carpet in front of her desk. President Rebeccah Nielsen had recently taken to refusing to leave her office and the private chambers attached to it, refusing all public appearances and declining to leave the reinforced security of her small domain within the Palace of Communications.

Ryan had received Chbihi's instructions with some concern. He had taken it as a sign of the paranoia afflicting Nielsen; but he was also wise enough to realise that those who used assassins as a battle-tactic also had to beware attracting their wrath, too. Nielsen had ordered Chbihi and Ryan to ensure that at all times she had eight heavily vetted and trusted troopers in her presence, in pairs tasked to watch each other as much as her. There were additional pairs of security troopers outside her office and quarters at all times, in every room. The Palace was on a lock-down. She had a number of personal force fields built into her clothing. Her servants had been dismissed. Even her three closest advisors had to submit to a harsh series of checks before being allowed into her presence.

"Is this information beyond doubt?" Vice-President Pereyra asked, already knowing the answer.

"That's a stupid question!" Nielsen snapped.

"It's come from numerous HPCGs across all of the Levitican Union. It was a timed and carefully planned assault," said Director Chbihi quietly. Her intelligence analysts had poured over the information provided by the stations as they were assaulted, beamed at super-fast speeds across space to Earth, and had passed it to Jaiden Ryan before they decided they could not hide it from the President any longer. She had to know, nothing could be gained by concealing it. Ryan had found it interesting Chbihi had even considered the suggestion.

"It is a timed and carefully planned insult," President Nielsen snapped. Her face was thinner, she had lost weight rapidly, and black-encircled red-webbed eyes stared up from the deaths-head visage she currently projected. Her usual careful stage-managed appearance had evaporated with her seclusion. "The Levitican Union must be punished. StarCom will not tolerate such a blatant slap in our face!"

She stared at her three advisors, lips a thin line, eyes wide.

They shifted, waiting for one to speak.

Eventually, Ryan cleared his throat. "The issue is that the Levitican Union is large, economically powerful and well resourced, and has a considerable although admittedly not fully integrated military. Solar system defences alone will be considerable in some targets, and many uninhabited systems are observed and regularly patrolled –"

"I do not care for excuses, or protests as to their strength," Nielsen hissed. "I want the Levitican Union burning."

"Operation Storm is fully under way," Ryan replied. "We have forces within striking distance, but not enough to mount a full assault on the entire nation. Perhaps a targeted strike and withdrawal –"

"- will not be sufficient," Nielsen finished. "The Levitican Union must be conquered, at all costs. Divert resources away from Operation Storm if you must. This must happen, Ryan."

"Even I know it is not wise to change a committed strategy half-way through its enactment," Vice-President Pereyra came to Ryan's defence.

"I suggest you keep out of military matters," said Nielsen coldly. "Ryan, make it happen."

Commander-In-Chief Ryan had prepared plans for this outcome, but he was not happy about it. He had to have one more try, but he would not dare the wrath of Nielsen much more than that. He knew an assault on the Levitican Union was a grievous error.

"This will mean that Operation Storm will not be fully completed," he said, "and will mean we have to bring some elements of the plan, particularly in the galactic north-east-east to an end. We will face stiffer competition than we have previously. I must say to you, Madam President, that although we can do this, all of your long-term plans will suffer as a result of this short-term reaction."

"Ryan," President Nielsen said slowly, "Make it happen, or I will find somebody who can make it happen over your very dead, and very cold, body. Are we clear with each other?"

He swallowed. The other two did not move at all.

"We can invade the Union within the week," he said. "I have already made preliminary plans. We can use long-range stargates to jump elements of our reserve fleet in for a co-ordinated attack with some of our forward elements. But I will have virtually no reinforcements should things go wrong, and there will be problems encountered."

"So it will happen within the week," President Nielsen sighed and leaned back in her chair. The zealous light had not left her eyes. "Good. The Levitican Union, this Lord Principal, the other Lords, and all their citizens shall know not to defy me."

She then leaned forward again. "One more thing, Commander-In-Chief."

"Yes, Madam President?"

"I want you to authorise the use of the Tears of the Moon on these highly visible targets." She slammed a data-pad on the desk before her. "I want the galaxy to see what happens when I am aggrieved."

Ryan was shocked.

"The Tears of the Moon are outlawed, by –" Pereyra began.

"Imperial Decrees hold no sway over me. Wake up, Vice-President, we are in a new world now," President Nielsen slapped a hand on her desk for emphasis.

"We did not want the galaxy to know we possessed such weaponry," said Director Chbihi in a cautionary but conciliatory manner. "To use them now will reveal our hand."

"My order is given. Use them on these targets."

Ryan lowered his eyes. Inside, his heart was breaking. "Yes, President Nielsen."

*

Rear-Admiral Adare stood in the mustering hall of the *Thor's Hammer*. It was located centrally, in the belly of the ship, and was long enough that a battlewalker could run full pelt along it without stopping. It was impossible to hear someone at the far end. It could hold over a thousand marines and their equipment easily, and still have plenty of room left over.

The *Thor's Hammer* had jumped into an uninhabited solar system with its squadron, under coded orders to rendezvous with a small frigate hunter group, being jumped an unimaginably vast distance from one of the Sol Stargates. The Sol Stargates were capable of reaching across the Core almost into the Mid-Sectors, such was their unparalleled range.

He had received updated plans about what their new mission was. Operation Storm had apparently been abandoned; whilst no commander was ever privy to the full battle-plan beyond their next immediate steps, for reasons of operational security, he could not believe that the assault into the Levitican Union had been planned. It must be a reaction to their seizure of StarCom's outposts, but the size of the force was immense.

It smacked to him of desperation, the leadership losing their focus. It was emotive rather than strategic thinking.

The coded orders to divert to this system before rendezvousing with his designated battle-group for the invasion of the Union had taken him by surprise. He was immensely curious at what or who was so important it warranted the use of a stargate to jump it out to them.

A lander from one of the frigates was currently docked in a spare port in the *Thor*'s belly. The big airlocks were just cycling open now. His curiosity was piqued considerably.

He recognised the sound of Special Agent La Rue's footsteps as she approached from behind him. It showed how much she dogged him, that he was becoming overly-familiar with her gait.

"Special Agent," he said. "Have you come to inspect the cargo? Or is it, or they, something you were expecting?"

"I wasn't expecting it. I know what it is, now, of course - I received a message from the frigate carrying it as soon as it jumped in. I still want to see one, though."

Adare was wearying of this game. How could someone in her position have such an ego that they had to satisfy it by lording their position and knowledge over somebody else? On the other hand, such people were easily manipulated.

"How do you manage to get these secret communications?" he asked.

"We work for StarCom," she replied. "The Praetorian Guard were the best in terms of warfare, StarCom is the best at communications. That's why the CID is one of the best intelligence agencies in the galaxy."

"Imperial Intelligence was better," Adare commented.

"Imperial Intelligence relied on StarCom's CID," La Rue shot back. "Without us, they could not have done half of what they did. Much of Imperial Intelligence joined us."

"And much of Imp-Intel did not," Adare said. He wondered briefly where those Imperial Intelligence agents who had not joined StarCom had gone.

The airlock doors were now fully open. The naval crew inside the lander's airlock made the crossing over to the *Thor*, one manipulating the controls of a heavy-duty flat-bed hover-platform.

On top of the platform was a casket. It was marked with signs which made Adare's eyes narrow.

"What is coming aboard my ship?" he said to La Rue.

"It's called the Tears of the Moon," she replied quietly.

"I've never heard of it," he said.

"Here's the file," said La Rue, handing over a small data-chip.

He took the chip in his left hand, then held it over his outstretched right hand, which was palm up. The implant in the palm activated, and with a small, quick conical flash of greenish-blue light, the palm-implant read the data-chip.

Even as it dumped its information into his head within a nanosecond, Adare was focusing his eyes on the casket. Inside it, he now knew, was a warhead.

"The Tears of the Moon," Adare repeated. "Agent La Rue, such weapons are outlawed."

"By a now defunct Imperial Decree," she said.

"It is horrendous," he said.

"It is a war-winner," La Rue replied.

"It will turn the galaxy against the StarCom Federation quicker than anything else we've done." He could not resist, hating the SCF as much as he did, and having the opportunity to bait La Rue.

"So when am I using it?" he asked.

*

The servant was still feeling a little bit groggy, having awoken barely twenty minutes before. Clark reached for the dermal hypojector on his table, and depressed the panel on top. The stimulants diffused through his skin and into his blood-stream. They were completely legal, and were medically proscribed.

He sighed and stood up from the sofa, stretching and rolling his head to loosen his neck. He was extremely stressed at the moment. He was one of the high-ranking butlers at the Sky Keep, responsible for ensuring Lord

Erik Towers was well-looked after. He had been one of Erik Towers' manservants for nearly fifty years, and he was highly trusted.

It was also a very responsible position. He had direct responsibility for the entirety of Erik Towers' household staff, nearly two hundred people at any one given time. He was constantly assessed for security concerns, as he had direct, daily access to Lord Erik Towers.

Head of Staff Clark Hall had taken his weekly rest-day in his own quarters in upper rental district of Tiananmen city. He had already called for the cab to take him up to the Sky Keep.

His door buzzer sounded, and the intercom automatically linked through to the person stood outside. "Taxi-cab for Mr Hall," the voice said.

He frowned. It was not his usual driver from the taxi firm, but then he supposed everyone was allowed a day off, not just him. "I'm coming," he called back, knowing the intercom would pick up his voice.

He picked up his smart long-tailed tailored jacket from the chair, shrugging it on as he used a wall switch to close the lounge. The sofas and chairs descended into the lower section of the room, the floor closing over them. The bed came down from the ceiling, ready for when he would return in six days time, most likely late at night and most likely extremely tired again. The windows, currently showing a wonderful view of the city, the Sky Keep, and the opposite mountain slope from the one his small, luxury flat was position on, darkened.

He went across the room to the door, and pressed his palm against it to unlock the exit. The door slid aside.

"Oh," he said, seeing the figure outside his door. "You could have waited downstairs, there was no need to come up."

The person in the uniform of the taxi company looked blankly at him for a moment, then in one rapid startling movement pushed him back into his home, stepping quickly inside.

The door was already closing, the man had an arm around his throat and a spare hand clasped across his mouth. Clark tried to struggle, but the short man was immensely strong. They were on the floor, the man half-kneeling as he strangled Clark.

Clark could see the picture in the mirror opposite. The man's face was changing, even his clothes morphing into a black, featureless synth-suit. He had no features. As Clark suffocated, his second to last thought was that he was being killed by a mythical Faceless assassin. His very last thought was wonderment that this was how it felt to die.

The Faceless assassin stood up from the body. He dragged the body through into the single main room, depositing it on the bed. Then, its right hand morphed into special equipment, a tube-like extension with a pad on the end. It ripped the Head of Staff's clothes open across the chest, and pressed the pad on the exposed skin.

It absorbed the DNA of the Head of Staff. It then moved the pad up to Clark Hall's head, and began the lengthier process of brain-mapping. The cybernetic biomorph would plunder the memories of Clark Hall, learning and imitating mannerisms, patterns of speech, previous conversations with all his daily contacts, movements around the Sky Keep, and every other possible thing it needed in order to successfully assume the life of the dead Clark Hall.

Shortly thereafter, the Faceless assassin stood up from the bed, its body morphing already. He went to the hall mirror and looked at himself, satisfied with the results – he was now a perfect copy of Clark Hall.

The door intercom chimed. "Taxi-cab for Mr Hall," the real taxi driver outside said.

"I'm coming," the assassin replied in Clark Hall's voice.

<Admiral Gavain,> the voice of Lieutenant Forrest came over the datasphere. <Apologies for the delay, sir, but I've connected to the Sky Keep now. Lady Sophia is available.>

<Not your fault,> said Gavain. <Patch it through.>

He was sat in the ready room of the *Vindicator*. They had jumped in-system nearly six hours ago, and after going through the usual security clearances following their unscheduled arrival, had been given permission to approach Alwathbah.

As soon as they were within local communications range, he had ordered an all-stop in compliance with Blackheath's shipping control regulations, and they had attempted to hail the Sky Keep. Lieutenant Forrest had a major battle on her hands trying to get access to Lady Sophia, and Gavain had retired to his ready room, careful not to show his exasperation at being kept waiting.

The holo-projection suite in his room kicked in, and Lady Sophia's image appeared. She was looking as grand and as beautiful as ever, in an elegant, stately dress, a small diamond-specked tiara crown in her hair.

"Lady Sophia," Admiral Gavain said by way of greeting. His voice was neutral.

"Admiral," she nodded. "One apologises for keeping you waiting, but you have not picked a good time to visit. My father has already had another explosion at me, regarding your unscheduled jump into Blackheath. Could you not radio ahead next time?"

"I will try, my Lady," said Admiral Gavain. "However I have concerns I must discuss with you immediately. In person, and not on a channel such as this, however secure you think it is."

"One can meet with you tomorrow if necessary," said Lady Sophia firmly, "but not today one is afraid, James."

"This is urgent," he replied.

"Everything is urgent," she said gently, "but it will have to wait, Admiral. Today is a very important day."

"Why?"

Lady Sophia did not look happy to James Gavain. "There is going to be an announcement by my father. It concerns the line of succession, and I cannot really say any more than that."

"This would be following the announcement of your marriage to Lord Micalek Zupanic?" Gavain asked. His mind had made the connection.

She just nodded once, not saying anything.

"Very well," Gavain continued. "In that case, can we arrange a meeting for tomorrow? It concerns the Levitican Union's seizure of StarCom assets, and how this may expose the Vindicator Mercenary Company assets here in Blackheath."

"One is not sure she follows –"

"On Tahrir," he pressed.

"Ah, one suddenly sees," said Lady Sophia. "In that case, certainly, James. One will have someone check one's diary, and fit you in for tomorrow. One will also arrange for you to have clearance to approach and orbit Alwathbah."

"Thank you, Lady Sophia. The heightened security does not surprise me, considering the Levitican Union's antics of late."

"One looks forward to seeing you." She looked to the side, and nodded to someone off camera. "Sorry, Admiral, but I must go now. My father is making the announcement in the next half-hour."

"See you tomorrow, my Lady. Gavain out." He sent a mental command to cancel the communications.

Then, he also instructed Lieutenant Forrest to provide him with a live-feed from the Blackheath news channels. He might as well watch the announcement, while he was in-system.

Lady Sophia, arm in arm with Lord Micalek, walked into the throne room. It was cathedral-like, fashioned in the style of medieval earth. At the moment it was clear of all furniture except the throne, but servants stood by the numerous doors, ready to bring in the tables for the feast that was planned after the announcement. The day would be full of celebrations, audiences both public and private, and entertainment. Numerous minor nobles and members of the upper classes would need reassurances on what the announcement would mean to them.

It was not every day that a House changed its line of succession. It was a shame Luke could not be here, as she would dearly have loved to see her brother and have his support, but it could not be. As a Lord Minister of the Levitican Union, and particularly being in charge of the Union's military, he had to stay in location in the war-rooms of Leviticus.

The throne was the centre of attention. There was a podium in front of it, and a special docking station for Lord Erik's droid-chair. He had not sat in the throne for many, many years, but it still served a ceremonial function if not a practical one. Holo-cameras from many different competing news channels were set up in front of the throne, directed at the podium.

"If you lead the way, Lady Sophia," said Lord Micalek gallantly.

She looked into his bewitching eyes, and could not help but smile. "Of course," she commented. They walked slowly across the throne room, down the centrally laid, wide red carpet. The crowds before them parted, and eventually they reached the cleared area in front of the podium.

Lord Erik Towers looked up from his script as they approached. "Lord Micalek, Sophia," he nodded curtly. "I am informed we go live in less than two minutes. Don't keep me waiting again."

Lord Micalek looked startled at the rebuke, but Lady Sophia squeezed his arm. "Sorry father, it was unavoidable business."

"Your bloody borgs again," he grunted, eyes narrowed. Then the storm was over as quickly as it had begun. "Get into position," he gestured at the dais.

As they climbed the steps, Lord Erik floating at the side of them in his hovering droid-chair, Lady Sophia frowned gently. "Is Clark Hall not here?" she asked. The Head of Staff was usually around somewhere. It was highly unusual for him to be absent in general, but particularly when there was an announcement to be made.

"He's had to deal with some problem in the kitchens," Erik Towers waved off the comment. "This is it, Sophia. Today I tell the Union that you are no longer my heir-apparent, and the line of succession will flow to Luke. You know this is not a reflection on my thoughts of you."

"Yes, father," she said, taking up a position behind his chair, where it had settled into the docking station. She knew the exact opposite, of course. It was not just political expediency, her marriage into the House of Zupanic that had caused this decision she knew.

Lord Micalek squeezed her arm in reassurance this time.

"Lord Erik," said the Deputy Head of Staff from the floor. "We'll be recording in ten seconds."

Erik just waved open-handed, to signal he was ready. He cleared his throat, and took a sip of water from the cup-holder built into his chair.

Lady Sophia put a smile that she did not really feel on her face, and waited for the count-down to finish. She was not entirely happy with being removed from the position of heir to House Towers, but then, the political landscape was already changing. Nothing would prevent her from becoming a Lord Minister in the future, or maybe even Lord

Principal of the Levitican Union, if she so desired. Her interests had always been in her commercial ventures, and she did not particularly lust after power like her brother or father did. It surprised her then that today was causing a lump in her throat.

"We are go!" the Deputy Head of Staff called out.

"Citizens of the Levitican Union, subjects of House Towers, and people of the colonised galaxy," Lord Erik Towers began strongly, "I thank you for your attention. We have seen much change of late, not the least being the forging of the Levitican Union, a nation which –"

The next chain of events happened extremely fast.

There was a massive explosion, and Lord Erik Towers disappeared in a sheet of flame. Even as the fireball was expanding, fiercely exploding out from his droid-chair, a personal force field that she did not even know Lord Micalek carried was suddenly activated, covering them both in a protective bubble which withstood the force of the bomb. She blinked against the flash and the heat, then kept her eyes closed and instinctively held on to Lord Micalek as he did her.

When she opened her eyes, the force field was deactivating again, and all was carnage. The throne had been destroyed, the podium blown clear across the room, and the dais now had a huge crater in it. It creaked under their feet, in danger of total collapse. The droid-chair was completely annihilated. Her father had been vaporised in the explosion, before he had even properly begun his speech.

There was blood everywhere. The holo-cameras were awry, although some were still filming. Many in the front rows had died instantly, and many others were heavily wounded. Some lucky people at the back of the crowd had sustained only light injuries from the flying shrapnel. Everywhere people were screaming in pain and terror, a terrible cacophony of wailing that sounded surreal in the ear-drum ringing after-effect of the explosion.

A holographic image suddenly appeared, showing the form of a Faceless assassin. A recording boomed, the audio if not the image being picked up by some of those holo-cameras still recording. "In the name of the StarCom Federation, seizure of StarCom assets is an act of aggression, and will be punished."

Soldiers from House Towers and House Zupanic were running forwards from the sides of the room into the charnel house before her, weapons unholstered as if it would do any good.

A group of six House Zupanic soldiers had surrounded them, and there was almost a nasty incident as House Towers soldiers insisted on joining the cordon around Micalek and Sophia.

"Lord, Lady," a sergeant in Levitican Union military uniform said, with a flash-patch that showed the flag of Zupanic. "Are you both uninjured?"

"I - I think so," said Lady Sophia, her accent dropping.

"We still need the medics to check you both out, let me call -"

"My father!" she screamed suddenly. "My father!"

"Lady Sophia, there's nothing we can do," said Lord Micalek. "Lady Sophia -"

"Find who did this!" she screamed. Tears were streaming down her face. "Find out who did this now, Micalek!"

"Yes, My Lady," he nodded, then reached forwards and took the communicator from the sergeant in front of him. He hugged her close to him, her entire body shaking with unrestrained grief, as he began barking orders out across the voice-net.

<All hands,> Admiral Gavain ordered, standing up from behind his desk, <Go to red alert.>

As he strode across the ready room and out onto the bridge, he felt the entire nature of the ship change through his connection to the datasphere. Every crew member jacked in to the datasphere as the red alert warning went out, crewmen waking up from slumber or stopping whatever they were doing as they hurried to their stations. Those already jacked in increased their alertness, ready for anything, and Gavain could feel their collective minds sharpen in preparation. The ship shields went up, weapons ports opened, blast shutters closed, torpedoes and missiles were loaded, chambers energised and magnetic coils charged. The engines went hot under the increased power demand they were placed under.

<Admiral on the bridge,> the new Commander Al-Malli announced. <The bridge is yours, Admiral,> she said.

<All hands, be informed;> Gavain broadcast on the general channel, <There has been an assassination of Lord Erik Towers, at the hands of the StarCom Federation. Be alert and prepared for incoming hostile starships - if StarCom follows their usual pattern, it is possible Blackheath could be invaded.>

He logged off the general channel, and ordered scanners to search for incoming jump signatures.

The Faceless assassin Clark Hall walked down the corridor, heading towards the carport. He did not stop to speak to anybody, but he knew that his progress would be tracked and recorded automatically. It would be remembered by all who saw the Head of Staff, that at the point when Erik Towers was assassinated, his head manservant was walking down to the carport instead of being at his side.

The assassin walked into the control room. There were two operatives presently on duty, both of whom were pale white. They had obviously heard the news. There was also one soldier on duty, his weapon at port.

Out in the carport, he could see several soldiers on duty, standing guard to make sure nobody could leave the Sky Keep.

"Head of Staff," the soldier said, his rank insignia identifying him as a corporal. "What are you doing here?"

"I've been told to convey a message in person down to military headquarters. I must hurry," his voice shook convincingly, "we can't let the killer escape."

"OK," said the corporal, "I'll just check those orders before the ops guys release your car, Mr Hall."

Clark Hall sighed heavily, as if in exasperation. "Can we check those in the office in private?" he asked. "No offence to these gentlemen, but the orders are not for public consumption."

"Alright," said the Corporal. He led the assassin into the private office, and turned his back to him as he operated the panel to close the office door.

A couple of seconds later, the Corporal was collapsing to the floor, dead. The assassin's form was already beginning to change, and within a minute he had assumed the identity of the soldier.

He waited a little longer, then went out into the control room.

"Guys," he said in the voice of the Corporal, "the orders check out. Release Mr Hall's car, immediately. I'll be in the office - all hell's broken loose. I've got to speak to command myself. I won't be long, call me if there's any problems, yeah?"

"Yes, Corporal," one of the operatives nodded.

The assassin walked back into the office, the door closing behind him. The assassin had already moved the Corporal's body and used a special device to disintegrate it, to prevent detection. Within a couple of minutes, disguised as Clark Hall again, the assassin would be flying away free from the Sky Keep, his entire mission successful.

He used his internal cybernetic implants to begin morphing his body back into the shape of the Head of Staff.

It was at that moment that the door behind him opened, and one of the operatives entered. "Corp - bloody hell!" the operative exclaimed.

The assassin whirred around with unbelievable speed, a monstrously depraved nightmare as he was still morphing from one body shape to another. His arm whipped out, a long blade extending rapidly, and slicing quickly through the neck of the operative. Even as the decapitated body was falling to the floor, the assassin was jumping out of the office, heading for the second operative.

The second operative had slammed a hand down on the alarm button. It did not save his life, but as his blood splurted up the inside window of the control room, the alarm was already sounding out across the carport. Elsewhere in the Sky Keep, the house security forces would already be responding. Downstairs in the carport proper, he could see soldiers already reacting, two of them beginning to raise their weapons up towards the control room cockpit.

The assassin had no other option but to use the fall-back plan, which was to fight his way out. It would be messy, he knew, and the Shadow Council of the Faceless would doubtless remonstrate harshly with him on his return. He had no other alternative, however.

He completed the morph into Clark Hall, then did something the Head of Staff could never have done. An organic projectile-throwing weapon had morphed into being in his right hand, and he fired it several times at the window, blowing some of the glass out and weakening the entire pane.

Then he leapt through the window, turning and tumbling in the air as he fell the huge drop to the floor. Soldiers were firing at him as he fell, but they missed, and he landed like a cat on both feet and crouching onto his free left hand. His right pumped several precise shots into the soldiers in front of him.

He was up and running, using the cover of the docked cars. He jumped up onto the boot of one, then across the roof of a second, launching himself right-footed off the bonnet of a third and spun in the air, two blades extending out from both arms. One speared into the back of a soldier, the other sliced at an angle into another soldier's head, shearing cleanly through the skull bone and brain.

As he landed the bio-weapon was back in his right hand, and he fired a series of shots at the three soldiers in front of him. They fell back, two killed outright by the shots, a third unusually going a bit wider than he planned.

He was unstoppable, he could easily do this all day, he exulted.

Lady Sophia entered the carport, Lord Micalek walking behind her. He was insisting that she should not see this, but she responded that a little more death today would not damage her sensitivities any further.

Bodies and blood lay all around the carport. A Captain of the guard saluted and then waved her over.

"There are over thirty-two dead, only four wounded, my Lady," said the Captain, anger and sorrow in his voice. He was bleeding, a bullet wound in his right arm. A medic was gingerly scanning it, in preparation for the removal of the bullet.

"Is this him?" asked Lady Sophia, looking at the body down on the floor.

"Yes," replied the Captain. "Be careful, Lady. We've sedated him to keep him under, but it's not Clark Hall. This is a biomorph, my Lady."

She knelt down besides the assassin. "A Faceless," she breathed.

She stood. "Take him to the cells, but put him in stasis. They have implants to terminate themselves in case of capture, and we want them removed before he is awakened."

"Yes, my Lady," said the Captain. He ignored the medic as he turned away and began giving orders.

Lady Sophia looked down at the assassin who, because her father had never finished his speech, had effectively made her the head of House Towers.

Chapter XVIII

Luke Towers sat in his own private office. It was not the official ministry office, but rather a smaller, much more functional room just off the main strategic command war-room. Four guards stood in the room, one in each corner. Every Lord Minister was under heavy supervision, and security had been tightened to unbelievable levels following the assassination of his father.

He was taking a short break from the war-room. He had been awake nearly thirty hours now, and was seriously considering leaving the premises - again, under heavy guard - to return to his own quarters for some rest.

He had been convinced that following his father's death, the StarCom Federation would launch their invasion. In the hours after the news had reached them, which was almost instantaneous with the control and usage of the HPCG stations, he and his staff had been on edge, checking constantly with every system in the Levitican Union, waiting for the first strike to land or at worst all communications to be lost with a system.

Nothing had happened. It appeared that the assassination was the only aim StarCom had in mind. There was no following invasion.

On his desk was a small, hand-sized holographic three-dimensional picture of his father. It was Erik Towers when Luke had been a boy, before his illness had confined him to a droid-chair. Luke stared at, unable and unwilling to cry or show any other outward emotion, merely furious that his ailing father had been taken before his time. He may only have had another few years left, but that did not take away the hurt.

It was as if a hole had opened up in his heart. He had lost his father. He did not fully comprehend it, he could not completely accept that it was true, or real. He had spoken to his sister via a star-spanning continuous hyper-pulse link, and she was as devastated as he was. He felt hollow, nothing felt real to him at the moment.

He was hurting, and he did not know how to deal with it. He desperately wanted to go to sleep, and perhaps when he woke up none of this would be happening.

The door opened, and Luke Towers looked up.

"Lord Principal Ramicek," he said tiredly, "how can I help you?"

"We've not spoken since the news came through," said Lord Ramicek, his own guards piling in after him. The room was now completely full of people. Luke thought about ordering some of them out, but then it would utterly counter the security precautions he had placed on every single member of the Council. Any one of the people in this room could be a Faceless assassin. This was the fear that the shadowy organisation produced.

"No, we haven't," Luke confirmed.

"Allow me to offer my most sincere condolences," said Ramicek. "When I lost my father, it was to the bomb blast that took my arm and half my face off." Luke looked at Ramicek in surprise; he had not heard of this before. The skin grafting and replacement arm were perfect. "There is nothing in the world that anyone can say or do to make the pain go away."

"No, there isn't, Lord."

"I have just recorded a message for broadcast, condemning the actions of the StarCom Federation and the assassination of Lord Erik. Would you like to review it before I send it for broadcast. Or add your own comments?"

Luke considered briefly. "That won't be necessary, Lord Principal. I'm sure that your broadcast will be fine. I've spoken to Sophia, and she will make an announcement tomorrow on behalf of House Towers."

"You look shattered, you need some rest. I've been told that you've been awake for hours." Lord Principal Ramicek pulled out a chair and sat down.

"I am," he replied. "I'll probably go to bed shortly. I think any immediate danger of a StarCom invasion has probably passed. Typically, when they have used assassination, it's directly before they jump their warships into the system or territory. Only occasionally - such as with the OutWorlds Alliance and the failed attempt on Al-Zuhairi - have they done it purely as a punishment."

"We are a strong nation," said Ramicek. "Perhaps they realised they could not take us on. Of course, there is another problem now. Well, a couple of problems, actually."

"Problems, Lord Principal?" Luke asked.

"Well, first, the assassination of your father is technically an act of war."

"It could be said that we committed the act of war when we took the StarCom HPCG stations and the stargates," Luke replied.

"This is true," Ramicek shrugged and held his hands wide. "But they did not declare war on us officially. They assassinated the head of one of our nation's Houses. I have stopped short of declaring war on StarCom, but we need to discuss it at the next Council meeting."

"I don't think it is wise to provoke them," said Luke, his words hollow as he spoke. "We must think of another action to take. If indeed StarCom do not end up invading us, anyway, in which case the declaration of war becomes a moot point."

"We cannot leave this unanswered," said Lord Principal Ramicek. He paused, then speared Luke with his gaze. "There is another problem, though, as I said."

"Yes, Lord Principal?"

"Your father was killed before he announced that the line of succession in House Towers had been changed. He had not signed any paperwork, any official act. No-one except my House and your House knows that Lady Sophia was to be removed as heir-apparent, and that you were to take her place. Where does this leave us, Luke, particularly in view of the fact that Sophia is due to marry my son Micalek? This would bring the two Houses together more than we originally wished when we made the original deal."

Luke closed his eyes. He should have seen this coming. With Lady Sophia as heir-apparent, now the head of the House, when she married Micalek she would become a Zupanic. House Towers and all its territory, under established intergalactic convention and Imperial Law, would become a part of House Zupanic.

"I will have to discuss this with my sister," he said, stalling. He already had, as Lady Sophia had raised the point when they spoke. She was showing remarkable clear-headedness in the current situation, but then she always did have the cooler, more logical practicality of the two of them. "But I suggest for now we leave the question, at least until after the funeral. The marriage is still some six months away, so we have time to talk and make our decisions. That's both of our Houses, Lord Principal."

"Very well," Lord Ramicek did not look pleased. "I was hoping we could discuss and sort it today, if possible, but I understand my timing may not be appropriate. Lady Sophia will be assuming the head of House Towers, however?"

"For the time being, and most likely forever," said Lord Minister Luke. "We can always come to some arrangement about the division of our House territory, to protect each House's landholdings."

"Ah –" began Lord Principal Ramicek.

Luke held up his hands. "But that is for you and my sister to discuss, as the heads of House Towers and House Zupanic, my Lord Principal. Not me."

"Very well," said Lord Ramicek. "We are one nation now, however, so let me put forwards the idea that perhaps our Houses can join properly through Micalek and Sophia? It sounds as if this may be more than just a political marriage, if what my son says is correct. They sound very close already."

"Stranger things have happened, Lord Principal." Luke was aware he was becoming rude. "Anyway, Lord Principal, I am tired and must retire to bed, or if the Federation do invade, I won't be fit to command the defence."

"Very well," Lord Ramicek repeated, slapping his hands on his thighs as he stood. "I wish you all the best, Lord Minister Luke. My thoughts are with you and your sister."

"Thank you, Lord Principal. Good night."

Ramicek laughed without humour. "It's actually the morning, Lord Luke. You definitely need the sleep."

*

Lady Sophia was wearing all black. It was raining, not unusual in Tiananmen city at this time of year. There had been some attempts at snow. Winter was not far away, and there was a bitter coldness to the air.

Lord Micalek stood by her side, in a greatcoat over his new Levitican Union military uniform. Although they were not supposed to have any public appearances, Lady Sophia had insisted that the state funeral for her father be carried out properly; as a concession they would not leave the courtyard of the Sky Keep, so the army could keep them safely protected.

Micalek had pointed out that this had not protected the double of Lord Al-Zuhairi.

After the funeral of her father, there would be the official crowning ceremony, where she was named as the new head of house. In Imperial times, she would have taken the title Lady Senator, and become a part of the Imperial Senate. That birthright had now disappeared with the collapse of the Red Imperium, but not all traditions could be overturned so quickly.

Even funerals, she reflected, were traditions which the human race had decided to keep. They originally had their basis in the old earth religions, most of which had died out apart from in a small number of far-flung colonies. As the family unit had also become less common across the galaxy, the need for funerals had also vanished. Only the upper classes and the house nobility observed any formal funeral rites. The type of funeral varied massively across the galaxy, depending on which part of Earth's many civilisations the House could trace its ancestry back to.

House Towers had an old Western slant to its traditions and values, and so the funeral service was roughly comparable to an ancient Christian service. Instead of a minister, the head of state conducted the service, even where it was an incoming House Lord overseeing the funeral of the former.

With Micalek as her support, she read the eulogy, emotion wracking her voice. The service was beamed all across the galaxy, and she won the sympathy of many across the stars. At that precise moment though, all she could concentrate on was the words, and the pain. Her world consisted of that courtyard, and the casket floating before her.

At the appropriate point, and after a minute's reflective silence, she depressed the panel on the podium in front of her.

Screens rose up around the casket from the special platform it was resting on. She could not feel the heat as the flames ignited below the casket, and indeed could not see inside the unit.

Eventually the screens lowered. The casket was no more, and her father's ashes had been carefully deposited into an urn. There would be a private ceremony later, where she would eject them into space from the airlock of her own private starship. Her new Head of Staff brought the ashes to her, and she raised them up so the crowd could see them.

They thumped their chests, and then straightened out their arms, repeating the gesture three times. The Imperial Salute was always repeated three times at funerals.

Letting her tears flow freely, she allowed Lord Micalek to escort her back inside the Sky Keep, to the throne room where she would be crowned. Another tradition, she thought, pointless, but important.

Lord Micalek approached Lady Sophia from behind, and carefully put his hands on her hips. He rested his chin on her shoulder. To the guards watching, it was obvious that they were intimate, as this was an invasion of space no woman would brook if it were not welcome.

"Are you alright, my love?" he asked.

"Yes," she said, putting one hand on his. The other was holding herself just below her breasts, a protective gesture. She could not take her eyes off the stasis tank.

"Why have you come down here?" he asked.

They stood in the cells, in a specially constructed medical room. A couple of medical orderlies and a doctor were on hand to monitor the stasis tank, to ensure its occupant did not suffer any biological issues or emergencies while it was held frozen in time.

"It's been a week since my father was assassinated," said Lady Sophia. "One just wanted to have a last look at him before we leave."

"Have they removed all of his suicide implants?" asked Lord Micalek.

"They think so," said Lady Sophia, "but one wants to make sure. It is difficult for the cybernetic surgeons to tell. The implants are like nothing they have ever seen before, completely organic, extremely advanced."

"He will be coming with us," said Lord Micalek.

Lady Sophia frowned, and turned to him. "What do you mean, Micalek?" she asked.

"I have made arrangements for him to be transferred across to the *LSS First Ship*," he said. "He will travel with us to the Dalcice System," he named the capital solar system of House Zupanic. "I know that when he is brought out of stasis for interrogation, you want to know immediately and have the information to hand. Maybe even speak to him. And besides, my mother's interrogators are unsurpassed."

"One sees," said Lady Sophia, then she nodded. "Yes, it makes sense.

We will be leaving Blackheath tomorrow. Before we go, by the way, one must see Admiral Gavain."

"Your mercenaries?" Lord Micalek asked.

"Yes. One was supposed to see him a week ago, and with everything happening, he has been very patient. Although one is sure he doesn't understand why - borgs, and especially Praetorians, do not have families. One knows they do not grasp the concept of family at all."

"Not all borgs are like that," whispered the borg Lord Micalek.

She smiled weakly. "One did not mean you," she said.

"So do not fall into the stereotypical thinking of all humanists," he teased gently.

"One is a free-thinker, neutral, not my father," she said quietly.

"I know. Let us go to bed, House Lady Sophia Towers, and get some rest before our journey commences tomorrow. They will take this Faceless assassin aboard the *First Ship* for us overnight, so let us not think any more of it."

*

Rear-Admiral Adare sat in the flag chair of the *Thor's Hammer* dreadnought. He was completely quiet, listening in to the crew as they spoke over the datasphere, reassuring himself that all was well with his ship.

The time was upon them, he knew.

He jacked into the neural net shared by the entire squadron, as he received the summons to attend a private conference. All the officers in command of every ship in the assembled battle-group were present, identified instantly by the neural signifier on the private channel.

<All ships,> Admiral Haas was saying. <I am giving the order, and the stargate is ready. Maintain formation, and accelerate to the selected jumping speed ..... now!> The private channel was closed down.

Rear-Admiral Adare gave the order, and the *Thor's Hammer* went from stationary up to almost full output immediately. They accelerated in time with the rest of the battle-group, heading directly for the Dandarra System's stargate.

Their target system was so far away, it would take a number of jumps for the starship battle-group to hit the target. By using the stargate, they could be catapulted much further. In terms of transit time, they would be in hyper-space for more than five weeks, an incredibly long faster-than-light journey, but in terms of real-space time it would be little more than a couple of minutes.

The battle-group consisted of three squadrons, all from the StarCom Federation Armed Forces' Third Fleet. That was his squadron, Admiral

Haas's, and Vice-Admiral Scanlon's. Behind them, coming in after naval success had been reported back, would be the 6th Fleet 1st Cohort, with the ground-based invasion force.

All three squadrons were in a standard assault V-formation, heading to the stargate in staggered waves. Each of the three would be jumped to separate locations within the target solar system, to ensure maximum coverage. It would be carnage, if all went to plan. The target system was heavily defended, but these were all ex-Praetorian Guard ships-of-the-line. It was virtually a full fleet action, the Third Fleet consisting of only five squadrons, configured as it was for large-scale assault and invasion operations.

He watched Vice-Admiral Scanlon's 1st Vanguard squadron get captured by the jump field of the Dandarra Stargate, blur, and then disappear in a flash of light, the ships elongating before they disappeared. Barely ten seconds later, the same thing happened as Admiral Haas's 2nd Main Squadron repeated the process with an eye-searing explosive flare.

Then it was his squadron's turn, and the 5th Rearguard Squadron was on its way to the Blackheath System.

*

Lord Minister Luke Towers was in the war-room in Levitican Megapolis when his worst fears came to fruition. An operator around the circular bank of monitoring desks, a strategic military holo-map rotating gently in the air at the centre of the pit, slapped the warning panel on his representative console.

He spoke into the voice-mic mounted on his desk, whilst Lord Minister Luke Towers watched. "All staff be aware," he announced, the dread clear in his voice, "I have a confirmed report from the Svenge-Talia System. Multiple incoming warp signatures have resolved themselves into twenty-five - yes, twenty-five - ships-of-the-line. We have a major incursion under way."

Luke Towers felt his heart stop for a moment, but then his training kicked in. He was the leader, and this had not been unexpected; but twenty-five ships!

"Get me identification on those ships as soon as you can," he ordered. "Sound the general alert, message all solar systems immediately that we are experiencing hostile action." He snapped a voice-mic around his larynx, so it could be picked up by the voice enhancers and amplified around the war-room. Suddenly the quietness of strategic command had been broken, and everyone was working hard at their assigned tasks.

"Lord Minister," another voice boomed around the room from another operator. "Multiple jump signatures in the Cannai System have resolved themselves into eighteen warships, identification pending."

"The HPCG in Svenge-Talia reports that we have identified them as StarCom Federation starships. Three squadrons, a vertical-V line formation, SCFAF Fifth Fleet."

"Lord Minister!" a panicked voice cried out. "We have jump signatures coming in here, at Newchrist!"

"Alert the defences," Luke ordered calmly. "I expect this to be a StarCom Federation invasion. Leviticus must be protected at all costs. Numbers?"

"Between twelve and fifteen ships," the operator said.

Another operator was receiving more information from the hyper-pulse communications generators in the Cannai System. As they were speaking, they were updating the information on the holo-map. Luke's eyes were glued to the holo-map as they spoke. "Cannai System reports two squadrons from the SCFAF Fifth Fleet, positive idents of designations being 6th Secondary and 7th Secondary Squadrons. Separate jump-points reported."

"Leviticus Theatre," the operator called out, "hostiles identified as Third Fleet, 3rd Main and 4th Secondary Squadrons. One jump point, fourteen ships confirmed."

Luke read the information being displayed on the holo-map. It was being updated constantly, and using his remote control data-pad, he could zero in on any specific theatre that he wanted to.

All of a sudden, his heart lurched for the second time as a big red mark flashed up over the Blackheath System.

"We have thirty starships confirmed in the Blackheath System," he heard the operator saying, "three jump points, spread across the system. Three squadrons, v-formation assault pattern."

Luke looked at the read-outs, and realised that he had been caught out by the StarCom Federation. They had landed in overwhelming force, concentrating it on his strongest points to cause maximum damage. None of his plans had allowed for such a vast and strong assault to take place. They must have halted operations all over a number of sectors in the Eastern Segment in order to carry out this invasion-in-force. StarCom had truly taken him by surprise.

It was unbelievable, but it was happening.

*

James Gavain was awoken by the ship going to red alert.

He jacked in immediately. <SitRep,> he demanded of Commander Al-Malli.

<We have multiple incoming jump signatures,> she reported. <The

house military is going bonkers, these aren't expected. Arrival in one minute twenty-two and counting.>

Gavain slept fully clothed, as did all navvies, and only needed to put his boots on. He emerged from his quarters, went calmly down the corridor, and walked onto the bridge.

As he entered, he assessed a map provided to his minds-eye. The scanners of the *Vindicator* had picked up the first jump incursion, at a point closest astronomically to Alwathbah. A second jump signature had formed close to the military base of the planet November, and then a third at a point equidistant between the planets Omaha and Utah, where the second of two large military starbases resided.

<Admiral on the bridge,> Commander Al-Malli said.

He sat down in the flag chair, and called up all the displays he wanted to see as virtual holographic representations in front of him.

He could see the situation clearly. They were currently orbiting Tahrir. He had been down to the surface to see Commodore Andersson and the progress with the Tahrir Base. The *LSS First Ship* was en-route to them, but was still some thirty minutes away. It was still closer to Alwathbah, with the potentially hostile ships coming in on the far side of the planet, just beyond the edge of its gravitational well.

He thought quickly, and made his decision.

<Our first and only priority is to safeguard Lady Sophia, and the *LSS First Ship*,> he ordered. <Set a heading for the *First Ship* on an intercept course. Inform system command that we will protect it. Our rules of engagement are to defend, we will not interfere in what is a local system matter.>

On a private channel, Commander Al-Malli contacted him. <Do we not need to protect the Tahrir Base?> she asked.

<The Commodore has his orders, he knows what to do,> Gavain said. <He'll sit quiet, observe, and only defend the base if it comes under attack, but will not make a move until he gets the coded signal.>

<Do we not need to protect the Blackheath System?> Al-Malli asked.

<We are not under contract to,> Gavain said. He felt slightly odd as he said it, but the reasoning was clear. <We are mercenaries. We protect Lady Sophia, our Director, but do not go any further. This is an issue for the Levitican Union to resolve.>

<Ships translating now,> said the scanners Lieutenant Agrawal.

<Identification on the closest?> Gavain asked.

The data was fed through to him as the computers worked on the images they were receiving. The enemy squadron was indeed StarCom Federation Armed Forces. The ten starships were identified as the 5th Rearguard Squadron, of the 3rd Fleet, known to be commanded by a Rear-Admiral called Silus Adare. The dreadnought *Thor's Hammer* was clearly identified, notorious from the news broadcasts of it destroying Exeter Alpha in the initial phase of the StarCom blitzkrieg.

There were twelve Levitican Union starships facing off against Adare's squadron, but the mix of classes and the superiority of ex-Praetorian technology meant that they were outclassed. The starbase in orbit around Alwathbah would even the odds somewhat, but Adare had a reputation as a capable commander. Gavain did not like the Union's odds, at least in this part of the solar system.

Aboard the *LSS First Ship*, the noble barge that belonged to House Towers, Lady Sophia and Lord Micalek had moved up to the small bridge of the ship, on the latter's insistence. Their breakfast had been interrupted as a red alert klaxon had sounded throughout the entire barge. Sophia had never heard one ring out on the *First Ship* before, but a sinking feeling in the pit of her stomach told her what was happening before they had it confirmed.

"Show me," Lord Micalek was demanding.

The Captain of the *First Ship* manipulated some controls on his command chair, and the holo-map changed to show the current positions of the enemy invaders.

"We have no weapons on the barge," she whispered to Micalek. "We're completely defenceless."

"The two Union warships there will cover our escape towards Tahrir," said Micalek, "but we have no option. We must jump out-system as soon as we can, and then jump again in case we're tracked on our heading."

"We can't!"

"We must."

"There is an incoming call from a ship identified as the *Vindicator*," the communications specialist shouted out, "they want to rendezvous with us."

"My mercenaries," Lady Sophia said.

"They're offering us protection out of the system."

"Can they be trusted?" Micalek asked.

"Yes."

"Do it," Lord Micalek commanded of the Captain. "Rendezvous with them, then we jump."

"Yes, my Lord."

Lord Micalek leaned forwards, his hands on the railing around the position of the Captain's chair. "What are they doing?" he asked, looking at the StarCom forces.

"What do you mean?"

"The Commie squadron is splitting. It makes no sense."

Silus Adare had given the order. The *Thor's Hammer* dreadnought had moved onto a direct heading for the capital world of Alwathbah, the *Snake-Eyes* – now fully repaired – and the *Underworld* and *Ubermacht* destroyers on a slightly different heading for the military starbase in orbit around the world. The fast frigates *Nero* and *Orion* had been tasked with chasing the ship identified as the House Towers noble barge, but would be intercepted before they reached it. The remainder of his squadron was moving to engage the Union starships heading towards Alwathbah. Of the twelve Union starships in the immediate vicinity, they were spread out to defend this portion of the system, and they were not attempting to consolidate before attacking, desperate to defend the noble barge and Alwathbah. They were coming in individually, so he felt confident in splitting his own squadron.

Besides which, he knew it was far too late for Alwathbah already.

<We are taking incoming fire from the starbase and the planetary surface,> the tactical officer announced. Although Adare had allowed Commodore Pacheco to command the *Thor,* he was still tracking the progress of the ship as well as the overall strategic command of his squadron.

<Admiral Haas reports contact around the planet November,> a comms officer said.

<*Underworld* and *Ubermacht* to target the starbase, weapons free> Adare commanded.

<*Snake-Eyes* engaging starbase,> a tactical officer said.

Admiral Adare turned to Pacheco. <We are within torpedo range of Alwathbah,> he said. <Let the records show that I gave the command to launch the Tears of the Moon.>

His gaze flicked to Special Agent La Rue. She was stood there, arms crossed, eyes wide as she waited to watch the devastation the Tears of the Moon would wreak.

<*Nero* and *Orion* engaging Union Targets One and Two.>

<Heavy incoming fire from Alwathbah orbital guns.>

<Tears of the Moon warhead loaded and locked, Admiral.>

Rear-Admiral Adare could not help but call up a visual of the planet. <Fire,> he ordered.

The torpedo streaked away from its launch-tube in the *Thor's Hammer* dreadnought, passing through the hole generated for it in the shields. The dreadnought was taking a heavy pounding from the military starbase, but it was more than capable of resisting this for a couple more minutes before its shields were breached.

The torpedo rocketed through the void. Its nose began to burn red as it punched into the atmosphere. Moving at incredible speeds, it emerged into the upper atmosphere, and still glowing red, the warhead detonated.

On the surface, those that were watching the night-sky fearfully saw the massive explosion in the blackness, unaware of what it portended.

The warhead had splintered, numerous smaller warheads streaking out from its payload. The sky became full of red streaks of fire, like an exceptionally heavy asteroid breaking up on approach. The red streaks covered an impressively wide area in a matter of seconds, making it look as if the clear, night sky was crying tears of blood.

The redness began to spread. A glow lit the entire planetary surface below. The red became a roiling cloud, of pure fire. It spread rapidly, until it filled the entire sky. It stretched from horizon to horizon, the night now completely gone.

From an orbital perspective, the fire was advancing rapidly, and would in less than a minute completely cover this half of the planet. In two, the entire planet would be under its influence.

The Tears of the Moon weapon had ignited the atmosphere of the planet Alwathbah, and was in the process of burning it completely away.

Shortly, the heavily populated planet would be nothing more than a fireball, and when the fire exhausted itself as the atmosphere was completely eliminated, nothing would be left on the surface.

<What is the population of the planet?> Admiral Gavain asked.

<Over nine billion people,> Commander Al-Malli said after a moment.

The bridge had fallen silent temporarily. Then Gavain realised that they were still in a war-zone, and he commanded his people to return their attention to duty.

<Send a coded message to the *First Ship*, with the following heading,> Gavain commanded. <We must jump as soon as possible.>

The military starbase around Alwathbah had furiously turned its weaponry on the *Thor's Hammer*, but the warships were retreating, turning to deal with the Levitican Union warships coming up behind them.

Adare's feint had worked, allowing the dreadnought to get in close enough to deliver the Tears of the Moon. The planet was already burnt out, and where once it had been temperate, a swirling mix of whites, blues and greens, it was now a dusty fireball of scorched earth. The oceans had boiled away in the unimaginably hot conflagration. Three minutes, and a world was dead.

"Unbelievable," breathed Special Agent La Rue. Adare thought she actually looked ill.

Personally, he felt nothing except interest, and perhaps a sense of achievement. He had never fired a Weapon of Planetary Destruction before. He had made the history books today, he knew. His name would be notorious. He did not care.

<*Orion* and *Nero* report that the *First Ship* is turning. Jump initiation capacitors are charging.>

<They are not to escape,> Adare ordered.

<They will not be able to intercept in time.>

He sighed. <Pull them back to defend the *Queen of Egypt*.>

<Aye, Admiral.>

<Track their heading. If we can determine their jump location, we will follow them.>

<They have been communicating with an ex-Praetorian ship, designated *Vindicator*.>

Rear-Admiral Adare turned back to his strategic map, and paid particular attention to the ship *SS Vindicator*, pulling a file on them. Previously commanded by Captain James Gavain, promoted after the Battle of Mars, it had disappeared whilst on its final mission following the Dissolution Order. Gavain had later re-appeared, and StarCom intelligence suggested he had become a mercenary, registered with Interstellar Merchants Guild. There was an interesting hit; one of the listed directors was House Lady Sophia Towers.

He looked again at the *First Ship*, and then the *Vindicator* battlecruiser, and realised what was happening. Gavain was protecting his co-director.

"See you again one day, James Gavain," Rear-Admiral Adare whispered to himself, as the *First Ship* and the *Vindicator* both jumped in unison.

Chapter XIX

Admiral Gavain looked up as the turbolift doors opened. The holo-viewer was currently showing an image of the *LSS First Ship*. It and the *SS Vindicator* were in the uninhabited system of Gevin. It was used for mining, and there were a couple of mining ships detected on long-range scanners, but they were to distant to be able to see the *Vindicator* and the *First Ship*.

House Lady Sophia and Lord Micalek walked onto his bridge. He could see the strain and stress in Lady Sophia's face, whilst Lord Micalek looked determined and angry. He noted how close the Zupanic lord stood to Lady Sophia when they reached the command dais.

"With your permission, Lady Sophia," Admiral Gavain said, fixing her with his neutral gaze, "We should now separate. The *First Ship* should jump to one of these three systems, and we can carry you on to your destination."

"James, why?" she asked.

"Because," Lord Micalek answered for her, "the StarCom Federation forces will have tracked the direction of our jump. There are only a handful of systems we could have jumped to with the limitation on the barge's jump capacitors. Your Admiral here wants to use it as a decoy whilst we jump further out."

"Yes, I do," Gavain nodded. He stood, bowed, and then offered his hand to the Lord. It was a gesture he was becoming more and more familiar with now his Praetorian Guard days were over.

"Pleased to meet you," Lord Micalek bowed and shook the hand. "Lady Sophia has told me much about you."

Gavain just nodded, passively accepting the comment. "Where do you wish us to take you, Lady Sophia?

"The Zubrenic System," said Lady Sophia firmly.

"Why Zubrenic?" Gavain asked.

"If Leviticus and the Newchrist System falls, that is where the Levitican Union Council will relocate to," Lord Micalek answered.

<Commander Al-Malli, set course for the Zubrenic System> Gavain ordered. <How many jumps?>

<Three at full charge,> the response came from the Commander. <Three days real-time, with a lay-over to recharge to full if you wish?>

<Recharge for the one jump remaining, we'll recharge at Zubrenic in safety.>

<Aye, sir. We will arrive tomorrow at 11:42>

The conversation had taken less than a second across the datasphere. Gavain said to the Lady and Lord, "We will have you there tomorrow.

After we have seen you to safety, we will recharge and then jump back out to rejoin the rest of my unit."

"Admiral," Lady Sophia said, exchanging a glance with Micalek, "could we talk with you in private?"

Gavain considered, "Yes, my Lady. This way," he stood, and handed command of the bridge over to Al-Malli.

He sat down behind his desk in the ready room, Lady Sophia taking the seat before him. Lord Micalek elected to stand, one hand placed reassuringly on her shoulder. Behind Gavain, there was a flash as the *First Ship* jumped out-system.

"What do you wish to discuss?" Gavain asked.

Lady Sophia looked up at Lord Micalek, then back to him. "The Levitican Union is under assault, James. We are facing overwhelming force. If what was happening in Blackheath is repeated throughout the Union – and we received reports that other systems had been attacked - we could be looking at the end of the Union. Certainly of House Towers. Did you see what those monsters did to Alwathbah?"

Gavain sighed, then called up a holo-image. It showed a torpedo, striking into a planet. "It was a WPD," he said, "called Tears of the Moon. It was experimental, developed a decade ago, according to the highly-classified Praetorian Guard files we have. It works by igniting the atmosphere of a planet, and the resultant fire-storm destroys the planetary surface. The planet is rendered uninhabitable, permanently, for eternity. The last entry on file says the project was abandoned following test failure. It was obviously restarted, and fell into the hands of the Federation. It looks as if it has been improved beyond the project parameters."

"It is pure evil," Lord Micalek commented. "Such wholesale destruction has not been seen since the days of the planet-crackers."

"The Tears of the Moon prevents space debris in the aftermath of its use," Gavain said, "which is why it was developed. It was a project of the False Emperor, the True Emperor curse his soul."

"We must resist the StarCom Federation with all of our strength," Lord Micalek said angrily.

"I am sure you will," said Admiral Gavain.

There was a long pause, and then Lady Sophia said, "We need your help, James. One - I, need your help."

He blinked once. "That is not possible," he said. "The terms of our deal, Lady Sophia."

"I will offer you a contract," said Lady Sophia. Her imperial accent was completely gone. "I will pay you, both for your advice to me and Luke in defending the Levitican Union, and for all and any actions in defence of the Levitican Union, whatever they may be."

"It would be suicide, the risks are too high," said Admiral Gavain. "As much as I would love to take a contract against StarCom."

"One billion Imperial Crowns," said Lady Sophia.

Gavain leaned back and crossed his arms. Nothing was said for a long moment. "Two billion, payable in advance," he said. "Half a billion more on the successful liberation of the Blackheath System. One billion more if - and I do stress if - the StarCom Federation advance is halted, and they are forced out of Levitican Union space. Complete salvage rights to any and all equipment in any theatre we have operated within, at my sole discretion, with no interference or protestations from the Levitican Union military. I would expect the Vindicator Mercenary Corporation's losses to be high."

"That was suspiciously quick," Lord Micalek raised his shaped, black eyebrows.

"I already have a plan," he replied. "I expected you to ask, and I have my interests on Tahrir to defend."

"It is a done deal," Lady Sophia said. "I will draw up the contract now, and we'll sign today, Admiral."

"Agreed," he leaned forward and shook her hand.

"I will counter-sign as well," said Lord Micalek. "It will carry more weight within the Levitican Union."

"And if Luke has had to evacuate from Newchrist, when we land in the Zubrenic System, he will also counter-sign," said Lady Sophia. "With the Lord Minister's signature, it will officially bind the Union to the contract."

"As you said, a done deal," Admiral Gavain gave a rare smile. Inside though, he was wondering whether he had not taken on much, much more than he was capable of achieving.

*

Commodore Harley Andersson leaned on the railing of his brand new Command Centre, within the depths of Tahrir Base. It was modelled almost exactly on his last ComCen aboard the Janus Shipyards, and he enjoyed the reassurance of the familiarity.

The Blackheath System had been completely overrun.

It was now six hours since the StarCom incursion. The squadron identified as belonging to Rear-Admiral Silus Adare had performed admirably, although they had lost one of their frigates, the *Nero*, to defending Union forces and had taken some damage. Two of Adare's ships were currently repairing at Lady Sophia's shipyards in orbit around Tahrir, whilst the others were providing orbital support to the ground forces that had landed on the planet.

Andersson had his intelligence from tapping into the military communications on Tahrir, and even that was a passive connection so as not to betray the location of the camouflaged base. Elements of the 6th

Fleet, 1st Cohort had jumped in, with Federal Guard units who were probably intended to hold the system once Third Fleet moved on to further the invasion.

Elsewhere in Blackheath, Admiral Haas had been successful in his assault on the military planet November, moving onto the planet October once ground forces had arrived in-system. Vice-Admiral Scanlon's squadron had encountered fierce resistance around the planet Omaha, where the other military starbase was located, with a fairly large proportion of the in-system fleet defences. He had lost two of his twelve ships, with another dead in the water and likely to be in repair for months. The planets Omaha and Utah were both suffering land assault.

The planetary assaults were likely to be successful, Andersson knew. With all naval forces wiped out in the system, the StarCom ships-of-the-line were all free to bombard the planets in support of their land armies. A small number of Union starships had jumped out-system when it became clear Blackheath was lost.

His own orders were clear. He was to remain in hiding in Tahrir Base, in the mountains and far removed from any likely targets for the enemy. The chameleonic field was functioning perfectly. He had thousands of people on-base, and they were all armed. He had to protect the contents of the base, the bio-vats and the advanced Praetorian Guard technology he had rescued from the Janus Shipyards.

Gavain would come back fighting, he had said, either under a Levitican Union contract or not, once the worst of the StarCom Federation forces had moved on. Neither of them had suspected that the StarCom assault would begin mere days after they first discussed the possibility. Andersson had urged Gavain to press for a contract, and James had seemed to relent from his previous position, appearing to accept the logic. If he had to fight his way into Blackheath to rescue his people and his equipment in Tahrir Base, he may as well do it under a contract than not.

Besides which, Harley knew that James did not particularly care much for the StarCom Federation. He would enjoy taking the fight to them.

Andersson sighed. Until he had the coded signal from Gavain, he was to do nothing but wait. He decided he would send out some marines, disguised as locals, to obtain intelligence. His job was to prepare for the return of Gavain, but he should understand what was happening on the rest of the planet, and know the positions, locations and activities of the StarCom ground forces.

Rear-Admiral Adare was reading the damage reports from his squadron. The *Nero* had been completely destroyed, although all life-pods had now been collected by Federal Guard corvettes. The *Snake-Eyes* strikecruiser had suffered tremendous damage again, and he was thinking of having its commanding officer replaced, and the *Underworld* had also suffered severe damage. Both were in the commercial shipyards above Tahrir, receiving emergency repairs.

The ground assault was well under way on Tahrir. Tahrcity had already been taken.

He opened a private communication to Commodore Pacheco. <Send me the data on the noble barge *First Ship*'s likely location,> he ordered.

The data was fed through to him. He reviewed it carefully. The heading that the *First Ship* was taking could lead it to any of seven systems, although if it was cross-referenced with the heading of the *Vindicator,* jumping as it had before they had rendezvoused in Blackheath space properly, there were only four possibilities.

If he took the assumption that *Vindicator* was going to meet with the *First Ship,* he had to ensure that any forces he sent in pursuit of the noble barge were equipped to deal with a battlecruiser.

He had contacted Admiral Haas on the matter, and Haas had concurred that the destruction of Lady Sophia's barge was of paramount importance, especially as they now had intelligence to suggest she was actually aboard it with Lord Micalek Zupanic when it had jumped out-system. They did have a small window to conduct the pursuit, before the next phase of the operation to invade Levitican space was executed. Haas had given the honour to Adare.

He would task the *Thor,* the *Revenging Angel,* the *Veritable,* and the *Serendipity* to jump to each of the four systems, as the heaviest warships he had, with the *Ubermacht, Queen of Egypt* and *Orion* supporting one ship each. The *Thor's Hammer* was easily a match for a battlecruiser on its own. They would jump far enough out-system that their warp signatures would not be detected, so they could run silent and surprise the enemy, whichever system they were hiding in.

He gave the orders for the pursuit.

*

Some hours later, the *LSS First Ship* was recharging near the sun of the uninhabited solar system JC-4122. The small barge was undefended, on its own, without any form of support or escort.

The jump signatures were registered on its scanners. The Captain tried desperately to disengage the recharging cycle and prime the main drive engines to escape out of the solar gravity well, going so far as to jettison the extended charging panels, but it was too late. There was not enough time - the ships coming in were military and not commercial vessels.

The StarCom Federation battlecruiser *Revenging Angel,* and the *Orion* frigate which had come so close to intercepting the *First Ship* in Blackheath, translated back into realspace. As their systems came back on-line, they scanned the system, discovered the *First Ship,* and immediately set a pursuit course.

The *Orion* frigate began firing on the *First Ship,* its aft shields flaring. Eventually, with a flaring of coruscating energy, the shields failed and the frigates weaponry punched easily into the rear of the noble barge, crippling it. It drifted on, losing power rapidly, momentum capable of carrying it forwards for eternity.

Until the single spread of three torpedoes from the *Revenging Angel* slammed into its superstructure, detonating with all the fury of their high-yield destruction. The barge cracked open, suffering the loss of all hands, the Captain of the barge giving his life willingly to protect his House Lady.

The Captain of the *Revenging Angel* believed that he had killed Lady Sophia and Lord Micalek. His only regret was the mercenary scum of the *Vindicator* had not been present for him to test his ship against.

*

The *SS Vindicator* completed its translation into the very edges of the Zubrenic System. Admiral Gavain's caution was designed to protect his ship and the Lady Sophia, and Lord Micalek, in case Zubrenic had come under attack.

Out on the edges of the solar system, the *Vindicator* successfully evaded detection. Gavain ordered long-range scans, to search for what was in-system. Zubrenic was just across the border into House Zupanic territory, inhabited with a vast number of small colonies on the numerous moons around a gas giant. Protected by vast asteroid fields, it took some time for the scans to penetrate the heavy clouds of rock and find the Levitican Union fleet in-system.

Gavain ordered the *Vindicator* to cease running silent, announcing its presence loudly.

Lady Sophia and Lord Micalek broadcast a joint communication, verified with code-words, and the Levitican Union forces stood down. The *Vindicator* made its way in-system at full propulsion, heading for the planet Zubrenica Prime, and then one of its larger moons.

The moon Zubrenica XIX was cold, without atmosphere, and had low gravity. It had also been heavily colonised over the past centuries, with over sixty percent of its surface covered in habitable dwellings, the most important moon in the system. The heavy industry in Zubrenic, coupled with its low civilian population and inaccessible, easily defensible approaches, made it perfect as the designated haven for the Council of the Levitican Union.

The *Vindicator* coasted in amongst the warships, following its designated course through the haphazard, hastily organised fleet of ships. Many were showing varying degrees of battle-damage.

When it came in close to Zubrenica XIX, a lander was launched from its belly. The shuttle flew in rapidly towards the surface of the moon, eventually being swallowed by the large military complex on its surface.

The war-room in the military base had been quickly brought out of moth-balls, activated and staffed with the arrival of the evacuees from Leviticus, Newchrist System. Some elements of the few survivors jumping out from Blackheath and Cannai had been re-directed towards Zubrenic, with most of those escaping Svenge-Talia heading for Fort Bastion.

Lord Minister Luke Towers wore his Levitican Union uniform, complete with the long cloak of his office and the ceremonial sword. He had been returning from a recording for the Union forces, when the message had come that his sister and betrothed were in-system. It was the small spark of thankful light, in his overwhelming night of darkness.

The war-room was low-lit, partly to reflect the fact that it was now standard night-time, but also because it fit his overall mood. He was trying hard not to show it to his people, but it was difficult not to - in the last forty-eight hours he had seen the strongest systems in the Levitican Union fall under the hammer of the StarCom Federation.

Only Fort Bastion remained as a single source of strength, against two full fleets. He did have other forces, scattered across Union space, but it would take some time to concentrate them and he was paralysed with indecision as to how to respond to the invasion. His advisors all had alternative views on what to do, and they were splitting along House lines.

His face was bathed in the green glow coming from the central holo-map, and it was just as well; he was pale, tired, and exhausted.

Gradually the other Lord Ministers arrived in the war-room. Zubrenica XIX was not designed for comfort, even the civilians who lived on-planet enduring Spartan conditions. They looked as rough as he did, exhausted, worried about the future. Only Lord Principal Ramicek and Lord Minister Obamu looked fresh; Luke suspected that both were using stims. Perhaps it was time he consulted with his own medical practitioners.

The doors to the war-room opened, the guards standing aside easily in the artificial gravity, and a number of figures entered. His face brightened considerably in the half-lit darkness as he saw his sister framed in the doorway, arm in arm with Lord Micalek Zupanic.

"Micci!" Lord Principal Ramicek was exclaiming, striding forwards, arms wide. Luke strongly suspected that it was done for effect. The Lord Principal had always struck him as a man very aware of how to play to the crowd and take advantage of the moment.

There was one other person with them, striding down the steps into the war-room's holo-pit.

"Sophia," Luke embraced his sister. The operators he had brought with him in the evacuation from Leviticus looked away. "I feared you were dead."

"One is not dead quite yet, brother," she replied, holding him in the hug a while longer than was necessary.

"Your message said you have brought the assassin who killed father?" he said.

"We think he's a Faceless, and he's in a stasis tank," said Sophia. "Lord Micalek has suggested we hand him other to his mother, Lady Wyn, so we can extract information from him."

"Of course," Luke nodded, then stepped away. He found it strange to hear his sister talking in such a cold way, but grief and vengeance can do that to people, he well knew.

The man stood behind her saluted, in the old Imperial style. "Admiral Gavain, Lord Minister."

"Yes, I remember you from the Sky Keep the day you first came to Blackheath," Lord Minister Luke said. "If you had a hand in ensuring my sister's safety - and the safety of Lord Micalek - I thank you deeply."

The Admiral removed his peaked cap and bowed crisply.

Lord Principal Ramicek glanced at the holo-map, then at Gavain, then at Lord Minister Luke. "This is still a highly-classified room, Lord Luke," he said. "Should we really have a mercenary, and a non-Union national, present?"

"Father," Lord Micalek said, "we have an arrangement. Admiral Gavain is under contract to us." He explained quickly.

"And do you agree to this?" Lord Ramicek asked Luke.

He looked at his sister, who gave the smallest of nods but smiled her winning smile. "Yes, without a doubt," he said. "We need all the help we can get, and a fresh perspective on strategy may help."

"He is very gifted," Lady Sophia said to Lord Ramicek. "You should see what James has already accomplished."

"So what's the status?" asked Lord Micalek, turning to Luke. "What've we missed?"

Luke pointed at the holo-map. "They hit us hard, all across the Levitican Union. Newchrist, Cannai and Blackheath they took immediately - from Newchrist we were lucky to escape. As we were leaving, they were destroying the underwater cities from orbit around Leviticus, so there will be nothing to return to . . . assuming we win."

"Defeatist talk, Lord Minister," was Gavain's only comment.

Lord Luke did not respond. "They used overwhelming force to quickly win those solar systems. Even in our worst projections we did not plan for two entire fleets to hit our space. In Svenge-Talia StarCom encountered greater difficulties, taking nearly an entire day to beat our forces, but Svenge-Talia has now fallen."

"A testament to the strength of House Obamu," said Lord Minister Moafa Obamu.

"There were mixed Levitican Union forces in Svenge-Talia, as with everywhere," Lord Brin Claes snapped, very uncharacteristically for him. The strain was telling on him.

"It is not important," Luke held up his hands. "All that matters is that we have taken significant losses. According to our intelligence, and with the benefit of hindsight, StarCom's Fifth Fleet began consolidating over a week ago to jump into Cannai and Svenge-Talia. The threat by Third Fleet was never identified, due mainly to their use of the stargates deep within StarCom Federation space.

"We know that the stargates have been used again, to jump Federal Guard reserve units and large elements of Sixth Fleet towards us. What we do not know, is where. At least that seems to be standard StarCom tactics to date; send in the ground forces and the reserve naval units after the systems have been taken.

"The StarCom units that hit the Newchrist System have already jumped out, and targeted three systems, two in Claes space and one in Zupanic. About an hour ago, the battle-group which struck Cannai also split, re-appearing in four systems, three Galetti and one Claes. It seems we are losing or have lost those systems already.

"One of my biggest concerns is the use of their Weapons of Planetary Destruction." Luke's voice went hoarse for a moment. "The destruction of Alwathbah was thankfully not repeated anywhere else."

"It has gone galaxy-wide," commented Lady Minister Monique Lapointe. "Everyone in the galaxy knows of the travesty that occurred on Alwathbah."

"We have added the name of Silus Adare to the most-wanted list," said Lady Minister Aria Galetti. "He must be caught, and tried for war-crimes."

"We have to win the war first," Gavain said suddenly. "I can give you a plan on how to do it."

"You've only just seen the map," Lord Principal Ramicek scoffed.

"One told you he was good," commented Lady Sophia, as Micalek touched her arm lightly in warning for the cheek.

"Incorrect," Admiral Gavain responded to Ramicek. "We tapped into your communications, your datasphere, even your computer mainframes and data-cores en-route. My techs are Praetorian - your computer systems did not detect our intrusion. If we can do that, so can StarCom's ex-Praetorian Guard."

Lord Luke paled. Everybody in the room was shocked.

"We will sell you the necessary technology to defend yourselves properly," said Admiral Gavain.

"Outrageous!" said Lady Minister Monique Lapointe.

"We had better pay it," said Lord Minister Luke, tensely. "We need that technology. No wonder they ripped through our defences so easily."

"We can discuss a price shortly," said Admiral Gavain.

"What is your plan?" Lord Luke asked.

"Very simply, draw them in, and then choke them," said Admiral Gavain. His eyes chilled Luke as he stared into their icy depths. "You are still numerically superior to them, if you can concentrate your forces effectively. It is always difficult to do when defending against a siege, but it can be done with adequate preparation. Their weakness is in holding the systems they take. Their lines of reinforcement and supply are too stretched, and they need those reinforcements to keep the systems they batter into submission with their elite Third and Fifth fleet units."

"Please, explain more," said Lord Minister Luke, crossing his arms.

Gavain pointed at numerous places on the map. "Pull these units forwards, to positions roughly here. In Galetti, Claes, Lapointe and Towers space, order your units to jump out immediately to these points when they are assaulted by the SCF, they are not to engage."

"You would have us retreat in the face of the enemy?" Lord Principal Ramicek almost hissed, losing his famous composure.

"It is a war of attrition you cannot win against a technologically superior enemy," said Gavain. "Your only hope is weight of numbers, and superior tactics." His voice changed as he continued to explain. "StarCom will most likely strike Fort Bastion; it is a system they cannot ignore due to its apparent strength. You must trap them there, bog them down at all costs. Have your reinforcements ready to jump in and turn it into a meat-grinder."

"You just said to avoid a war of attrition," pointed out Lord Luke.

"Because whilst that is happening," said Admiral Gavain, "I will be taking out their supply lines, the two stargates at Dandarra and Xanaduce. I will ensure they cannot reinforce or hold the systems they have already taken. You draw them in, and using my unit as a quick strike force, I will strangle them. Then you can reclaim the systems you have given up. We use similar tactics - except we concentrate our forces at their weakest points, turn the tables so they are forced into defending the systems they hold, and we have the advantage."

"How will you assault their two long-range stargates?" asked Lord Principal Ramicek. "We've lost our nearest stargates at Blackheath and Cannai. The stargate in my territory is too far away for you to get there, and in any case you would not be able to reach Dandarra or Xanaduce - StarCom will most likely assault Fort Bastion before then."

Gavain explained, talking calmly, coolly, and collectedly, explaining each and every point with precision.

There was silence when he had finished.

Lord Minister Luke nodded abruptly, uncrossing his arms. "We're doing it," he said, looking straight at Admiral Gavain. "The fate of the Levitican Union rests in your hands, Admiral."

Chapter XX

<We will be reaching the terminus point in three .... two .... one .... exit!> the helmsman shouted.

Commander Julia Kavanagh could not help but grip the arms of her command chair with the tension. She loved having command of her own ship, but she still felt unsure about the new situation sometimes. She wondered if that was why James had placed her under the command of Captain Elena Jarman for this mission.

She felt the wrenching, that little shock as it seemed that half the brain caught up with the rest as they exited the jump. <*Sorceror* has achieved successful translation,> said her navigations officer.

<Restricted scanning,> she ordered. She wished and hoped she was showing the same kind of commanding aura that Gavain did when he was in charge on the *Vindicator*. She tried to emulate him, but one of the things Gavain had said to her before they parted was that she had to find our own style of command. <Have we been detected? Has the *Solace* translated successfully?>

<The *Solace* is off our port bow, as expected, Commander,> her senior scanners officer announced.

<Sir, no sign of detection.>

<Then feed me the tactical map,> Kavanagh demanded. She reviewed it carefully. The two strikecruisers were in the shadow of the Blackheath System's primary sun. A scanners black-spot had been created, where no astral body, starbase or commercial space station could easily see this region of space. The automated defence beacons had been destroyed during the StarCom Federation invasion of the system. It had been a risk to jump in where they had, particularly so close to the gravity well of the sun, as the beacons could have been reactivated or they could be faced with a StarCom naval patrol, but it would appear they had been successful in avoiding the attraction of unwelcome attention.

<The *Solace* is hailing us,> her comms officer said.

<Acknowledged. Connect me.> She waited, and then Captain Elena Jarman appeared before her.

<All correct, Commander Kavangh?>

<Yes, Captain.>

<Then we run silent and head towards our designated positions, on our given vectors. Good luck, and good hunting.>

<The same to you, Captain.>

<Jarman out.>

Commander Kavanagh straightened her uniform and leaned back in the chair. She wished she had been given the opportunity to say her farewells to Ulrik Andryukhin, but the next she saw of him, he would be hurtling past her in a strike-pod.

<All hands, I am giving the order to go silent.>

The *Sorceror* powered down all but basic systems on her command, and then using minimal amounts of propulsion, ghosted in on its attack vector, deeper into the occupied Blackheath System.

*

Inside the solar system that was Fort Bastion, nothing except the large orbital bodies on their repetitive and personal rotations, small asteroids on their astral journeys, and occasional space debris floating aimlessly onwards, moved.

Fort Bastion was named so because although it had some small civilian component to it, it was a primarily a large military complex, formerly of House Towers origin before the inception of the Levitican Union. It had once been a testing ground for new Imperial weaponry, hence the space debris.

The system was full of asteroid fields, which constantly shifted in the solar currents coming from the sun. They distorted the gravity fields, making hyperspace travel in and out of the system extremely dangerous without updated information. Of the three rock-based planets, two were too close and too hot, and only one was inhabited, and even then the surface of the planet was uninhabitable to human life, making ground invasion difficult and thus giving House Towers centuries of access to one of the toughest training grounds in the cosmos. The moons were not much more welcoming.

Fort Bastion had nearly five starbases within its perimeter, covering every approach into the system, and two military-grade shipyards. There were numerous automated guns secreted within the asteroids and the rings of the four gas planets. Gun platforms floated at special locations within the system. Camouflaged mine fields were constantly rotated, and explosives placed to detonate other asteroids or space debris. Automated defence beacons were strung throughout the system. The entire system was deadly.

Fort Bastion had many surprises to its name, and much martial prowess. It was particularly so at the moment, with the largest single mustered fleet of the Levitican Union still intact, resident within its boundary. Ships from all the houses clustered together in the inner circle of the system.

The jump signatures of the incoming StarCom Federation ships-of-the-line were detected many minutes ahead of their arrival.

Rear-Admiral Adare checked the data read-outs being flung at him by the various bridge crew. The *Thor's Hammer* had made a safe translation out of its terminus point, and there were no immediate threats. The rest of his rearguard squadron had successfully made the translation from hyper-space.

Vice-Admiral Scanlon and Admiral Haas's units were also in-system, at the expected locations. Each of the three squadrons had come in at completely different jump-points, far out beyond the worst ravages of the system. It had been decided to give away the advantage of surprise, partly to avoid the heavy defences further in-system, where the asteroid fields, mines, debris, and automated defences were located.

It was also partly because they could not guarantee where the constantly shifting jumping hazards in-system were. The only way to safely translate in was to do so on the edges, and then travel in-system at full propulsion. It would be a difficult fight, he knew.

He confirmed his squadron's course, and once all his warships had confirmed that they were fully functional following the jump, gave the permission to advance.

*

Lord Minister Luke Towers read the report that his operative had handed him. "I see," he nodded. He turned to Lord Principal Ramicek. "StarCom forces have just jumped into Fort Bastion," he said.

"The game is afoot," commented Lord Principal Ramicek. "I hope your mercenary is correct about this." The comment was addressed to his son.

"We all hope he is," said Lady Sophia, answered in place of Micalek.

Luke Towers left them, walking back across the war-room to the central holo-pit. As he walked, he demanded that a continuous hyper-pulse link be set up with Admiral Gavain. An operative hurried to do his bidding.

Luke leant on the rail around the holo-pit, clenching it lightly as he watched the first phase of Gavain's master plan take shape. In the past week since Gavain had suggested the plan, he had struggled with doubt. StarCom forces had continued to wreak havoc in the Levitican Union, taking more Claes and Galetti systems. The incursion had begun to spread into Lapointe territory. One more Towers system had fallen. House Obamu had suffered a major multi-pronged thrust, from the elements of the StarCom Fifth Fleet that had struck Svenge-Talia.

Each time, there was limited engagement before the navy pulled out. It meant much of Luke's ground army was rescued, of course, but also it was turning into a public relations disaster as they were not confronting the invaders. Many of the citizens in the Levitican Union were questioning what their leadership was doing to halt the StarCom advance. There had been riots, the most numerous and violent in Zupanic space.

The Union was beginning to fracture, he knew. A victory was needed.

The holo-map focused in on the Fort Bastion system. Symbols reported the forces that had translated in. Out of the front-line units StarCom had invaded with, the remainder had reappeared in the assault on Fort Bastion. It was the same three squadrons that had assaulted Blackheath, led by Haas, Scanlon, and the war-criminal Silus Adare.

"The mercenary commander is available, Lord Minister," an operator said.

"Thank you," Lord Luke replied, manipulating the controls in front of him. The holo-map disappeared, and a much larger-than-life image of Admiral James Gavain appeared in front him. The giant figure was resplendent in his Praetorian Guard-modelled red and black uniform, sat on the bridge of what was presumably his starship. In return, he would see Luke, with the Zupanics, Sophia, and the war-room behind them.

"Admiral Gavain, are your forces ready?" asked Lord Minister Luke.

"Yes, Lord Minister," Gavain nodded. "My advance team should have been in place for several days now, and we are ready to launch the assault at your command."

"You have it. Fort Bastion has just come under attack."

There was not even a smile from Gavain, a satisfied I-told-you-so grin. He was completely cold. "Understood, Lord Minister. How long will it be until their forces are committed and cannot escape Fort Bastion's gravity wells?"

Luke consulted the data in front of him. "They will be unable to jump out-system in under one hour, but they will be fully committed in four hours forty minutes when they are inside the outer defensive ring. At that point my reserves will reveal themselves, and the first engagement of Fort Bastion will begin." That point was distant from the centre of the system, where the strength of his force lay.

He hoped that the defensive technology Gavain had sold them at a ridiculously high price would work, and they would not fall prey to the battle-grade data-viruses that the ex-Praetorian StarCom ships were carrying.

Luke also did not add that the intention of turning the battle at Fort Bastion into a days or weeks-long engagement would cost the Union dearly. Many of his forces outside of Bastion were still in transit to their jump-points. The intention was to have StarCom commit as much of their front-line units as they could.

"We will jump in forty minutes, then. The trap is sprung."

"Good luck, Admiral."

"Likewise," Gavain's image disappeared with no more than that.

*

Chief of Station Aldris was a very, very worried man.

His life had been turned upside down when the Levitican Union had stormed the Blackheath Stargate. He had already been disillusioned with the StarCom Federation, so when the Levitican Union had offered all the former StarCom staff on the stargates and the HPCG stations a free pardon if they agreed to serve them, he had leapt at the chance. He had agreed to three years of service, the training of a successor and the sharing of technological know-how, and then he could retire to a nice plot of land somewhere. Perhaps in the rural areas of Alwathbah.

The sudden arrival of the StarCom Federation Armed Forces, the destruction of Alwathbah and the seizure of the entire system had resulted in many sleepless nights for the last week. He had watched as elements of 6th Fleet had arrived, carrying the ground forces for the land invasion which was apparently now drawing to a close, and the Federal Guard reserve ships. He had no choice but eventually to stand by as Federal Guard navvies had landed aboard his stargate.

Then the agents from the Central Intelligence Department had arrived. They were interviewing and interrogating all of his staff. As far as he knew, he had not been sold out yet for being a 'collaborator' with the Levitican Union, but every day he woke up, he knew it was only a matter of time until they discovered how readily and quickly he had abandoned the StarCom Federation and handed its precious Blackheath Stargate and himself over to the enemy willingly.

So it was that he was sat on the ComCen, feeling physically ill and completely unable to concentrate on his job, when the unexpected jump-signatures were registered on the scanners.

All naval comings and goings by StarCom ships were known and reported in advance by system control on the planet October, and there had been no such notifications in the morning briefing. The system itself was still in lock-down, so there was no commercial traffic whatsoever.

"Where are the jump-signatures?" he asked.

"None are in designated jump-points, sir," his scanners adept said. "We have two to four ships coming in at Tahrir .... and three to six ships coming in close to us!"

It must be a counter-attack he thought. It had to be. The Levitican Union was coming back.

"Do we raise shields?" his Deputy Chief of Station asked. "These aren't expected, sir."

He saw the Special Agent look at him, waiting for him to give the order.

Chief of Station Aldris hesitated, trying desperately to think of a way of keeping those shields down in order to help the Union, but he had no need to worry. The decision was already taken out of his hands.

Captain Elena Jarman, of the Vindicator Mercenary Corporation strikecruiser *SS Solace*, was actually in her ready-room when the call came through from the bridge over the datasphere. They had been running silent for days now, and the datasphere was muted, only essential communications and link-ups allowed.

<Commander, incoming jump-signatures, at the correct positions!> her second-in-command sounded elated.

It was the signal they had been told to wait for, she knew. She immediately began to head to the bridge. <Launch the strike-pods at the target. All hands, battle-stations,> she called.

"What are you going to do, Chief of Station?" the Special Agent from StarCom's CID asked. "Raise the shields? Why do you hesitate?"

Aldris could see no alternative. He had to give the order, and hope that the incoming ships, if they were hostile, were successful in re-taking Blackheath.

"Raise –" he began.

"There's something out there!" someone screamed. "I think they've just fired at us!"

Out in the depths of space, the strike-pods streamed away from the strikecruisers *Solace* and the *Sorceror*. It was an extremely long distance from which to launch them, but any closer and they would have risked detection.

In the same second, both ships launched two low-yield torpedoes each. The torpedoes streaked past the strike-pods, still flying towards the Blackheath Stargate, zeroing in rapidly on the four shield generators.

Space rippled and both ships revealed themselves.

Commander Julia Kavanagh could not keep the excitement from her voice, as she gave the order to adjust to a new heading. Captain Jarman aboard the *Solace* had sent through her orders, and Kavanagh was following them to the letter.

<Shield generators destroyed,> someone reported, <Stargate defenceless.>

<Strike-pods land in six seconds.>

She could feel the *Sorceror* turning on its axis, bringing weaponry to bear. It and the *Solace* were moving slowly, ready to provide a screen for the incoming ships jumping near the stargate.

There were a number of Federal Guard starships in the system, but mostly they were destroyers, frigates, corvettes, military transporters, or other support ships. Close-by, and in the mission time, the only significant threat presented to them were two hopelessly outclassed frigates. StarCom had obviously not expected anyone to threaten the Blackheath Stargate.

The strike-pods struck home, punching through the stargate's outer hull. They drilled in, and then released their cargo. The mercenary Marines boarded the special space station, and began to wreak havoc.

They only had a limited time to achieve their objective.

Captain Jonathan O'Connor, commanding officer of the mercenary star-carrier *Quintessential*, sat confidently in the command chair. He loved being a part of the Vindicator Mercenary Corporation, and did not regret his decision to join James Gavain's outfit at all. He was glad he had followed Harley into the Blackheath System those months ago, when it had been House Towers territory. It was the very system they were now assaulting.

<Successful translation achieved, Captain,> helm reported.

<Two hostiles in close proximity, torpedoes being fired at our location,> tactical reported.

<Tag them Red One and Red Two,> Captain O'Connor commanded. <Launch all flight craft, now. Has the *Monstrosity* completed translation?> he referred to the military transporter. The *Monstrosity* was capable of defending itself, but he had to ensure it survived this encounter. They were up against two Federal Guard ships, a destroyer and a frigate. There were doubtless more out of sight, around the curvature of Tahrir.

<Yes, sir.>

<Impact in three seconds ....>

O'Connor actually felt the impacts as the torpedoes slammed into his beloved ship. They had no shields, so there was no defence. This was always going to be the danger coming in so close to Tahrir. The enemy had had enough time to respond, and were now engaging them at long range.

The reason why the *Quintessential* had been chosen as close support for the strike on the planet Tahrir, was that it was a heavy capital ship with the weaponry to match, and it had the advantage that it could launch its numerous starfighters and starbombers seconds after exit from hyper-space, even though it had no shields. Whilst the capital weaponry was coming on-line and the shields were being charged, the smaller attack craft could wreak havoc on the enemy and defend the two VMC ships.

<All fighters launched,> came the report.

<*Monstrosity* is on a high-speed course for the planet Tahrir.>

<Protect the transporter at all costs!> he commanded.

Chief of Station Aldris whimpered as the turbolift doors to his Command

Centre blew inwards, and a black and red-painted space Marine stepped confidently through the breach.

"Surrender –" it began to broadcast.

The Special Agent from the CID began to fire a small hand-laser, uselessly. He was big, and very physically imposing, but he was dwarfed by the Marine.

The Marine strode forwards through the fire, much of it being deflected off a personal force field. The Marine simply snipped the tines of his or hers heavy power-claw, and Aldris actually screamed as the Special Agent fell into two halves, deeply crimson red blood spraying and exploding everywhere.

Satisfied there was no more resistance, the Marine focused its terrifying T-visor upon him. It was like looking at an alien being. Aldris could see his reflection in the mirror glass of the visored helmet.

"You are the Chief of Station?" it asked through its external voice-casters.

"Y – y – yes," stammered Aldris. He was not that interested in the military, but he knew that the marine was not carrying the colours of the Levitican Union.

The claw, still dripping with blood, raised up and Aldris screamed again. A small port in the claw opened, and a data-chip extended outwards from the recess.

"Follow the orders coded on this data-chip, and we will leave," the Marine said.

Admiral James Gavain looked on approvingly, as his staff performed admirably. They had been in-system less than a minute, and all was going according to plan.

The *Vindicator* and the *Kinslayer* interdictor had jumped in together, in formation, and begun moving towards the Blackheath Stargate. Behind them, the *Remembrance* battlecruiser and the *Undefeatable* had also materialised, and were following at a safe distance in the second wave, approaching the stargate.

The *Solace* and the *Sorceror* were now attempting to engage the two frigates, protecting the stargate and the four ships approaching it. No doubt the StarCom Federation ships in-system were wondering what was happening, as it was not a standard battle formation.

The *Quintessential* and the *Monstrosity* were taking fire, but were rapidly approaching Tahrir. In another two minutes, the *Monstrosity* would be within launch-range of the planet.

Under the control of the Vindicator Mercenaries, the Blackheath Stargate activated. It generated the special structural integrity fields, to provide an additional envelope of security around the ships it was about to catapult across space, warp accelerators fired and the jump initiation capacitors in the launching pylons snatched the *Vindicator* and the *Kinslayer* starships in their grasp.

With a blinding flash of light, the *Vindicator* and the *Kinslayer* vanished, propelled into hyper-space.

Commander Kavanagh registered that the report came through, across the datasphere, that the first two ships had exited the Blackheath System.

Captain Jarman had taken the *Solace* back towards the Blackheath Stargate, to pick up the Marines that were currently aboard the facility once they had completed their mission. The *Sorceror* was on its own, but the strikecruiser could take on the two frigates easily.

Emperor-speed you on your way, Jamie, she thought, even as the *Sorceror*'s shields, now fully active, took the brunt of a weak broadside from the frigate tagged as Red Three.

<The *Monstrosity* is within the striking distance of Tahrir,> the report came through.

Captain Jonathan O'Connor snapped his attention away from the battle damage reports. His fighter screen was taking damage from the Federal Guard destroyer and frigate, but now his capital ship's weaponry systems were on-line, he had begun to punish the destroyer. The frigate was suffering wave after wave of heavy bombing runs.

<The interference cloud is active?> he asked.

<Fully, Captain,> came the response. They had set up a cloud of scanner-interfering particles, chaff and electronic noise, to disguise the actions of the *Monstrosity*.

The M-class super-transporter was equipped with some of the very best Praetorian technology. The strike-pods it carried were capable of stealthed insertions. With the additional cover of the interference the *Quintessential* was running, the strike-pods could land safely in the uninhabited and unwatched regions of Tahrir. The enemy satellite net had already been disabled by specially tasked fighter wings.

The strike-pods launched, burning quickly into the atmosphere of Tahrir. Exactly two thousand Marines made their way down to the planetary surface, all of them ejected within the first ten seconds of his order.

Good luck, General Andryukhin, O'Connor thought.

<Pull back from Tahrir,> he ordered. <All units, disengage. Flight squadrons, staggered withdrawal, return home.>

The Blackheath Stargate's launching pylons crackled with raw energy, coruscating beams of light snapping out, capturing the *Remembrance* and the *Undefeatable*, and the starships jumped out-system.

"Thank you," said the Marine to Chief of Station Aldris. "We will be back."

The Marine clumped away across the Command Centre. "Who are you?" Aldris called out.

The Marine carried on its way, ignoring him completely. The rest of its squad followed him, and the bridge of the stargate facility was suddenly empty. No-one moved, no-one said a word.

Aldris was confused. His heart felt weak. He had already had enough of this damned interstellar war of secession.

He glanced down at the orders the Marine had given him. The first ships they had catapulted into hyper-space had been sent to Dandarra, the second pair to Xanaduce. The only thing both systems had in common was that they were both very deep into StarCom territory, and both had stargates.

Of course, he thought, not making any connection, the two systems contained the only two stargates in StarCom territory that could come anywhere near to reaching conquered Levitican Union space.

<*Solace* reports that they have collected the boarding parties,> the comms officer informed Commander Kavanagh. <Captain Jarman is ordering us to jump. Mission accomplished.>

<Turn to this heading, full speed ahead, and then jump,> Commander Kavanagh ordered. <All power to rear batteries.>

<Aye, sir,> came the response.

Despite herself, she looked on the holo-map at Tahrir. She knew that her beloved, Lieutenant-General Ulrik Andryukhin, was leading the two thousand marines that had just been dropped onto Tahrir. She hoped he would live and survive the hostile territory, and that she would see him again.

<We are clear of the planet Tahrir's gravity well,> came the report.

<We are ready to jump, sir.>

Captain Jonathan O'Connor checked the holo-map. The *Solace* and the *Sorceror* had both left the system. Only the *Monstrosity* and the *Quintessential* remained. They were not being pursued by the destroyer or the frigate, both of which were heavily damaged and were obviously unwilling to continue the fight.

<Jump,> he ordered.

Seconds later, the last of the Vindicator Mercenary ships jumped out of the Blackheath System.

*

The Xanaduce System was deep within conquered StarCom Federation territory. It was considered a pacified system, but even so, because of its importance it was protected by three Federal Guard naval frigates and an ageing strikecruiser, a captured starbase, and had a sizeable army outpost on the planet below the base.

At any one given time, there was always the possibility that there would be a passing StarCom Federation unit consisting of ships-of-the-line. Damaged ships came back through Dandarra, before heading on further into StarCom space, Corewards. Ships going to the front-line headed in the opposite direction. Xanaduce had been re-opened for interstellar trade, so the stargate in Xanaduce was seeing heavy use once again as commercial trade re-asserted itself.

It was partly luck that there was absolutely no shipping near the stargate when they had jumped in.

Commander De Graaf felt satisfied with how the mission had gone, and had felt himself bask in Captain Danae Markos' praise. They had jumped in as close as they dared to the stargate. The defensive forces in-system were so distant, there had never been any real danger.

The combined firepower of the *Remembrance* battlecruiser and his *Undefeatable* destroyer had overwhelmed the shields of the stargate in a relatively short period of time. They had launched Marines towards the stargate, and overpowered it.

As Commander De Graaf observed the Marines returning to their motherships, he knew that they had carried out an unenviable mission. There were non-combatants aboard that stargate, members of the StarCom organisation admittedly, but not in a military capacity. The Marines had orders to kill every last person aboard the facility, and they had done that with unswerving devotion to duty. It had apparently been brutal.

The *Undefeatable* had laid a large number of mines around the stargate, even as the in-system forces had tried desperately to respond. They had not expected such an assault. De Graaf reminded himself that it was StarCom who were the aggressors in this war; besides which, he was a mercenary, on a contract.

He loved his new life, and was thankful to Gavain for giving him another chance. He was responding to Gavain's trust with a desire to prove himself, and to carry out his duties to the best of his ability.

At a predetermined time, the stargate computers automatically triggered, and the launching pylons grasped the two mercenary ships, and threw them back into hyper-space, heading back towards the Levitican Union.

A minute later, the proximity mines exploded. The stargate slowly broke apart, aided by the thermal bombs planted on its primary and secondary power generators. There was no way for StarCom to discover where they had jumped to, and no way for StarCom to use the stargate to launch further forces, reinforcements or supplies into Levitican Union space easily.

De Graaf hoped that Gavain's mission in Dandarra had gone just as successfully.

Chapter XXI

Lieutenant-General Andryukhin walked down the ramp of the *King Cobra* hover-armoured personnel carrier. As he did the marine mounted in the twin-lascannon pod on top rotated the mount, staring at the surroundings.

General Andryukhin looked up, seeing the faint haze in the air that betrayed the presence of the chameleonic force field. His power-armour booted feet stamped down onto the newly laid metacrete surface, polished into a perfect flatness. The mountain the shelf was cut into rose up into the air, and it was already covered thickly with snow. There was a deep chillness to the air, his suit's computer informed him.

The courtyard was full of vehicles, from repulsortanks to HAPCs, battlewalkers to long-range artillery pieces, anti-air platforms to mobile orbital lasers, and many more types of vehicles besides. Many of the Marines who had dropped onto the planet Tahrir were out walking in the open, greeting comrades and generally being relieved that they had made it safely to the base.

A small *Leopard*-class hover-jeep, a vehicle used for everything from scouting, special forces insertions and general run-arounds, glided to a halt before him. A figure vaulted the jeep, and saluted him crisply. Commodore Harley Andersson was barely recognisable through the oxygenator visor.

Andryukhin returned the Imperial salute, his chest armour ringing as the gauntlet slammed into it. "Commodore," he said. "Tahrir Base is certainly as fricking impressive as I had been told. You've done some bloody hard work here."

"This is just the surface base. It's nearly ten times as big below ground," the voice-caster built into the oxygenator unit ground out. "We've got plenty of space for the Marines you brought with you."

"How many have come in?"

"About sixty percent, but we know there are more on their way. Walk this way, General - shall we get into the warmth?"

"Lead the way," Ulrik Andryukhin gestured with his power-claw. He followed Andersson as they walked to the jeep, riding in the back with the Commodore as it set off.

The strike-pods had been carefully shielded from detection, although doubtlessly they would eventually be tracked. The StarCom forces on Tahrir were far too distant to catch up with the landing sites for the Marines. Andryukhin himself had travelled nearly sixteen hours at the top speed of the *King Cobra* to make it to the base, they had been dropped so far from its location.

StarCom may have picked up on the fact that some strike-pods had been fired at Tahrir, but even that was not certain. The *Monstrosity* and the *Quintessential* had used special interference to prevent the detection of their launch, and the satellite net was all but destroyed. His Marines were all on orders to be extremely covert, disassembling their strike-pods and burying the equipment before heading for Tahrir Base.

The *Leopard*-class jeep glided to a halt again, and they both disembarked, Andersson thanking the driver politely. They entered a large building, itself close to the inner edge of the base and built partially into the steep incline of the mountain.

Andersson removed the oxygenator and the visor, and then pulled down the specially sealed thermosuit hood. "Welcome to the upper command post," he said, taking Andryukhin through the operations room to his office at the back.

"We were ready for the assault into Blackheath," said Andersson, "and Jamie left me a couple of standing orders. We were to be prepared for any course of action, but I must admit, I wasn't really expecting to be told to keep within the base. Nor was I expecting two thousand Marines to drop covertly onto the planet. I take it the game-plan's changed?"

"Fucking hell too right it has," General Andryukhin swore. "Harley, everything's changed." Andryukhin explained about the contract they had taken, and Andersson whistled at the money Gavain was charging. Andryukhin then moved on to the future plans, and what Gavain was going to do next.

"I always said that he was bright," Harley leaned back in his suspensor-chair and smiled proudly. "Emperor, but I love that man. He was tipped for greatness you know, he would have done very well if the Praetorian Guard had survived."

"It seems to be working so far."

"But you've not explained what you're doing here on Tahrir. I already have a thousand Marines on base, I didn't need the protection. We have a small army here, now."

"Which we'll be using," said Andryukhin. "Jamie intends to come back Harley, but until he does, we need provisions for long-range operations. We need to undermine the StarCom land forces on-planet, and be in position to take strategic locations all over the planet. When Jamie comes back, we have to be ready."

"Small-unit operations?" Andersson asked.

"Yes," Andryukhin replied. "We have to get into position whilst evading the main StarCom land forces."

"Well, I have all the intelligence you need."

"I was hoping you would, we're going to need it," said Andryukhin. "We have less than six hours to plan and brief my troops, and to wait for the rest to arrive, before we head back out again."

"We'd better get to work, then," Andersson grinned.

"We're going to hand the Commies their fucking heads," Andryukhin smiled savagely.

*

Admiral Gavain waited for the all-clear to sound after the jump, before he passed control of the bridge of the *Vindicator* back to Commander Al-Malli. They had been highly successful in the Dandarra mission, jumping in and out before the local forces had assaulted them.

As he walked to his ready-room, he accessed the report sent over by Captain Markos, who had apparently also had a similarly successful mission in the Xanaduce System.

Both strike forces had used the stargates to propel them to terminus points a couple of jumps away from their combined, pre-arranged rendezvous point. The naval ships of the Vindicator Mercenary Corporation were now reunited, in the system they would launch from when they returned to the Blackheath System. There was little chance of the StarCom forces recovering data from the destroyed stargates, but it was important to be careful.

All Gavain had to do now was wait for the signal from Lord Minister Luke to assault the Blackheath System. There was a message waiting for him from Lord Luke, saying that Fort Bastion had come under assault two days ago, but the trap had worked and the fighting was stalling.

All they needed now was for StarCom to commit more forces into the meat-grinder that Fort Bastion had already become, and the Levitican Union counter-attack could begin in earnest.

*

Commander-In-Chief Jaiden Ryan met Vice-President Pereyra in the corridor, as he was walking towards the President's office. "You've been summoned as well?" he asked.

"Oh yes," said Pereyra. She looked tense, Ryan could see it in the way she was walking. She had to shorten her gait to match his slower progress. He was sure he was putting on weight. "Not that I have much power any more. She's taken it all herself."

"Director Chbihi is already in the office, I understand," commented Ryan. There was a question in his voice.

"Malika is no more favoured than we are," said Pereyra. "I was speaking to her before - she is as concerned about the President's behaviour as we are."

"We cannot continue like this," said Ryan, stepping as close to treachery as he dared.

"We will talk later, it's not safe," said Pereyra. "But I agree. As does Malika."

The guards outside President Nielsen's office allowed the doors to be opened after they had passed the incredibly onerous security precautions. Ryan and Pereyra stepped into the office, and then crossed the expansive gap to approach Nielsen's desk at the other end.

President Nielsen looked even worse, if that was possible. Her hand was shaking as she sipped from a dark liquid, and there was a hypojector close by her right hand. It must be sedatives, Ryan thought. Dark rings were visible under her eyes, and her hair was not prepared. She looked more cadaverous than ever. Her left eye twitched spasmodically.

"Ryan!" she snapped. "Explain what is happening on the Levitican front to me?"

"It has become a step too far, as I feared," he replied without hesitation. "We abandoned Operation Storm in the north-eastern vector of the Core to launch Operation Vengeance, the invasion of the Levitican Union. We have over-stretched our forces, and now we are coming close to the collapse of the entire galactic vector.

"We cannot hold the territory we have taken. Not only were we stretching the Federal Guard too thin, but now we cannot reinforce or resupply the systems we have taken in the Union. Levitican mercenaries have destroyed both stargates, the only two stargates we could use, to get reinforcements quickly to Levitican space. Now we have to engage in a month-long journey. Our blitzkrieg tactics will not support such a long logistics chain."

"It is intolerable that they have insulted me so by destroying the stargates!" Nielsen suddenly screeched. "Are they barbarians?"

Ryan wisely said nothing about the Tears of the Moon.

"Our situation has not gone unnoticed," the sibilant Malika Chbihi said. "My spy network informs me that the triple-way Korhonen, Cervantia, and Hausenhof war is possibly going to end. They are looking at territory we have taken with jealous eyes, as easier pickings. They know we are too weak in the north-eastern vector of the Core to withstand their approach, especially now our Third, Fifth and Sixth Fleets are tied down, and the Federal Guard reservists are stretched beyond their ability. I have numerous reports of uprisings and rebellions about to rear their heads."

"So what is your response?" Nielsen asked.

"Reinforcing the Levitican operation is now out-of-the-question," Ryan said promptly. "I will use those supporting, reserve forces of the Federal Guard to protect against Korhonen et al aggression, with the new Ninth and Tenth Fleets.

"In Levitican space, I have ordered a slow-down in the planned invasion programme, and a halt to other elements of it as I must divert forces to an unexpected theatre. Fort Bastion may prove to be my Waterloo. The fighting there is intense, and there are more Levitican forces appearing. I believe it to have been a trap. I must commit more forces to win the system. Losses are mounting. My only consolation is that we are exacting a heavy toll on the Levitican defences, but I believe there may be a counter-attack imminent in systems we have already taken."

Nielsen's eyes narrowed. "You want to ask me if we can withdraw?" she guessed.

Ryan lowered his eyes. "Yes, Madam President. It all hangs in the balance. If a counter-attack occurs, we may lose our chance."

"Your request is denied. We may have an advantage," and here Nielsen smiled a terribly forced smile at Director Chbihi. "Explain to the Commander-In-Chief."

Ryan looked at Chbihi questioningly.

"We have been contacted by the laughably titled Lord Principal Ramicek Zupanic," said Director Chbihi. "He has attempted to sell out the Levitican Union. In return for leaving Zupanic space intact, and returning the system we have already taken, he will ensure his forces leave the war, and he will break the agreement that formed the Union."

"The end of the Union, and the withdrawal of a portion of the Union forces. Will that help win your war, Ryan?" Nielsen asked.

"It could swing things in our favour," he said. In the invasion plan, they were going to leave House Zupanic space until last, as it was the most distant from the invasion path. However, if the Zupanic military forces suddenly withdrew, it may have an effect in the Fort Bastion system, and perhaps the surprise could suddenly swing things his way.

"Then I will signal our assent," said Nielsen. "He has said that once our forces withdraw from the Zupanic system we took, he will order his own armed forces to immediately return to Zupanic space. A day or two later he will renounce the Levitican Union. It will tear the nation apart," she gloated.

*

The *LSS Knightsword* translated from the terminus point into realspace. The dreadnought was the flagship of Lord Luke Towers, and was one of three dreadnoughts owned by the Levitican Union. All three had been House Towers ships previously. One was now floating dead in space out towards the edge of the Fort Bastion System, shattered into pieces, but its sistership the *Knighthood* was still in service in Fort Bastion, albeit also showing signs of heavy damage.

The *Knightsword* had come in at a safe location, deep within Fort

Bastion. StarCom forces had no such advantage, not daring to jump directly into any areas within the system that they had not already passed through, in case they were mined.

Lord Minister Luke Towers gave permission for his pre-recorded message to be broadcast to everyone within the Fort Bastion system. The *Knightsword* was his personal warship, and he wanted to let everyone in-system know that he was present. It would boost morale.

Whilst the *Knightswords* computers uploaded the most recent military intelligence, Luke headed to the ready room to review the data on his own. He sat at the desk, and then keyed the information into the holo-projector display before him.

He reviewed the strategic information first. The StarCom advance had ground to a halt. Some twelve hours previously, another two squadrons had jumped into the Fort Bastion System. StarCom were getting desperate to win this battle, he could see that. He now had over half of their remaining ships-of-the-line locked into the battle at Fort Bastion.

It was time to commit his reserves he knew. Another eight ships had moved within jumping range of Fort Bastion. He recorded an order for them to engage, and carefully selected the jump-point as being close to the StarCom Federation Fifth Fleet's 1st Vanguard squadron. There was a mine field between the jump point and the 1st Vanguard, and hidden asteroid guns nearby. Perhaps they would fall for the same trick twice, he thought, the first time they had tried it yesterday having been proven to be a great success. If not, there was nothing lost.

The siege of Fort Bastion had ground down into siege warfare, and it was bloody. They were now well into the fourth day of battle, and it had become a series of raiding sorties, advances and withdrawals. StarCom forces were going very carefully, and had they had taken heavy damage and some not insignificant losses.

There was a personal message for him from an agent being run by his father's spy-master. That surprised him. The agent, according to the message, was risking a great deal personally in order to get this to him. He opened the message, and read it.

He stood, ordered a whiskey from the food simulator, sat down and read it again. Then he drained the whiskey, and then read it one more time to make sure.

He could not believe it.

He reviewed the strategic data. The message from his spy was corroborated.

There was no option. He prepared, signed and sealed a number of orders, and sent them out. He had to launch the counter-invasion now. Some four ship-of-the-line squadrons were still active in the rest of

Levitican space, but six had been committed to Fort Bastion. He had to strike now, as he had no reason to doubt the spy's message.

He pressed a communicator pad. "Set up a continuous hyper-pulse message with Admiral Gavain, now."

Adare entered his quarters, tired. They were in the middle of a war-zone, but the operations in Fort Bastion were proving more difficult than StarCom Federation tacticians had imagined.

As the lighting came on, he saw something that he registered instantly as out of place.

He walked over to the table, and picked up a piece of paper. There was writing on it.

Of course, he thought, how ingenious. In a time when every communication was electronic, or capable of being overheard or recorded, what better way to get a secret message to somebody undetected. The piece of paper was from Lieutenant-Colonel Lamans.

For a moment he wondered if it was a test. It could be Special Agent La Rue, attempting to ascertain his loyalty. The note told Adare that everything was ready, and the plans were in place.

He scribbled out a reply, using the pencil which had been left next to the note. He would give the signal as to when, and they were all to be ready.

*

The alert woke Admiral Gavain. It was an automatic call from the datasphere. He jacked in, rubbing the sleep from his eyes as he did so.

<There is a continuous hyper-pulse comms coming in for you, Admiral,> comms officer Lieutenant Forrest told him.

It could only be Lord Minister Luke, he knew. <Put it through,> he said, standing up. He was fully dressed, but wore his black skin-tight undershirt. He was still shrugging on his uniform jacket as the holo-projection of Lord Minister Luke appeared in front of him.

"Admiral Gavain," Lord Luke looked incredibly angrily. "I am in the Fort Bastion System, so I am not free to speak. I know we probably have secure communications, but you never know - StarCom could crack this pulse channel."

"I understand, Lord Minister."

"You have a green-light to launch the mission," Luke said simply.

Gavain paused, folding his arms. "It seems a little .... premature, surely?" he asked.

"It might be, but events have forced my hand," said Lord Minister Luke. "How soon can you launch?"

"We are ready," said Admiral Gavain. "Within three minutes."

"Emperor-speed, as I believe you would say. All the best, Admiral."

After Lord Luke had disappeared, Gavain wondered what could have happened. Lord Luke had looked extremely angry. Unfortunately, as they were hiding in the SD4-M2 System - their old training grounds - they did not have access to any automatic beacons in order to pick up news. They did not know what was happening in the Levitican Union battle, as they were incommunicado, awaiting the order to launch back into the Blackheath System.

Well, thought Gavain, whatever the reason, the order has been given. We are in contract, and an order is an order.

<Commander Al-Malli,> he called across the private channel.

<Yes, Admiral?>

<Signal the squadron. We have mission go. Initiate the jump sequence.>

<Aye, aye, sir!>

Chapter XXII

Commodore Michael Murphy rubbed the sleep out of his eyes. It was coming up to 06:00 Imperial Standard hours, and he was due to take command of the ship. He had awoken early, unable to sleep. The bio-engineered cybernetic Praetorians did not need large amounts of sleep in any case, but he had found of late that he was unable to keep to any normal pattern. He was stressed.

He emerged onto the bridge of the *SFSS Universal*, the destroyer that he used as his flagship, with two marines following him. A former loyalist to the second Emperor, he had been on the wrong end of the civil war, and like some, had been offered release from the Saturnian prisons if he accepted the StarCom offer of a place in their military. It had come with two guards and a CID Special Agent, the latter of whom was already on the bridge.

<Commodore on the bridge,> his second in command announced. <You are early, sir.>

<I could not sleep,> he replied on the private channel.

"Good morning," he said cordially to the Special Agent, who looked at him coldly, then shrugged ever so slightly.

He hated being watched so. It had allowed him to keep his life, joining the StarCom Federation, but he resented it hugely.

He sat in the command chair, and called up a status report. As the theatre commander in the Blackheath System, he now had overall command of the operations in-system, following the death of the Rear-Admiral who had been charged with the role, following the strike where the mercenaries had utilised the Blackheath Stargate.

Commodore Murphy still puzzled about the engagement near Tahrir. He had originally suspected that it had been a cover for dropping forces on-planet, but so far, none had appeared on the surface and no trace of any hostile incursion had been detected. He suspected now it was a diversion, to allow the mercenaries to capture and use the Blackheath Stargate. He was well aware that their successful mission had led to the jeopardisation of the entire operation to invade the Levitican Union, with no reinforcements or resupply now possible for a month.

He put the thoughts out of his mind, and concentrated. He was a member of the Federal Guard fleet, a massive organisation of ships that operated in small units, holding and consolidating StarCom's grip in systems where the front-line ships had smashed resistance. All the ships in the system were under his command.

He had a frigate on a constant roving patrol around the various mining operations on Dante, Yin and Yang. He doubted there would be an attack there, but it was more to keep the populations and the miners under control.

He had an interdictor, a frigate and a strikecruiser in close proximity to the Blackheath Stargate, ex-Praetorian ships all, having placed his best ships where he needed them. The military world of November was further defended by two strikecruisers, ex-House military. He had three ex-house military frigates on patrol between Omaha and Utah, although there was currently an insurgency underway on both planets, so there were significant ground forces present, and thusly one E-class military transporter from Sixth Fleet in orbit around each

Tahrir was still an active site of battle, with House Towers military fighting a desperate action against the StarCom invaders, the last major one in-system. The *Universal* itself was in orbit, along with another destroyer and two frigates. The *Universal* was the only ex-Praetorian ship, the others being house military. The ex-Praetorian battlecruiser *Carnivorous* and a strikecruiser named the *Shadow* were in the shipyards, being repaired, both from Third Fleet and left behind as the main ships-of-the-line squadron had moved on into Fort Bastion.

In orbit around Tahrir were also no less than six military transporters, two M-class super-transporters, and four house military. They were stationary, with little to do whilst the marines and soldiery of the StarCom Federation engaged in the fight for Tahrir. Besides the elite Praetorian marines from Sixth Fleet, there were regiments of soldiers from conquered territories who had come over to the Federation, units from Houses Weiberg, Tremane, Hannover and Ymar.

Other support ships in-system consisted of two cargo-freighters, a medical-frigate, and a repairship, all from Sixth Fleet. The gigantic repair-ship was near the planet November, latched around one of the patrolling frigates like a limpet to a shark, and the medical-frigate was in orbit around Tahrir for obvious reasons. There were also six corvettes from the Federal Guard, in various locations around the system. Corvettes were hyper-space and planetary-landing capable small naval units, fast units that had little front line battle-value but were useful for scouting missions, running messages, and ferrying people to and from locations in a war-zone.

All in all, Commodore Murphy reflected, there was quite a considerable StarCom presence in the system. He would have preferred to have more ex-Praetorian ships under his command, however, but the Blackheath System was nearing pacification on the ground as well as in space. His main concern was another incursion by Levitican Union ships.

<Jump signatures!> his scanners officer suddenly called out, as if in answer to his thought.

His peaceful morning ruined, Murphy demanded, <Where?>

<Close to Tahrir, sir!>

<All hands, red alert! Put all forces in theatre on battle-stations,> Commodore Murphy ordered.

He reviewed the battle-map quickly. The jump signatures were indeed coming in close to Tahrir, but he noted they were far enough out that the enemy would have time to raise shields before any of his ships could get within weapons range. He felt a sinking feeling as the read-out told him that there were between seven and twelve possible ships coming in from the size of the jump signatures.

"What is your tactical analysis?" his Special Agent asked.

"This is no raid," Commodore Murphy replied. "They're coming in to stay, this time. They're targeting Tahrir." It was classic Praetorian offensive tactics he knew, concentrate a strong force on a particular point.

<Order an in-system jump from the strikecruisers around November,> he ordered. He dared not pull too many forces away from defensive points around the system, in case more enemy ships were in-bound. <Wait until the enemy ships are fully translated, jump to these co-ordinates.> He also ordered the frigate on patrol around Dante, Yin and Yang to do the same. <*Carnivorous* and *Shadow* to disengage from the shipyards, immediately. Transporters to retreat to safe distance, except for the M-classes, I want their fire support.>

<Exit!> the helmsman Vries called out across the datasphere.

<Transmit the signal,> Admiral Gavain ordered calmly. He checked; all ships had translated in within two seconds of each other, in near-perfect timing. <Squadron, set course for Tahrir on the pre-determined attack vector.>

His priority target was Tahrir. If they had that planet, he would have a foot-hold into the system. His secondary target was the military world of November, but he was willing to take a gamble on that one.

They transmitted a wide-band signal on a frequency which slammed through the planetary atmosphere of Tahrir, even as Gavain was quickly reading the tactical situation.

Commodore Harley Andersson's patch into the largely defunct satellite network on the other side of the planet Tahrir had informed him of the sudden movement of the Federal Guard starships in orbit.

He had called the entire base to alert, not that there were many staff left on site any more. When the signal was received by the base's highly powered communications receptors, he punched the air in excitement.

"Nice to see you, Jamie," he whispered to himself.

<Contact all Marine units. Tell them they are go!> he ordered. In the process of doing so, they risked giving away the position of the Tahrir

Base, but it was unavoidable. The base broke comms silence.

<Commodore,> his comms lieutenant called for his attention. <Something odd. The hostile ships have transmitted a signal towards Tahrir, and there has been an answering signal back.>

Commodore Murphy thought fast. <Tell all ground forces to prepare for a Levitican Union counter-assault,> he warned, guessing incorrectly. <Scanners? Who are they?> He stared at the tactical display in front of him. The enemy ships had translated into the system in a double-line formation, not exactly standard, but they were already moving towards Tahrir. He had ordered his ships to form up near the shipyards, so hopefully when the *Carnivorous* and the *Shadow* were released from their docks, they could join the fight quickly.

<The lead ship is identified as *Vindicator,* commander James Gavain, Vindicator Mercenary Corporation,> his scanners officer replied. <All ships are ex-Praetorian. Another battlecruiser and two strike cruisers in the first line, a starcarrier, interdictor and destroyer in the second.>

Similar forces as to before, Michael Murphy thought. The *Monstrosity* military super-transporter they had used before was absent, which probably meant they intended to have the naval battle first, before engaging land units.

Andryukhin received the word from Commodore Andersson, and grinned. He reached for the helmet hanging at his belt, and fastened it into place, the seals bonding together.

They were under camouflage, protected by special chameleonic force fields, at the base of the hills that led across the one kilometre plain to the space lift installation. The megapolis of Tahrcity was distant on the horizon, its cityscape striking and beautiful with the pink streaks of the early dawn behind.

Over the past couple of days, his forces had moved in closer and closer to the city, finally laying up in their given positions. A large proportion of his force was residing outside Tahrcity, with others located all over the planet, ready to strike at the reserve lines and support outposts for the tens of thousands of soldiery on-planet. The main battle was taking place with the retreating Levitican Union forces, over a thousand kilometres north, sheltering from the naval forces in orbit. They were perhaps a day or two away from surrender, being hunted down like vermin as they hid.

It was all about to change.

He patched into his own unit, a special strike force. <We have go> he signalled. <Attack!>

<They are forming up near the shipyards,> Lieutenant Agrawal told him.

<A defensive semi-circular formation, Admiral. Signs that the ships in dock are readying to disengage.>

<Jump signatures!> someone shouted.

<Where?> Gavain did not lose his composure, but he knew this was not a good sign. Could it be a trap?

<Behind us .....> the incredulity then entered Agrawal's voice. <Two strikecruisers located near November, and the frigate near Yang, have suddenly disappeared, Admiral. I suspect it is them from the signatures, translation in less than ten seconds.>

<Are they mad?> Commander Al-Malli asked on a private channel. <It's a highly risky manoeuvre to do an in-system jump. If it goes wrong, they could destroy their ships.>

<If it goes right, they have us trapped,> was Gavain's response.

Lieutenant Zuo Li-Chan operated the massive arms of the *Executioner*-class battlewalker, feeling the regular fast heart-beat vibrations as the driver ran it towards the space lift installations walls. <All units, free fire!> she commanded.

The early morning light was ripped asunder as multiple beams streaked towards the walls. The space lift was being defended by a token Federation force, lazy and confident as they were so far behind the front lines.

The walls came crashing down under the onslaught. The Federation ex-Praetorian *Revenant* stood by them came awake, moving away quickly to avoid the fall.

At one hundred metres, Lieutenant Zuo fired the twin-MACs on the right arm, and the super-heavy siege weapon of the left-shoulder mounted plasmacannon. The ball-like projectiles of the MACs slammed in unison into the *Revenant*, which was still unshielded, almost driving it off-balance and tipping it, the driver forced to make it fall to one knee with a crashing thud, even as the plasma blast sheared into the cockpit which projected forwards from the main body like the beak of a raven.

As the *Executioner* thundered past, Marine Lieutenant Zuo twisted its upper body, shearing the power-sword on the left arm through the weakened cockpit. The crew were incinerated by the crackling blade, and the *Revenant* began to topple forwards.

The *King Cobra* HAPC shot underneath the falling *Revenant*, jumping into the air and over the collapsing walls. It landed inside the compound of the space lift installation, other *Cobra* HAPCs following it into the facility's inner courtyard.

The assault ramps popped, and Lieutenant-General Andryukhin jumped out, booted feet slamming into the ground. <Towards the control

station,> he ordered his unit.

The cargo doors leading inside the main building were closing rapidly, but Zuo Li-Chan's *Executioner* fired at them. With a rending screech of metal, the doors blew inwards. Andryukhin led the charge inside, power claw hissing as the Federation troopers ran to meet them.

<We are within firing range,> Gavain's tactical officer informed him.

Admiral Gavain checked, and saw that they had reach long-distance torpedo range on the enemy. They had identified the *Universal* as the commanding officer's flagship. <Target Red One, torpedoes away,> he ordered.

<Three seconds until we have jump arrival,> Lieutenant Agrawal warned.

Torpedoes streaked away from the forward launching ports of the *Vindicator*, the *Remembrance*, the *Solace* and the *Sorceror*. They crossed torpedoes coming in from the defending Federation naval units.

There was a blinding flash of light behind the mercenary ships, as the incoming Federation ships translated into real-space.

When the flash of light had cleared, it became obvious that something had gone horribly wrong. They had mis-jumped. The two strikecruisers from November, and the frigate jumping in from near Yang, had translated at almost exactly the same time and place, coming from separate directions.

The incoming warpfields had crossed, two of the ships attempting to occupy a space too close to each other in realspace. They had been drawn towards each other, their jumps thrown off-course, both attempting to materialise in the same physical location. The result was catastrophic.

The resultant explosion as the warpfields collapsed and the ships detonated caught the second strikecruiser, drawing it into the conflagration as it translated. There were multiple explosions in space, all three ships tearing each other apart spectacularly.

<No!> cried Commodore Murphy, actually raising his hands to head in horror.

Seconds later the incoming torpedoes not destroyed by protective fire slammed into the *Universal*s shields. They deflected most, but three torpedoes sliced through, detonating on the fore hull almost simultaneously. The nose of the *Universal* was ringed in fire, and the ship's forward acceleration slowed. Murphy had to grasp the arm of his chair to protect against the impact.

<Signal the *Apollo* and the *Monstrosity*,> Gavain ordered. <Tell them all is

clear for them to jump in and assault the planet November.>

<Unbelievable,> Commander Al-Malli breathed.

<That's why in-system jumps are not advisable,> Admiral Gavain commented.

General Andryukhin stood on the lifting platform of the space lift installation, the ceiling grids opening above his head. They were peeling back, rising into the air like the petals of a flower opening.

It had taken less than five minutes for his strike force to claim the installation. Now he and his marines were clustered on the space lift platform. His armoured units were already racing towards Tahrcity. The assault on the capital had already begun. All over the planet, his Marines were catching the Federation land forces completely unprepared.

He signalled Andersson's technicians in the control room. <Send us,> he ordered.

With a whirr, the space lift activated. Beams of energy threw themselves into the air, latching onto the shipyards far above. Barely moments later, as the shipyards systems automatically responded and locked in, the box-like self-contained platform began to rise upwards, slowly at first but then with increasing speed.

Andryukhin and over two hundred of his Marines were on their way to the shipyards. He looked out of the reinforced window, seeing the planet Tahrir already dwindling rapidly.

Aboard the *Sorceror*, Commander Kavanagh thumped the arm of her chair and smiled. "Go, Ulrik," she commented, watching on a small long-range viewscreen as the space-lift activated. It was already possible to see the space lift platform punching up through the atmosphere, a big rectangular structure being propelled upwards in-between the forcefield beams.

<We are reaching secondary engagement range with the enemy forces,> her tactical officer announced.

At almost the same moment, the orders were received from Admiral Gavain. The two strikecruisers were to surge ahead, and engage the destroyers at short range whilst the battlecruisers came in.

<Adjust to this heading,> Commander Kavanagh ordered. <Be advised, primary target is Red One,> she named the *Universal*, <all weapons-free, all weapons-free.>

As the space-lift platform docked at the shipyards, the *Sorceror* pulled ahead of the main battle line. It began to fire all weaponry as it rapidly closed the distance with the slow-moving Federation destroyer, the *Solace* on a similar parallel path.

Commodore Murphy saw what was happening. Having recovered from the shock of seeing his reserve forces destroy themselves, he ordered the units in orbit around the Blackheath Stargate to advance at full speed towards Tahrir. He was outgunned, and he needed the support.

Even as he gave the order, he saw the fighters and bombers streaking away from the mercenary star-carrier.

<Target the *Sorceror* and fire!> he ordered. He tasked his other destroyer to target the *Sorceror,* whilst his two frigates and the two M-class military transporters were to shelter behind and come up and under the destroyer line, once the *Sorceror* was in range. They would all target the *Sorceror,* and hopefully knock it out of the fight.

He needed the *Carnivorous* and the *Shadow* out of the shipyards and on the battlefield if he was to stand any hope of fending off the mercenary ships.

Andryukhin fired his rotary battlecannon, sweeping it left to right as he ran across the open cargo-hall. The space lift was designed to transport large provisions up to the shipyards. They were not meeting heavy resistance so far, but he knew it was only a matter of time. The Federation forces on the space station would begin to react, like a body firing white cells at an invading virus.

<Company Alpha with me, to the *Carnivorous.* Company Beta, head for the *Shadow,*> he ordered.

Admiral Gavain read the urgent warning that the *Sorceror* was beginning to lose its forward shields, but before he could order her to do so, Commander Kavanagh quite sensibly turned her ship, trying to bring a port broadside to bear on the Federation destroyer *Universal.*

<We are within secondary engagement range of Red One,> he was informed.

<Target Red One, all weapons-free,> Commander Al-Malli ordered.

<Jump signatures detected close to the planet November,> a scanners officer said.

That was the *Apollo* frigate and the *Monstrosity,* he knew. Within three minutes, the *Monstrosity* would be launching eight thousand Marines towards the military planet, almost exactly the same number as the enemy forces currently in-situ. It would be an even fight, he knew.

He re-directed his attention back to the fight around Tahrir. The docking clamps were blowing free of the *Carnivorous* battlecruiser. Come on Ulrik, he thought.

There was a blinding flash of light, and the military transporter *Monstrosity* translated into realspace, the *Apollo* frigate exiting its own terminus point at a safe distance slightly behind. They were at battle-speed as they exiting, pointing directly at the planet November.

The *Monstrosity* closed the distance within a couple of minutes, and began to launch strike-pods, which streaked down to the surface. The atmosphere of November began to look as if it had suffered a meteor strike, a meteor which had shattered and broken up as it hit the atmospheric envelope.

The *Apollo* under Lt-Commander Wybeck engaged the repair-ship, which was currently latched around a defenceless frigate. Although they had been disengaging, under the fire of the *Apollo* guns, they had no choice but to surrender and power down.

Andryukhin charged through the umbilical cord onto the bridge of the *Carnivorous*, firing his rotary cannon aggressively into the Marines before him. They were beginning to meet heavy resistance. This was an ex-Praetorian ship, and now they were fighting people who had exactly the same equipment and training as they did.

<Port shields failing,> came the warning call.

Commander Kavanagh ordered a roll, to bring the starboard side into direct firing position on the *Universal*, and to protect her damaged ship. Damage reports were coming in - there had been no less than five hull breaches, all relatively minor, but the strikecruiser *Sorceror* was about to start taking heavy damage. She contained the panic she felt, knowing that she was under direct fire from six Federation ships.

She looked at the *Carnivorous* battlecruiser, which had now slipped its moorings and was beginning to power away from the shipyards. If her beloved had not made it aboard, when the *Carnivorous* and the *Shadow* joined the fight, she and Captain Jarman were in serious trouble. The *Solace* was doing its best to hurt the *Universal*, but there were too many of them.

The *Vindicator* and the *Remembrance* turned away from each other in almost perfect unison, the former bringing its starboard batteries to bear, and the *Remembrance* its port. They opened up with a blistering hail of fire, directly onto the *Universal*. Supported by the long-distance fire from the *Undefeatable* and the *Kinslayer*, the damage they started doing to the destroyer was phenomenal.

<Shields failing, shields failing, catastrophic failure!>

Commodore Michael Murphy directed his attention away from the strategic picture to the immediate danger. All shields were failing on the *Universal*. He had no hope of defending against the onslaught he was coming under.

<Break-off,> he ordered. <Bring us about, get us back to the shipyards. Sound general reverse, all units>

Captain Danae Markos of the *Remembrance* saw the *Universal* beginning to turn. The *Solace* and the *Sorceror* strikecruisers had overshot the enemy units, and were coming about to try and make their way back towards the VMC line.

<Port torpedoes, strike these co-ordinates, staggered launch> she ordered her weapons teams.

The torpedoes streaked away from the *Remembrance*, ten of them. Designed for long range engagement, they covered the distance in an unbelievably short period of time. One after another they impacted into the fore and upper hull of the turning *Universal*, but rather than being on a dispersal pattern, they all homed in on the same point.

The first couple opened up the reinforced hull of the destroyer like a tin can, the next ploughing deeper and deeper into the infrastructure. There was a series of explosions as the *Universal* was ripped into deck after deck.

Commodore Michael Murphy, jacked into the datasphere, felt his ship rumble as the hull was breached, then heard the massive explosions as deck after deck was torn away above him. The damage reports were instantaneous, but he knew his doom was impending.

He was knocked out of his seat, sprawling forwards ignominiously as the *Universal* continued to suffer torpedo strike after torpedo strike. He rolled onto his back, and said a last prayer to the Emperor.

He raised his hands over his head as the fiery explosion burst into the bridge, the torpedo detonating a deck above them, and he screamed as he was incinerated, the entire room turning into an inferno.

General Andryukhin slammed full-bodied into the Federation marine before him, colliding with a clunking of metal, a heavy duty laser beam slicing over his head as they fell to the deck of the *Carnivorous*' bridge. The marine under him tried to batter him away, but Andryukhin desperately drove the tines of his power claw into the StarCom soldiers side.

Andryukhin reared up. His helmet had been fitted with two small lasers for close in-fighting, and these triggered, boring into the head of the marine under him. They ripped into the helmet, blinding the Federation soldier.

General Andryukhin powered up, firing his rotary cannon across the bridge of the *Carnivorous*. He raised his right foot and stamped it angrily down on the weakened helmet of the Federation marine, and there was a crunch as it caved in.

Streaking tracer shots ripped through the bridge crew, sending body parts and people flying in all manner of directions. The rest of his squads were coming up behind him. He saw Sergeant Jack Inman fling himself towards the captain of the ship, getting cut down by a Federation marine using a sword. The two halves of Jack Inman, cut from shoulder to hip, slid apart and to the floor in a shower of blood.

Corporal Calaman fired her heavy-duty lascannon into the Federation Marine, and he staggered back, half his upper body missing. One more blast, and the Marine almost disintegrated.

Andryukhin de-cycled his rotary cannon, realising as the battle anger faded that they had taken the bridge.

<Strike force,> he commanded, <We are ready to go. Life pods.> He looked down at the body of Inman, and then turned to Calaman. <You're acting Sergeant. Plant the data-virus directly into the computer core, set the bombs, and we go.>

Commander De Graaf kept the *Undefeatable* at an even level with the *Kinslayer*, using his heavier weaponry to batter the *Universal* from afar. The ship was continuing to turn, and was beginning to be a danger to the Federation ships which were trying to retreat.

He ordered a blistering pattern of fire into the ailing ship, protecting Commander Kavanagh and Captain Jarman as their strikecruisers fell into line with the advancing battlecruisers of the *Vindicator* and the *Remembrance*.

He was watching the *Carnivorous* come into range, when suddenly a series of life-pods ejected from the ship. "Well done, Ulrik," he punched the air, surprising his bridge crew.

Spinning in space as the life-pod ejected, Andryukhin looked through the port-hole at the *Carnivorous*. Life-pods were also ejecting from the *Shadow* strikecruiser.

All of a sudden its shields began to fall, and lights started to go off all across the ship. He grinned ferally. The data-virus they had planted not only deactivated the ship, but would spread across the Federation data-sphere, wreaking similar havoc on the other units. The *Carnivorous* powered down, and with its bridge currently about to explode, they had no hope of getting it re-started. The data-virus that Commodore Andersson's technicians had engineered was much more effective than anything they had taken with them when they had landed on the surface of Tahrir.

Starfighters launched from the *Quintessential* streaked past, trying to protect the life-pods that had ejected. This was the most dangerous point of his entire mission, he realised. They were in small, indefensible craft, in the middle of a fully fledged battle. He was powerless to effect his future now.

He broke open an old-fashioned deck of cards, and beckoned Naomi Calaman to join him.

Admiral Gavain examined the strategic situation carefully. The *Universal* was still trying to fight, its weapons teams not necessarily realising that they had lost their bridge, but they were not firing at anywhere like efficiency or with full arsenal. The *Carnivorous* and the *Shadow* were out of the fight, knocked out by his strike-teams.

The virus had spread across the Federation datasphere. Although the firewalls on an ex-Praetorian starship were of the best in the galaxy, when a virus had been planted inside the main core, they were of no use whatsoever. The reinforcements coming in from the Blackheath Stargate, the strikecruiser, interdictor and frigate, were fighting it off to varying levels of success. The frigates around Omaha and Utah were too far out to be affected. The numerous corvettes in-system were failing.

He watched as the reports started coming in. The destroyer and the two frigates, with the two military transporters, were suffering heavily, their systems under heavy assault by the virus. The medical frigate was already dead in the water.

<Signal the *Titan of Stars*, tell them to jump in for the Tahrir assault. I want our forces landing on the Federation ground forces immediately.>

<Aye, Admiral.>

<Patch me through to the enemy fleet in system, each ship individually.>

Gavain waited, until he got the all-clear.

<StarCom Federation starship,> he said, his voice being directly targeted to each ship. <I am Admiral Gavain of the Vindicator Mercenary Corporation, currently contracted to the defence of the Levitican Union. If you surrender now, your lives will be spared and you will be accorded prisoner-of-war status in accordance with interstellar convention. De-power your ship, completely deactivate power generators, and send all your command staff to my location in a shuttle.>

He waited, and then the calls started coming in.

Chapter XXIII

Commander De Graaf was sat on the bridge of his destroyer, the *Undefeatable,* sipping a hot drink peacefully. Every so often a call came in from the forces on the surface of Tahrir, asking for a supportive orbital strike. When these calls came, his weapons officers would target the location and fire pin-point turbolaser beams down to the surface.

The *Titan* had jumped in-system, and deployed its three thousand marines on top of the one thousand already engaging the bulk of the Federation land army. Levitican Union forces had rallied, no longer under threat from orbit, and had turned. The precise tactical strikes by the covert forces on Tahrir had crippled the enemy defences on the planet. Within the day, they would have Tahrir back in their control.

The strikecruiser *Sorceror* under Julia Kavanagh had been the worst damaged out of the VMC forces, the *Solace* taking some hits. The *Remembrance* and the *Vindicator* battlecruisers had emerged relatively unscathed. Andryukhin's actions had saved them all some serious damage.

He shook his head in wonderment. It had been a daring plan, but it had worked. There was no end to his respect for James Gavain now, and he was determined not to let the man's trust in him disappear. He had been teetotal now for more than a month.

The fighting on November was fierce, but Levitican Union reinforcements had jumped in and deployed less than a half hour ago. The VMC units were handing over battlefield operations to them now, about to pull out, re-board the *Monstrosity,* and head for Tahrir. Omaha and Utah planets were also now receiving the dropships and landers from incoming Union military transporters.

Some of the Federation naval forces had jumped out-system rather than surrender, but many had been unable to do so. There had been some fighting on the *Shadow,* as their troops had refused to accept the command staff's surrender.

De Graaf admired Gavain, but he could not help but wonder what he would be like when he did not have the upper hand. Now they had the Blackheath System in their control, they could become a target for any Federation reprisals - although thanks to their actions in knocking out the stargates in Dandarra and Xanaduce, the Federation could not get reinforcements into Blackheath. He wondered what was happening elsewhere in the Levitican Union; multiple star systems had been assaulted at the same time as they had hit Blackheath. Was the StarCom Federation invasion of the Union collapsing?

*

Commander-In-Chief Jaiden Ryan held his head in his hands, sat in his office within the Palace of Communications. Reports were still coming in, but the entire operation to conquer the Levitican Union had turned sour. It had truly been a step too far.

A large proportion of his forces were bogged down in Fort Bastion, being mangled by the heavy Levitican Union presence and their considerable defences. They had developed a resistance to the electronic warfare his advanced Praetorian front-line units were using, and this had helped to tip the balance in their favour. A win was still possible he judged, but at a cost he was unwilling to bear. It would be a pyrrhic victory, if any, and was still at best projection a week or maybe two away.

If he could have placed reinforcements into the Fort Bastion system, that may have been different, but he now had none to send. The stargates at Xanaduce and Dandarra were out of action, destroyed, so there was no way he could send in units from deeper in the Core.

The Union counter-attack had been vicious. They had retaken numerous star systems, battering his Federal Guard reserves and now engaging his land forces. Blackheath and Cannai had both fallen. Those of his front-line units not engaged in Fort Bastion had come under attack, and whilst there had been one success on the behalf of Fifth Fleet, it was only a foot-note to the disaster that was befalling his operation.

The supposed betrayal by House Zupanic had not materialised yet. Even if it occurred, he knew it would not swing the balance. The situation in the war had changed rapidly; he suspected that even if Lord Ramicek had intended to betray the Union, he would have reassessed that decision rapidly, as soon as Lord Minister Luke had begun his counter-attack. The StarCom Federation was on the verge of losing the war altogether.

He had been out-thought by Lord Minister Luke Towers. He was impressed, even as he knew that he was looking at the collapse of the war. Disaster in the Levitican Union spelt disaster in the entire Eastern Segment and north-eastern galactic vector. Solar systems were rising up in droves now, and the entire vector out from Sol was now under threat.

He raised his head. There was only one real option. He still had the best part of five squadrons in Fort Bastion, the remnants of two fleets. They were heavily damaged, battle-worn, but they could be rescued. He had shattered Federal Guard, and some of Sixth Fleet's land forces still intact.

President Nielsen would not like it, but he had a responsibility to the men and women under his command.

His mind was made up. They would retreat from Levitican Union space.

He looked at the situation with this resolve at the fore-front of his thinking. The best way was to secure the stargates at Cannai and Blackheath. He looked at Fort Bastion. He could send the 1st Vanguard under Vice-Admiral Scanlon to Cannai, to recapture and to hold, with Rear-Admiral Adare of the 5th Rearguard to do the same in Blackheath.

They would have to hold the stargates for the rest of the forces in Fort Bastion to pull out, and the other forces scattered across the Levitican Union.

He recorded the orders, and sent them out to the hyper-pulse communications generators, to be sent Priority Alpha.

Then he leaned back in his chair, awaiting the inevitable summons to President Nielsen. He wondered if she would have him removed, or executed.

*

Rear-Admiral Adare was on the bridge of the *Thor's Hammer*. Lieutenant-Colonel Lamans stood at parade-ground rest beside him, but there was no indication from him that any messages had passed between them. Special Agent La Rue and her two marines stood near him, and he wondered again if he had been set up by them. Commander Zehin could apparently be trusted, but Commodore Pacheco was die-hard StarCom Federation.

Adare put all such thoughts out of his mind. The battle in Fort Bastion was not proceeding well. They had been told to withdraw back out to the edge of the solar system, along with Vice-Admiral Scanlon's squadron. Both Scanlon and he had suffered damage in the days long engagement in Bastion.

The Levitican Union campaign had cost his squadron. The frigate *Nero* had been lost, and the *Orion* was going to be scuttled. The *Queen of Egypt* was at fifty percent efficiency, and the *Underworld* destroyer was barely functioning. The rest of the ships in the squadron had suffered varying degrees of damage. Only the super-heavy armour of the *Thor* had prevented his own ship suffering unsustainable battle-damage.

He did not truly care about the rest of the squadron, or the rest of the StarCom Federation Armed Forces for that matter. All he cared about was himself. On all the signs so far though, he would not survive Fort Bastion.

<Incoming hyper-pulse, Priority Alpha,> his comms officer said.

<Private channel,> he ordered.

He listened to the message from Commander-in-Chief Ryan himself, and could not help but smile. He downloaded it onto a data-chip, and passed it to Special Agent La Rue.

<Address all ships,> he commanded. <We are leaving Fort Bastion. Our new mission is to take and hold the Blackheath Stargate. Jump in thirty minutes.>

He then disengaged from the channel, and began planning his second assault into the Blackheath System. The Levitican Union system was certainly taking a hammering in this war. His orders were clear; take and hold the Blackheath Stargate at all costs, and do not engage beyond holding the stargate. All other targets were to be ignored unless they threatened the asset. It was vital for the Federation withdrawal from the Levitican Union.

From intelligence gleaned so far, Admiral Gavain of the Vindicator Mercenary Corporation was in-system.

"I told you we would meet again," he said to himself.

*

Commander-In-Chief Ryan entered President Nielsen's office with considerable trepidation. The Director of the intelligence services, Malika Chbihi, and the Vice-President were already present. President Nielsen was half-standing out of her chair, in mid-rant.

As he entered and the doors closed behind him, she stopped, eyes narrowing dangerously as she stared at him. He did not let his pace falter as he approached her desk, the guards in the room following his progress. There were eight of them, spaced around the room in various alcoves.

"What have you done!" she hissed at him, pointing a trembling figure in an accusatory manner.

He looked at her calmly. He knew he was probably facing at the least dismissal, but most likely death. She had a way of dealing with those who displeased her. She was looking terrible, worse than ever, like a cadaverous queen ruling over the kingdom of the dead. She had no weight on her, and her voice was cracking.

"I had no choice," he said quietly, coming to a stop between Pereyra and Malika before the desk.

"There is always a choice. How dare you be so treacherous? To order the withdrawal from Levitican space without my approval is high treason, Jaiden Ryan," she growled.

"We are losing," he said plainly. "We might be able to win the battle in Bastion, but we have lost the war. It is my assessment –"

"Director," Nielsen cut him off, addressing Malika Chbihi. "Have the Commander-In-Chief arrested, and taken to the cells, to await summary execution."

There was a long moment of silence.

"No," said Director Chbihi.

Nielsen sat back down fully in her chair. "What do you mean, no?" her eyes were wide.

"This has gone far enough," said Vice-President Pereyra. "You are out of control, Rebeccah. You are no longer fit to govern the StarCom Federation."

President Nielsen looked as if she were about to have a heart-attack. Ryan was as equally surprised, and was looking from the Director to the Vice-President in almost as much shock.

"Guards!" she suddenly shouted. "Arrest them all!"

There was another long pause.

"What are you waiting for?" she screeched. "Shoot them! Now!"

The guards did not move, but they did begin to change. Their bodies began to morph, features changing, bones breaking and re-setting, Their clothes changed, their forms becoming different, and then, within ten seconds, only eight Faceless assassins stood in the room where once there had been her loyal guard.

One of them walked forwards. Nielsen actually clutched a hand below her breast, as if her heart were literally about to give up. Her mouth was as wide as her eyes, and she looked as if she were struggling for breath.

Ryan could not believe his eyes.

The Faceless assassin who had walked up to her desk, leaned over it, one hand on each side of the desk. "President Nielsen," said the assassin. "Your insurance is cancelled."

President Nielsen fell backwards, off the suspensor chair. The assassin walked around, knelt down, and put a hand to her neck. It looked up, it's terrible, blank black eyes looking at the three most senior members of the Federation before it.

"She is suffering heart failure," it said. Its right hand morphed quickly, becoming a blade. He sliced it through her neck, neatly decapitating her. As the blood flowed out across the marble floor, it stood and added, "but now she is dead."

As one, the assembled Faceless turned and left the room, with the exception of the leader. It stood before the three. Ryan had never met a Faceless assassin before, although he had heard of their myth since he was a new-born, fresh out of the vat.

"Vice-President Pereyra," the leader said. "The contract is complete. We expect your half of the payment from StarCom Federation coffers to be transferred immediately. We will claim the other half from First Lord Al-Zuhairi, as per your arrangement."

Ryan gasped. Pereyra had conspired with First Lord Al-Zuhairi of the OutWorlds Alliance to kill the President.

"It will be done," said Pereyra.

The Faceless assassin left the room, with the eyes of all three following him.

When Ryan turned back, Pereyra was sat in the President's chair. "Sorry, Ryan, but we had to keep you innocent of this," she said gesturing to Director Chbihi. "Now, we have to stop this insane war."

*

<Admiral!> said Lieutenant Agrawal, <Incoming jump signatures.>

<Show me,> he replied. Gavain broke off from his conversation with Commander Al-Malli, and turned around. The holo-map sprung into life before his eyes, and he calmly reviewed the data. He had considered the possibility of a Federation counter-attack, but had not viewed it as likely.

There were several signatures being recorded, a number of ships coming in close to the Blackheath Stargate. Of all the possible places he thought might be attacked, he had guessed at the planet November or Tahrir, not the stargate.

<Red alert. Form up, two line formation,> he ordered, <centre on the stargate, and ahead half-power.>

Even at full power, they would not be able to reach the stargate before the enemy forces translated in, and he wanted to be sure this was not a feint to lure him away from Tahrir.

Space split asunder, and the squadron emerged from hyper-space.

Adare reviewed the situation quickly, ordering identification of the hostile ships in-system. When the tag came up naming the *Vindicator*, he smiled.

"What do you intend to do, Admiral?" Special Agent La Rue asked.

"My orders were to secure the stargate," he said, "so that is what we will do."

<All ships, turn to this heading, V-formation> he ordered on the datasphere.

He could feel Special Agent La Rue watching the data transfer. "Our orders were to secure and guard the stargate," she said. "Why are you changing heading towards Tahrir and the enemy?"

"The best way to secure the stargate, is to destroy the enemy," he said. "We outnumber and outclass them."

"We are damaged."

He called up a holographic image of the mercenary ships. "So are they," he said.

<Identification coming through,> Lieutenant Agrawal said.

Gavain read the data. The squadron was identified as Third Fleet, Fifth Rearguard. They were led by the Rear-Admiral Silus Adare, the very man wanted for the war-crime of planetary annihilation. The squadron was now veering away from the stargate, and heading towards his ships.

He had no option.

<All ships, prepare for action, full speed ahead,> he gave the order.

Adare glanced at Lieutenant-Colonel Lamans, and saw the man stare back at him. He had not left the bridge as he was supposed to, to join his marines downstairs. Lamans raised an eyebrow questioningly, and carefully, he shook his head ever so slightly.

Admiral Gavain stared at the map carefully, having given command of the ships operations to Al-Malli. His mind was racing, thinking of what he would do in which circumstances. The enemy were coming in at him in a V-formation, with the *Thor's Hammer* in the lead, then the two battlecruisers. The strikecruisers came next, then the two destroyers, one of which was struggling to keep up and should obviously not even be attempting to fight. There was a star-carrier nestled inside the arrowhead formation, but even that looked heavily damaged.

Despite the obviously dilapidated state of the squadron, they still outgunned his own, primarily because of the dreadnought. The *Thor* was showing the least signs of damage, and would be the hardest target. Gavain also knew his own ships needed repair.

His ships were advancing in a double-line formation, his battlecruisers in the centre, and the strikecruisers on the flanks. Both strikecruisers were severely damaged, the *Sorceror* in particular in desperate need of attention. In the second line were his star-carrier, interdictor, destroyer, and trailing behind both lines the frigate. His support ships were staying out of the fight completely.

The odds were stacked against him, and he would take heavy losses today, he knew.

He stared at the representation of the *Thor's Hammer*, knowing that it was the killer, and cursing Adare and all he stood for.

<Two minutes until we reach torpedo range,> he was informed.

<All ships, torpedoes on the *Thor*,> Gavain ordered.

Chapter XXIV

The *Thor's Hammer* glided through the explosions, its prow emerging from the fire like a dragon exiting its cave. It shields were still sparkling as it's forward torpedo launchers lit up, and then eschewed its deadly cargo. The torpedoes tracked in towards the *Vindicator,* crossing the distance rapidly.

<Enemy fighters launching . . . estimate two hundred ....>

They are under strength, Gavain thought. <Order O'Connor to have our fighter screen intercept them, I want bombers on the *Thor* as soon as we have its shield down,> he ordered.

The *Vindicator* rocked.

<Impact, seven torpedoes, damage minimal, shields holding.>

<Return fire,> Commander Al-Malli ordered.

<All ships to hold the line,> Gavain ordered. <*Sorceror* and *Solace,* prepare to advance. All ships to target the *Thor,* it is designated as the primary target.>

Torpedoes flashed across the distance between the two squadrons, the battlecruisers *Veritable* and *Revenging Angel* opening up on the *Vindicator.* Seconds later the destroyers *Underworld* and *Ubermacht* began to launch theirs, then the *Thor,* then the battlecruisers again.

Wave after wave of lethal projectiles streamed in towards the *Vindicator.* Fighters streamed past it, attempting to intercept the lethal weaponry but with little effect. In less than half a minute they would have contact with the enemy starfighters coming in towards them, but their fight would be as a small side-show in comparison to the leviathans rushing towards each other.

<We are entering secondary engagement range, Admiral,> Commodore Pacheco informed him.

<Fire on the *Vindicator,*> Adare confirmed his orders. <All ships, *Vindicator* is the primary target.>

<Forward shields failing!> Gavain heard the call from his senior tactical officer, the newly promoted Lieutenant Woolfe.

<First line, hard port and all-stop,> Gavain ordered. <Present starboard-side now. Second line, all-stop.>

Rear-Admiral Adare watched as the enemy ships slowed and turned quickly, presenting their starboard sides. They were about to broadside the *Thor.*

"What are they doing?" asked Special Agent La Rue from behind him.

He felt a flash of irritation. "He's taking a risky manoeuvre, forcing us to either slow or evade by planting his squadron directly in front of us. They have the advantage, bringing broadsides to bear on us. Would you mind if I concentrated, Special Agent?"

"Yes, of course," she said, falling silent.

The second line were diving under the first, but coming to a stop as well, further back, allowing the destroyer's longer-range weaponry to wreak havoc on the *Thor's Hammer.*

<Forward shields failing.>

<Orders, Rear-Admiral Adare?> Commodore Pacheco asked.

<Continue, we can take it and more,> he ordered. <However, all ships, prepare to adjust heading to the following vector, and roll.>

This might just turn out to be your lucky day, Gavain, Admiral Adare thought. <All ships, disperse fire.>

<Disperse fire, Admiral?>

<Maximum damage to all ships, Commodore Pacheco,> Adare responded. He glanced at Lamans, who was staring at him again, and once more, he gently shook his head.

<They are changing fire pattern, Admiral,> Lieutenant Woolfe warned Gavain.

Gavain saw what was happening. As predicted, Adare was taking his arrowhead formation up and over his own ships' position – he had not counted on the enemy squadron splitting fire. Some of his other ships could not take this.

With some horror, Gavain watched as the dreadnought began to roll. The direction it was taking brought its formidable starboard weaponry to bear on his port flank, where the strikecruiser *Solace* under Commander Kavanagh was located.

He desperately gave orders for the turn, ordering his first line ships to split and accelerate, to engage the enemy units individually, but it was too late.

<Full broadside, target *Sorceror*,> Adare ordered.

<Aye, aye sir.>

The fearsome broadside of the dreadnought *Thor's Hammer* opened up on the damaged *Solace* at the closest range yet of the engagement. Torpedoes struck home first, slamming into the shields, followed rapidly by multiple beams from the turbolasers, every single battery spitting azure death.

With a glittering, the *Sorceror*'s shields failed spectacularly, and some of the laser beams began to strike home.

Powerful magnetic accelerator cannons roared soundlessly, propelling ball-like projectiles into the hull. Disruptor emitters wreaked havoc on the hull, and then more torpedoes struck in on the unprotected *Sorceror*. Already heavily damaged, it could not tolerate the fusillade it suddenly found itself under.

<Warning - imminent meltdown!> Commander Kavanagh's engineering officer suddenly shouted. <Twenty seconds and counting.>

Commander Kavanagh gasped. Her strikecruiser's main drive engines and power generators were overheating, struck numerous times, unable to withstand the tremendous barrage of firepower that the *Thor's Hammer* had suddenly levelled at it.

<All hands,> she ordered, <All hands - abandon ship!>

Her ship shook so violently, it felt as if the entire world were ending.

<All hands, abandon ship!> she repeated, standing up from the command chair. The lifepods for the bridge crew were located at the aft of the bridge. Every single crew member was streaming towards the rear, but as they ran, the ship shook violently again from more broadsides.

She was lifted up off her feet, and for a sickening moment, she floated in the air, before her head banged off the ceiling. She collapsed to the floor, dazed, wondering what was happening.

<Five seconds!> her chief engineer called out.

"Ulrik," she whispered, before she fell unconscious.

Lieutenant-General Andryukhin, who had been directing the mop-up operation on Tahrir when the enemy squadron landed in Blackheath, watched the *Sorceror* break apart. The explosion was spectacular, even at this distance.

He felt something very unaccustomed. Tears were welling up in his eyes, and he was glad his helmet was in place to hide his emotion from his staff. He stood still, in complete shock, as he watched the death of his lover.

*

"Lord Minister, I think you might want to listen to this," said the comms officer aboard the *Knightsword*.

Lord Minister Luke Towers looked around, still leaning on the railing before the holo-map of the Fort Bastion solar system. "What is it?" he asked.

"A continuous hyper-pulse, Priority Alpha - it's from Earth, a general broadcast," the comms officer said.

"Put it on the main holo-viewer," Lord Minister Luke ordered.

He stood back, hands on hips as an image appeared before him. The gigantic head and shoulders that appeared in the middle of his bridge was not that of President Nielsen, but that of Vice-President Pereyra.

"- Nielsen is dead," the Vice-President was saying. "I am now the President of the StarCom Federation. On behalf of StarCom, I offer sincere condolences to all in the galaxy who have suffered loss at the hands of our armed forces, and I extend the hand of peace to all involved. As of several minutes ago, I have ordered all military operations to cease, and I ask those nations with whom we are currently actively at war to accept a truce whilst we withdraw from your territory –"

"Lord Minister Luke, an incoming hail from the enemy flagship."

"On my personal communicator," he said, unhooking it from his belt and raising it to his chest. A small image of a man in StarCom Federation uniform stood before him.

"Lord Minister, I am Admiral Haas," the man introduced himself, "Commanding officer of the StarCom Federation forces in the Fort Bastion theatre."

"I know who you are, Heinrich Haas," said Lord Minister Luke.

"Are you watching the broadcast from Earth?"

"Yes, I have it on the viewer now."

"Will you accept the truce whilst we withdraw?"

Luke hesitated. "How will you withdraw?"

"Allow us to use the Blackheath and Cannai stargates to retreat. We currently have an active operation under way in both to seize them. We were about to retreat from Levitican territory in any case, Lord Minister."

"Stop the fighting in Blackheath and Cannai, and you can withdraw under a truce," said Lord Minister Luke. "We can discuss terms at a later point, after the firing has stopped."

"I will do my best. May we use your HPCG connection to broadcast to the two systems?" Admiral Haas asked.

"Of course," said Lord Minister Luke.

The communication ended.

"Data-scrub the communication for viruses before putting it on the HPCG," Luke commanded sternly.

He looked up at the gigantic head of the new President Giovanna Pereyra. "Once again," she was saying, "I can only express my deepest and most humble apologies for all the pain, loss and death that was caused by the StarCom Federation under the direction of President Nielsen. We will make reparations where we are able to. I am sorry for what you have suffered in our name."

*

Gavain stared at the fireball that had been the *Sorceror*, the inferno caused by the explosion rapidly dying out in the void of space, feeding off the oxygen within the ship even as it was turned inside-out, the superstructure failing spectacularly as it was pulled apart by the vacuum.

He tried to force himself not to think of Jules Kavanagh, but for the briefest of moments, he saw before his eyes some of the moments they had shared together. Her support to him, her knowing way of looking at him, of reading him when no-one else could.

He blinked, and saw the holographic image of the *Thor's Hammer* on the display before him. Nothing had changed - Adare was a war-criminal, the *Thor* was the heaviest ship ranged against them, and he was the primary target. That he was Jules Kavanagh's killer was of secondary importance. Gavain had a duty to his people, to try and get as many of them out of this battle as possible.

<*Remembrance* and *Vindicator* to target *Thor*. De Graaf, Meier, target the *Underworld*, it is heavily damaged, knock it out of the fight and quick. *Solace*, protect the second line, engage the enemy battlecruisers.>

Gavain knew the *Solace* would take horrendous damage, but they had to reduce the enemy firepower coming in at them. Knocking out the *Underworld* destroyer was his best option, using his battlecruiser and the *Remembrance* to keep the dreadnought distracted.

He knew he could not win this fight. He wondered when he would have to signal the withdrawal, and how many more ships and people he would lose.

Admiral Silus Adare smiled without humour. Admiral Gavain was losing, he knew.

He glanced up. Special Agent La Rue was not paying him any attention, instead staring at the holo-map with intensity. His two bodyguard marines, Dum and Dee, were stood behind him.

The *Vindicator* and the *Remembrance* were desperately trying to engage his dreadnought, and they were taking heavy damage to their shields. Shortly, he knew that his heavier class of ship would batter through both. The *Thor* was in a heavy engagement - Adare knew he might not have a better opportunity than this.

Perhaps this would be Admiral Gavain's lucky day after all.

He glanced at Lieutenant-Colonel Lamans, his smile widening and becoming genuine, before he nodded sharply, just the once.

Lamans moved in a blur, his super-enhanced body reacting to the signal with inhuman speed. The blades mounted on both his right and left fore-arms extended as he whirled round.

The first blade cut through the unprotected head and face of the first marine, the one that Adare had christened Dum. It continued on, striking into the neck of Dee, even as his second blade plunged straight into the chest and heart of Dum, penetrating the thick chest armour with unparalleled force.

With a scraping of sparks, Lamans withdrew the blade, whirling back around in the opposite direction, swiping the second marine with a vicious backhand slash with his second blade, before then plunging the first blade into Dee's chest.

Both marines dropped to the floor, mortally wounded, Dum crying out in agony. It was the first sound Adare had ever heard from him.

"What –" Commodore Pacheco was beginning to say, before Commander Zehra Sahin pulled her side-arm from its holster and shot him at point-blank range through the side of the head.

Special Agent La Rue was turning round, to meet Adare's fist as he rose from the chair. The uppercut punch knocked her back, and he followed it up with a quick double punch, before giving her vicious martial art kick to the side of the head. She collapsed to the floor.

"I'll save you for later," he said. All across the bridge, marines and bridge-crew loyal to him and Lieutenant-Colonel Lamans were turning on those they had been forced to call comrades. It was his own civil war, Adare reflected, those who hated the StarCom Federation rising up against those who supported it.

He bodily lifted Commodore Pacheco from his command chair, and took his place. As far as he was concerned, he was no longer commanding the Third Fleet's Fifth Rearguard Squadron; his only concern was the command of the *Thor's Hammer*. All over the ship, people loyal to him were taking control. He was no longer a part of the Federation at all.

Commander De Graaf had not known Julia Kavanagh that long in comparison to the others, but her loss nevertheless affected him. It had been almost an entire year since he had first met her. He did not think she had particularly cared for him or thought much of him, and the loss of opportunity to prove how much he had changed made him feel cheated.

<*Underworld*'s shields are failing!> a scanners Sub-Lieutenant announced.

<We will have to take the starboard turbolasers off-line in ten seconds, Commander,> his senior tactical officer warned. <They are overheating.>

<Continue to fire on the *Underworld*,> he ordered. <Push past the safety limit. We must eliminate it, now!>

He knew that Gavain's plan depended on him and his ship reducing the enemy numbers, and the Federation starship *Underworld* was the most damaged of the entire enemy squadron. Taking it out would rob the enemy of a significant volume of fire-power, although there was still the behemoth that was the dreadnought *Thor's Hammer*.

He shifted attention briefly, watching as Gavain's *Vindicator* and Markos' *Remembrance* desperately engaged the *Thor*. The *Vindicator* was about to lose its starboard shields, and as it had turned to follow the *Thor*, had exposed its rear to the enemy battlecruisers, which were now targeting both him and Markos's *Remembrance*.

<Turbolaser battery four going critical, evacuating operating crew,> he heard.

<Torpedoes! *Underworld*!> De Graaf cried.

The ship rocked as the turbolaser battery exploded.

Lieutenant-Commander Meier of the *Kinslayer* interdictor was adding his fire-power to the destroyer *Undefeatable*'s, but the latter's ordnance was much greater. Torpedoes streaked into the defenceless *Underworld*, a series of explosions blossoming all down its hull.

<Target has critical structural stress at the following points,> he heard a junior tactical officer say on the datasphere to the tactical command team.

<All batteries, target here,> De Graaf interrupted, mentally signalling the point he wanted them to go for.

Turbolaser beams and MAC projectiles ripped across the void, slamming into the *Underworld* at the precise point he had chosen. Finally, already with heavy damage from its numerous battles, the *Underworld* began to shudder and shake, gutting itself as a series of internal explosions wracked it, all power fading as its engineers desperately shut down the generators or face the prospect of the ship's drives going critical.

<The *Underworld*'s going!> Commander De Graaf called out. <We've done it. Good work, crew!>

There was a brief cheer on the bridge. They needed all they could celebrate in this engagement.

<Drop shields,> Admiral Silus Adare commanded. <Prepare for jump to these co-ordinates.>

<We are under heavy fire, Admiral,> said Commander Sahin. <As soon as we drop shields to jump ->

<We can more than take it,> said Silus Adare. <Stop all firing. Communications, patch me through to Gavain on the *Vindicator*.>

Gavain checked the report that the enemy destroyer was out of the fight. It was indeed powering down, having sustained massive damage at the hands of Commander De Graaf and Lieutenant-Commander Meier. De Graaf in particular deserved the victory, having pushed his ship to its limits in order to secure the kill.

<Shift targets to the *Ubermacht*,> he commanded the two, before breaking off the connection.

Lieutenant Forrest was addressing him, <We have an incoming call

from the *Thor*, sir,> she said, the incredulity soaking her data-message to him.

<The *Thor* is dropping shields!>

<Dreadnought engaging its structural integrity fields .... yes, they are preparing to jump!>

Gavain could not believe it. <Heavy fire on the *Thor*,> he ordered calmly. <Accept the hail.>

In less than a nano-second, an image of the hated Admiral Silus Adare appeared before him on the bridge. Momentarily the battle receded into the back of Gavain's mind, as he paid full attention to the communications link.

<Admiral James Gavain, it is a pleasure at last to speak to you.>

<I wish I could say the same. You are a war-criminal, wanted for the destruction of the planet Alwathbah. What are you doing, Adare? Your ship is preparing for a jump.>

<I'm leaving, James,> Adare taunted him with the familiar use of his name. There was an unpleasant sneer on the other man's face. <I am no longer a member of the StarCom Federation.>

Gavain suspected a trap. <Regardless, you are wanted ->

<Mercenary, does your contract include bringing me to justice?>

<No, but ->

<Then I suspect it consists of defending this system. I suggest you pay attention to the bottom line, James. I am about to transmit to you the bypass codes for the firewalls on the rest of my squadron. They will transmit as we jump. If you have any sense, leave me be and let the *Thor* escape.>

Gavain checked the situation. The *Thor* was powering ahead, away from its own squadron and the battle as it prepared to jump. It was too late for him to signal the interdictor *Kinslayer*, to charge it to prevent the jump. He could turn his ships and face the rest of the enemy squadron.

He took a gamble, and made a choice. <Cease fire on the *Thor*,> he commanded. <*Vindicator* and *Remembrance* to come about. Target the enemy battlecruisers.> With his attention momentarily returned to the battle, he saw that the *Solace* strikecruiser was taking heavy damage to its hull, receiving a battering from the *Veritable* and the *Revenging Angel*. His own ship and Markos's could make a difference and save the strikecruiser, if the *Thor* was genuinely leaving the fight.

He returned to the private communication with Adare. <Why are you doing this?> he asked. <Is this real, or a trap?>

<I hate the StarCom Federation as much as you.> Adare replied.

<Then why serve them?>

<I had no choice. But I do now.>

<Were you forced into destroying Alwathbah?> Gavain asked. <Killing

billions of people?>

Adare smirked. <No, that was just because I could,> the man said. <I see you are turning away from me. Well done, Admiral, you will not regret it. We jump in twenty seconds, you will have the bypass codes one second before we leave this system, for good.>

<Very well, traitor.>

<You were the traitor,> Admiral Adare suddenly snarled. <One day, you and me will have a reckoning over the Emperor, Gavain.>

<But not today, I think.>

<No, not today. Oh, and Gavain?>

<Yes?>

<My condolences on the loss of the *Sorceror*. I hope you didn't lose anybody on board dear to you.>

<You bastard,> said Gavain, but the link was already terminated.

He plunged back into awareness of the battle. The *Solace* strikecruiser was faring badly, having been boarded by Marines launched from the *Veritable*. He could see the tell-tale pockmarks where the strikepods had latched onto the strikecruiser.

<The *Thor* is jumping!> he was informed.

<We received a data-burst from the *Thor* as it jumped,> his data-tac officer said. <We're holding it in the buffers, about to delete it ->

<No,> Gavain ordered. <Quarantine it, scrub it for viruses, and then let me know what it is. Supposedly we have just been given the bypass codes for the enemy squadron.>

With a blinding flash of light, the *Thor's Hammer* left the Blackheath System.

The *Vindicator* and the *Remembrance* battlecruisers had returned to the main fight, having abandoned the pursuit of the dreadnought minutes ago, and both were now subjecting the StarCom Federation battlecruiser *Revenging Angel* ṭo a terrible barrage of fire. The enemy battlecruisers were pulling away from engaging the *Solace*, trying to turn to face the incoming mercenary ships. They engaged in a short-range firefight, which is a terrible thing to behold with ship-borne weaponry.

<Sir,>, data-tac officer Woolfe said, <the transmission checks out, they are bypass codes.>

Gavain's eyes widened. There was no doubt, the *Thor's Hammer* dreadnought had indeed jumped out-system. It had not reappeared anywhere else in Blackheath; it was gone. A strange twist of fate, the treachery of a madman in command of a Federation dreadnought, might just turn this battle in his favour.

Gavain, normally so calm and collected in front of his crew, actually clenched a fist as he ordered, <Fire the bypass codes at the enemy. Take them down, now!>

Invisible in space, on numerous hostile carrier-waves, the *Vindicator* transmitted the bypass codes. They were automatically picked up by every Federation starship's comms receptor, and loaded into a secure buffer.

The codes passed through the buffers, deactivating the firewalls. The programmes ran through the datasphere the StarCom ships had established, jumping from system to system, deactivating every single thing they could find.

Of the StarCom ships, the *Ubermacht* was the first to drop its shields completely, shut down the computer core, cut all power to its weaponry batteries, and switch off its power generators. Its main drive engines flared and then spluttered out, the ship floating dead in the water, continuing on its vector, but adrift in space.

Barely a second later the *Queen of Egypt* followed suit. The *Snake-Eyes* was successful in taking the infected systems off-line, but struggling to get secondary systems up. The *Serendipity* went completely dead. The *Revenging Angel* managed to maintain its weaponry systems, but the drives and shields deactivated. The *Veritable* went completely dark and silent.

The storm of weapons fire suddenly became one-sided, the mercenary ships taking full advantage of the situation.

<Fire all batteries at the *Ubermacht,*> De Graaf hissed, <Close distance. Supporting fire on the *Veritable.*>

<All fighters and bombers, target the destroyer and the star-carrier,> Jonathan O'Connor, aboard the *Quintessential* ordered. <Do your best, before they get secondary, isolated systems up and running, this is our chance.>

<All fire, repeat all fire, on the *Veritable,*> Captain Danae Markos ordered. <The Admiral wants that ship destroyed. No prisoners.>

The mercenary Captain Elena Jarman stared down at her chest, going instantly into shock. She stood on the blackened, fire-ravaged, blood-drenched bridge of her ship, the strikecruiser *Solace.* The enemy Marine in front of her had a power claw, and he had plunged it into her torso. Strangely, it did not hurt.

She looked up into the T-visor of his helmet, as the Marine, bedecked in the colours of the StarCom Federation and bearing the flash-patch of the *Revenging Angel* battlecruiser on his left shoulder, energised the power claw. It tore her innards to shreds as the tines opened, and her body literally exploded in a shower of gore and burnt meat.

<Marines, prepare to launch at the *Revenging Angel,*> Commander Al-Malli ordered, looking at Gavain.

He nodded. <They kept their shields, but as soon as they're down, I want that ship boarded,> he ordered.

At that moment, the *Solace* went quiet as the bridge was captured by the boarders.

<Marines to launch at the *Solace* as well,> he ordered quietly. <*Apollo* come up, keep the *Solace* under your guns, launch supporting forces to repel boarders.>

<Aye, aye, sir,> said Lieutenant-Commander Wybeck. She turned to her bridge crew. <You heard the Admiral. Full power, get us in range of the *Solace*. We're in danger of losing the ship to the boarders.>

<*Veritable* super-structure failing,> Gavain was told.

<*Queen of Egypt* under heavy bomber runs,> someone else said.

Gavain knew the tide of the battle had turned, despite the possible loss of the *Solace*. <I want the *Queen of Egypt* boarded,> he said. <Launch landers from the *Remembrance*. Fighters from *Quintessential* to provide cover.>

<Admiral Gavain, we have an incoming hail from the Captain of the *Revenging Angel*.>

<Marines have landed on the *Angel*.>

<*Veritable* is breaking up, repeat, *Veritable* breaking up. They are out of the fight.>

Gavain signalled that he accepted the hail from the enemy Captain.

The enemy Captain appeared before him, and introduced himself as a Captain Niesche.

Captain Niesche could not believe that the *Thor* had jumped out-system. The double betrayal of Admiral Adare, by not only jumping out of the battle, but also in giving the enemy the codes to bypass their firewalls and security systems, was unbelievable. It had turned the battle.

However, Niesche had also received a HPCG communication, first a general hyper-pulse sent from StarCom, and then a second from the Fort Bastion system and Admiral Haas.

He spoke quickly, doing his best to convince the hard-faced Admiral of the mercenaries before him of what had happened in the rest of the galaxy.

<Is this true?> Gavain asked, closing the communication down whilst he

spoke to his bridge-crew.

<Checking .....> Lieutenant Forrest looked up quickly. <Sir, there was a general broadcast from Earth, but our filter system assumed it was propaganda .... I'm sorry. The enemy ships did receive a coded hyper-pulse from out-system about a minute ago.>

Gavain frowned. <It is not your fault, Lieutenant. It does not change anything.>

<Sir, there is a comms from HPCG Tahrir coming in,> Forrest suddenly said.

<Through to me,> he ordered. He reviewed it quickly, then shifted ever so slightly in his chair.

It was from Lord Minister Luke. It appeared to confirm what Captain Niesche was saying. There had indeed been a general truce called. The war was over.

Before he contacted Niesche to tell him to stand down and hand his ship over to the mercenary Marines currently storming it, Gavain checked the time the truce was called. He realised it had been called seconds before the *Sorceror* had been destroyed. Kavanagh had literally died as the war ended.

Most of the blood-shed in the Blackheath System could have been avoided, if only interstellar communications and the politicians behind them had worked faster.

The Vindicator Mercenary Corporation had been victorious, but at a tremendous and mostly unnecessary cost.

Chapter XXV

It was snowing on Tahrir Base. A large proportion of Tahrir had now entered winter, but it was always snowing in the southern polar mountains. Tahrir Base's chameleonic field had been dropped temporarily for the funeral service, there being no risk of detection with the satellite net above the region almost utterly destroyed and collateral damage from the multiple invasions Tahrir had suffered recently.

Admiral Gavain was wearing full dress uniform, standing on the back of the *Leopard*-class hoverjeep as it cruised gently down the central aisle of the parade ground. The aisle had been created by the careful division of the assembled crews of the starships, who had been brought to the surface of the planet especially for this service.

As the jeep glided past, the naval officers, crew, and marines turned towards him and saluted, a rippling wave of Imperial salutes charting his progress towards the stage at the head of the parade ground.

Gavain still hated being planet-side, but whenever they could, Praetorian tradition demanded it. Ejections of bodies into space only happened when on operational duty, or when there was a body.

The jeep coasted to a stop, and Gavain dismounted.

He strode up to Ulrik Andryukhin, and placed a hand on his shoulder. His old friend stared back at him, Gavain reading the pain in his eyes. James could only guess at what Ulrik was feeling right now. He wanted to say something, opened his mouth, but Ulrik just gently shook his head and half-shrugged one shoulder.

It did not matter. Julia Kavanagh was gone, and words were not enough.

It hurt him that her death had come precisely at the point when Vice-President Pereyra - now President, he supposed - had been announcing the end to StarCom aggression. If only Lord Minister Luke, or Admiral Haas, had come to their agreement and issued their orders sooner. It was not their fault, of course, it was nobody's fault.

If you were going to lay fault at anyone's door, he thought, then blame fate and her sister destiny. Destiny had led to the end of the Red Empire, the Dissolution of the Praetorian Guard, and the creation of the Vindicator Mercenary Corporation, and fate - and his orders - had led to Kavanagh's ship being badly damaged, unable to engage in a second battle to defend Blackheath so quickly after its first to re-take the system.

Gavain turned, and strode up the steps to the podium mounted on the main stage. He cleared his throat, and began to speak.

"Men and women of the Vindicator Mercenary Corporation," he began, "We are gathered here today, to commemorate the heroic actions and mourn the loss of many of our comrades ....."

*

Lady Sophia Towers sat in the gardens of the palace of the Zupanics. The palace had once belonged to another House, one that had fallen to House Zupanic a century ago, during a sanctioned war that had taken place in the First Emperor's rule.

The palace was a temporary home to the Council of the Levitican Union, until they could agree on a new capital system for the young nation. The system of Zubrenic had been the fall-back position following the StarCom invasion and the destruction of the megapolis on Leviticus.

She heard gravel crunching, and she looked up, a welcoming smile on her face. The *LSS Knightsword* had jumped in several hours ago, carrying her brother from the Fort Bastion system. Lord Minister Luke strode towards her, his face a grim, almost furious mask.

Her smile faltered.

"Luke," she said, uncrossing her legs and standing to greet him with a hug. He was stiff and unwelcoming. "It is good to see you - but what's wrong?"

"Where is Lord Micalek?" he asked. "I understand you two are never separated nowadays."

"Luke!" she admonished, frowning. "Whatever is the matter? We won the war - thanks to you. And one has not seen you since you left for the front. What in the name of the True Emperor is wrong?"

He sighed heavily, and his frown dissipated slightly. He took her hands, and sat on the bench, pulling her down with him. "I'm sorry, Sophia," he said, "we may have won the war, but everything is far from good."

"You are speaking in riddles," she said. "As well as concerning me greatly."

He nodded. "I apologise, but I'm very worried. All is not as it seems, Sophia. I have come into some information which you need to know."

She suddenly straightened. She was the head of House Towers, a noble, a woman of breeding, education, and great responsibility. "What is it, brother?" she asked. "Is it StarCom?"

"If only," he said. "All goes well, there. The remnants of their fleets are currently jumping out via Blackheath and Cannai back towards the Core, towards Earth and Sol. We're letting them in-system one ship at a time, in a phased and timed withdrawal. There has been no trouble so far. The truce is holding."

"So what is it then?"

"There is no easy way to say this," he said. "So I will just say it. We have been betrayed, Sophia, not just once, or twice, but three times."

"Betrayed? By whom?"

"House Zupanic."

She instantly thought of Lord Micalek, and the feelings she had been experiencing towards the devilishly handsome and charming young Lord suddenly became jeopardised. She braced herself. "Explain to me, Luke," she commanded her younger brother.

Lord Minister Luke began, speaking low and with care. "The first betrayal you know about. House Zupanic conspired to put themselves at the head of the Levitican Union."

She almost laughed with relief. "We knew that," she said.

"We did," he nodded. "We knew they had conspired with the other Houses, against the spirit of our agreement, if not the words, that saw your hand promised to Lord Micalek. What we did not know or guess at was the betrayal to the StarCom Federation."

"What do you mean?" she was horror-stricken at the words, her relief crashing into disbelief.

"I received a warning, whilst I was in Fort Bastion. Lord Ramicek Zupanic approached President Nielsen, offering to withdraw his forces from the front line and back to Zupanic space, abandoning the rest of us to the mercy of StarCom. It would have shattered the Union. We would currently be waving the Federation flag, if he had done it."

"So why didn't he ...." she began, "You ordered the counter-attack early so that if he did withdraw his forces, we would still stand a chance against the StarCom Federation?"

"I did," Luke confirmed. "StarCom upheld their part of the bargain, in withdrawing from a system they had captured in Zupanic territory. Note that apart from that, not a single Zupanic system suffered in the invasion of the Union. Ramicek hesitated, and once he saw that we were driving the Federation back and winning, he reneged on his deal with President Nielsen."

Lady Sophia wanted to swear, but her upbringing prevented it. A thought suddenly occurred to her. "Did Lord Micalek know of this?" she asked.

"I'm uncertain," said Lord Luke. "What I do know is that a number of people in House Zupanic - Ramicek, certainly his wife Lady Wyn, and maybe other family members - all knew of the third betrayal. The greatest of them all."

"Which is?"

"The Faceless assassin that was captured after the assassination of our father. The Zupanics took him, or it, on the grounds that they could interrogate him. They did, but our father had his own spies in Ramicek's house. That spy network has reported back to me that the interrogation did not take place, and one of them has found out why. They have no need to interrogate the assassin, in any way, for any information, at least about our father's death. They removed the Faceless operative from you and me so we could not discover the truth."

Lady Sophia guessed. "No," she whispered.

"Yes," Lord Luke nodded. "The hit was made to look like StarCom retribution. But it wasn't. There was almost a week between the assassination and the commencement of the invasion, which is not how StarCom operated under Nielsen. The killer was in the employ of House Zupanic. House Zupanic assassinated our father."

Lady Sophia forced her mind to work, despite the shock. "They did it so I would become head of the household, before you were named heir-apparent," she said, a shiver running up and down her spine.

"I believe so," said Lord Minister Luke. "I do not have conclusive evidence that Lord Micalek was involved, but .... the 'interrogation' of the Faceless assassin was his suggestion, he benefits on behalf of House Zupanic by being your husband, and gaining access to our territory .... it doesn't look good, Sophia."

Lady Sophia looked away. She had been so happy. The war was over, won by her brother, she was the head of House Towers, and about to be married to a powerful man in a House that would secure the future of the Levitican Union in general, and her people in particular.

Now she saw it for what it was.

They had won the war, but lost the peace.

*

Admiral Gavain stood at the far end of the room on Tahrir Base, holding the fluted glass of real alcohol in one hand. He was not really a big drinker, but it was traditional at a wake, so he had a glass for appearances. The senior and middle-ranking officers were in the room, whilst individual wakes would be held by the friends of those who had been lost all over the base over the next few days. Just allowing the shore-leave for all of his mercenaries had been a logistical nightmare.

He was also ill-at-ease at social functions, even ones such as this to commemorate and remember the dead. He stood mainly on his own. Inevitably, his thoughts turned to the future, and he gazed out of the window at the slowly emptying parade ground beyond.

The future. What would that consist of, he wondered.

Out of his forces, he had lost thousands of people, not just in the last, unexpected naval action, but also on the ground in their counter-invasion of Blackheath. Commodore Andersson had put the accelerated growth bio-vats to work; in a number of months, the first of their replacements would be 'born' on the Tahrir Base.

He had lost Commander Kavanagh, a very dear and close friend, as well as one other member of his command staff, Elena Jarman of the *Solace*. The *Solace*'s bridge had been captured and then destroyed by the Marines, but the strikecruiser, despite taking heavy damage, had been reclaimed and was undergoing heavy repair in the shipyards. All of his ships needed repair, and were in a queue.

He had also lost the *Sorceror* strikecruiser. However, thanks to the contract he had negotiated with the Towers and Zupanic families on behalf of the Levitican Union, he and his unit had first pick of all salvage created as a result of any direct action they had participated in.

All of his losses in terms of vehicles and equipment such as battlewalkers, repulsortanks and more had been made good by the actions on Tahrir and the planet November. He had replacements for all, and had actually expanded his land forces in terms of equipment, if not the people to use it.

In naval ships, he had claimed the *Carnivorous*, an old but still serviceable and effective Praetorian battlecruiser, and the *Shadow* S-class strikecruiser. He had claimed the *Revenging Angel*, the second of Adare's battlecruisers, the *Veritable*, being destroyed in the last moments of his defence of Blackheath. The *Queen of Egypt* star-carrier was now his, as was the *Universal* and *Ubermacht* destroyer. He now owned the *Snake-Eyes* strike-cruiser, the *Serendipity* damaged beyond serviceable repair. He had claimed six Federal Guard corvettes as his as well, in addition to a medical frigate, a repair-ship, an assault frigate, and one more M-class military transporter. The rest of the salvage, or bounty, he was in the process of selling to the Levitican Union.

Most of the ships required heavy repair, but Lady Sophia had hyper-pulsed and vastly reduced the rates of her shipyards for him, although he did not have priority usage. It would take many months to fully repair the fleet, and drain a significant proportion of his money. It would take years of bio-vats, or months of recruitment, to get up to full strength.

He raised his glass. Despite the trials of recent history, the future looked bright. He turned around, to survey the room.

There was Commander De Graaf, with a soft drink in his hands. He had noted not only how well De Graaf had responded to his warning about his behaviour and his drinking, and how the man had set about rectifying the problems. He had been vital during the last action of the Levitican War, and had out-performed even Gavain's expectations. His reservations towards Lucas De Graaf had been largely dispelled.

He was talking to Ulrik Andryukhin, in itself a minor miracle. Gavain did not often reveal that he knew or even recognised what was happening amongst his staff – there, he missed Jules, as she had always known him the best on that score – but he knew De Graaf and Andryukhin had an intense dislike for each other. Perhaps it was gone for good, or maybe it was only a temporary thing due to circumstance, but they were in deep conversation, De Graaf doing most of the talking.

Andryukhin looked lost. It was something Gavain had never seen his friend display. He had been in love with Kavanagh, James guessed. It was difficult to say. They had a deep friendship, but of late, there had not been the time for discussion. He hoped Andryukhin would recover – that they would all recover – from her loss within time.

Commodore Harley Andersson stood, talking quietly with Captain Jonathan O'Connor and Petra Raimes. They were missing Elena Jarman, Gavain had no doubt. Perhaps the loss of people so close would be an underline, and gel the VMC even closer together than ever before. He gazed at Andersson, hoping they would have time to themselves later.

His other command staff were present as well. They had all done well, but the loss of two of their number had served to remind them how dangerous their occupation was. He was proud of them.

It had been one long, torturous and emotional year. Much had changed. Nothing would ever be the same again, not for anyone in the galaxy. The Red Imperium was dead, the Emperor was dead, and multiple civil wars of secession were raging across the galaxy. The aggression of the StarCom Federation had been halted, but there were other conflicts, both military and political, taking place.

He thought about where he had been mentally when the Dissolution Order had come through. Almost a year ago, he had fought against the False Emperor. He had been thanked, and then dismissed by his own, life-long organisation. He had floated bereft of purpose for months, before Lady Sophia had made him an offer. With a bit of guidance from Commodore Andersson, he had taken it. He had forged a new life for himself, and for his crew, and had expanded his power beyond all conceivable belief.

Despite all the losses and the dramatic changes of the last year, there was a future for him and his in this war-torn galaxy, and he was grabbing it with both hands.

Liked The Book?

Age of Secession

I would love to have your reviews and feedback, if you would like to post this in the place where you bought the book. It all helps to spread the news about the Age of Secession.

Visit the website www.ageofsecession.com, for lots of new content and Age of Secession-related material. News, new releases, background to the series, and more being added all the time!

Roger Ruffles himself would love to hear from you, so either follow him on Twitter @RogerRuffles, or write to him at ageofsecession@gmail.com

If Facebook is more of your thing, there is also the Age of Secession page, at www.facebook.com/AgeOfSecession.

The Age of Secession Continues .....

ROSICRUX
Part II - Vindicator Trilogy

OUT NOW

Admiral James Gavain is enmeshed in the politics of the post-Dissolution colonised galaxy, an unwilling and reluctant participant. His main concern now is for forging a future for the people under his command, a mercenary company for sale to the highest bidder in a rapidly disintegrating colonial galaxy.

As pirates swamp the Eastern Segment, preying on the weak, a pattern begins to emerge. All is not as it seems. Whilst his ships engage on a contract which plunges the mercenary company into a conspiracy far deeper than could be imagined, Ulrik Andryukhin leads the marines on a ground campaign which exposes the darker side of humanity - intolerance for anything that is different. The old enmity between the augmented and the unaugmented is running strong, and genocide is the preferred solution.

Balancing the difficulties of a star-spanning conspiracy and the outrage of a friend grieving for a lost lover, Gavain also discovers his newfound ally and supporter Lady Sophia is playing a dangerous game. Married into House Zupanic, famed for their murderous and fatal political machinations, she is looking for power within the young Levitican Union, and vengeance for the assassination of a member of her own House.

Coming Soon to the Age of Secession .....

PAY DIRT: DISHONEST INTENTIONS

IN 2018

Life is tough for many in the Age of Secession, and for some it has become much tougher since the Emperors of House Constantin fell from grace.

Iain Briggs is a con-man, along with friends Dominic Gaiman and Marin Todor. They have moved from trick to trick, from planet to star system to intergalactic House since the Red Empire of Mars fell, each scam being bigger than the last.

The rise of the Vindicate Empire offers them their biggest and most dangerous opportunity yet, as this Fifth Empire looks to build landgates and starterminals across the colonised galaxy in every direction. It will revolutionise space travel, allowing trade to pass from one side of the colonised galaxy to another within a day, rather than in years.

Constructing a pathway across the stars, they will face the jealousies of leaders, the murderous intent of criminals, the hidden and dangerous motives of pirates, the wrath of the security forces of the nations they are working both for and against. This is the biggest job of all, and if any of them are to escape with their lives, they will have to succeed in a way they could not imagine when they started.

Most would see pay dirt as succeeding in one of the biggest construction jobs in mankind's history. They will see pay dirt as escaping with their lives, from an ever-deepening web of dishonest intentions.

Out Soon!

Go to facebook, twitter, or **www.ageofsecession.com**
for more details

Coming Later to the Age of Secession .....

In 2018/2019

Augmented Genocide

As the billions of Erdogan refugees make their home in the growing systems of the Mercenary Lord, back at home the Zhou-Zheng Compact have opened their deathcamps and are slowly exterminating their conquered people. There is not a single Erdogan family who has not suffered a loss, a relative dying in a work-camp.

This is the story of those who fought, against the Genocide of the Augmented.

The Lost Kindred

The Lost Kindred were abandoned.

It all began centuries before the Age of Secession started, but it will come to a head now. As the colonised galaxy turns upon itself, the Thirteen Kindred will return in greater force than ever before.

And the Kinsmen are angry that they were ever abandoned in the first place.

Adare's Legacy: Kingdom of Blood

It is to the Bandit Kingdoms of the Badlands that Caterina arrives with a child she did not want, but is now determined to protect whatever his origins. Abandoned by her former nation, all alone in a harsh and hostile galaxy, she finds she has to be as black-hearted as the pirates she now keeps company with.

She will stop at nothing to ensure that there is a legacy for the child of Silus Adare.

The Kingdom of Blood.

Collective Misdirection

It began with a virus, a simple line of quantum-locked code. It spread silently, the interconnected hive minds of the Nacrimosa Collective being a perfect breeding ground. Then one day, someone somewhere pressed a button, and an entire nation froze in terror as their minds shut down.

Who brought the Collective to its knees? The galaxy is being lied to, misdirected somehow, and what appears to be an opportunity for some might be more of a poisoned chalice than it first appears.

The Collective Misdirection must be exposed, before it is too late.

Printed in Great Britain
by Amazon

19099609R00183